Kiss Me Again, Stranger

DOUBLEDAY & COMPANY, INC., GARDEN CITY, NEW YORK

DRAWINGS BY MARGOT TOMES

DOUBLEDAY & COMPANY, INC., GARDEN CITY, NEW YORK

KISS
ME
AGAIN,
STRANGER

by Daphne du Maurier

A COLLECTION
OF EIGHT
STORIES
LONG AND SHORT

Library of Congress Catalog Card Number 53–5038

Contents

Kiss

Me

Again,

Stranger

I LOOKED AROUND for a bit, after leaving the Army and before settling down, and then I found myself a job up Hampstead way, in a garage it was, at the bottom of Haverstock Hill near Chalk Farm, and it suited me fine. I'd always been one for tinkering with engines, and in R.E.M.E. that was my work and I was trained to it—it had always come easy to me, anything mechanical.

My idea of having a good time was to lie on my back in my greasy overalls under a car's belly, or a lorry's, with a spanner in my hand, working on some old bolt or screw, with the smell of oil about me, and someone starting up an engine, and the other chaps around clattering their tools and whistling. I never minded the smell or the dirt. As my old Mum used to say when I'd be that way as a kid, mucking about with a grease can, "It won't hurt him, it's clean dirt," and so it is, with engines.

The boss at the garage was a good fellow, easygoing, cheerful, and he saw I was keen on my work. He wasn't much of a mechanic himself, so he gave me the repair jobs, which was what I liked.

I didn't live with my old Mum—she was too far off, over Shepperton way, and I saw no point in spending half the day getting to and from my work. I like to be handy, have it on the spot, as it were. So I had a bedroom with a couple called Thompson, only about ten minutes' walk away from the garage. Nice people, they were. He was in the shoe business—cobbler, I suppose he'd be called—and Mrs. Thompson cooked the meals and kept the house for him over the shop. I used to eat with them, breakfast and supper—we always had a cooked supper—and being the only lodger, I was treated as family.

I'm one for routine. I like to get on with my job, and then when the day's work's over settle down to a paper and a smoke and a bit of music on the wireless, variety or something of the sort, and then turn in early. I never had much use for girls, not even when I was doing my time in the Army. I was out in the Middle East, too, Port Said and that.

No, I was happy enough living with the Thompsons, carrying on much the same day after day, until that one night, when it happened. Nothing's been the same since. Nor ever will be. I don't know . . .

The Thompsons had gone to see their married daughter up at Highgate. They asked me if I'd like to go along, but somehow I didn't fancy barging in, so instead of staying home alone after leaving the garage I went down to the picture palace and, taking a look at the poster, saw it was cowboy and Indian stuff—there was a picture of a cowboy sticking a knife into the Indian's guts. I like that—proper baby I am for westerns—so I paid my one and twopence and went inside. I handed my slip of paper to the usherette and said, "Back row, please," because I like sitting far back and leaning my head against the board.

Well, then I saw her. They dress the girls up no end in some of these places, velvet tams and all, making them proper guys. They hadn't made a guy out of this one, though. She had copper hair, page-boy style I think they call it, and blue eyes, the kind that look short-sighted but see further than you think, and go dark by night, nearly black, and her mouth was sulky-looking, as if she was fed up, and it would take someone giving her the world to make her smile. She hadn't freckles, nor a milky skin, but warmer than that, more like a peach, and natural too. She was small and slim, and her velvet coat—blue it was—fitted her close, and the cap on the back of her head showed up her copper hair.

I bought a programme—not that I wanted one, but to delay going in through the curtain—and I said to her, "What's the picture like?"

She didn't look at me. She just went on staring into nothing, at the opposite wall. "The knifing's amateur," she said, "but you can always sleep."

I couldn't help laughing. I could see she was serious though. She wasn't trying to have me on or anything.

"That's no advertisement," I said. "What if the manager heard you?"

Then she looked at me. She turned those blue eyes in my direction; still fed-up they were, not interested, but there was something in them I'd not seen before, and I've never seen it since, a kind of laziness, like someone waking from a long dream and glad to find you there. Cats' eyes have that gleam sometimes when you stroke them, and they purr and curl themselves into a ball and let you do anything you want. She looked at me this way a moment, and there was a smile lurking somewhere behind her mouth if you gave it a chance, and tearing my slip of paper in half, she said, "I'm not paid to advertise. I'm paid to look like this and lure you inside."

She drew aside the curtains and flashed her torch in the darkness. I couldn't see a thing. It was pitch black, like it always is at first until you get used to it and begin to make out the shapes of the other people sitting there, but there were two great heads on the screen and some chap saying to the other, "If you don't come clean I'll put a bullet through you," and somebody broke a pane of glass and a woman screamed.

"Looks all right to me," I said, and began groping for somewhere to sit.

She said, "This isn't the picture, it's the trailer for next week," and she flicked on her torch and showed me a seat in the back row, one away from the gangway.

I sat through the advertisements and the newsreel, and then some chap came and played the organ, and the colours of the curtains over the screen went purple and gold and green—funny, I suppose they think they have to give you your money's worth—and looking around, I saw the house was half empty—and I guessed the girl had been right, the big picture wasn't going to be much, and that's why nobody much was there.

Just before the hall went dark again she came sauntering down the aisle. She had a tray of ice creams, but she didn't even bother to call them out and try to sell them. She could have been walking in her sleep, so when she went up the other aisle I beckoned to her.

"Got a sixpenny one?" I said.

She looked across at me. I might have been something dead under her feet, and then she must have recognised me, because that half smile came back again, and the lazy look in the eye, and she walked round the back of the seats to me.

"Wafer or cornet?" she said.

I didn't want either, to tell the truth. I just wanted to buy something from her and keep her talking.

"Which do you recommend?" I asked.

She shrugged her shoulders. "Cornets last longer," she said, and put one in my hand before I had time to give her my choice.

"How about one for you too?" I said.

"No, thanks," she said, "I saw them made."

And she walked off, and the place went dark, and there I was sitting with a great sixpenny cornet in my hand, looking a fool. The damn thing slopped all over the edge of the holder, spilling on to my shirt, and I had to ram the frozen stuff into my mouth as quick as I could for fear it would all go on my knees, and I turned sideways, because someone came and sat in the empty seat beside the gangway.

I finished it at last, and cleaned myself up with my pocket handkerchief, and then concentrated on the story flashing across the screen. It was a western all right, carts lumbering over prairies, and a train full of bullion being held to ransom, and the heroine in breeches one moment and full evening dress the next. That's the way pictures should be, not a bit like real life at all; but as I watched the story I began to notice the whiff of scent in the air, and I didn't know what it was or where it came from, but it was there just the same. There was a man to the right of me, and on my left were two empty seats, and it certainly wasn't the people in front, and I couldn't keep turning round and sniffing.

I'm not a great one for liking scent. It's too often cheap and nasty, but this was different. There was nothing stale about it, or stuffy, or strong; it was like the flowers they sell up in the West End in the big flower shops before you get them on the barrows—three bob a bloom sort of touch, rich chaps buy them for actresses and such—and it was so darn good, the smell of it there in that murky old picture palace full of cigarette smoke, that it nearly drove me mad.

At last I turned right round in my seat, and I spotted where it came from. It came from the girl, the usherette; she was leaning on the back board behind me, her arms folded across it.

"Don't fidget," she said. "You're wasting one and twopence. Watch the screen."

But not out loud so that anyone could hear. In a whisper, for me alone. I couldn't help laughing to myself. The cheek of it! I knew where the scent came from now, and somehow it made me enjoy the picture more. It was as though she was beside me in one of the empty seats and we were looking at the story together.

When it was over and the lights went on, I saw I'd sat through the last showing and it was nearly ten. Everyone was clearing off for the night. So I waited a bit, and then she came down with her torch and started squinting under the seats to see if anybody had dropped a glove or a purse, the way they do and only remember about afterwards when they get home, and she took no more notice of me than if I'd been a rag which no one would bother to pick up.

I stood up in the back row, alone—the house was clear now—and when she came to me she said, "Move over, you're blocking the gangway," and flashed about with her torch, but there was nothing there, only an empty packet of Player's which the cleaners would throw away in the morning. Then she straightened herself and looked me up and down, and taking off the ridiculous cap from the back of her head that suited her so well, she fanned herself with it and said, "Sleeping here tonight?" and then went off, whistling under her breath, and disappeared through the curtains.

It was proper maddening. I'd never been taken so much with a girl in my life. I went into the vestibule after her, but she had gone through a door to the back, behind the box-office place, and the commissionaire chap was already getting the doors to and fixing them for the night. I went out and stood in the street and waited. I felt a bit of a fool, because the odds were that she would come out with a bunch of others, the way girls do. There was the one who had sold me my ticket, and I dare say there were other usherettes up in the balcony, and perhaps a cloakroom attendant too, and they'd all be giggling together, and I wouldn't have the nerve to go up to her.

In a few minutes, though, she came swinging out of the place alone. She had a mac on, belted, and her hands in her pockets, and she had no hat. She walked straight up the street, and she didn't look to right or left of her. I followed, scared that she would turn round and see me off, but she went on walking, fast and direct, staring straight in front of her, and as she moved her copper page-boy hair swung with her shoulders.

Presently she hesitated, then crossed over and stood waiting for a bus. There was a queue of four or five people, so she didn't see me join the queue, and when the bus came she climbed on to it, ahead of the others, and I climbed too, without the slightest notion where it was going, and I couldn't have cared less. Up the stairs she went with me after her, and settled herself in the back seat, yawning, and closed her eyes.

I sat myself down beside her, nervous as a kitten, the point being that I never did that sort of thing as a rule and expected a rocket, and when the conductor stumped up and asked for fares I said, "Two sixpennies, please," because I reckoned she would never be going the whole distance and this would be bound to cover her fare and mine too.

He raised his eyebrows—they like to think themselves smart, some of these fellows—and he said, "Look out for the bumps when the driver changes gear. He's only just passed his test." And he went down the stairs chuckling, telling himself he was no end of a wag, no doubt.

The sound of his voice woke the girl, and she looked at me out of her sleepy eyes, and looked, too, at the tickets in my hand—she must have seen by the colour they were sixpennies—and she smiled, the first real smile I had got out of her that evening, and said without any sort of surprise, "Hullo, stranger."

I took out a cigarette, to put myself at ease, and offered her one, but she wouldn't take it. She just closed her eyes again, to settle herself to sleep. Then, seeing there was no one else to notice up on the top deck, only an Air Force chap in the front slopped over a newspaper, I put out my hand and pulled her head down on my shoulder, and got my arm round her, snug and comfortable, thinking of course she'd throw it off and blast me to hell. She didn't, though. She gave a sort of laugh to herself, and settled down like as if she might have been in an armchair, and she said, "It's not every night I get a free ride and a free pillow. Wake me at the bottom of the hill, before we get to the cemetery."

I didn't know what hill she meant, or what cemetery, but I wasn't going to wake her, not me. I had paid for two sixpennies, and I was darn well going to get value for my money.

So we sat there together, jogging along in the bus, very close and very pleasant, and I thought to myself that it was a lot more fun than sitting at home in the bed-sit reading the football news, or spending an evening up Highgate at Mr. and Mrs. Thompson's daughter's place.

Presently I got more daring, and let my head lean against hers, and tightened up my arm a bit, not too obvious-like, but nicely. Anyone coming up the stairs to the top deck would have taken us for a courting couple.

Then, after we had had about fourpenny-worth, I got anxious. The old bus wouldn't be turning round and going back again when we reached the sixpenny limit; it would pack up for the night, we'd have come to the terminus. And there we'd be, the girl and I, stuck out somewhere at the back of beyond, with no return bus, and I'd got about six bob in my pocket and no more. Six bob would never pay for a taxi, not with a tip and all. Besides, there probably wouldn't be any taxis going.

What a fool I'd been not to come out with more money. It was silly, perhaps, to let it worry me, but I'd acted on impulse right from the start, and if only I'd known how the evening was going to turn out I'd have had my wallet filled. It wasn't often I went out with a girl, and I hate a fellow who can't do the thing in style. Proper slap-up do at a Corner House—they're good these days with that help-yourself service —and if she had a fancy for something stronger than coffee or orange-ade, well, of course as late as this it wasn't much use, but nearer home I knew where to go. There was a pub where my boss went, and you paid for your gin and kept it there, and could go in and have a drink from your bottle when you felt like it. They have the same sort of racket at the posh night clubs up West, I'm told, but they make you pay through the nose for it.

Anyway, here I was riding a bus to the Lord knows where, with my girl beside me—I called her "my girl" just as if she really was and we were courting—and bless me if I had the money to take her home. I began to fidget about, from sheer nerves, and I fumbled in one pocket after another, in case by a piece of luck I should come across a half-crown, or even a ten-bob note I had forgotten all about, and I suppose I disturbed her with all this, because she suddenly pulled my ear and said, "Stop rocking the boat."

Well, I mean to say . . . It just got me. I can't explain why. She held my ear a moment before she pulled it, like as though she were feeling the skin and liked it, and then she just gave it a lazy tug. It's the kind of thing anyone would do to a child, and the way she said it, as if she had known me for years and we were out picnicking together, "Stop rocking the boat." Chummy, matey, yet better than either.

"Look here," I said, "I'm awfully sorry, I've been and done a darn silly thing. I took tickets to the terminus because I wanted to sit beside you, and when we get there we'll be turned out of the bus, and it will be miles from anywhere, and I've only got six bob in my pocket."

"You've got legs, haven't you?" she said.

"What d'you mean, I've got legs?"

"They're meant to walk on. Mine were," she answered.

Then I knew it didn't matter, and she wasn't angry either, and the evening was going to be all right. I cheered up in a second, and gave her a squeeze, just to show I appreciated her being such a sport—most girls would have torn me to shreds—and I said, "We haven't passed a cemetery, as far as I know. Does it matter very much?"

"Oh, there'll be others," she said. "I'm not particular."

I didn't know what to make of that. I thought she wanted to get out at the cemetery stopping point because it was her nearest stop for home, like the way you say, "Put me down at Woolworth's," if you live handy. I puzzled over it for a bit, and then I said, "How do you mean, there'll be others? It's not a thing you see often along a bus route."

"I was speaking in general terms," she answered. "Don't bother to talk, I like you silent best."

It wasn't a slap on the face, the way she said it. Fact was, I knew what she meant. Talking's all very pleasant with people like Mr. and Mrs. Thompson, over supper, and you say how the day has gone, and one of you reads a bit out of the paper, and the other says, "Fancy, there now," and so it goes on, in bits and pieces, until one of you yawns, and somebody says, "Who's for bed?" Or it's nice enough with a chap like the boss, having a cuppa midmorning, or about three when there's nothing doing, "I tell you what I think, those blokes in the government are making a mess of things, no better than the last lot," and then we'll be interrupted with someone coming to fill up with petrol. And I like talking to my old Mum when I go and see her, which I don't do often enough, and she tells me how she spanked my bottom when I was a kid, and I sit on the kitchen table like I did then, and she bakes rock cakes and gives me peel, saying, "You always were one for peel." That's talk, that's conversation.

But I didn't want to talk to my girl. I just wanted to keep my arm round her the way I was doing, and rest my chin against her head, and that's what she meant when she said she liked me silent. I liked it too.

One last thing bothered me a bit, and that was whether I could kiss her before the bus stopped and we were turned out at the terminus. I mean, putting an arm round a girl is one thing, and kissing her is another. It takes a little time as a rule to warm up. You start off with a long evening ahead of you, and by the time you've been to a picture or a concert, and then had something to eat and to drink, well, you've got yourselves acquainted, and it's the usual thing to end up with a bit of kissing and a cuddle, the girls expect it. Truth to tell, I was never much of a one for kissing. There was a girl I walked out with back home, before I went into the Army, and she was quite a good sort, I liked her. But her teeth were a bit prominent, and even if you shut your eyes and tried to forget who it was you were kissing, well, you knew it was her, and there was nothing to it. Good old Doris from next door. But the opposite kind are even worse, the ones that grab you and nearly eat you. You come across plenty of them when you're in uniform. They're much too eager, and they muss you about, and you get the feeling they can't wait for a chap to get busy about them. I don't mind saying it used to make me sick. Put me dead off, and that's a fact. I suppose I was born fussy. I don't know.

But now, this evening in the bus, it was all quite different. I don't know what it was about the girl—the sleepy eyes, and the copper hair, and somehow not seeming to care if I was there, yet liking me at the same time; I hadn't found anything like this before. So I said to myself, "Now, shall I risk it, or shall I wait?" and I knew, from the way the driver was going and the conductor was whistling below and saying good night to the people getting off, that the final stop couldn't be far away; and my heart began to thump under my coat, and my neck grow hot below the collar—darn silly, only a kiss, you know, she couldn't kill me—and then . . . It was like diving off a springboard. I thought, "Here goes," and I bent down, and turned her face to me, and lifted her chin with my hand, and kissed her good and proper.

Well, if I was poetical, I'd say what happened then was a revelation. But I'm not poetical, and I can only say that she kissed me back, and it lasted a long time, and it wasn't a bit like Doris.

Then the bus stopped with a jerk, and the conductor called out in a singsong voice, "All out, please." Frankly, I could have wrung his neck.

She gave me a kick on the ankle. "Come on, move," she said, and I stumbled from my seat and racketted down the stairs, she following behind, and there we were, standing in a street. It was beginning to rain too, not badly, but just enough to make you notice and want to turn up the collar of your coat, and we were right at the end of a great wide street, with deserted unlighted shops on either side, the end of the world it looked to me, and sure enough there was a hill over to the left, and at the bottom of the hill a cemetery. I could see the railings and the white tombstones behind, and it stretched a long way, nearly halfway up the hill. There were acres of it.

"God darn it," I said, "is this the place you meant?"

"Could be," she said, looking over her shoulder vaguely, and then she took my arm. "What about a cup of coffee first?" she said.

First . . . ? I wondered if she meant before the long trudge home, or was this home? It didn't really matter. It wasn't much after eleven. And I could do with a cup of coffee, and a sandwich too. There was a stall across the road, and they hadn't shut up shop.

We walked over to it, and the driver was there too, and the conductor, and the Air Force fellow who had been up in front on the top deck. They were ordering cups of tea and sandwiches, and we had the same, only coffee. They cut them tasty at the stalls, the sandwiches, I've noticed it before, nothing stingy about it, good slices of ham between thick white bread, and the coffee is piping hot, full cups too, good value, and I thought to myself, "Six bob will see this lot all right."

I noticed my girl looking at the Air Force chap, sort of thoughtful-like, as though she might have seen him before, and he looked at her too. I couldn't blame him for that. I didn't mind either; when you're out with a girl it gives you a kind of pride if other chaps notice her. And you couldn't miss this one. Not my girl.

Then she turned her back on him, deliberate, and leant with her elbows on the stall, sipping her hot coffee, and I stood beside her doing the same. We weren't stuck-up or anything; we were pleasant and polite enough, saying good evening all round, but anyone could tell that we were together, the girl and I, we were on our own. I liked that. Funny, it did something to me inside, gave me a protective feeling. For all they knew, we might have been a married couple on our way home.

They were chaffing a bit, the other three and the chap serving the sandwiches and tea, but we didn't join in.

"You want to watch out, in that uniform," said the conductor to the Air Force fellow, "or you'll end up like those others. It's late, too, to be out on your own."

They all started laughing. I didn't quite see the point, but I supposed it was a joke.

"I've been awake a long time," said the Air Force fellow. "I know a bad lot when I see one."

"That's what the others said, I shouldn't wonder," remarked the driver, "and we know what happened to them. Makes you shudder. But why pick on the Air Force, that's what I want to know?"

"It's the colour of our uniform," said the fellow. "You can spot it in the dark."

They went on laughing in that way. I lighted up a cigarette, but my girl wouldn't have one.

"I blame the war for all that's gone wrong with the women," said the coffee-stall bloke, wiping a cup and hanging it up behind. "Turned a lot of them balmy, in my opinion. They don't know the difference between right or wrong."

" 'Tisn't that, it's sport that's the trouble," said the conductor. "Develops their muscles and that, what weren't never meant to be developed. Take my two youngsters, f'r instance. The girl can knock the boy down any time, she's a proper little bully. Makes you think."

"That's right," agreed the driver, "equality of the sexes, they call it, don't they? It's the vote that did it. We ought never to have given them the vote."

"Garn," said the Air Force chap, "giving them the vote didn't turn the women balmy. They've always been the same under the skin. The people out East know how to treat 'em. They keep 'em shut up out there. That's the answer. Then you don't get any trouble."

"I don't know what my old woman would say if I tried to shut her up," said the driver. And they all started laughing again.

My girl plucked at my sleeve and I saw she had finished her coffee. She motioned with her head towards the street.

"Want to go home?" I said.

Silly. I somehow wanted the others to believe we were going home. She didn't answer. She just went striding off, her hands in the pockets of her mac. I said good night and followed her, but not before I noticed the Air Force fellow staring after her over his cup of tea.

She walked off along the street, and it was still raining, dreary somehow, made you want to be sitting over a fire somewhere snug, and when she had crossed the street and had come to the railings outside the cemetery she stopped, and looked up at me, and smiled.

"What now?" I said.

"Tombstones are flat," she said, "sometimes."

"What if they are?" I asked, bewildered-like.

"You can lie down on them," she said.

She turned and strolled along, looking at the railings, and then she came to one that was bent wide, and the next beside it broken, and she glanced up at me and smiled again.

"It's always the same," she said. "You're bound to find a gap if you look long enough."

She was through that gap in the railings as quick as a knife through butter. You could have knocked me flat.

"Here, hold on," I said, "I'm not as small as you."

But she was off and away, wandering among the graves. I got through the gap, puffing and blowing a bit, and then I looked around, and bless me if she wasn't lying on a long flat gravestone, with her arms under her head and her eyes closed.

Well, I wasn't expecting anything. I mean, it had been in my mind to see her home and that. Date her up for the next evening. Of course, seeing as it was late, we could have stopped a bit when we came to the doorway of her place. She needn't have gone in right away. But lying there on the gravestone wasn't hardly natural.

I sat down and took her hand.

"You'll get wet lying there," I said. Feeble, but I didn't know what else to say.

"I'm used to that," she said.

She opened her eyes and looked at me. There was a street light not far away, outside the railings, so it wasn't all that dark, and anyway, in spite of the rain, the night wasn't pitch black, more murky somehow. I wish I knew how to tell about her eyes, but I'm not one for fancy talk. You know how a luminous watch shines in the dark. I've got one myself. When you wake up in the night, there it is on your wrist, like a friend. Somehow my girl's eyes shone like that, but they were lovely too. And they weren't lazy cats' eyes any more. They were loving and gentle, and they were sad, too, all at the same time.

"Used to lying in the rain?" I said.

"Brought up to it," she answered. "They gave us a name in the shelters. The dead-end kids, they used to call us in the war days."

"Weren't you never evacuated?" I asked.

"Not me," she said. "I never could stop anyplace. I always came back."

"Parents living?"

"No. Both of them killed by the bomb that smashed my home." She didn't speak tragic-like. Just ordinary.

"Bad luck," I said.

She didn't answer that one. And I sat there, holding her hand, wanting to take her home.

"You been on your job some time at the picture house?" I asked.

"About three weeks," she said. "I don't stop anywhere long. I'll be moving on again soon."

"Why's that?"

"Restless," she said.

She put up her hands suddenly and took my face and held it. It was gentle the way she did it, not as you'd think.

"You've got a good kind face. I like it," she said to me.

It was queer. The way she said it made me feel daft and soft, not sort of excited like I had been in the bus, and I thought to myself, "Well, maybe this is it, I've found a girl at last I really want. But not for an evening, casual. For going steady."

"Got a bloke?" I asked.

"No," she said.

"I mean, regular." '

"No, never."

It was a funny line of talk to be having in a cemetery, and she lying there like some figure carved on the old tombstone.

"I haven't got a girl either," I said. "Never think about it, the way other chaps do. Faddy, I guess. And then I'm keen on my job. Work in a garage—mechanic, you know—repairs, anything that's going. Good pay. I've saved a bit, besides what I send my old Mum. I live in digs. Nice people, Mr. and Mrs. Thompson, and my boss at the garage is a nice chap too. I've never been lonely, and I'm not lonely now. But since I've seen you, it's made me think. You know, it's not going to be the same any more."

She never interrupted once, and somehow it was like speaking my thoughts aloud.

"Going home to the Thompsons' is all very pleasant and nice," I said, "and you couldn't wish for kinder people. Good grub, too, and we chat a bit after supper, and listen to the wireless. But d'you know, what I want now is different. I want to come along and fetch you from the cinema, when the programme's over, and you'd be standing there by the curtains, seeing the people out, and you'd give me a bit of a wink to show me you'd be going through to change your clothes and I could wait for you. And then you'd come out into the street, like you did tonight, but you wouldn't go off on your own, you'd take my arm, and if you didn't want to wear your coat I'd carry it for you, or a parcel maybe, or whatever you had. Then we'd go off to the Corner House or some place for supper, handy. We'd have a table reserved—they'd know us, the waitresses and them; they'd keep back something special, just for us."

I could picture it too, clear as anything. The table with the ticket on, "Reserved." The waitress nodding at us, "Got curried eggs to-night." And we going through to get our trays, and my girl acting like she didn't know me, and me laughing to myself.

"D'you see what I mean?" I said to her. "It's not just being friends, it's more than that."

I don't know if she heard. She lay there looking up at me, touching my ear and my chin in that funny, gentle way. You'd say she was sorry for me.

"I'd like to buy you things," I said, "flowers sometimes. It's nice to

see a girl with a flower tucked in her dress; it looks clean and fresh. And
for special occasions, birthdays, Christmas, and that, something you'd
seen in a shopwindow, and wanted, but hadn't liked to go in and ask
the price. A brooch perhaps, or a bracelet, something pretty. And I'd
go in and get it when you weren't with me, and it'd cost much more
than my week's pay, but I wouldn't mind."

I could see the expression on her face, opening the parcel. And she'd
put it on, what I'd bought, and we'd go out together, and she'd be
dressed up a bit for the purpose, nothing glaring I don't mean, but
something that took the eye. You know, saucy.

"It's not fair to talk about getting married," I said, "not in these
days, when everything's uncertain. A fellow doesn't mind the uncer-
tainty, but it's hard on a girl. Cooped up in a couple of rooms maybe,
and queueing and rations and all. They like their freedom, and being
in a job, and not being tied down, the same as us. But it's nonsense the
way they were talking back in the coffee stall just now. About girls not
being the same as in old days, and the war to blame. As for the way
they treat them out East—I've seen some of it. I suppose that fellow
meant to be funny, they're all smart alecks in the Air Force, but it was
a silly line of talk, I thought."

She dropped her hands to her side and closed her eyes. It was getting
quite wet there on the tombstone. I was worried for her, though she
had her mac of course, but her legs and feet were damp in her thin
stockings and shoes.

"You weren't ever in the Air Force, were you?" she said.

Queer. Her voice had gone quite hard. Sharp, and different. Like as
if she was anxious about something, scared even.

"Not me," I said. "I served my time with R.E.M.E. Proper lot they
were. No swank, no nonsense. You know where you are with them."

"I'm glad," she said. "You're good and kind. I'm glad."

I wondered if she'd known some fellow in the R.A.F. who had let
her down. They're a wild crowd, the ones I've come across. And I remembered the way she'd looked at the boy drinking his tea at the stall.
Reflective, somehow. As if she was thinking back. I couldn't expect
her not to have been around a bit, with her looks, and then brought up
to play about the shelters, without parents, like she said. But I didn't
want to think of her being hurt by anyone.

"Why, what's wrong with them?" I said. "What's the R.A.F. done to you?"

"They smashed my home," she said.

"That was the Germans, not our fellows."

"It's all the same, they're killers, aren't they?" she said.

I looked down at her lying on the tombstone, and her voice wasn't hard any more, like when she'd asked me if I'd been in the Air Force, but it was tired, and sad, and oddly lonely, and it did something queer to my stomach, right in the pit of it, so that I wanted to do the darnedest silliest thing and take her home with me, back to where I lived with Mr. and Mrs. Thompson, and say to Mrs. Thompson—she was a kind old soul, she wouldn't mind—"Look, this is my girl. Look after her." Then I'd know she'd be safe, she'd be all right, nobody could do anything to hurt her. That was the thing I was afraid of suddenly, that someone would come along and hurt my girl.

I bent down and put my arms round her and lifted her up close.

"Listen," I said, "it's raining hard. I'm going to take you home. You'll catch your death lying here on the wet stone."

"No," she said, her hands on my shoulders, "nobody ever sees me home. You're going back where you belong, alone."

"I won't leave you here," I said.

"Yes, that's what I want you to do. If you refuse I shall be angry. You wouldn't want that, would you?"

I stared at her, puzzled. And her face was queer in the murky old light there, whiter than before, but it was beautiful, Jesus Christ, it was beautiful. That's blasphemy. But I can't say it no other way.

"What do you want me to do?" I asked.

"I want you to go and leave me here, and not look back," she said, "like someone dreaming, sleepwalking, they call it. Go back walking through the rain. It will take you hours. It doesn't matter; you're young and strong and you've got long legs. Go back to your room, wherever it is, and get into bed, and go to sleep, and wake and have your breakfast in the morning, and go off to work, the same as you always do."

"What about you?"

"Never mind about me. Just go."

"Can I call for you at the cinema tomorrow night? Can it be like what I was telling you, you know . . . going steady?"

She didn't answer. She only smiled. She sat quite still, looking into

my face, and then she closed her eyes and threw back her head and
said, "Kiss me again, stranger."

I left her, like she said. I didn't look back. I climbed through the
railings of the cemetery, out on to the road. No one seemed to be
about, and the coffee stall by the bus stop had closed down, the boards
were up.

I started walking the way the bus had brought us. The road was
straight, going on for ever. A High Street it must have been. There
were shops on either side, and it was right away northeast of London,
nowhere I'd ever been before. I was proper lost, but it didn't seem to
matter. I felt like a sleepwalker, just as she said.

I kept thinking of her all the time. There was nothing else, only her
face in front of me as I walked. They had a word for it in the Army,
when a girl gets a fellow that way so he can't see straight or hear right
or know what he's doing; and I thought it a lot of cock, or it only
happened to drunks, and now I knew it was true and it had happened
to me. I wasn't going to worry any more about how she'd get home;
she'd told me not to, and she must have lived handy, she'd never have
ridden out so far else, though it was funny living such a way from her
work. But maybe in time she'd tell me more, bit by bit. I wouldn't
drag it from her. I had one thing fixed in my mind, and that was to
pick her up the next evening from the picture palace. It was firm and
set, and nothing would budge me from that. The hours in between
would just be a blank for me until 10 P.M. came round.

I went on walking in the rain, and presently a lorry came along and
I thumbed a lift, and the driver took me a good part of the way before
he had to turn left in the other direction, and so I got down and
walked again, and it must have been close on three when I got home.

I would have felt bad, in an ordinary way, knocking up Mr. Thompson to let me in, and it had never happened before either, but I was
all lit up inside from loving my girl, and I didn't seem to mind. He came
down at last and opened the door. I had to ring several times before he
heard, and there he was, grey with sleep, poor old chap, his pyjamas
all crumpled from the bed.

"Whatever happened to you?" he said. "We've been worried, the
wife and me. We thought you'd been knocked down, run over. We

came back here and found the house empty and your supper not touched."

"I went to the pictures," I said.

"The pictures?" He stared up at me in the passageway. "The pictures stop at ten o'clock."

"I know," I said. "I went walking after that. Sorry. Good night."

And I climbed up the stairs to my room, leaving the old chap muttering to himself and bolting the door, and I heard Mrs. Thompson calling from her bedroom, "What is it? Is it him? Is he come home?"

I'd put them to trouble and to worry, and I ought to have gone in there and then and apologised, but I couldn't somehow, it wouldn't have come right; so I shut my door and threw off my clothes and got into bed, and it was like as if she was with me still, my girl, in the darkness.

They were a bit quiet at breakfast the next morning, Mr. and Mrs. Thompson. They didn't look at me. Mrs. Thompson gave me my kipper without a word, and he went on looking at his newspaper.

I ate my breakfast, and then I said, "I hope you had a nice evening up at Highgate?" and Mrs. Thompson, with her mouth a bit tight, she said, "Very pleasant, thank you, we were home by ten," and she gave a little sniff and poured Mr. Thompson out another cup of tea.

We went on being quiet, no one saying a word, and then Mrs. Thompson said, "Will you be in to supper this evening?" and I said, "No, I don't think so. I'm meeting a friend," and then I saw the old chap look at me over his spectacles.

"If you're going to be late," he said, "we'd best take the key for you."

Then he went on reading his paper. You could tell they were proper hurt that I didn't tell them anything, or say where I was going.

I went off to work, and we were busy at the garage that day, one job after the other came along, and any other time I wouldn't have minded. I liked a full day and often worked overtime, but today I wanted to get away before the shops closed; I hadn't thought about anything else since the idea came into my head.

It was getting on for half-past four, and the boss came to me and said, "I promised the doctor he'd have his Austin this evening; I said you'd be through with it by seven-thirty. That's O.K., isn't it?"

My heart sank. I'd counted on getting off early, because of what I wanted to do. Then I thought quickly that if the boss let me off now, and I went out to the shop before it closed, and came back again to do the job on the Austin, it would be all right, so I said, "I don't mind working a bit of overtime, but I'd like to slip out now, for half an hour, if you're going to be here. There's something I want to buy before the shops shut."

He told me that suited him, so I took off my overalls and washed and got my coat and I went off to the line of shops down at the bottom of Haverstock Hill. I knew the one I wanted. It was a jeweller's, where Mr. Thompson used to take his clock to be repaired, and it wasn't a place where they sold trash at all, but good stuff, solid-silver frames and that, and cutlery.

There were rings, of course, and a few fancy bangles, but I didn't like the look of them. All the girls in the N.A.A.F.I. used to wear bangles with charms on them, quite common it was, and I went on staring in at the window and then I spotted it, right at the back.

It was a brooch. Quite small, not much bigger than your thumbnail, but with a nice blue stone on it and a pin at the back, and it was shaped like a heart. That was what got me, the shape. I stared at it a bit, and there wasn't a ticket to it, which meant it would cost a bit, but I went in and asked to have a look at it. The jeweller got it out of the window for me, and he gave it a bit of a polish and turned it this way and that, and I saw it pinned on my girl, showing up nice on her frock or her jumper, and I knew this was it.

"I'll take it," I said, and then asked him the price.

I swallowed a bit when he told me, but I took out my wallet and counted the notes, and he put the heart in a box wrapped up careful with cotton wool, and made a neat package of it, tied with fancy string. I knew I'd have to get an advance from the boss before I went off work that evening, but he was a good chap and I was certain he'd give it to me.

I stood outside the jeweller's, with the packet for my girl safe in my breast pocket, and I heard the church clock strike a quarter to five. There was time to slip down to the cinema and make sure she understood about the date for the evening, and then I'd beat it fast up the road and get back to the garage, and I'd have the Austin done by the time the doctor wanted it.

When I got to the cinema my heart was beating like a sledge hammer and I could hardly swallow. I kept picturing to myself how she'd look, standing there by the curtains going in, with that velvet jacket and the cap on the back of her head.

There was a bit of a queue outside, and I saw they'd changed the programme. The poster of the western had gone, with the cowboy throwing a knife in the Indian's guts, and they had instead a lot of girls dancing, and some chap prancing in front of them with a walking stick. It was a musical.

I went in, and didn't go near the box office but looked straight to the curtains, where she'd be. There was an usherette there all right, but it wasn't her. This was a great tall girl who looked silly in the clothes, and she was trying to do two things at once—tear off the slips of tickets as the people went past, and hang on to her torch at the same time.

I waited a moment. Perhaps they'd switched over positions and my girl had gone up to the circle. When the last lot had got in through the curtains and there was a pause and she was free, I went up to her and I said, "Excuse me, do you know where I could have a word with the other young lady?"

She looked at me. "What other young lady?"

"The one who was here last night, with copper hair," I said.

She looked at me closer then, suspicious-like.

"She hasn't shown up today," she said. "I'm taking her place."

"Not shown up?"

"No. And it's funny you should ask. You're not the only one. The police were here not long ago. They had a word with the manager, and the commissionaire too, and no one's said anything to me yet, but I think there's been trouble."

My heart beat different then. Not excited, bad. Like when someone's ill, took to hospital, sudden.

"The police?" I said. "What were they here for?"

"I told you, I don't know," she answered, "but it was something to do with her, and the manager went with them to the police station, and he hasn't come back yet. This way, please, circle on the left, stalls to the right."

I just stood there, not knowing what to do. It was like as if the floor had been knocked away from under me.

The tall girl tore another slip off a ticket and then she said to me, over her shoulder, "Was she a friend of yours?"

"Sort of," I said. I didn't know what to say.

"Well, if you ask me, she was queer in the head, and it wouldn't surprise me if she'd done away with herself and they'd found her dead. No, ice creams served in the interval, after the newsreel."

I went out and stood in the street. The queue was growing for the cheaper seats, and there were children too, talking, excited. I brushed past them and started walking up the street, and I felt sick inside, queer. Something had happened to my girl. I knew it now. That was why she had wanted to get rid of me last night, and for me not to see her home. She was going to do herself in, there in the cemetery. That's why she talked funny and looked so white, and now they'd found her, lying there on the gravestone by the railings.

If I hadn't gone away and left her she'd have been all right. If I'd stayed with her just five minutes longer, coaxing her, I'd have got her round to my way of thinking and seen her home, standing no nonsense, and she'd be at the picture palace now, showing the people to their seats.

It might be it wasn't as bad as what I feared. It might be she was found wandering, lost her memory and got picked up by the police and taken off, and then they found out where she worked and that, and now the police wanted to check up with the manager at the cinema to see if it was so. If I went down to the police station and asked them there, maybe they'd tell me what had happened, and I could say she was my girl, we were walking out, and it wouldn't matter if she didn't recognise me even, I'd stick to the story. I couldn't let down my boss, I had to get that job done on the Austin, but afterwards, when I'd finished, I could go down to the police station.

All the heart had gone out of me, and I went back to the garage hardly knowing what I was doing, and for the first time ever the smell of the place turned my stomach, the oil and the grease, and there was a chap roaring up his engine, before backing out his car, and a great cloud of smoke coming from his exhaust, filling the workshop with stink.

I went and got my overalls, and put them on, and fetched the tools, and started on the Austin, and all the time I was wondering what it was that had happened to my girl, if she was down at the police station, lost and lonely, or if she was lying somewhere . . . dead. I kept seeing her face all the time like it was last night.

It took me an hour and a half, not more, to get the Austin ready for the road, filled up with petrol and all, and I had her facing outwards to the street for the owner to drive out, but I was all in by then, dead tired, and the sweat pouring down my face. I had a bit of a wash and put on my coat, and I felt the package in the breast pocket. I took it out and looked at it, done so neat with the fancy ribbon, and I put it back again, and I hadn't noticed the boss come in—I was standing with my back to the door.

"Did you get what you want?" he said, cheerful-like and smiling. He was a good chap, never out of temper, and we got along well.

"Yes," I said.

But I didn't want to talk about it. I told him the job was done and the Austin was ready to drive away. I went to the office with him so that he could note down the work done, and the overtime, and he offered me a fag from the packet lying on his desk beside the evening paper.

"I see Lady Luck won the three-thirty," he said. "I'm a couple of quid up this week."

He was entering my work in his ledger, to keep the pay roll right.

"Good for you," I said.

"Only backed it for a place, like a clot," he said. "She was twenty-five to one. Still, it's all in the game."

I didn't answer. I'm not one for drinking, but I needed one bad just then. I mopped my forehead with my handkerchief. I wished he'd get on with the figures, and say good night, and let me go.

"Another poor devil's had it," he said. "That's the third now in three weeks, ripped right up the guts, same as the others. He died in hospital this morning. Looks like there's a hoodoo on the R.A.F."

"What was it, flying jets?" I asked.

"Jets?" he said. "No, damn it, murder. Sliced up the belly, poor sod. Don't you ever read the papers? It's the third one in three weeks, done identical, all Air Force fellows, and each time they've found 'em near a graveyard or a cemetery. I was saying just now, to that chap who came in for petrol, it's not only men who go off their rockers and turn sex maniacs, but women too. They'll get this one all right though, you see. It says in the paper they've a line on her and expect an arrest shortly. About time, too, before another poor blighter cops it."

He shut up his ledger and stuck his pencil behind his ear.

"Like a drink?" he said. "I've got a bottle of gin in the cupboard."

"No," I said, "no, thanks very much. I've . . . I've got a date."

"That's right," he said, smiling, "enjoy yourself."

I walked down the street and bought an evening paper. It was like what he said about the murder. They had it on the front page. They said it must have happened about 2 A.M. Young fellow in the Air Force, in northeast London. He had managed to stagger to a call box and get through to the police, and they found him there on the floor of the box when they arrived.

He made a statement in the ambulance before he died. He said a girl called to him, and he followed her, and he thought it was just a bit of love-making—he'd seen her with another fellow drinking coffee at a stall a little while before—and he thought she'd thrown this other fellow over and had taken a fancy to him, and then she got him, he said, right in the guts.

It said in the paper that he had given the police a full description of her, and it said also that the police would be glad if the man who had been seen with the girl earlier in the evening would come forward to help in identification.

I didn't want the paper any more. I threw it away. I walked about the streets till I was tired, and when I guessed Mr. and Mrs. Thompson had gone to bed I went home, and groped for the key they'd left on a piece of string hanging inside the letter box, and I let myself in and went upstairs to my room.

Mrs. Thompson had turned down the bed and put a Thermos of tea for me, thoughtful-like, and the evening paper, the late edition.

They'd got her. About three o'clock in the afternoon. I didn't read the writing, nor the name nor anything. I sat down on my bed and took up the paper, and there was my girl staring up at me from the front page.

Then I took the package from my coat and undid it, and threw away the wrapper and the fancy string, and sat there looking down at the little heart I held in my hand.

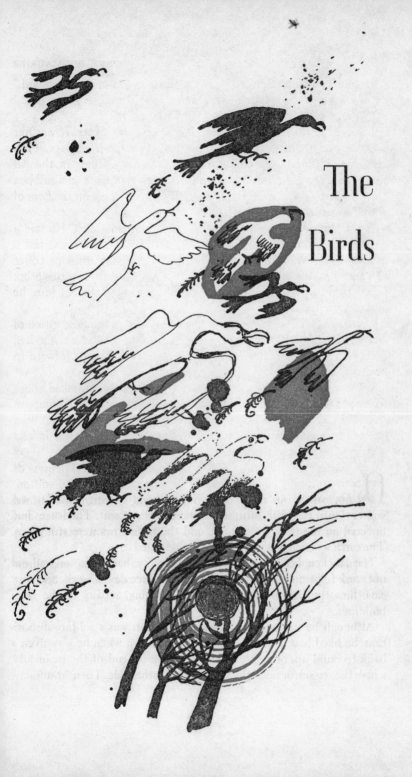

The
Birds

On december the third the wind changed overnight and it was winter. Until then the autumn had been mellow, soft. The leaves had lingered on the trees, golden-red, and the hedgerows were still green. The earth was rich where the plough had turned it.

Nat Hocken, because of a wartime disability, had a pension and did not work full-time at the farm. He worked three days a week, and they gave him the lighter jobs: hedging, thatching, repairs to the farm buildings.

Although he was married, with children, his was a solitary disposition; he liked best to work alone. It pleased him when he was given a bank to build up, or a gate to mend at the far end of the peninsula, where the sea surrounded the farmland on either side. Then, at midday, he would pause and eat the pasty that his wife had baked for him, and, sitting on the cliff's edge, would watch the birds. Autumn was best for this, better than spring. In spring the birds flew inland, purposeful, intent; they knew where they were bound, the rhythm and ritual of their life brooked no delay. In autumn those that had not migrated overseas but remained to pass the winter were caught up in the same driving urge, but because migration was denied them followed a pattern of their own. Great flocks of them came to the peninsula, restless, uneasy, spending themselves in motion; now wheeling, circling in the sky, now settling to feed on the rich new-turned soil, but even when they fed it was as though they did so without hunger, without desire. Restlessness drove them to the skies again.

Black and white, jackdaw and gull, mingled in strange partnership, seeking some sort of liberation, never satisfied, never still. Flocks of starlings, rustling like silk, flew to fresh pasture, driven by the same necessity of movement, and the smaller birds, the finches and the larks, scattered from tree to hedge as if compelled.

Nat watched them, and he watched the sea birds too. Down in the bay they waited for the tide. They had more patience. Oyster catchers, redshank, sanderling, and curlew watched by the water's edge; as the slow sea sucked at the shore and then withdrew, leaving the strip of seaweed bare and the shingle churned, the sea birds raced and ran upon the beaches. Then that same impulse to flight seized upon them too. Crying, whistling, calling, they skimmed the placid sea and left the shore. Make haste, make speed, hurry and begone; yet where, and to what purpose? The restless urge of autumn, unsatisfying, sad, had put a spell upon them and they must flock, and wheel, and cry; they must spill themselves of motion before winter came.

"Perhaps," thought Nat, munching his pasty by the cliff's edge, "a message comes to the birds in autumn, like a warning. Winter is coming. Many of them perish. And like people who, apprehensive of death before their time, drive themselves to work or folly, the birds do likewise."

The birds had been more restless than ever this fall of the year, the agitation more marked because the days were still. As the tractor traced its path up and down the western hills, the figure of the farmer silhouetted on the driving seat, the whole machine and the man upon it would be lost momentarily in the great cloud of wheeling, crying birds.

There were many more than usual, Nat was sure of this. Always, in autumn, they followed the plough, but not in great flocks like these, nor with such clamour.

Nat remarked upon it when hedging was finished for the day. "Yes," said the farmer, "there are more birds about than usual; I've noticed it too. And daring, some of them, taking no notice of the tractor. One or two gulls came so close to my head this afternoon I thought they'd knock my cap off! As it was, I could scarcely see what I was doing, when they were overhead and I had the sun in my eyes. I have a notion the weather will change. It will be a hard winter. That's why the birds are restless."

Nat, tramping home across the fields and down the lane to his cottage, saw the birds still flocking over the western hills, in the last glow of the sun. No wind, and the grey sea calm and full. Campion in bloom yet in the hedges, and the air mild. The farmer was right, though, and it was that night the weather turned. Nat's bedroom faced east. He woke just after two and heard the wind in the chimney. Not the storm and bluster of a sou' westerly gale, bringing the rain, but east wind, cold and dry. It sounded hollow in the chimney, and a loose slate rattled on the roof. Nat listened, and he could hear the sea roaring in the bay. Even the air in the small bedroom had turned chill: a draught came under the skirting of the door, blowing upon the bed. Nat drew the blanket round him, leant closer to the back of his sleeping wife, and stayed wakeful, watchful, aware of misgiving without cause.

Then he heard the tapping on the window. There was no creeper on the cottage walls to break loose and scratch upon the pane. He listened, and the tapping continued until, irritated by the sound, Nat got out of bed and went to the window. He opened it, and as he did so something brushed his hand, jabbing at his knuckles, grazing the skin. Then he saw the flutter of the wings and it was gone, over the roof, behind the cottage.

It was a bird; what kind of bird he could not tell. The wind must have driven it to shelter on the sill.

He shut the window and went back to bed, but, feeling his knuckles wet, put his mouth to the scratch. The bird had drawn blood. Frightened, he supposed, and bewildered, the bird, seeking shelter, had stabbed at him in the darkness. Once more he settled himself to sleep.

Presently the tapping came again, this time more forceful, more insistent, and now his wife woke at the sound and, turning in the bed, said to him, "See to the window, Nat, it's rattling."

"I've already seen to it," he told her; "there's some bird there trying to get in. Can't you hear the wind? It's blowing from the east, driving the birds to shelter."

"Send them away," she said, "I can't sleep with that noise."

He went to the window for the second time, and now when he opened it there was not one bird upon the sill but half a dozen; they flew straight into his face, attacking him.

He shouted, striking out at them with his arms, scattering them; like the first one, they flew over the roof and disappeared. Quickly he let the window fall and latched it.

"Did you hear that?" he said. "They went for me. Tried to peck my eyes." He stood by the window, peering into the darkness, and could see nothing. His wife, heavy with sleep, murmured from the bed.

"I'm not making it up," he said, angry at her suggestion. "I tell you the birds were on the sill, trying to get into the room."

Suddenly a frightened cry came from the room across the passage where the children slept.

"It's Jill," said his wife, roused at the sound, sitting up in bed. "Go to her, see what's the matter."

Nat lit the candle, but when he opened the bedroom door to cross the passage the draught blew out the flame.

There came a second cry of terror, this time from both children, and stumbling into their room, he felt the beating of wings about him in the darkness. The window was wide open. Through it came the birds, hitting first the ceiling and the walls, then swerving in mid-flight, turning to the children in their beds.

"It's all right, I'm here," shouted Nat, and the children flung themselves, screaming, upon him, while in the darkness the birds rose and dived and came for him again.

"What is it, Nat, what's happened?" his wife called from the further bedroom, and swiftly he pushed the children through the door to the passage and shut it upon them, so that he was alone now in their bedroom with the birds.

He seized a blanket from the nearest bed and, using it as a weapon, flung it to right and left about him in the air. He felt the thud of bodies, heard the fluttering of wings, but they were not yet defeated, for again and again they returned to the assault, jabbing his hands, his head, the little stabbing beaks sharp as pointed forks. The blanket became a weapon of defence; he wound it about his head, and then in greater darkness beat at the birds with his bare hands. He dared not stumble to the door and open it, lest in doing so the birds should follow him.

How long he fought with them in the darkness he could not tell, but at last the beating of the wings about him lessened and then withdrew, and through the density of the blanket he was aware of light. He waited, listened; there was no sound except the fretful crying of one of the children from the bedroom beyond. The fluttering, the whirring of the wings had ceased.

He took the blanket from his head and stared about him. The cold grey morning light exposed the room. Dawn and the open window had called the living birds; the dead lay on the floor. Nat gazed at the little corpses, shocked and horrified. They were all small birds, none of any size; there must have been fifty of them lying there upon the floor. There were robins, finches, sparrows, blue tits, larks, and bramblings, birds that by nature's law kept to their own flock and their own territory, and now, joining one with another in their urge for battle, had destroyed themselves against the bedroom walls, or in the strife had been destroyed by him. Some had lost feathers in the fight; others had blood, his blood, upon their beaks.

Sickened, Nat went to the window and stared out across his patch of garden to the fields.

It was bitter cold, and the ground had all the hard black look of frost. Not white frost, to shine in the morning sun, but the black frost that the east wind brings. The sea, fiercer now with the turning tide, white-capped and steep, broke harshly in the bay. Of the birds there was no sign. Not a sparrow chattered in the hedge beyond the garden gate, no early missel-thrush or blackbird pecked on the grass for worms. There was no sound at all but the east wind and the sea.

Nat shut the window and the door of the small bedroom, and went back across the passage to his own. His wife sat up in bed, one child asleep beside her, the smaller in her arms, his face bandaged. The curtains were tightly drawn across the window, the candles lit. Her face looked garish in the yellow light. She shook her head for silence.

"He's sleeping now," she whispered, "but only just. Something must have cut him, there was blood at the corner of his eyes. Jill said it was the birds. She said she woke up, and the birds were in the room."

His wife looked up at Nat, searching his face for confirmation. She looked terrified, bewildered, and he did not want her to know that he was also shaken, dazed almost, by the events of the past few hours.

"There are birds in there," he said, "dead birds, nearly fifty of them. Robins, wrens, all the little birds from hereabouts. It's as though a madness seized them, with the east wind." He sat down on the bed beside his wife, and held her hand. "It's the weather," he said, "it must be that, it's the hard weather. They aren't the birds, maybe, from here around. They've been driven down from upcountry."

"But, Nat," whispered his wife, "it's only this night that the weather turned. There's been no snow to drive them. And they can't be hungry yet. There's food for them out there in the fields."

"It's the weather," repeated Nat. "I tell you, it's the weather."

His face, too, was drawn and tired, like hers. They stared at one another for a while without speaking.

"I'll go downstairs and make a cup of tea," he said.

The sight of the kitchen reassured him. The cups and saucers, neatly stacked upon the dresser, the table and chairs, his wife's roll of knitting on her basket chair, the children's toys in a corner cupboard.

He knelt down, raked out the old embers, and relit the fire. The glowing sticks brought normality, the steaming kettle and the brown teapot comfort and security. He drank his tea, carried a cup up to his wife. Then he washed in the scullery, and, putting on his boots, opened the back door.

The sky was hard and leaden, and the brown hills that had gleamed in the sun the day before looked dark and bare. The east wind, like a razor, stripped the trees, and the leaves, crackling and dry, shivered and scattered with the wind's blast. Nat stubbed the earth with his boot. It was frozen hard. He had never known a change so swift and sudden. Black winter had descended in a single night.

The children were awake now. Jill was chattering upstairs and young Johnny crying once again. Nat heard his wife's voice, soothing, comforting. Presently they came down. He had breakfast ready for them, and the routine of the day began.

"Did you drive away the birds?" asked Jill, restored to calm because of the kitchen fire, because of day, because of breakfast.

"Yes, they've all gone now," said Nat. "It was the east wind brought them in. They were frightened and lost, they wanted shelter."

"They tried to peck us," said Jill. "They went for Johnny's eyes."

"Fright made them do that," said Nat. "They didn't know where they were in the dark bedroom."

"I hope they won't come again," said Jill. "Perhaps if we put bread for them outside the window they will eat that and fly away."

She finished her breakfast and then went for her coat and hood, her schoolbooks and her satchel. Nat said nothing, but his wife looked at him across the table. A silent message passed between them.

"I'll walk with her to the bus," he said. "I don't go to the farm today."

And while the child was washing in the scullery he said to his wife, "Keep all the windows closed, and the doors too. Just to be on the safe side. I'll go to the farm. Find out if they heard anything in the night." Then he walked with his small daughter up the lane. She seemed to have forgotten her experience of the night before. She danced ahead of him, chasing the leaves, her face whipped with the cold and rosy under the pixie hood.

"Is it going to snow, Dad?" she said. "It's cold enough."

He glanced up at the bleak sky, felt the wind tear at his shoulders.

"No," he said, "it's not going to snow. This is a black winter, not a white one."

All the while he searched the hedgerows for the birds, glanced over the top of them to the fields beyond, looked to the small wood above the farm where the rooks and jackdaws gathered. He saw none.

The other children waited by the bus stop, muffled, hooded like Jill, the faces white and pinched with cold.

Jill ran to them, waving. "My Dad says it won't snow," she called, "it's going to be a black winter."

She said nothing of the birds. She began to push and struggle with another little girl. The bus came ambling up the hill. Nat saw her on to it, then turned and walked back towards the farm. It was not his day for work, but he wanted to satisfy himself that all was well. Jim, the cowman, was clattering in the yard.

"Boss around?" asked Nat.

"Gone to market," said Jim. "It's Tuesday, isn't it?"

He clumped off round the corner of a shed. He had no time for Nat. Nat was said to be superior. Read books, and the like. Nat had forgotten it was Tuesday. This showed how the events of the preceding night had shaken him. He went to the back door of the farmhouse and heard Mrs. Trigg singing in the kitchen, the wireless making a background to her song.

"Are you there, missus?" called out Nat.

She came to the door, beaming, broad, a good-tempered woman.

"Hullo, Mr. Hocken," she said. "Can you tell me where this cold is coming from? Is it Russia? I've never seen such a change. And it's going on, the wireless says. Something to do with the Arctic Circle."

"We didn't turn on the wireless this morning," said Nat. "Fact is, we had trouble in the night."

"Kiddies poorly?"

"No . . ." He hardly knew how to explain it. Now, in daylight, the battle of the birds would sound absurd.

He tried to tell Mrs. Trigg what had happened, but he could see from her eyes that she thought his story was the result of a nightmare.

"Sure they were real birds," she said, smiling, "with proper feathers and all? Not the funny-shaped kind that the men see after closing hours on a Saturday night?"

"Mrs. Trigg," he said, "there are fifty dead birds, robins, wrens, and such, lying low on the floor of the children's bedroom. They went for me; they tried to go for young Johnny's eyes."

Mrs. Trigg stared at him doubtfully.

"Well there, now," she answered, "I suppose the weather brought them. Once in the bedroom, they wouldn't know where they were to. Foreign birds maybe, from that Arctic Circle."

"No," said Nat, "they were the birds you see about here every day."

"Funny thing," said Mrs. Trigg, "no explaining it, really. You ought to write up and ask the *Guardian*. They'd have some answer for it. Well, I must be getting on."

She nodded, smiled, and went back into the kitchen.

Nat, dissatisfied, turned to the farm gate. Had it not been for those corpses on the bedroom floor, which he must now collect and bury somewhere, he would have considered the tale exaggeration too.

Jim was standing by the gate.

"Had any trouble with the birds?" asked Nat.

"Birds? What birds?"

"We got them up our place last night. Scores of them, came in the children's bedroom. Quite savage they were."

"Oh?" It took time for anything to penetrate Jim's head. "Never heard of birds acting savage," he said at length. "They get tame, like, sometimes. I've seen them come to the windows for crumbs."

"These birds last night weren't tame."

"No? Cold, maybe. Hungry. You put out some crumbs."

Jim was no more interested than Mrs. Trigg had been. It was, Nat thought, like air raids in the war. No one down this end of the country knew what the Plymouth folk had seen and suffered. You had to endure something yourself before it touched you. He walked back along the lane and crossed the stile to his cottage. He found his wife in the kitchen with young Johnny.

"See anyone?" she asked.

"Mrs. Trigg and Jim," he answered. "I don't think they believed me. Anyway, nothing wrong up there."

"You might take the birds away," she said. "I daren't go into the room to make the beds until you do. I'm scared."

"Nothing to scare you now," said Nat. "They're dead, aren't they?"

He went up with a sack and dropped the stiff bodies into it, one by one. Yes, there were fifty of them, all told. Just the ordinary common birds of the hedgerow, nothing as large even as a thrush. It must have been fright that made them act the way they did. Blue tits, wrens—it was incredible to think of the power of their small beaks jabbing at his face and hands the night before. He took the sack out into the garden and was faced now with a fresh problem. The ground was too hard to dig. It was frozen solid, yet no snow had fallen, nothing had happened in the past hours but the coming of the east wind. It was unnatural, queer. The weather prophets must be right. The change was something connected with the Arctic Circle.

The wind seemed to cut him to the bone as he stood there uncertainly, holding the sack. He could see the white-capped seas breaking down under in the bay. He decided to take the birds to the shore and bury them.

When he reached the beach below the headland he could scarcely stand, the force of the east wind was so strong. It hurt to draw breath, and his bare hands were blue. Never had he known such cold, not in all the bad winters he could remember. It was low tide. He crunched his way over the shingle to the softer sand and then, his back to the wind, ground a pit in the sand with his heel. He meant to drop the birds into it, but as he opened up the sack the force of the wind carried them, lifted them, as though in flight again, and they were blown away from him along the beach, tossed like feathers, spread and scattered, the bodies of the fifty frozen birds. There was something ugly in the sight. He did not like it. The dead birds were swept away from him by the wind.

"The tide will take them when it turns," he said to himself.

He looked out to sea and watched the crested breakers, combing green. They rose stiffly, curled, and broke again, and because it was ebb tide the roar was distant, more remote, lacking the sound and thunder of the flood.

Then he saw them. The gulls. Out there, riding the seas.

What he had thought at first to be the whitecaps of the waves were gulls. Hundreds, thousands, tens of thousands . . . They rose and fell in the trough of the seas, heads to the wind, like a mighty fleet at anchor, waiting on the tide. To eastward, and to the west, the gulls were there. They stretched as far as his eye could reach, in close formation, line upon line. Had the sea been still they would have covered the bay like a white cloud, head to head, body packed to body. Only the east wind, whipping the sea to breakers, hid them from the shore.

Nat turned and, leaving the beach, climbed the steep path home. Someone should know of this. Someone should be told. Something was happening, because of the east wind and the weather, that he did not understand. He wondered if he should go to the call box by the bus stop and ring up the police. Yet what could they do? What could anyone do? Tens and thousands of gulls riding the sea there in the bay because of storm, because of hunger. The police would think him mad, or drunk, or take the statement from him with great calm. "Thank you. Yes, the matter has already been reported. The hard weather is driving the birds inland in great numbers." Nat looked about him. Still no sign of any other bird. Perhaps the cold had sent them all from upcountry? As he drew near to the cottage his wife came to meet him at the door. She called to him, excited. "Nat," she said, "it's on the wireless. They've just read out a special news bulletin. I've written it down."

"What's on the wireless?" he said.

"About the birds," she said. "It's not only here, it's everywhere. In London, all over the country. Something has happened to the birds."

Together they went into the kitchen. He read the piece of paper lying on the table.

"Statement from the Home Office at 11 A.M. today. Reports from all over the country are coming in hourly about the vast quantity of birds flocking above towns, villages, and outlying districts, causing obstruction and damage and even attacking individuals. It is thought that the Arctic air stream, at present covering the British Isles, is causing birds to migrate south in immense numbers, and that intense hunger may drive these birds to attack human beings. Householders are warned to see to their windows, doors, and chimneys, and to take reasonable precautions for the safety of their children. A further statement will be issued later."

A kind of excitement seized Nat; he looked at his wife in triumph.

"There you are," he said. "Let's hope they'll hear that at the farm. Mrs. Trigg will know it wasn't any story. It's true. All over the country. I've been telling myself all morning there's something wrong. And just now, down on the beach, I looked out to sea and there are gulls, thousands of them, tens of thousands—you couldn't put a pin between their heads—and they're all out there, riding on the sea, waiting."

"What are they waiting for, Nat?" she asked.

He stared at her, then looked down again at the piece of paper. "I don't know," he said slowly. "It says here the birds are hungry." He went over to the drawer where he kept his hammer and tools.

"What are you going to do, Nat?"

"See to the windows and the chimneys too, like they tell you."

"You think they would break in, with the windows shut? Those sparrows and robins and such? Why, how could they?"

He did not answer. He was not thinking of the robins and the sparrows. He was thinking of the gulls. . . .

He went upstairs and worked there the rest of the morning, boarding the windows of the bedrooms, filling up the chimney bases. Good job it was his free day and he was not working at the farm. It reminded him of the old days, at the beginning of the war. He was not married then, and he had made all the black-out boards for his mother's house in Plymouth. Made the shelter too. Not that it had been of any use when the moment came. He wondered if they would take these precautions up at the farm. He doubted it. Too easygoing, Harry Trigg and his missus. Maybe they'd laugh at the whole thing. Go off to a dance or a whist drive.

"Dinner's ready." She called him, from the kitchen.

"All right. Coming down."

He was pleased with his handiwork. The frames fitted nicely over the little panes and at the bases of the chimneys.

When dinner was over and his wife was washing up, Nat switched on the one o'clock news. The same announcement was repeated, the one which she had taken down during the morning, but the news bulletin enlarged upon it. "The flocks of birds have caused dislocation in all areas," read the announcer, "and in London the sky was so dense at ten o'clock this morning that it seemed as if the city was covered by a vast black cloud.

"The birds settled on roof tops, on window ledges, and on chimneys. The species included blackbird, thrush, the common house sparrow, and, as might be expected in the metropolis, a vast quantity of pigeons and starlings, and that frequenter of the London river, the black-headed gull. The sight has been so unusual that traffic came to a standstill in many thoroughfares, work was abandoned in shops and offices, and the streets and pavements were crowded with people standing about to watch the birds."

Various incidents were recounted, the suspected reason of cold and hunger stated again, and warnings to householders repeated. The announcer's voice was smooth and suave. Nat had the impression that this man, in particular, treated the whole business as he would an elaborate joke. There would be others like him, hundreds of them, who did not know what it was to struggle in darkness with a flock of birds. There would be parties tonight in London, like the ones they gave on election nights. People standing about, shouting and laughing, getting drunk. "Come and watch the birds!"

Nat switched off the wireless. He got up and started work on the kitchen windows. His wife watched him, young Johnny at her heels.

"What, boards for down here too?" she said. "Why, I'll have to light up before three o'clock. I see no call for boards down here."

"Better be sure than sorry," answered Nat. "I'm not going to take any chances."

"What they ought to do," she said, "is to call the Army out and shoot the birds. That would soon scare them off."

"Let them try," said Nat. "How'd they set about it?"

"They have the Army to the docks," she answered, "when the dockers strike. The soldiers go down and unload the ships."

"Yes," said Nat, "and the population of London is eight million or more. Think of all the buildings, all the flats and houses. Do you think they've enough soldiers to go round shooting birds from every roof?"

"I don't know. But something should be done. They ought to do something."

Nat thought to himself that "they" were no doubt considering the problem at that very moment, but whatever "they" decided to do in London and the big cities would not help the people here, three hundred miles away. Each householder must look after his own.

"How are we off for food?" he said.

"Now, Nat, whatever next?"

"Never mind. What have you got in the larder?"

"It's shopping day tomorrow, you know that. I don't keep uncooked food hanging about, it goes off. Butcher doesn't call till the day after. But I can bring back something when I go in tomorrow."

Nat did not want to scare her. He thought it possible that she might not go to town tomorrow. He looked in the larder for himself, and in the cupboard where she kept her tins. They would do for a couple of days. Bread was low.

"What about the baker?"

"He comes tomorrow too."

He saw she had flour. If the baker did not call she had enough to bake one loaf.

"We'd be better off in old days," he said, "when the women baked twice a week, and had pilchards salted, and there was food for a family to last a siege, if need be."

"I've tried the children with tinned fish, they don't like it," she said.

Nat went on hammering the boards across the kitchen windows. Candles. They were low in candles too. That must be another thing she meant to buy tomorrow. Well, it could not be helped. They must go early to bed tonight. That was, if . . .

He got up and went out of the back door and stood in the garden, looking down towards the sea. There had been no sun all day, and now, at barely three o'clock, a kind of darkness had already come, the sky sullen, heavy, colourless like salt. He could hear the vicious sea drumming on the rocks. He walked down the path, halfway to the beach. And then he stopped. He could see the tide had turned. The rock that had shown in midmorning was now covered, but it was not the sea that held his eyes. The gulls had risen. They were circling, hundreds of them, thousands of them, lifting their wings against the wind. It was the gulls that made the darkening of the sky. And they were silent. They made not a sound. They just went on soaring and circling, rising, falling, trying their strength against the wind.

Nat turned. He ran up the path, back to the cottage.

"I'm going for Jill," he said. "I'll wait for her at the bus stop."

"What's the matter?" asked his wife. "You've gone quite white."

"Keep Johnny inside," he said. "Keep the door shut. Light up now, and draw the curtains."

"It's only just gone three," she said.

"Never mind. Do what I tell you."

He looked inside the tool shed outside the back door. Nothing there of much use. A spade was too heavy, and a fork no good. He took the hoe. It was the only possible tool, and light enough to carry.

He started walking up the lane to the bus stop, and now and again glanced back over his shoulder.

The gulls had risen higher now, their circles were broader, wider, they were spreading out in huge formation across the sky.

He hurried on; although he knew the bus would not come to the top of the hill before four o'clock he had to hurry. He passed no one on the way. He was glad of this. No time to stop and chatter.

At the top of the hill he waited. He was much too soon. There was half an hour still to go. The east wind came whipping across the fields from the higher ground. He stamped his feet and blew upon his hands. In the distance he could see the clay hills, white and clean, against the heavy pallor of the sky. Something black rose from behind them, like a smudge at first, then widening, becoming deeper, and the smudge became a cloud, and the cloud divided again into five other clouds, spreading north, east, south, and west, and they were not clouds at all; they were birds. He watched them travel across the sky, and as one section passed overhead, within two or three hundred feet of him, he knew, from their speed, they were bound inland, upcountry; they had no business with the people here on the peninsula. They were rooks, crows, jackdaws, magpies, jays, all birds that usually preyed upon the smaller species; but this afternoon they were bound on some other mission.

"They've been given the towns," thought Nat; "they know what they have to do. We don't matter so much here. The gulls will serve for us. The others go to the towns."

He went to the call box, stepped inside, and lifted the receiver. The exchange would do. They would pass the message on.

"I'm speaking from Highway," he said, "by the bus stop. I want to report large formations of birds travelling upcountry. The gulls are also forming in the bay."

"All right," answered the voice, laconic, weary.

"You'll be sure and pass this message on to the proper quarter?"

"Yes . . . yes . . ." Impatient now, fed-up. The buzzing note resumed.

"She's another," thought Nat, "she doesn't care. Maybe she's had to answer calls all day. She hopes to go to the pictures tonight. She'll squeeze some fellow's hand, and point up at the sky, and 'Look at all them birds!' She doesn't care."

The bus came lumbering up the hill. Jill climbed out, and three or four other children. The bus went on towards the town.

"What's the hoe for, Dad?"

They crowded around him, laughing, pointing.

"I just brought it along," he said. "Come on now, let's get home. It's cold, no hanging about. Here, you. I'll watch you across the fields, see how fast you can run."

He was speaking to Jill's companions, who came from different families, living in the council houses. A short cut would take them to the cottages.

"We want to play a bit in the lane," said one of them.

"No, you don't. You go off home or I'll tell your Mammy."

They whispered to one another, round-eyed, then scuttled off across the fields. Jill stared at her father, her mouth sullen.

"We always play in the lane," she said.

"Not tonight, you don't," he said. "Come on now, no dawdling."

He could see the gulls now, circling the fields, coming in towards the land. Still silent. Still no sound.

"Look, Dad, look over there, look at all the gulls."

"Yes. Hurry, now."

"Where are they flying to? Where are they going?"

"Upcountry, I dare say. Where it's warmer."

He seized her hand and dragged her after him along the lane.

"Don't go so fast. I can't keep up."

The gulls were copying the rooks and crows. They were spreading out in formation across the sky. They headed, in bands of thousands, to the four compass points.

"Dad, what is it? What are the gulls doing?"

They were not intent upon their flight, as the crows, as the jackdaws had been. They still circled overhead. Nor did they fly so high. It was as though they waited upon some signal. As though some decision had yet to be given. The order was not clear.

"Do you want me to carry you, Jill? Here, come pick-a-back."

This way he might put on speed; but he was wrong. Jill was heavy. She kept slipping. And she was crying too. His sense of urgency, of fear, had communicated itself to the child.

"I wish the gulls would go away. I don't like them. They're coming closer to the lane."

He put her down again. He started running, swinging Jill after him. As they went past the farm turning he saw the farmer backing his car out of the garage. Nat called to him.

"Can you give us a lift?" he said.

"What's that?"

Mr. Trigg turned in the driving seat and stared at them. Then a smile came to his cheerful, rubicund face.

"It looks as though we're in for some fun," he said. "Have you seen the gulls? Jim and I are going to take a crack at them. Everyone's gone bird-crazy, talking of nothing else. I hear you were troubled in the night. Want a gun?"

Nat shook his head.

The small car was packed. There was just room for Jill, if she crouched on top of petrol tins on the back seat.

"I don't want a gun," said Nat, "but I'd be obliged if you'd run Jill home. She's scared of the birds."

He spoke briefly. He did not want to talk in front of Jill.

"O.K.," said the farmer, "I'll take her home. Why don't you stop behind and join the shooting match? We'll make the feathers fly."

Jill climbed in, and, turning the car, the driver sped up the lane. Nat followed after. Trigg must be crazy. What use was a gun against a sky of birds?

Now Nat was not responsible for Jill, he had time to look about him. The birds were circling still above the fields. Mostly herring gull, but the black-backed gull amongst them. Usually they kept apart. Now they were united. Some bond had brought them together. It was the black-backed gull that attacked the smaller birds, and even newborn lambs, so he'd heard. He'd never seen it done. He remembered this now, though, looking above him in the sky. They were coming in towards the farm. They were circling lower in the sky, and the black-backed gulls were to the front, the black-backed gulls were leading. The farm, then, was their target. They were making for the farm.

Nat increased his pace towards his own cottage. He saw the farmer's car turn and come back along the lane. It drew up beside him with a jerk.

"The kid has run inside," said the farmer. "Your wife was watching for her. Well, what do you make of it? They're saying in town the Russians have done it. The Russians have poisoned the birds."

"How could they do that?" asked Nat.

"Don't ask me. You know how stories get around. Will you join my shooting match?"

"No, I'll get along home. The wife will be worried else."

"My missus says if you could eat gull there'd be some sense in it," said Trigg, "we'd have roast gull, baked gull, and pickle 'em into the bargain. You wait until I let off a few barrels into the brutes. That'll scare 'em."

"Have you boarded your windows?" asked Nat.

"No. Lot of nonsense. They like to scare you on the wireless. I've had more to do today than to go round boarding up my windows."

"I'd board them now, if I were you."

"Garn. You're windy. Like to come to our place to sleep?"

"No, thanks all the same."

"All right. See you in the morning. Give you a gull breakfast."

The farmer grinned and turned his car to the farm entrance.

Nat hurried on. Past the little wood, past the old barn, and then across the stile to the remaining field.

As he jumped the stile he heard the whir of wings. A black-backed gull dived down at him from the sky, missed, swerved in flight, and rose to dive again. In a moment it was joined by others, six, seven, a dozen, black-backed and herring mixed. Nat dropped his hoe. The hoe was useless. Covering his head with his arms, he ran towards the cottage. They kept coming at him from the air, silent save for the beating wings. The terrible, fluttering wings. He would feel the blood on his hands, his wrists, his neck. Each stab of a swooping beak tore his flesh. If only he could keep them from his eyes. Nothing else mattered. He must keep them from his eyes. They had not learnt yet how to cling to a shoulder, how to rip clothing, how to dive in mass upon the head, upon the body. But with each dive, with each attack, they became bolder. And they had no thought for themselves. When they dived low and missed, they crashed, bruised and broken, on the ground. As Nat ran he stumbled, kicking their spent bodies in front of him.

He found the door; he hammered upon it with his bleeding hands. Because of the boarded windows no light shone. Everything was dark.

"Let me in," he shouted, "it's Nat. Let me in."

He shouted loud to make himself heard above the whir of the gulls' wings.

Then he saw the gannet, poised for the dive, above him in the sky. The gulls circled, retired, soared, one after another, against the wind. Only the gannet remained. One single gannet above him in the sky. The wings folded suddenly to its body. It dropped like a stone. Nat screamed, and the door opened. He stumbled across the threshold, and his wife threw her weight against the door.

They heard the thud of the gannet as it fell.

His wife dressed his wounds. They were not deep. The backs of his hands had suffered most, and his wrists. Had he not worn a cap they would have reached his head. As to the gannet . . . the gannet could have split his skull.

The children were crying, of course. They had seen the blood on their father's hands.

"It's all right now," he told them. "I'm not hurt. Just a few scratches. You play with Johnny, Jill. Mammy will wash these cuts."

He half shut the door to the scullery so that they could not see. His wife was ashen. She began running water from the sink.

"I saw them overhead," she whispered. "They began collecting just as Jill ran in with Mr. Trigg. I shut the door fast, and it jammed. That's why I couldn't open it at once when you came."

"Thank God they waited for me," he said. "Jill would have fallen at once. One bird alone would have done it."

Furtively, so as not to alarm the children, they whispered together as she bandaged his hands and the back of his neck.

"They're flying inland," he said, "thousands of them. Rooks, crows, all the bigger birds. I saw them from the bus stop. They're making for the towns."

"But what can they do, Nat?"

"They'll attack. Go for everyone out in the streets. Then they'll try the windows, the chimneys."

"Why don't the authorities do something? Why don't they get the Army, get machine guns, anything?"

"There's been no time. Nobody's prepared. We'll hear what they have to say on the six o'clock news."

Nat went back into the kitchen, followed by his wife. Johnny was playing quietly on the floor. Only Jill looked anxious.

"I can hear the birds," she said. "Listen, Dad."

Nat listened. Muffled sounds came from the windows, from the door. Wings brushing the surface, sliding, scraping, seeking a way of entry. The sound of many bodies, pressed together, shuffling on the sills. Now and again came a thud, a crash, as some bird dived and fell. "Some of them will kill themselves that way," he thought, "but not enough. Never enough."

"All right," he said aloud, "I've got boards over the windows, Jill. The birds can't get in."

He went and examined all the windows. His work had been thorough. Every gap was closed. He would make extra certain, however. He found wedges, pieces of old tin, strips of wood and metal, and fastened them at the sides to reinforce the boards. His hammering helped to deafen the sound of the birds, the shuffling, the tapping, and more ominous—he did not want his wife or the children to hear it— the splinter of cracked glass.

"Turn on the wireless," he said, "let's have the wireless."

This would drown the sound also. He went upstairs to the bedrooms and reinforced the windows there. Now he could hear the birds on the roof, the scraping of claws, a sliding, jostling sound.

He decided they must sleep in the kitchen, keep up the fire, bring down the mattresses, and lay them out on the floor. He was afraid of the bedroom chimneys. The boards he had placed at the chimney bases might give way. In the kitchen they would be safe because of the fire. He would have to make a joke of it. Pretend to the children they were playing at camp. If the worst happened, and the birds forced an entry down the bedroom chimneys, it would be hours, days perhaps, before they could break down the doors. The birds would be imprisoned in the bedrooms. They could do no harm there. Crowded together, they would stifle and die.

He began to bring the mattresses downstairs. At sight of them his wife's eyes widened in apprehension. She thought the birds had already broken in upstairs.

"All right," he said cheerfully, "we'll all sleep together in the kitchen tonight. More cosy here by the fire. Then we shan't be worried by those silly old birds tapping at the windows."

He made the children help him rearrange the furniture, and he took the precaution of moving the dresser, with his wife's help, across the window. It fitted well. It was an added safeguard. The mattresses could now be lain, one beside the other, against the wall where the dresser had stood.

"We're safe enough now," he thought. "We're snug and tight, like an air-raid shelter. We can hold out. It's just the food that worries me. Food, and coal for the fire. We've enough for two or three days, not more. By that time . . ."

No use thinking ahead as far as that. And they'd be giving directions on the wireless. People would be told what to do. And now, in the midst of many problems, he realised that it was dance music only coming over the air. Not Children's Hour, as it should have been. He glanced at the dial. Yes, they were on the Home Service all right. Dance records. He switched to the Light programme. He knew the reason. The usual programmes had been abandoned. This only happened at exceptional times. Elections and such. He tried to remember if it had happened in the war, during the heavy raids on London. But of course. The B.B.C. was not stationed in London during the war.

The programmes were broadcast from other, temporary quarters. "We're better off here," he thought; "we're better off here in the kitchen, with the windows and the doors boarded, than they are up in the towns. Thank God we're not in the towns."

At six o'clock the records ceased. The time signal was given. No matter if it scared the children, he must hear the news. There was a pause after the pips. Then the announcer spoke. His voice was solemn, grave. Quite different from midday.

"This is London," he said. "A National Emergency was proclaimed at four o'clock this afternoon. Measures are being taken to safeguard the lives and property of the population, but it must be understood that these are not easy to effect immediately, owing to the unforeseen and unparalleled nature of the present crisis. Every householder must take precautions to his own building, and where several people live together, as in flats and apartments, they must unite to do the utmost they can to prevent entry. It is absolutely imperative that every individual stay indoors tonight and that no one at all remain on the streets, or roads, or anywhere withoutdoors. The birds, in vast numbers, are attacking anyone on sight, and have already begun an assault upon buildings; but these, with due care, should be impenetrable. The population is asked to remain calm and not to panic. Owing to the exceptional nature of the emergency, there will be no further transmission from any broadcasting station until 7 A.M. tomorrow."

They played the National Anthem. Nothing more happened. Nat switched off the set. He looked at his wife. She stared back at him.

"What's it mean?" said Jill. "What did the news say?"

"There won't be any more programmes tonight," said Nat. "There's been a breakdown at the B.B.C."

"Is it the birds?" asked Jill. "Have the birds done it?"

"No," said Nat, "it's just that everyone's very busy, and then of course they have to get rid of the birds, messing everything up, in the towns. Well, we can manage without the wireless for one evening."

"I wish we had a gramophone," said Jill, "that would be better than nothing."

She had her face turned to the dresser backed against the windows. Try as they did to ignore it, they were all aware of the shuffling, the stabbing, the persistent beating and sweeping of wings.

"We'll have supper early," suggested Nat, "something for a treat. Ask Mammy. Toasted cheese, eh? Something we all like?"

He winked and nodded at his wife. He wanted the look of dread, of apprehension, to go from Jill's face.

He helped with the supper, whistling, singing, making as much clatter as he could, and it seemed to him that the shuffling and the tapping were not so intense as they had been at first. Presently he went up to the bedrooms and listened, and he no longer heard the jostling for place upon the roof.

"They've got reasoning powers," he thought; "they know it's hard to break in here. They'll try elsewhere. They won't waste their time with us."

Supper passed without incident, and then, when they were clearing away, they heard a new sound, droning, familiar, a sound they all knew and understood.

His wife looked up at him, her face alight. "It's planes," she said; "they're sending out planes after the birds. That's what I said they ought to do all along. That will get them. Isn't that gunfire? Can't you hear guns?"

It might be gunfire out at sea. Nat could not tell. Big naval guns might have an effect upon the gulls out at sea, but the gulls were inland now. The guns couldn't shell the shore because of the population.

"It's good, isn't it," said his wife, "to hear the planes?" And Jill, catching her enthusiasm, jumped up and down with Johnny. "The planes will get the birds. The planes will shoot them."

Just then they heard a crash about two miles distant, followed by a second, then a third. The droning became more distant, passed away out to sea.

"What was that?" asked his wife. "Were they dropping bombs on the birds?"

"I don't know," answered Nat. "I don't think so."

He did not want to tell her that the sound they had heard was the crashing of aircraft. It was, he had no doubt, a venture on the part of the authorities to send out reconnaissance forces, but they might have known the venture was suicidal. What could aircraft do against birds that flung themselves to death against propeller and fuselage, but hurtle to the ground themselves? This was being tried now, he sup-

posed, over the whole country. And at a cost. Someone high up had
lost his head.

"Where have the planes gone, Dad?" asked Jill.

"Back to base," he said. "Come on, now, time to tuck down for
bed."

It kept his wife occupied, undressing the children before the fire,
seeing to the bedding, one thing and another, while he went round
the cottage again, making sure that nothing had worked loose. There
was no further drone of aircraft, and the naval guns had ceased. "Waste
of life and effort," Nat said to himself. "We can't destroy enough of
them that way. Cost too heavy. There's always gas. Maybe they'll try
spraying with gas, mustard gas. We'll be warned first, of course, if they
do. There's one thing, the best brains of the country will be on to it
tonight."

Somehow the thought reassured him. He had a picture of scientists,
naturalists, technicians, and all those chaps they called the back-room
boys, summoned to a council; they'd be working on the problem now.
This was not a job for the government, for the chiefs of staff—they
would merely carry out the orders of the scientists.

"They'll have to be ruthless," he thought. "Where the trouble's
worst they'll have to risk more lives, if they use gas. All the livestock,
too, and the soil—all contaminated. As long as everyone doesn't panic.
That's the trouble. People panicking, losing their heads. The B.B.C.
was right to warn us of that."

Upstairs in the bedrooms all was quiet. No further scraping and
stabbing at the windows. A lull in battle. Forces regrouping. Wasn't
that what they called it in the old wartime bulletins? The wind hadn't
dropped, though. He could still hear it roaring in the chimneys. And
the sea breaking down on the shore. Then he remembered the tide.
The tide would be on the turn. Maybe the lull in battle was because
of the tide. There was some law the birds obeyed, and it was all to do
with the east wind and the tide.

He glanced at his watch. Nearly eight o'clock. It must have gone
high water an hour ago. That explained the lull: the birds attacked
with the flood tide. It might not work that way inland, upcountry,
but it seemed as if it was so this way on the coast. He reckoned the
time limit in his head. They had six hours to go without attack. When

the tide turned again, around one-twenty in the morning, the birds would come back. . . .

There were two things he could do. The first to rest, with his wife and the children, and all of them snatch what sleep they could, until the small hours. The second to go out, see how they were faring at the farm, see if the telephone was still working there, so that they might get news from the exchange.

He called softly to his wife, who had just settled the children. She came halfway up the stairs and he whispered to her.

"You're not to go," she said at once, "you're not to go and leave me alone with the children. I can't stand it."

Her voice rose hysterically. He hushed her, calmed her.

"All right," he said, "all right. I'll wait till morning. And we'll get the wireless bulletin then too, at seven. But in the morning, when the tide ebbs again, I'll try for the farm, and they may let us have bread and potatoes, and milk too."

His mind was busy again, planning against emergency. They would not have milked, of course, this evening. The cows would be standing by the gate, waiting in the yard, with the household inside, battened behind boards, as they were here at the cottage. That is, if they had time to take precautions. He thought of the farmer, Trigg, smiling at him from the car. There would have been no shooting party, not tonight.

The children were asleep. His wife, still clothed, was sitting on her mattress. She watched him, her eyes nervous.

"What are you going to do?" she whispered.

He shook his head for silence. Softly, stealthily, he opened the back door and looked outside.

It was pitch dark. The wind was blowing harder than ever, coming in steady gusts, icy, from the sea. He kicked at the step outside the door. It was heaped with birds. There were dead birds everywhere. Under the windows, against the walls. These were the suicides, the divers, the ones with broken necks. Wherever he looked he saw dead birds. No trace of the living. The living had flown seaward with the turn of the tide. The gulls would be riding the seas now, as they had done in the forenoon.

In the far distance, on the hill where the tractor had been two days before, something was burning. One of the aircraft that had crashed; the fire, fanned by the wind, had set light to a stack.

He looked at the bodies of the birds, and he had a notion that if he heaped them, one upon the other, on the window sills they would make added protection for the next attack. Not much, perhaps, but something. The bodies would have to be clawed at, pecked, and dragged aside before the living birds could gain purchase on the sills and attack the panes. He set to work in the darkness. It was queer; he hated touching them. The bodies were still warm and bloody. The blood matted their feathers. He felt his stomach turn, but he went on with his work. He noticed grimly that every windowpane was shattered. Only the boards had kept the birds from breaking in. He stuffed the cracked panes with the bleeding bodies of the birds.

When he had finished he went back into the cottage. He barricaded the kitchen door, made it doubly secure. He took off his bandages, sticky with the birds' blood, not with his own cuts, and put on fresh plaster.

His wife had made him cocoa and he drank it thirstily. He was very tired.

"All right," he said, smiling, "don't worry. We'll get through."

He lay down on his mattress and closed his eyes. He slept at once. He dreamt uneasily, because through his dreams there ran a thread of something forgotten. Some piece of work, neglected, that he should have done. Some precaution that he had known well but had not taken, and he could not put a name to it in his dreams. It was connected in some way with the burning aircraft and the stack upon the hill. He went on sleeping, though; he did not awake. It was his wife shaking his shoulder that awoke him finally.

"They've begun," she sobbed, "they've started this last hour. I can't listen to it any longer alone. There's something smelling bad too, something burning."

Then he remembered. He had forgotten to make up the fire. It was smouldering, nearly out. He got up swiftly and lit the lamp. The hammering had started at the windows and the doors, but it was not that he minded now. It was the smell of singed feathers. The smell filled the kitchen. He knew at once what it was. The birds were coming down the chimney, squeezing their way down to the kitchen range.

He got sticks and paper and put them on the embers, then reached for the can of paraffin.

"Stand back," he shouted to his wife. "We've got to risk this."

He threw the paraffin on to the fire. The flame roared up the pipe, and down upon the fire fell the scorched, blackened bodies of the birds.

The children woke, crying. "What is it?" said Jill. "What's happened?"

Nat had no time to answer. He was raking the bodies from the chimney, clawing them out on to the floor. The flames still roared, and the danger of the chimney catching fire was one he had to take. The flames would send away the living birds from the chimney top. The lower joint was the difficulty, though. This was choked with the smouldering, helpless bodies of the birds caught by fire. He scarcely heeded the attack on the windows and the door: let them beat their wings, break their beaks, lose their lives, in the attempt to force an entry into his home. They would not break in. He thanked God he had one of the old cottages, with small windows, stout walls. Not like the new council houses. Heaven help them up the lane in the new council houses.

"Stop crying," he called to the children. "There's nothing to be afraid of, stop crying."

He went on raking at the burning, smouldering bodies as they fell into the fire.

"This'll fetch them," he said to himself, "the draught and the flames together. We're all right, as long as the chimney doesn't catch. I ought to be shot for this. It's all my fault. Last thing, I should have made up the fire. I knew there was something."

Amid the scratching and tearing at the window boards came the sudden homely striking of the kitchen clock. Three A.M. A little more than four hours yet to go. He could not be sure of the exact time of high water. He reckoned it would not turn much before half-past seven, twenty to eight.

"Light up the Primus," he said to his wife. "Make us some tea, and the kids some cocoa. No use sitting around doing nothing."

That was the line. Keep her busy, and the children too. Move about, eat, drink; always best to be on the go.

He waited by the range. The flames were dying. But no more blackened bodies fell from the chimney. He thrust his poker up as far as it could go and found nothing. It was clear. The chimney was clear. He wiped the sweat from his forehead.

"Come on now, Jill," he said, "bring me some more sticks. We'll have a good fire going directly." She wouldn't come near him, though. She was staring at the heaped singed bodies of the birds.

"Never mind them," he said, "we'll put those in the passage when I've got the fire steady."

The danger of the chimney was over. It could not happen again, not if the fire was kept burning day and night.

"I'll have to get more fuel from the farm tomorrow," he thought. "This will never last. I'll manage, though. I can do all that with the ebb tide. It can be worked, fetching what we need, when the tide's turned. We've just got to adapt ourselves, that's all."

They drank tea and cocoa and ate slices of bread and Bovril. Only half a loaf left, Nat noticed. Never mind though, they'd get by.

"Stop it," said young Johnny, pointing to the windows with his spoon, "stop it, you old birds."

"That's right," said Nat, smiling, "we don't want the old beggars, do we? Had enough of 'em."

They began to cheer when they heard the thud of the suicide birds.

"There's another, Dad," cried Jill, "he's done for."

"He's had it," said Nat. "There he goes, the blighter."

This was the way to face up to it. This was the spirit. If they could keep this up, hang on like this until seven, when the first news bulletin came through, they would not have done too badly.

"Give us a fag," he said to his wife. "A bit of a smoke will clear away the smell of the scorched feathers."

"There's only two left in the packet," she said. "I was going to buy you some from the Co-op."

"I'll have one," he said, "t'other will keep for a rainy day."

No sense trying to make the children rest. There was no rest to be got while the tapping and the scratching went on at the windows. He sat with one arm round his wife and the other round Jill, with Johnny on his mother's lap and the blankets heaped about them on the mattress.

"You can't help admiring the beggars," he said; "they've got persistence. You'd think they'd tire of the game, but not a bit of it."

Admiration was hard to sustain. The tapping went on and on and a new rasping note struck Nat's ear, as though a sharper beak than any hitherto had come to take over from its fellows. He tried to remember the names of birds; he tried to think which species would go for this particular job. It was not the tap of the woodpecker. That would be light and frequent. This was more serious, because if it continued long the wood would splinter as the glass had done. Then he remembered the hawks. Could the hawks have taken over from the gulls? Were there buzzards now upon the sills, using talons as well as beaks? Hawks, buzzards, kestrels, falcons—he had forgotten the birds of prey. He had forgotten the gripping power of the birds of prey. Three hours to go, and while they waited, the sound of the splintering wood, the talons tearing at the wood.

Nat looked about him, seeing what furniture he could destroy to fortify the door. The windows were safe because of the dresser. He was not certain of the door. He went upstairs, but when he reached the landing he paused and listened. There was a soft patter on the floor of the children's bedroom. The birds had broken through. . . . He put his ear to the door. No mistake. He could hear the rustle of wings and the light patter as they searched the floor. The other bedroom was still clear. He went into it and began bringing out the furniture, to pile at the head of the stairs should the door of the children's bedroom go. It was a preparation. It might never be needed. He could not stack the furniture against the door, because it opened inward. The only possible thing was to have it at the top of the stairs.

"Come down, Nat, what are you doing?" called his wife.

"I won't be long," he shouted. "Just making everything shipshape up here."

He did not want her to come; he did not want her to hear the pattering of the feet in the children's bedroom, the brushing of those wings against the door.

At five-thirty he suggested breakfast, bacon and fried bread, if only to stop the growing look of panic in his wife's eyes and to calm the fretful children. She did not know about the birds upstairs. The bedroom, luckily, was not over the kitchen. Had it been so, she could not have failed to hear the sound of them up there, tapping the boards. And the silly, senseless thud of the suicide birds, the death and glory boys, who flew into the bedroom, smashing their heads against the walls. He knew them of old, the herring gulls. They had no brains.

The black-backs were different; they knew what they were doing. So did the buzzards, the hawks . . .

He found himself watching the clock, gazing at the hands that went so slowly round the dial. If his theory was not correct, if the attack did not cease with the turn of the tide, he knew they were beaten. They could not continue through the long day without air, without rest, without more fuel, without . . . His mind raced. He knew there were so many things they needed to withstand siege. They were not fully prepared. They were not ready. It might be that it would be safer in the towns after all. If he could get a message through on the farm telephone to his cousin, only a short journey by train upcountry, they might be able to hire a car. That would be quicker—hire a car between tides . . .

His wife's voice, calling his name, drove away the sudden, desperate desire for sleep.

"What is it? What now?" he said sharply.

"The wireless," said his wife. "I've been watching the clock. It's nearly seven."

"Don't twist the knob," he said, impatient for the first time. "It's on the Home where it is. They'll speak from the Home."

They waited. The kitchen clock struck seven. There was no sound. No chimes, no music. They waited until a quarter past, switching to the Light. The result was the same. No news bulletin came through.

"We've heard wrong," he said. "They won't be broadcasting until eight o'clock."

They left it switched on, and Nat thought of the battery, wondered how much power was left in it. It was generally recharged when his wife went shopping in the town. If the battery failed they would not hear the instructions.

"It's getting light," whispered his wife. "I can't see it, but I can feel it. And the birds aren't hammering so loud."

She was right. The rasping, tearing sound grew fainter every moment. So did the shuffling, the jostling for place upon the step, upon the sills. The tide was on the turn. By eight there was no sound at all. Only the wind. The children, lulled at last by the stillness, fell asleep. At half-past eight Nat switched the wireless off.

"What are you doing? We'll miss the news," said his wife.

"There isn't going to be any news," said Nat. "We've got to depend upon ourselves."

He went to the door and slowly pulled away the barricades. He drew the bolts and, kicking the bodies from the step outside the door, breathed the cold air. He had six working hours before him, and he knew he must reserve his strength for the right things, not waste it in any way. Food, and light, and fuel; these were the necessary things. If he could get them in sufficiency, they could endure another night.

He stepped into the garden, and as he did so he saw the living birds. The gulls had gone to ride the sea, as they had done before; they sought sea food, and the buoyancy of the tide, before they returned to the attack. Not so the land birds. They waited and watched. Nat saw them, on the hedgerows, on the soil, crowded in the trees, outside in the field, line upon line of birds, all still, doing nothing.

He went to the end of his small garden. The birds did not move. They went on watching him.

"I've got to get food," said Nat to himself. "I've got to go to the farm to find food."

He went back to the cottage. He saw to the windows and the doors. He went upstairs and opened the children's bedroom. It was empty, except for the dead birds on the floor. The living were out there, in the garden, in the fields. He went downstairs.

"I'm going to the farm," he said.

His wife clung to him. She had seen the living birds from the open door.

"Take us with you," she begged. "We can't stay here alone. I'd rather die than stay here alone."

He considered the matter. He nodded.

"Come on, then," he said. "Bring baskets, and Johnny's pram. We can load up the pram."

They dressed against the biting wind, wore gloves and scarves. His wife put Johnny in the pram. Nat took Jill's hand.

"The birds," she whimpered, "they're all out there in the fields."

"They won't hurt us," he said, "not in the light."

They started walking across the field towards the stile, and the birds did not move. They waited, their heads turned to the wind.

When they reached the turning to the farm, Nat stopped and told his wife to wait in the shelter of the hedge with the two children.

"But I want to see Mrs. Trigg," she protested. "There are lots of things we can borrow if they went to market yesterday; not only bread, and . . ."

"Wait here," Nat interrupted. "I'll be back in a moment."

The cows were lowing, moving restlessly in the yard, and he could see a gap in the fence where the sheep had knocked their way through, to roam unchecked in the front garden before the farmhouse. No smoke came from the chimneys. He was filled with misgiving. He did not want his wife or the children to go down to the farm.

"Don't gib now," said Nat, harshly, "do what I say."

She withdrew with the pram into the hedge, screening herself and the children from the wind.

He went down alone to the farm. He pushed his way through the herd of bellowing cows, which turned this way and that, distressed, their udders full. He saw the car standing by the gate, not put away in the garage. The windows of the farmhouse were smashed. There were many dead gulls lying in the yard and around the house. The living birds perched on the group of trees behind the farm and on the roof of the house. They were quite still. They watched him.

Jim's body lay in the yard . . . what was left of it. When the birds had finished, the cows had trampled him. His gun was beside him. The door of the house was shut and bolted, but as the windows were smashed it was easy to lift them and climb through. Trigg's body was close to the telephone. He must have been trying to get through to the exchange when the birds came for him. The receiver was hanging loose, the instrument torn from the wall. No sign of Mrs. Trigg. She would be upstairs. Was it any use going up? Sickened, Nat knew what he would find.

"Thank God," he said to himself, "there were no children."

He forced himself to climb the stairs, but halfway he turned and descended again. He could see her legs protruding from the open bedroom door. Beside her were the bodies of the black-backed gulls, and an umbrella, broken.

"It's no use," thought Nat, "doing anything. I've only got five hours, less than that. The Triggs would understand. I must load up with what I can find."

He tramped back to his wife and children.

"I'm going to fill up the car with stuff," he said. "I'll put coal in it, and paraffin for the Primus. We'll take it home and return for a fresh load."

"What about the Triggs?" asked his wife.

"They must have gone to friends," he said.

"Shall I come and help you, then?"

"No; there's a mess down there. Cows and sheep all over the place. Wait, I'll get the car. You can sit in it."

Clumsily he backed the car out of the yard and into the lane. His wife and the children could not see Jim's body from there.

"Stay here," he said, "never mind the pram. The pram can be fetched later. I'm going to load the car."

Her eyes watched his all the time. He believed she understood, otherwise she would have suggested helping him to find the bread and groceries.

They made three journeys altogether, backwards and forwards between their cottage and the farm, before he was satisfied they had everything they needed. It was surprising, once he started thinking, how many things were necessary. Almost the most important of all was planking for the windows. He had to go round searching for timber. He wanted to renew the boards on all the windows at the cottage. Candles, paraffin, nails, tinned stuff; the list was endless. Besides all that, he milked three of the cows. The rest, poor brutes, would have to go on bellowing.

On the final journey he drove the car to the bus stop, got out, and went to the telephone box. He waited a few minutes, jangling the receiver. No good, though. The line was dead. He climbed on to a bank and looked over the countryside, but there was no sign of life at all, nothing in the fields but the waiting, watching birds. Some of them slept—he could see the beaks tucked into the feathers.

"You'd think they'd be feeding," he said to himself, "not just standing in that way."

Then he remembered. They were gorged with food. They had eaten their fill during the night. That was why they did not move this morning. . . .

No smoke came from the chimneys of the council houses. He thought of the children who had run across the fields the night before.

"I should have known," he thought; "I ought to have taken them home with me."

He lifted his face to the sky. It was colourless and grey. The bare trees on the landscape looked bent and blackened by the east wind. The cold did not affect the living birds waiting out there in the fields.

"This is the time they ought to get them," said Nat; "they're a sitting target now. They must be doing this all over the country. Why don't our aircraft take off now and spray them with mustard gas? What are all our chaps doing? They must know, they must see for themselves."

He went back to the car and got into the driver's seat.

"Go quickly past that second gate," whispered his wife. "The postman's lying there. I don't want Jill to see."

He accelerated. The little Morris bumped and rattled along the lane. The children shrieked with laughter.

"Up-a-down, up-a-down," shouted young Johnny.

It was a quarter to one by the time they reached the cottage. Only an hour to go.

"Better have cold dinner," said Nat. "Hot up something for yourself and the children, some of that soup. I've no time to eat now. I've got to unload all this stuff."

He got everything inside the cottage. It could be sorted later. Give them all something to do during the long hours ahead. First he must see to the windows and the doors.

He went round the cottage methodically, testing every window, every door. He climbed on to the roof also, and fixed boards across every chimney, except the kitchen. The cold was so intense he could hardly bear it, but the job had to be done. Now and again he would look up, searching the sky for aircraft. None came. As he worked he cursed the inefficiency of the authorities.

"It's always the same," he muttered, "they always let us down. Muddle, muddle, from the start. No plan, no real organisation. And we don't matter down here. That's what it is. The people upcountry have priority. They're using gas up there, no doubt, and all the aircraft. We've got to wait and take what comes."

He paused, his work on the bedroom chimney finished, and looked out to sea. Something was moving out there. Something grey and white amongst the breakers.

"Good old Navy," he said, "they never let us down. They're coming down-channel, they're turning in the bay."

He waited, straining his eyes, watering in the wind, towards the sea. He was wrong, though. It was not ships. The Navy was not there. The gulls were rising from the sea. The massed flocks in the fields, with ruffled feathers, rose in formation from the ground and, wing to wing, soared upwards to the sky.

The tide had turned again.

Nat climbed down the ladder and went inside the kitchen. The family were at dinner. It was a little after two. He bolted the door, put up the barricade, and lit the lamp.

"It's nighttime," said young Johnny.

His wife had switched on the wireless once again, but no sound came from it.

"I've been all round the dial," she said, "foreign stations, and that lot. I can't get anything."

"Maybe they have the same trouble," he said, "maybe it's the same right through Europe."

She poured out a plateful of the Triggs' soup, cut him a large slice of the Triggs' bread, and spread their dripping upon it.

They ate in silence. A piece of the dripping ran down young Johnny's chin and fell on to the table.

"Manners, Johnny," said Jill, "you should learn to wipe your mouth."

The tapping began at the windows, at the door. The rustling, the jostling, the pushing for position on the sills. The first thud of the suicide gulls upon the step.

"Won't America do something?" said his wife. "They've always been our allies, haven't they? Surely America will do something?"

Nat did not answer. The boards were strong against the windows, and on the chimneys too. The cottage was filled with stores, with fuel, with all they needed for the next few days. When he had finished dinner he would put the stuff away, stack it neatly, get everything shipshape, handy-like. His wife could help him, and the children too. They'd tire themselves out, between now and a quarter to nine, when the tide would ebb; then he'd tuck them down on their mattresses, see that they slept good and sound until three in the morning.

He had a new scheme for the windows, which was to fix barbed wire in front of the boards. He had brought a great roll of it from the farm. The nuisance was, he'd have to work at this in the dark, when the lull came between nine and three. Pity he had not thought of it before. Still, as long as the wife slept, and the kids, that was the main thing.

The smaller birds were at the window now. He recognised the light tap-tapping of their beaks and the soft brush of their wings. The hawks ignored the windows. They concentrated their attack upon the door. Nat listened to the tearing sound of splintering wood, and wondered how many million years of memory were stored in those little brains, behind the stabbing beaks, the piercing eyes, now giving them this instinct to destroy mankind with all the deft precision of machines.

"I'll smoke that last fag," he said to his wife. "Stupid of me, it was the one thing I forgot to bring back from the farm."

He reached for it, switched on the silent wireless. He threw the empty packet on the fire, and watched it burn.

The Little
Photographer

THE MARQUISE lay on her chaise longue on the balcony of the hotel. She wore only a wrapper, and her sleek gold hair, newly set in pins, was bound close to her head in a turquoise bandeau that matched her eyes. Beside her chair stood a little table, and on it were three bottles of nail varnish all of a different shade.

She had dabbed a touch of colour on to three separate fingernails, and now she held her hand in front of her to see the effect. No, the varnish on the thumb was too red, too vivid, giving a heated look to her slim olive hand, almost as if a spot of blood had fallen there from a fresh-cut wound.

In contrast, her forefinger was a striking pink, and this too seemed to her false, not true to her present mood. It was the elegant rich pink of drawing-rooms, of ball gowns, of herself standing at some reception, slowly moving to and fro her ostrich feather fan, and in the distance the sound of violins.

The middle finger was touched with a sheen of silk neither crimson nor vermilion, but somehow softer, subtler; the sheen of a peony in bud, not yet opened to the heat of the day but with the dew of the morning upon it still. A peony, cool and close, looking down upon lush grass from some terraced border, and later, at high noon, the petals unfolding to the sun.

Yes, that was the colour. She reached for cotton wool and wiped away the offending varnish from her other fingernails, and then slowly, carefully, she dipped the little brush into the chosen varnish and, like an artist, worked with swift, deft strokes.

When she had finished she leant back in her chaise longue, exhausted, waving her hands before her in the air to let the varnish harden—a strange gesture, like that of a priestess. She looked down at her toes, appearing from her sandals, and decided that presently, in a few moments, she would paint them too; olive hands, olive feet, subdued and quiet, surprised into sudden life.

Not yet, though. She must rest, relax. It was too hot to move from the supporting back of the chaise longue and lean forward, crouching, Eastern fashion, for the adorning of her feet. There was plenty of time. Time, in fact, stretched before her in an unwinding pattern through the whole long, languorous day.

She closed her eyes.

The distant sound of hotel life came to her as in a dream, and the sounds were hazy, pleasant, because she was part of that life yet free as well, bound no longer to the tyranny of home. Someone on a balcony above scraped back a chair. Below, on the terrace, the waiters set up the gay striped umbrellas over the little luncheon tables; she could hear the maître d'hôtel call directions from the dining-room. The *femme de chambre* was doing the rooms in the adjoining suite. Furniture was moved, a bed creaked, the *valet de chambre* came out on to the next balcony and swept the boards with a straw brush. Their voices murmured, grumbled. Then they went away. Silence again. Nothing but the lazy splash of the sea as effortlessly it licked the burning sand; and somewhere, far away, too distant to make an irritation, the laughter of children playing, her own amongst them.

A guest ordered coffee on the terrace below. The smoke of his cigar
came floating upwards to the balcony. The Marquise sighed, and her
lovely hands drooped down like lilies on either side of the chaise
longue. This was peace, this was contentment. If she could hold the
moment thus for one more hour . . . But something warned her, when
the hour was past, the old demon of dissatisfaction, of tedium, would
return, even here where she was free at last, on holiday.

A bumblebee flew on to the balcony, hovered over the bottle of
nail varnish, and entered the open flower, picked by one of the children, lying beside it. His humming ceased when he was inside the
flower. The Marquise opened her eyes and saw the bee crawl forth, intoxicated. Then dizzily once more he took the air and hummed his
way. The spell was broken. The Marquise picked up the letter from
Edouard, her husband, that had fallen on to the floor of the balcony.
". . . And so, my dearest, I find it impossible to get to you and the
children after all. There is so much business to attend to here at home,
and you know I can rely on no one but myself. I shall, of course, make
every effort to come and fetch you at the end of the month. Meanwhile, enjoy yourself, bathing and resting. I know the sea air will do
you good. I went to see Maman yesterday, and Madeleine, and it
seems the old curé . . ."

The Marquise let the letter fall back again on to the balcony floor.
The little droop at the corner of her mouth, the one telltale sign that
spoilt the smooth lovely face, intensified. It had happened again. Always his work. The estate, the farms, the forests, the businessmen that
he must see, the sudden journeys that he must take, so that in spite of
his devotion for her he had no time to spare, Edouard, her husband.

They had told her, before her marriage, how it would be. "*C'est un
homme très sérieux, Monsieur le Marquis, vous comprenez.*" How
little she had minded, how gladly she had agreed, for what could be
better in life than a marquis who was also *un homme sérieux*? What
more lovely than that château and those vast estates? What more im-
posing than the house in Paris, the retinue of servants, humble, bowing, calling her Madame la Marquise? A fairy-tale world to someone
like herself, brought up in Lyons, the daughter of a hard-working sur-
geon, an ailing mother. But for the sudden arrival of Monsieur le
Marquis she might have found herself married to her father's young
assistant, and that same day-by-day in Lyons continuing forever.

A romantic match, surely. Frowned on at first by his relatives, most certainly. But Monsieur le Marquis, *homme sérieux*, was past forty. He knew his own mind. And she was beautiful. There was no further argument. They married. They had two little girls. They were happy. Yet sometimes . . . The Marquise rose from the chaise longue and, going into the bedroom, sat down before the dressing table and removed the pins from her hair. Even this effort exhausted her. She threw off her wrapper and sat naked before her mirror. Sometimes she found herself regretting that day-by-day in Lyons. She remembered the laughter, the joking with other girls, the stifled giggles when a passing man looked at them in the street, the confidences, the exchange of letters, the whispering in bedrooms when her friends came to tea.

Now, as Madame la Marquise, she had no one with whom to share confidences, laughter. Everyone about her was middle-aged, dull, rooted to a life long-lived that never changed. Those interminable visits of Edouard's relatives to the château. His mother, his sisters, his brothers, his sisters-in-law. In the winter, in Paris, it was just the same. Never a new face, never the arrival of a stranger. The only excitement was the appearance, perhaps, at luncheon of one of Edouard's business friends, who, surprised at her beauty when she entered the salon, flickered a daring glance of admiration, then bowed and kissed her hand.

Watching such a one during luncheon, she would make a fantasy to herself of how they would meet in secret, how a taxi would take her to his apartment, and, entering a small, dark *ascenseur*, she would ring a bell and vanish into a strange unknown room. But, the long luncheon over, the business friend would bow and go his way. And afterwards she would think to herself he was not even passably good-looking; even his teeth were false. But the glance of admiration, swiftly suppressed—she wanted that.

Now she combed her hair before the mirror and, parting it on one side, tried a new effect; a ribbon, the colour of her fingernails, threaded through the gold. Yes, yes . . . And the white frock, later, and that chiffon scarf, thrown carelessly over the shoulders, so that when she went out on to the terrace, followed by the children and the English governess, and the maître d'hôtel, bowing, led the way to the little table at the corner under the striped umbrella, people would stare, would whisper, and the eyes would follow her as deliberately she

would stoop to one of the children, pat its curls in a fond maternal
gesture, a thing of grace, of beauty.

But now, before the mirror, only the naked body and the sad, sulky
mouth. Other women would have lovers. Whispers of scandal came to
her ears, even during those long heavy dinners, with Edouard at the
far end of the table. Not only in the smart riffraff society to which she
never penetrated, but even amongst the old noblesse to which she now
belonged. "*On dit, vous savez . . .*" and the suggestion, the murmur,
passed from one to the other, with a lifted eyebrow, a shrug of the
shoulder.

Sometimes, after a tea party, a guest would leave early, before six
o'clock, giving as an excuse that she was expected elsewhere, and the
Marquise, echoing regrets, bidding the guest au revoir, would wonder,
"Is she going to a rendezvous?" Could it be that in twenty minutes—
less, perhaps—that dark, rather ordinary little comtesse would be shivering, smiling secretly, as she let her clothes slip to the floor?

Even Elise, her friend of lycée days in Lyons, married now six years,
had a lover. She never wrote of him by name. She always called him
"*mon ami.*" Yet they managed to meet twice a week, on Mondays and
Thursdays. He had a car and drove her into the country, even in
winter. And Elise would write to the Marquise and say, "But how
plebeian my little affair must seem to you, in high society. How many
admirers you must have, and what adventures! Tell me of Paris, and
the parties, and who is the man of your choice this winter." The
Marquise would reply, hinting, suggesting, laughing off the question,
and launch into a description of her frock, worn at some reception.
But she did not say that the reception ended at midnight, that it was
formal, dull, and that all she, the Marquise, knew of Paris was the
drives she took in the car with the children, and the drives to the
couturier to be fitted for yet another frock, and the drives to the coiffeur to have her hair rearranged and set to perhaps a different style. As
to life at the château, she would describe the rooms, yes, the many
guests, the solemn long avenue of trees, the acres of woodland; but not
the rain in spring, day after day, nor the parching heat of early summer, when silence fell upon the place like a great white pall.

"Ah! Pardon, *je croyais que Madame était sortie . . .*" He had come
in without knocking, the *valet de chambre*, his straw brush in his hand,
and now he backed out of the room again, discreetly, but not before

he had seen her there, naked before the mirror. And surely he must have known she had not gone out, when only a few moments before she had been lying on the balcony? Was it compassion she saw in his eyes as well as admiration before he left the room? As though to say, "So beautiful, and all alone? We are not used to that in this hotel, where people come for pleasure. . . ."

Heavens, it was hot. No breeze even from the sea. Trickles of perspiration ran down from her arms to her body.

She dressed languidly, putting on the cool white dress, and then, strolling out on to the balcony once more, pulled up the sun blind, let the full heat of the day fall upon her. Dark glasses hid her eyes. The only touch of colour lay on her mouth, her feet, her hands, and in the scarf thrown about her shoulders. The dark lenses gave a deep tone to the day. The sea, by natural eye a periwinkle blue, had turned to purple, and the white sands to olive brown. The gaudy flowers in their tubs upon the terrace had a tropical texture. As the Marquise leant upon the balcony the heat of the wooden rail burnt her hands. Once again the smell of a cigar floated upwards from some source unknown. There was a tinkle of glasses as a waiter brought apéritifs to a table on the terrace. Somewhere a woman spoke, and a man's voice joined with the woman's, laughing.

An Alsatian dog, his tongue dripping moisture, padded along the terrace towards the wall, searching for a cold stone slab on which to lie. A group of young people, bare and bronzed, the salt from the warm sea scarce dried upon their bodies, came running up from the sands, calling for martinis. Americans, of course. They flung their towels upon the chairs. One of them whistled to the Alsatian, who did not move. The Marquise looked down upon them with disdain, yet merged with her disdain was a kind of envy. They were free to come and go, to climb into a car, to move onward to some other place. They lived in a state of blank, ferocious gaiety. Always in groups. Six or eight of them. They paired off, of course; they pawed each other, forming into couples. But—and here she gave full play to her contempt—their gaiety held no mystery. In their open lives there could be no moment of suspense. No one waited, in secret, behind a half-closed door.

The savour of a love affair should be quite otherwise, thought the Marquise, and breaking off a rose that climbed the trellis of the balcony, she placed it in the opening of her dress, below her neck. A

love affair should be a thing of silence, soft, unspoken. No raucous
voice, no burst of sudden laughter, but the kind of stealthy curiosity
that comes with fear, and when the fear has gone, a brazen confidence.
Never the give-and-take between good friends, but passion between
strangers . . .

One by one they came back from the sands, the visitors to the hotel.
The tables began to fill up. The terrace, hot and deserted all the morning, became alive once more. And guests, arriving by car for luncheon only, mingled with the more familiar figures belonging to the
hotel. A party of six in the right-hand corner. A party of three below.
And now more bustle, more chatter, more tinkling of glasses and
clatter of plates, so that the splash of the sea, which had been the
foremost sound since early morning, now seemed secondary, remote.
The tide was going out, the water rippling away across the sands.

Here came the children with their governess, Miss Clay. They
prinked their way like little dolls across the terrace, followed by Miss
Clay in her striped cotton dress, her crimped hair straggling from her
bathe, and suddenly they looked up to the balcony, they waved their
hands. "Maman . . . Maman . . ." She leant down, smiling at them;
and then, as usual, the little clamour brought distraction. Somebody
glanced up with the children, smiling, some man at a left-hand table
laughed and pointed to his companion, and it began, the first wave of
admiration that would come again in full measure when she descended, the Marquise, the beautiful Marquise and her cherubic children, whispers wafting towards her in the air like the smoke from the
cigarettes, like the conversation the guests at the other tables shared
with one another. This, then, was all that déjeuner on the terrace
would bring to her, day after day, the ripple of admiration, respect,
and then oblivion. Each and all went his way, to swim, to golf, to
tennis, to drive, and she was left, beautiful, unruffled, with the children
and Miss Clay.

"Look, Maman, I found a little starfish on the beach. I am going to
take him home with me when we go."

"No, no, that isn't fair, it's mine. I saw it first."

The little girls, with flushed faces, fell out with one another.

"Hush, Céleste and Hélène: you make my head ache."

"Madame is tired? You must rest after lunch. It will do you good, in such heat." Miss Clay, tactful, bent down to scold the children. "Everyone is tired. It will do us all good to rest," she said.

Rest . . . "But," thought the Marquise, "I never do anything else. My life is one long rest." *Il faut reposer. Repose-toi, ma chérie, tu as mauvaise mine.* Winter and summer, those were the words she heard. From her husband, from the governess, from sisters-in-law, from all those aged, tedious friends. Life was one long sequence of resting, of getting up, and of resting again. Because with her pallor, with her reserve, they thought her delicate. Heavens above, the hours of her married life she had spent resting, the bed turned down, the shutters closed. In the house in Paris, in the château in the country. Two to four, resting, always resting.

"I'm not in the least tired," she said to Miss Clay, and for once her voice, usually melodious and soft, was sharp, high-pitched. "I shall go walking after lunch. I shall go into the town."

The children stared at her, round-eyed, and Miss Clay, her goat-face startled to surprise, opened her mouth in protest:

"You'll kill yourself, in the heat. Besides, the few shops always close between one and three. Why not wait until after tea? Surely it would be wiser to wait until after tea? The children could go with you and I could do some ironing."

The Marquise did not answer. She rose from the table, and now, because the children had lingered over déjeuner—Céleste was always slow with her food—the terrace was almost deserted. No one of any importance would watch the progress back to the hotel.

The Marquise went upstairs and once again touched her face with powder, circled her mouth, dipped her forefinger in scent. Next door she could hear the droning of the children as Miss Clay settled them to rest and closed the shutters. The Marquise took her handbag, made of plaited straw, put in it her purse, a roll of film, a few odds and ends, and, tiptoeing past the children's room, went downstairs again and out of the hotel grounds to the dusty road.

The gravel forced its way at once into her open sandals and the glare of the sun beat down upon her head, and at once what had seemed to her, on the spur of the moment, an unusual thing to do struck her now, in the doing of it, as foolish, pointless. The road was deserted, the sands were deserted, the visitors who had played and walked all morning, while she had lain idle on her balcony, were now taking their ease in their rooms, like Miss Clay and the children. Only the Marquise trod the sun-baked road into the little town.

And here it was even as Miss Clay had warned her. The shops were closed, the sun blinds were all down, the hour of siesta, inviolate, unbroken, held sway over the shops and their inhabitants.

The Marquise strolled along the street, her straw handbag swinging from her hand, the one walker in a sleeping, yawning world. Even the café at the corner was deserted, and a sand-coloured dog, his face between his paws, snapped with closed eyes at the flies that bothered him. Flies were everywhere. They buzzed at the window of the *pharmacie*, where dark bottles, filled with mysterious medicine, rubbed glass shoulders with skin tonic, sponges, and cosmetics. Flies danced behind the panes of the shop filled with sunshades, spades, pink dolls, and rope-soled shoes. They crawled upon the empty bloodstained slab of the butcher's shop, behind the iron shutter. From above the shop came the jarring sound of the radio, suddenly switched off, and the heavy sigh of someone who would sleep and would not be disturbed. Even the *bureau de poste* was shut. The Marquise, who had thought to buy stamps, rattled the door to no purpose.

Now she could feel the sweat trickling under her dress, and her feet, in the thin sandals, ached from the short distance she had walked. The sun was too strong, too fierce, and as she looked up and down the empty street, and at the houses, with the shops between, every one of them closed from her, withdrawn into the blessed peace of their siesta, she felt a sudden longing for any place that might be cool, that might be dark—a cellar, perhaps, where there was dripping water from a tap. The sound of water falling to a stone floor would soothe her nerves, now jagged from the sun.

Frustrated, almost crying, she turned into an alleyway between two shops. She came to steps leading down to a little court where there was no sun, and paused there a moment, her hand against the wall, so cold and firm. Beside her there was a window, shuttered, against which she leant her head, and suddenly, to her confusion, the shutter was withdrawn and a face looked out upon her from some dark room within.

"*Je regrette . . .*" she began, swept to absurdity that she should be discovered here, intruding, like one peering into the privacy and squalor of life below a shop. And then her voice dwindled and died away, foolishly, for the face that looked out upon her from the open window was so unusual, so gentle, that it might have come straight from a stained-glass saint in a cathedral. His face was framed in a cloud of dark curled hair, his nose was small and straight, his mouth a sculptured mouth, and his eyes, so solemn, brown, and tender, were like the eyes of a gazelle.

"*Vous désirez, Madame la Marquise?*" he said in answer to her unfinished words.

He knows me, she thought in wonder, he has seen me before, but even this was not so unexpected as the quality of his voice, not rough, not harsh, not the voice of someone in a cellar under a shop, but cultivated, liquid, a voice that matched the eyes of the gazelle.

"It was so hot up in the street," she said. "The shops were closed and I felt faint. I came down the steps. I am very sorry, it is private, of course."

The face disappeared from the window. He opened a door somewhere that she had not seen, and suddenly she found a chair beneath her and she was sitting down, inside the doorway, and it was dark and cool inside the room, even like the cellar she had imagined, and he was giving her water from an earthenware cup.

"Thank you," she said, "thank you very much." Looking up, she saw that he was watching her, with humility, with reverence, the pitcher of water in his hand; and he said to her in his soft, gentle voice, "Is there anything else I can get for you, Madame la Marquise?"

She shook her head, but within her stirred the feeling she knew so well, the sense of secret pleasure that came with admiration, and, conscious of herself for the first time since he had opened the window, she drew her scarf closer about her shoulders, the gesture deliberate, and she saw the gazelle eyes fall to the rose tucked in the bodice of her dress.

She said, "How do you know who I am?"

He answered, "You came into my shop three days ago. You had your children with you. You bought a film for your camera."

She stared at him, puzzled. She remembered buying the film from the little shop that advertised Kodaks in the window, and she remembered too the ugly, shuffling, crippled woman who had served her behind the counter. The woman had walked with a limp, and afraid that the children would notice and laugh, and that she herself, from nervousness, would be betrayed to equally heartless laughter, she had ordered some things to be sent to the hotel, and then departed.

"My sister served you," he said in explanation. "I saw you from the inner room. I do not often go behind the counter. I take photographs of people, of the countryside, and then they are sold to the visitors who come here in the summer."

"Yes," she said, "I see, I understand."

And she drank again from the earthenware cup, and drank, too, the adoration in his eyes.

"I have brought a film to be developed," she said. "I have it here in my bag. Would you do that for me?"

"Of course, Madame la Marquise," he said. "I will do anything for you, whatever you ask. Since that day you came into my shop I . . ." Then he stopped, a flush came over his face, and he looked away from her, deeply embarrassed.

The Marquise repressed a desire to laugh. It was quite absurd, his admiration. Yet, funny . . . it gave her a sense of power.

"Since I came into your shop, what?" she asked.

He looked at her again. "I have thought of nothing else, but nothing," he said to her, and with such intensity that it almost frightened her.

She smiled; she handed back the cup of water. "I am quite an ordinary woman," she said. "If you knew me better, I should disappoint you." How odd it is, she thought to herself, that I am so much mistress of this situation, I am not at all outraged or shocked. Here I am, in the cellar of a shop, talking to a photographer who has just expressed his admiration for me. It is really most amusing, and yet he, poor man, is in earnest, he really means what he says.

"Well," she said, "are you going to take my film?"

It was as though he could not drag his eyes away from her, and boldly she stared him out of face, so that his eyes fell and he flushed again.

"If you will go back the way you came," he said, "I will open up the shop for you." And now it was she who let her eyes linger upon him; the open vest, no shirt, the bare arms, the throat, the head of curling hair, and she said, "Why cannot I give you the film here?"

"It would not be correct, Madame la Marquise," he said to her.

She turned, laughing, and went back up the steps to the hot street.

She stood on the pavement, she heard the rattle of the key in the door behind, she heard the door open. And then presently, in her own time, having deliberately stood outside to keep him waiting, she went into the shop, which was stuffy now, and close, unlike the cool quiet cellar.

He was behind the counter and she saw, with disappointment, that he had put on his coat, a grey cheap coat worn by any man serving in a shop, and his shirt was much too stiff, and much too blue. He was ordinary, a shopkeeper, reaching across the counter for the film.

"When will you have them ready?" she said.

"Tomorrow," he answered, and once again he looked at her with his dumb brown eyes. And she forgot the common coat and the blue stiff shirt, and saw the vest under the coat, and the bare arms.

"If you are a photographer," she said, "why don't you come to the hotel and take some photographs of me and my children?"

"You would like me to do that?" he asked.

"Why not?" she answered.

A secret look came into his eyes and went again, and he bent below the counter, pretending to search for string. But she thought, smiling to herself, "This is exciting to him, his hands are trembling"; and for the same reason her heart beat faster than before.

"Very well, Madame la Marquise," he said, "I will come to the hotel at whatever time is convenient to you."

"The morning, perhaps, is best," she said, "at eleven o'clock."

Casually she strolled away. She did not even say good-bye.

She walked across the street and, looking for nothing in the window of a shop opposite, she saw, through the glass, that he had come to the door of his own shop and was watching her. He had taken off his jacket and his shirt. The shop would be closed again, the siesta was not yet over. Then she noticed, for the first time, that he too was crippled, like his sister. His right foot was encased in a high fitted boot. Yet, curiously, the sight of this did not repel her, nor bring her to nervous laughter, as it had done before when she had seen the sister. His high boot had a fascination, strange, unknown.

The Marquise walked back to the hotel along the dusty road.

At eleven o'clock the next morning the concierge of the hotel sent up word that Monsieur Paul, the photographer, was below in the hall, and awaited the instructions of Madame la Marquise. The instructions were sent back that Madame la Marquise would be pleased if Monsieur Paul would go upstairs to the suite. Presently she heard the knock on the door, hesitant, timid.

"*Entrez*," she called, and standing, as she did, on the balcony, her arms around the two children, she made a tableau, ready set, for him to gaze upon.

Today she was dressed in silk shantung the colour of chartreuse, and her hair was not the little-girl hair of yesterday, with the ribbon, but parted in the centre and drawn back to show her ears, with the gold clips upon them.

He stood in the entrance of the doorway, he did not move. The children, shy, gazed with wonder at the high boot, but they said nothing. Their mother had warned them not to mention it.

"These are my babies," said the Marquise. "And now you must tell us how to pose, and where you want us placed."

The children did not make their usual curtsey, as they did to guests. Their mother had told them it would not be necessary. Monsieur Paul was a photographer, from the shop in the little town.

"If it would be possible, Madame la Marquise," he said, "to have one pose just as you are standing now. It is quite beautiful. So very natural, so full of grace."

"Why, yes, if you like. Stand still, Hélène."

"Pardon. It will take a few moments to fix the camera."

His nervousness had gone. He was busy with the mechanical tricks of his trade. And as she watched him set up the tripod, fix the velvet cloth, make the adjustments to his camera, she noticed his hands, deft and efficient, and they were not the hands of an artisan, of a shopkeeper, but the hands of an artist.

Her eyes fell to the boot. His limp was not so pronounced as the sister's, he did not walk with that lurching, jerky step that produced stifled hysteria in the watcher. His step was slow, more dragging, and the Marquise felt a kind of compassion for his deformity, for surely the misshapen foot beneath the boot must pain him constantly, and the high boot, especially in hot weather, crush and sear his flesh.

"Now, Madame la Marquise," he said, and guiltily she raised her eyes from the boot and struck her pose, smiling gracefully, her arms embracing the children.

"Yes," he said, "just so. It is very lovely."

The dumb brown eyes held hers. His voice was low, gentle. The sense of pleasure came upon her just as it had done in the shop the day before. He pressed the bulb. There was a little clicking sound.

"Once more," he said.

She went on posing, the smile on her lips; and she knew that the reason he paused this time before pressing the bulb was not from professional necessity, because she or the children had moved, but because it delighted him to gaze upon her.

"There," she said, and breaking the pose, and the spell, she moved towards the balcony, humming a little song.

After half an hour the children became tired, restless.

The Marquise apologised. "It's so very hot," she said, "you must excuse them. Céleste, Hélène, get your toys and play on the other corner of the balcony."

They ran chattering to their own room. The Marquise turned her back upon the photographer. He was putting fresh plates into his camera.

"You know what it is with children," she said. "For a few minutes it is a novelty, then they are sick of it, they want something else. You have been very patient, Monsieur Paul."

She broke off a rose from the balcony and, cupping it in her hands, bent her lips to it.

"Please," he said with urgency, "if you would permit me, I scarcely like to ask you . . ."

"What?" she said.

"Would it be possible for me to take one or two photographs of you alone, without the children?"

She laughed. She tossed the rose over the balcony to the terrace below.

"But of course," she said, "I am at your disposal. I have nothing else to do."

She sat down on the edge of the chaise longue and, leaning back against the cushion, rested her head against her arm.

"Like this?" she said.

He disappeared behind the velvet cloth, and then, after an adjustment to the camera, came limping forward.

"If you will permit me," he said, "the hand should be raised a little, so . . . And the head, just slightly on one side."

He took her hand and placed it to his liking; and then gently, with hesitation, put his hand under her chin, lifting it. She closed her eyes. He did not take his hand away. Almost imperceptibly his thumb moved, lingering, over the long line of her neck, and his fingers followed the movement of the thumb. The sensation was featherweight, like the brushing of a bird's wing against her skin.

"Just so," he said, "that is perfection."

She opened her eyes. He limped back to his camera.

The Marquise did not tire as the children had done. She permitted Monsieur Paul to take one photograph, then another, then another. The children returned, as she had bidden them, and played together at the far end of the balcony, and their chatter made a background to the business of the photography, so that, both smiling at the prattle of the children, a kind of adult intimacy developed between the Marquise and the photographer, and the atmosphere was not so tense as it had been.

He became bolder, more confident of himself. He suggested poses and she acquiesced, and once or twice she placed herself badly and he told her of it.

"No, Madame la Marquise. Not like that. Like this."

Then he would come over to the chair, kneel beside her, move her foot perhaps, or turn her shoulder, and each time he did so his touch became more certain, became stronger. Yet when she forced him to meet her eyes he looked away, humble and diffident, as though he was ashamed of what he did, and his gentle eyes, mirroring his nature, would deny the impulse of his hands. She sensed a struggle within him, and it gave her pleasure.

At last, after he had rearranged her dress the second time, she noticed that he had gone quite white and there was perspiration on his forehead.

"It is very hot," she said, "perhaps we have done enough for today."

"If you please, Madame la Marquise," he answered, "it is indeed very warm. I think it is best that we should stop now."

She rose from the chair, cool and at her ease. She was not tired, nor was she troubled. Rather was she invigorated, full of a new energy. When he had gone she would walk down to the sea and swim. It was very different for the photographer. She saw him wipe his face with his handkerchief, and as he packed up his camera and his tripod, and put them in the case, he looked exhausted and dragged his high boot more heavily than before.

She made a pretence of glancing through the snapshots he had developed for her from her own film.

"These are very poor," she said lightly. "I don't think I handle my camera correctly. I should take lessons from you."

"It is just a little practice that you need, Madame la Marquise," he said. "When I first started I had a camera much the same as yours. Even now, when I take exteriors, I wander out on the cliffs above the sea, with a small camera, and the effects are just as good as with the larger one."

She put the snapshots down on the table. He was ready to go. He carried the case in his hand.

"You must be very busy in the season," she said. "How do you get time to take exteriors?"

"I make time, Madame la Marquise," he said. "I prefer it, actually, to taking studio portraits. It is only occasionally that I find true satisfaction in photographing people. Like, for instance, today."

She looked at him and she saw again the devotion, the humility, in his eyes. She stared at him until he dropped his eyes, abashed.

"The scenery is very beautiful along the coast," he said. "You must have noticed it, when walking. Most afternoons I take my small camera and go out on to the cliffs, above the big rock that stands there so prominent, to the right of the bathing beach."

He pointed from the balcony, and she followed the direction of his hand. The green headland shimmered hazily in the intense heat.

"It was only by chance that you found me at home yesterday," he said. "I was in the cellar, developing prints that had been promised for visitors who were to leave today. But usually I go walking on the cliffs at that time."

"It must be very hot," she said.

"Perhaps," he answered. "But above the sea there is a little breeze. And best of all, between one and four there are so few people. They are all taking their siesta in the afternoon. I have all that beautiful scenery to myself."

"Yes," said the Marquise, "I understand."

For a moment they both stood silent. It was as though something unspoken passed between them. The Marquise played with her chiffon handkerchief, then tied it loosely round her wrist, a casual, lazy gesture.

"Sometime I must try it for myself," she said at last, "walking in the heat of the day."

Miss Clay came on to the balcony, calling the children to come and be washed before déjeuner. The photographer stepped to one side, deferential, apologising. And the Marquise, glancing at her watch, saw that it was already *midi*, and that the tables below on the terrace were filled with people and the usual bustle and chatter were going on, the tinkle of glasses, the rattle of plates, and she had noticed none of it.

She turned her shoulder to the photographer, dismissing him, deliberately cool and indifferent now that the session was over and Miss Clay had come to fetch the children.

"Thank you," she said. "I shall call in at the shop to see the proofs in a few days' time. Good morning."

He bowed, he went away, an employee who had fulfilled his orders.

"I hope he has taken some good photographs," said Miss Clay. "The Marquis will be very pleased to see the results."

The Marquise did not answer. She was taking off the gold clips from her ears that now, for some reason, no longer matched her mood. She would go down to déjeuner without jewellery, without rings; she felt, for today, her own beauty would suffice.

Three days passed, and the Marquise did not once descend into the little town. The first day she swam, she watched the tennis in the afternoon. The second day she spent with the children, giving Miss Clay leave of absence to take a tour by charabanc to visit the old walled cities, further inland, along the coast. The third day she sent Miss Clay and the children into the town to enquire for the proofs, and they returned with them wrapped in a neat package. The Marquise examined them. They were very good indeed, and the studies of herself the best she had ever had taken.

Miss Clay was in raptures. She begged for copies to send home to England. "Who would believe it," she exclaimed, "that a little photographer by the sea like this could take such splendid pictures? And then you go and pay heaven knows what to real professionals in Paris."

"They are not bad," said the Marquise, yawning. "He certainly took a lot of trouble. They are better of me than they are of the children." She folded the package and put it away in a drawer. "Did Monsieur Paul seem pleased with them himself?" she asked the governess.

"He did not say," replied Miss Clay. "He seemed disappointed that you had not gone down for them yourself; he said they had been ready since yesterday. He asked if you were well, and the children told him Maman had been swimming. They were quite friendly with him."

"It's much too hot and dusty down in the town," said the Marquise.

The next afternoon, when Miss Clay and the children were resting and the hotel itself seemed asleep under the glare of the sun, the Marquise changed into a short sleeveless frock, very simple and plain, and softly, so as not to disturb the children, went downstairs, her small box camera slung over her arm, and, walking through the hotel grounds on to the sands, she followed a narrow path that led upwards, to the greensward above. The sun was merciless. Yet she did not mind. Here on the springy grass there was no dust, and presently, by the cliff's edge, the bracken, growing thicker, brushed her bare legs.

The little path wound in and out amongst the bracken, at times coming so close to the cliff's edge that a false step, bringing a stumble, would spell danger. But the Marquise, walking slowly, with the lazy swing of the hips peculiar to her, felt neither frightened nor exhausted. She was merely intent on reaching a spot that overlooked the great rock standing out from the coast in the middle of the bay. She was quite alone on the headland. No one was in sight. Away behind her, far below, the white walls of the hotel and the rows of bathing cabins on the beach looked like bricks played with by children. The sea was very smooth and still. Even where it washed upon the rock in the bay it left no ripple.

Suddenly the Marquise saw something flash in the bracken ahead of her. It was the lens of a camera. She took no notice. Turning her back, she pretended to examine her own camera, and took up a position as though to photograph the view. She took one, took another, and then she heard the swish of someone walking towards her through the bracken.

She turned, surprised. "Why, good afternoon, Monsieur Paul," she said.

He had discarded the cheap stiff jacket and the bright blue shirt. He was not on business. It was the hour of the siesta, when he walked, as it were, incognito. He wore only the vest and a pair of dark blue trousers, and the grey squash hat, which she had noticed with dismay the morning he had come to the hotel, was also absent. His thick dark hair made a frame to his gentle face. His eyes had such a rapturous expression at the sight of her that she was forced to turn away to hide her smile.

"You see," she said lightly, "I have taken your advice, and strolled up here to look at the view. But I am sure I don't hold my camera correctly. Show me how."

He stood beside her and, taking her camera, steadied her hands, moving them to the correct position.

"Yes, of course," she said, and then moved away from him, laughing a little, for it had seemed to her that when he stood beside her and guided her hands she had heard his heart beating, and the sound brought excitement, which she wished to conceal from him.

"Have you your own camera?" she said.

"Yes, Madame la Marquise," he answered. "I left it over in the bracken there, with my coat. It is a favourite spot of mine, close to the edge of the cliff. In spring I come here to watch the birds and take photographs of them."

"Show me," she said.

He led the way, murmuring "Pardon," and the path he had made for himself took them to a little clearing, like a nest, hidden on all sides by bracken that was now waist-high. Only the front of the clearing was open, and this was wide to the cliff face and the sea.

"But how lovely," she said, and, passing through the bracken into the hiding place, she looked about her, smiling, and sitting down, gracefully, naturally, like a child at a picnic, she picked up the book that was lying on top of his coat beside his camera.

"You read much?" she said.

"Yes, Madame la Marquise," he answered. "I am very fond of reading." She glanced at the cover, and read the title. It was a cheap romance, the sort of book she and her friends had smuggled into their satchels at the lycée in old days. She had not read that sort of stuff for years. Once again she had to hide her smile. She put the book back on the coat.

"Is it a good story?" she asked him.

He looked down at her solemnly, with his great eyes like a gazelle's.

"It is very tender, Madame la Marquise," he said.

Tender . . . What an odd expression. She began to talk about the proofs of the photographs, and how she preferred one to another, and all the while she was conscious of an inner triumph that she was in such command of the situation. She knew exactly what to do, what to say, when to smile, when to look serious. It reminded her strangely of childhood days, when she and her young friends would dress up in their mothers' hats and say, "Let's pretend to be ladies." She was pretending now; not to be a lady, as then, but to be—what? She was not sure. But something other than the self who now, for so long, was in truth a real lady, sipping tea in the salon at the château, surrounded by so many ancient things and people that each one of them had the mustiness of death.

The photographer did not talk much. He listened to the Marquise. He agreed, nodded his head, or simply remained silent, and she heard her own voice trilling on in a sort of wonder. He was merely a witness she could ignore, a nonentity, while she listened to the brilliant, charming woman that had suddenly become herself.

At last there came a pause in the one-sided conversation, and he said to her shyly, "May I dare to ask you something?"

"Of course," she said.

"Could I photograph you here, alone, with this background?"

Was that all? How timid he was, and how reluctant. She laughed. "Take as many as you want," she said. "It is very pleasant sitting here. I may even go to sleep."

"*La belle au bois dormant*," he said quickly, and then, as if ashamed of his familiarity, he murmured "Pardon" once more and reached for the camera behind her.

This time he did not ask her to pose, to change position. He photographed her as she sat, lazily nibbling at a stem of grass, and it was he who moved, now here, now there, so that he had shots of her from every angle, full-face, profile, three-quarter.

She began to feel sleepy. The sun beat down upon her uncovered head, and the dragonflies, gaudy and green and gold, swung and hovered before her eyes. She yawned and leant back against the bracken.

"Would you care for my coat as a pillow for your head, Madame la Marquise?" he asked her.

Before she could reply he had taken his coat, folded it neatly, and placed it in a little roll against the bracken. She leant back against it, and the despised grey coat made a softness to her head, easy and comfortable.

He knelt beside her, intent upon his camera, doing something to the film, and she watched him, yawning, between half-closed eyes, and noticed that as he knelt he kept his weight upon one knee only, thrusting the deformed foot in the high boot to one side. Idly, she wondered if it hurt to lean upon it. The boot was highly polished, much brighter than the leather shoe upon the left foot, and she had a sudden vision of him taking great pains with the boot every morning when he dressed, polishing it, rubbing it, perhaps, with a wash-leather cloth.

A dragonfly settled on her hand. It crouched, waiting, a sheen upon its wings. What was it waiting for? She blew upon it and it flew away. Then it came back again, hovering, insistent.

Monsieur Paul had put aside his camera, but he was still kneeling in the bracken beside her. She was aware of him, watching her, and she thought to herself, "If I move he will get up, and it will all be over."

She went on staring at the glittering, shivering dragonfly, but she knew that in a moment or two she must look somewhere else, or the dragonfly would go, or the present silence would become so tense and so strained that she would break it with a laugh and so spoil everything. Reluctantly, against her will, she turned to the photographer, and his large eyes, humble and devoted, were fixed upon her with all the deep abasement of a slave.

"Why don't you kiss me?" she said, and her own words startled her, shocked her into sudden apprehension.

He said nothing. He did not move. He went on gazing at her. She closed her eyes, and the dragonfly went from her hand.

Presently, when the photographer bent to touch her, it was not what she expected. There was no sudden crude embrace. It was just as though the dragonfly had returned, and now with silken wings brushed and stroked the smooth surface of her skin.

When he went away it was with tact and delicacy. He left her to herself so that there should be no aftermath of awkwardness, of embarrassment, no sudden strain of conversation.

The Marquise lay back in the bracken, her hands over her eyes, thinking about what had happened to her, and she had no sense of shame. She was clear-headed and quite calm. She began to plan how she would walk back to the hotel in a little while, giving him good time to gain the sands before her, so that if by chance people from the hotel should see him they would not connect him with her, who would follow after, say in half an hour.

She got up, rearranged her dress, took out her powder compact from her pocket, with her lipstick, and, having no mirror, judged carefully how much powder to put upon her face. The sun had lost its power, and a cool breeze blew inland from the sea.

"If the weather holds," thought the Marquise as she combed her hair, "I can come out here every day, at the same time. No one will ever know. Miss Clay and the children always rest in the afternoon. If we walk separately and go back separately, as we have done today, and come to this same place, hidden by the bracken, we cannot possibly be discovered. There are over three weeks still to the holiday. The great thing is to pray for this hot weather to continue. If it should rain . . ."

As she walked back to the hotel she wondered how they would manage, should the weather break. She could not very well set out to walk the cliffs in a mackintosh, and then lie down while the rain and the wind beat the bracken. There was of course the cellar, beneath the shop. But she might be seen in the village. That would be dangerous. No, unless it rained in torrents, the cliff was safest.

That evening she sat down and wrote a letter to her friend Elise. ". . . This is a wonderful place," she wrote, "and I am amusing myself as usual, and without my husband, *bien entendu!*" But she gave no details of her conquest, though she mentioned the bracken and the hot afternoon. She felt that if she left it vague Elise would picture to herself some rich American, travelling for pleasure, alone, without his wife.

The next morning, dressing herself with great care—she stood for a long while before her wardrobe, finally choosing a frock rather more elaborate than was usual for the seaside, but this was deliberate on her part—she went down into the little town, accompanied by Miss Clay and the children. It was market day, and the cobbled streets and the square were full of people. Many came from the countryside around, but there were quantities of visitors, English and American, who strolled to see the sights, to buy souvenirs and picture-postcards, or to sit down at the café at the corner and look about them.

The Marquise made a striking figure, walking in her indolent way in her lovely dress, hatless, carrying a sunshade, with the two little girls prancing beside her. Many people turned to look at her, or even stepped aside to let her pass, in unconscious homage to her beauty. She dawdled in the market place and made a few purchases, which Miss Clay put into the shopping bag she carried, and then, still casual, still answering with gay, lazy humour the questions of the children, she turned into the shop which displayed Kodaks and photographs in the window.

It was full of visitors waiting their turn to be served, and the Marquise, who was in no hurry, pretended to examine a book of local views, while at the same time she could see what was happening in the shop. They were both there, Monsieur Paul and his sister, he in his stiff shirt, an ugly pink this time, worse even than the blue, and the cheap grey coat, while the sister, like all women who served behind a counter, was in drab black, a shawl over her shoulders.

He must have seen her come into the shop, because almost at once he came forward from the counter, leaving the queue of visitors to the care of his sister, and was by her side, humble, polite, anxious to know in what manner he could serve her. There was no trace of familiarity, no look of knowledge in his eyes, and she took care to assure herself of this by staring directly at him. Then deliberately, bringing the children and Miss Clay into the conversation, asking Miss Clay to make her choice of the proofs which were to be sent to England, she kept him there by her side, treating him with condescension, with a sort of hauteur, even finding fault with certain of the proofs, which, so she told him, did not do the children justice, and which she could not possibly send to her husband, the Marquis. The photographer apologised. Most certainly the proofs mentioned did not do the children justice. He would be willing to come again to the hotel and try again, at no extra charge, of course. Perhaps on the terrace or in the gardens the effect would be better.

One or two people turned to look at the Marquise as she stood there. She could feel their eyes upon her, absorbing her beauty, and still in a tone of condescension, coldly, almost curtly, she told the photographer to show her various articles in his shop, which he hastened to do in his anxiety to please.

The other visitors were becoming restive, they shuffled their feet waiting for the sister to serve them, and she, hemmed about with customers, limped wretchedly from one end of the counter to the other, now and again raising her head, peering to see if her brother, who had so suddenly deserted her, would come to the rescue.

At last the Marquise relented. She had had her fill. The delicious furtive sense of excitement that had risen in her since her entrance to the shop died down and was appeased.

"One of these mornings I will let you know," she said to Monsieur Paul, "and then you can come out and photograph the children again. Meanwhile, let me pay what I owe. Miss Clay, attend to it, will you?"

And she strolled from the shop, not bidding him good morning, putting out her hands to the two children.

She did not change for déjeuner. She wore the same enchanting frock, and the hotel terrace, more crowded than ever because of the many visitors who had come on an excursion, seemed to her to buzz and hum with a murmur of conversation, directed at her and her beauty, and at the effect she made, sitting there at the table in the corner. The maître d'hôtel, the waiters, even the manager himself, were drawn towards her, obsequious, smiling, and she could hear her name pass from one to the other.

All things combined to her triumph: the proximity of people, the smell of food and wine and cigarettes, the scent of the gaudy flowers in their tubs, the feel of the hot sun beating down, the close sound of the splashing sea. When she rose at last with the children and went upstairs, she had a sense of happiness that she felt must only come to a prima donna after the clamour of long applause.

The children, with Miss Clay, went to their rooms to rest; and swiftly, hurriedly, the Marquise changed her frock and her shoes and tiptoed down the stairs and out of the hotel, across the burning sands to the path and the bracken headland.

He was waiting for her, as she expected, and neither of them made any reference to her visit in the morning, or to what brought her there on the cliff this afternoon. They made at once for the little clearing by the cliff's edge and sat down of one accord, and the Marquise, in a tone of banter, described the crowd at lunch, and the fearful bustle and fatigue of the terrace with so many people, and how delicious it was to get away from them all to the fresh clean air of the headland, above the sea.

He agreed with her humbly, watching her as she spoke of such mundane matters as though the wit of the world flowed in her speech, and then, exactly as on the previous day, he begged to take a few photographs of her, and she consented, and presently she lay back in the bracken and closed her eyes.

There was no sense of time to the long, languorous afternoon. Just as before, the dragonflies winged about her in the bracken, and the sun beat down upon her body, and with her sense of deep enjoyment at all that happened went the curiously satisfying knowledge that what she did was without emotion of any sort. Her mind and her affections were quite untouched. She might almost have been relaxing in a beauty parlour, back in Paris, having the first telltale lines smoothed from her face and her hair shampooed, although these things brought only a lazy contentment and no pleasure.

Once again he departed, leaving her without a word, tactful and discreet, so that she could arrange herself in privacy. And once again, when she judged him out of sight, she rose to her feet and began the long walk back to the hotel.

Her good luck held and the weather did not break. Every afternoon, as soon as déjeuner was over and the children had gone to rest, the Marquise went for her promenade, returning about half-past four, in time for tea. Miss Clay, at first exclaiming at her energy, came to accept the walk as a matter of routine. If the Marquise chose to walk in the heat of the day, it was her own affair; certainly it seemed to do her good. She was more human towards her, Miss Clay, and less nagging to the children. The constant headaches and attacks of migraine were forgotten, and it seemed that the Marquise was really enjoying this simple seaside holiday alone with Miss Clay and the two little girls.

When a fortnight had passed, the Marquise discovered that the first delight and bliss of her experience were slowly fading. It was not that Monsieur Paul failed her in any way, but that she herself was becoming used to the daily ritual. Like an inoculation that "took" at the first with very great success, on constant repetition the effect lessened, dulled, and the Marquise found that to recapture her enjoyment she was obliged to treat the photographer no longer as a nonentity, or as she would a coiffeur who had set her hair, but as a person whose feelings she could wound. She would find fault with his appearance, complain that he wore his hair too long, that his clothes were cheap, ill-cut, or even that he ran his little shop in the town with inefficiency, that the material and paper he used for his prints were shoddy.

She would watch his face when she told him this, and she would see anxiety and pain come into his large eyes, pallor to his skin, a look of dejection fall upon his whole person as he realised how unworthy he was of her, how inferior in every way, and only when she saw him thus did the original excitement kindle in her again.

Deliberately she began to cut down the hours of the afternoon. She would arrive late at the rendezvous in the bracken and find him waiting for her with that same look of anxiety on his face, and if her mood was not sufficiently ripe for what should happen she would get through the business quickly, with an ill grace, and then dispatch him hastily on his return journey, picturing him limping back, tired and unhappy, to the shop in the little town.

She permitted him to take photographs of her still. This was all part of the experience, and she knew that it troubled him to do this, to see her to perfection, so she delighted in taking advantage of it, and would sometimes tell him to come to the hotel during the morning, and then she would pose in the grounds, exquisitely dressed, the children beside her, Miss Clay an admiring witness, the visitors watching from their rooms or from the terrace.

The contrast of these mornings, when as an employee he limped back and forth at her bidding, moving the tripod first here, first there, while she gave him orders, with the sudden intimacy of the afternoons in the bracken under the hot sun, proved, during the third week, to be her only stimulation.

Finally, a day breaking when quite a cold breeze blew in from the sea, and she did not go to the rendezvous as usual but rested on her balcony reading a novel, the change in the routine came as a real relief.

The following day was fine and she decided to go to the headland, and for the first time since they had encountered one another in the cool dark cellar below the shop he upbraided her, his voice sharp with anxiety.

"I waited for you all yesterday afternoon," he said. "What happened?"

She stared at him in astonishment.

"It was an unpleasant day," she replied. "I preferred to read on my balcony in the hotel."

"I was afraid you might have been taken ill," he went on. "I very nearly called at the hotel to enquire for you. I hardly slept last night, I was so upset."

He followed her to the hiding place in the bracken, his eyes still anxious, lines of worry on his brow, and though in a sense it was a stimulation to the Marquise to witness his distress, at the same time it irritated her that he should so forget himself to find fault in her conduct. It was as though her coiffeur in Paris, or her masseur, expressed anger when she broke an appointment fixed for a certain day.

"If you think I feel myself bound to come here every afternoon, you are very much mistaken," she said. "I have plenty of other things to do."

At once he apologised, he was abject. He begged her to forgive him.

"You cannot understand what this means to me," he said. "Since I have known you, everything in my life is changed. I live only for these afternoons."

His subjection pleased her, whipping her to a renewal of interest, and pity came to her too, as he lay by her side, pity that this creature should be so utterly devoted, depending on her like a child. She touched his hair, feeling for a moment quite compassionate, almost maternal. Poor fellow, limping all this way because of her, and then sitting in the biting wind of yesterday, alone and wretched. She imagined the letter she would write to her friend Elise.

"I am very much afraid I have broken Paul's heart. He has taken this little *affaire des vacances au sérieux*. But what am I to do? After all, these things must have an end. I cannot possibly alter my life because of him. *Enfin*, he is a man, he will get over it." Elise would picture the beautiful blond American playboy climbing wearily into his Packard, setting off in despair to the unknown.

The photographer did not leave her today, when the afternoon session had ended. He sat up in the bracken and stared out towards the great rock jutting out into the sea.

"I have made up my mind about the future," he said quietly.

The Marquise sensed the drama in the air. Did he mean he was going to kill himself? How very terrible. He would wait, of course, until she had left the hotel and had returned home. She need never know.

"Tell me," she said gently.

"My sister will look after the shop," he said. "I will make it all over to her. She is very capable. For myself, I shall follow you, wherever you go, whether it is to Paris, or to the country. I shall be close at hand; whenever you want me, I shall be there."

The Marquise swallowed. Her heart went still.

"You can't possibly do that," she said. "How would you live?"

"I am not proud," he said. "I know, in the goodness of your heart, you would allow me something. My needs would be very small. But I know that it is impossible to live without you, therefore the only thing to do is to follow you, always. I will find a room close to your house in Paris, and in the country too. We will find ways and means of being together. When love is as strong as this there are no difficulties."

He spoke with his usual humility, but there was a force behind his words that was unexpected, and she knew that for him this was no false drama, ill-timed to the day, but true sincerity. He meant every word. He would in truth give up the shop, follow her to Paris, follow her also to the château in the country.

"You are mad," she said violently, sitting up, careless of her appearance and her dishevelled hair. "Once I have left here I am no longer free. I cannot possibly meet you anywhere, the danger of discovery would be too great. You realise my position? What it would mean to me?"

He nodded his head. His face was sad, but quite determined. "I have thought of everything," he answered, "but as you know, I am very discreet. You need never be apprehensive on that score. It has occurred to me that it might be possible to obtain a place in your service as footman. It would not matter to me, the loss of personal dignity. I am not proud. But in such a capacity our life together could continue much as it does now. Your husband, the Marquis, must be a very busy man, often out during the day, and your children and the English miss no doubt go walking in the country in the afternoon. You see, everything would be very simple if we had the courage."

The Marquise was so shocked that she could not answer. She could not imagine anything more terrible, more disastrous, than that the photographer should take a place in the house as footman. Quite apart from his disability—she shuddered to think of him limping round the table in the great *salle à manger*—what misery she would suffer knowing that he was there, in the house, that he was waiting for her to go up to her room in the afternoon, and then, timidly, the knock upon the door, the hushed whisper. The degradation of this—this creature—there was really no other word for him—in the house, always waiting, always hoping.

"I am afraid," she said firmly, "that what you are suggesting is utterly impossible. Not only the idea of coming to my house as a servant, but of our ever being able to meet again once I return home. Your own common sense must tell you so. These afternoons have been—have been pleasant, but my holiday is very nearly over. In a few days' time my husband will be coming to fetch me and the children, and that finishes everything."

To show finality she got up, brushed her crumpled frock, combed her hair, powdered her nose, and, reaching for her bag, fumbled inside it for her note case.

She drew out several ten-thousand-franc notes.

"This is for the shop," she said, "any little fittings it may require. And buy something for your sister. And remember, I shall always think of you with great tenderness."

To her consternation his face went dead white, then his mouth began to work violently and he rose to his feet.

"No, no," he said, "I will never take them. You are cruel, wicked, to suggest it." And suddenly he began to sob, burying his face in his hands, his shoulders heaving with emotion.

The Marquise watched him helplessly, uncertain whether to go or to stay. His sobs were so violent that she was afraid of hysteria, and she did not know what might happen. She was sorry for him, deeply sorry, but even more sorry for herself, because now, on parting, he cut such a ridiculous figure in her eyes. A man who gave way to emotion was pitiable. And it seemed to her that the clearing in the bracken took on a sordid, shameful appearance, which once had seemed so secret and so warm. His shirt, lying on a stem of bracken, looked like old linen spread by washerwomen in the sun to dry. Beside it lay his tie and the cheap trilby hat. It needed only orange peel and silver paper from a chocolate carton to complete the picture.

"Stop that noise," she said in sudden fury. "For God's sake pull yourself together."

The crying ceased. He took his hands away from his ravaged face. He stared at her, trembling, his brown eyes blind with pain. "I have been mistaken in you," he said. "I know you now for what you are. You are a wicked woman and you go about ruining the lives of innocent men like myself. I shall tell your husband everything."

The Marquise said nothing. He was unbalanced, mad. . . .

"Yes," said the photographer, still catching at his breath, "that is what I shall do. As soon as your husband comes to fetch you I will tell him everything. I will show him the photographs I have taken here on the headland. I will prove to him without a doubt that you are false to him, that you are bad. And he will believe me. He cannot help but believe me. What he does to me does not matter. I cannot suffer more than I suffer now. But your life, that will be finished, I promise you. He will know, the English miss will know, the manager of the hotel will know; I will tell everybody how you have been spending your afternoons."

He reached for his coat, he reached for his hat, he slung his camera around his shoulder, and panic seized the Marquise, rose from her heart to her throat. He would do all that he threatened to do; he would wait there in the hall of the hotel by the reception desk, he would wait for Edouard to come.

"Listen to me," she began, "we will think of something, we can perhaps come to some arrangement . . ."

But he ignored her. His face was set and pale. He stooped, by the opening at the cliff's edge, to pick up his stick, and as he did so the terrible impulse was born in her, and flooded her whole being, and would not be denied. Leaning forward, her hands outstretched, she pushed his stooping body. He did not utter a single cry. He fell, and was gone.

The Marquise sank back on her knees. She did not move. She waited. She felt the sweat trickle down her face, to her throat, to her body. Her hands were also wet. She waited there in the clearing, upon her knees, and presently, when she was cooler, she took her handkerchief and wiped away the sweat from her forehead, and her face, and her hands.

It seemed suddenly cold. She shivered. She stood up and her legs were firm; they did not give way, as she feared. She looked about her, over the bracken, and no one was in sight. As always, she was alone upon the headland. Five minutes passed, and then she forced herself to the brink of the cliff and looked down. The tide was in. The sea was washing the base of the cliff below. It surged, and swept the rocks, and sank, and surged again. There was no sign of his body on the cliff face, nor could there be, because the cliff was sheer. No sign of his body in the water, and had he fallen and floated it would have shown there, on the surface of the still blue sea. When he fell he must have sunk immediately.

The Marquise turned back from the opening. She gathered her things together. She tried to pull the flattened bracken to its original height, and so smooth out the signs of habitation, but the hiding place had been made so long that this was impossible. Perhaps it did not matter. Perhaps it would be taken for granted that people came out upon the cliff and took their ease.

Suddenly her knees began to tremble and she sat down. She waited a few moments, then glanced at her watch. She knew that it might be important to remember the time. A few minutes after half-past three. If she was asked, she could say, "Yes, I was out on the headland at about half-past three, but I heard nothing." That would be the truth. She would not be lying. It would be the truth.

She remembered with relief that today she had brought her mirror in her bag. She glanced at it fearfully. Her face was chalk-white, blotched and strange. She powdered carefully, gently; it seemed to make no difference. Miss Clay would notice something was wrong. She dabbed dry rouge on to her cheeks, but this stood out like the painted spots on a clown's face.

"There is only one thing to do," she thought, "and that is to go straight to the bathing cabin on the beach, and undress, and put on my swimming suit, and bathe. Then if I return to the hotel with my hair wet, and my face wet too, it will seem natural, and I shall have been swimming, and that also will be true."

She began to walk back along the cliff, but her legs were weak, as though she had been lying ill in bed for many days, and when she came to the beach at last she was trembling so much she thought she would fall. More than anything she longed to lie down on her bed, in the hotel bedroom, and close the shutters, even the windows, and hide there by herself in the darkness. Yet she must force herself to play the part she had decided.

She went to the bathing cabin and undressed. Already there were several people lying on the sands, reading or sleeping, the hour of siesta drawing to its close. She walked down to the water's edge, kicked off her rope-soled shoes, drew on her cap, and as she swam to and fro in the still, tepid water, and dipped her face, she wondered how many of the people on the beach noticed her, watched her, and afterwards might say, "But don't you remember, we saw a woman come down from the headland in the middle of the afternoon?"

She began to feel very cold, but she continued swimming, backwards and forwards, with stiff, mechanical strokes, until suddenly, seeing a little boy who was playing with a dog point out to sea, and the dog run in barking towards some dark object that might have been a piece of timber, nausea and terror combined to turn her faint, and she stumbled from the sea back to the bathing cabin and lay on the wooden floor, her face in her hands. It might be, she thought, that had she gone on swimming she would have touched him with her feet, as his body came floating in towards her on the water.

In four days' time the Marquis was due to arrive by car and pick up his wife, the governess, and the children, and drive them home. The Marquise put a call through to him at the château and asked if it would be possible for him to come sooner. Yes, the weather was still good, she said, but somehow she had become tired of the place. It was now getting too full of people, it was noisy, and the food had gone off. In fact she had turned against it. She longed to be back at home, she told her husband, amongst her own things, and the gardens would be looking lovely.

The Marquise regretted very much that she was bored, but surely she could stick it out for just the four days, he said. He had made all his arrangements, and he could not come sooner. He had to pass through Paris anyway for an important business meeting. He would promise to reach her by the morning of the Thursday, and then they could leave immediately after lunch.

"I had hoped," he said, "that you would want to stay on for the week end, so that I too could get some bathing. The rooms are held surely until the Monday?"

But no, she had told the manager, she said, that they would not require the rooms after Thursday, and he had already let them to someone else. The place was crowded. The charm of it had gone, she assured him. Edouard would not care for it at all, and at the week end it became quite insupportable. So would he make every effort to arrive in good time on the Thursday, and then they could leave after an early lunch?

The Marquise put down the receiver and went out to the balcony to the chaise longue. She took up a book and pretended to read, but in reality she was listening, waiting for the sound of footsteps, voices, at the entrance to the hotel, and presently for her telephone to ring, and it would be the manager asking her, with many apologies, if she would mind descending to his office. The fact was, the matter was delicate . . . but the police were with him. They had some idea that she could help them. The telephone did not ring. There were no voices. No footsteps. Life continued as before. The long hours dragged through the interminable day. Lunch on the terrace, the waiters bustling, obsequious, the tables filled with the usual faces or with new visitors to take the place of old, the children chattering, Miss Clay reminding them of their manners. And all the while the Marquise listened, waited. . . .

She forced herself to eat, but the food she put in her mouth tasted of sawdust. Lunch over, she mounted to her room, and while the children rested she lay on the chaise longue on the balcony. They descended to the terrace again for tea, but when the children went to the beach for their second bathe of the day she did not go with them. She had a little chill, she told Miss Clay; she did not fancy the water. So she went on sitting there, on her balcony.

When she closed her eyes at night and tried to sleep, she felt his stooping shoulders against her hands once more, and the sensation that it had given her when she pushed them hard. The ease with which he fell and vanished, one moment there, and the next, nothing. No stumble, no cry.

In the daytime she used to strain her eyes towards the headland, in search of figures walking there amongst the bracken—would they be called "a cordon of police"? But the headland shimmered under the pitiless sun, and no one walked there in the bracken.

Twice Miss Clay suggested going down into the town in the mornings to make purchases, and each time the Marquise made an excuse.

"It's always so crowded," she said, "and so hot. I don't think it's good for the children. The gardens are more pleasant, the lawn at the back of the hotel is shady and quiet."

She herself did not leave the hotel. The thought of the beach brought back the pain in her belly, and the nausea. Nor did she walk.

"I shall be quite all right," she told Miss Clay, "when I have thrown off this tiresome chill."

She lay there on the balcony, turning over the pages of the magazines she had read a dozen times.

On the morning of the third day, just before déjeuner, the children came running on to the balcony, waving little windmill flags.

"Look, Maman," said Hélène, "mine is red, and Céleste's is blue. We are going to put them on our sand castles after tea."

"Where did you get them?" asked the Marquise.

"In the market place," said the child. "Miss Clay took us to the town this morning instead of playing in the garden. She wanted to pick up her snapshots that were to be ready today."

A feeling of shock went through the Marquise. She sat very still.

"Run along," she said, "and get ready for déjeuner."

She could hear the children chattering to Miss Clay in the bathroom. In a moment or two Miss Clay came in. She closed the door behind her. The Marquise forced herself to look up at the governess. Miss Clay's long, rather stupid face was grave and concerned.

"Such a dreadful thing has happened," she said, her voice low. "I don't want to speak of it in front of the children. I am sure you will be very distressed. It's poor Monsieur Paul."

"Monsieur Paul?" said the Marquise. Her voice was perfectly calm. But her tone had the right quality of interest.

"I went down to the shop to fetch my snapshots," said Miss Clay, "and I found it shut. The door was locked and the shutters were up. I thought it rather odd, and I went into the *pharmacie* next door and asked if they knew whether the shop was likely to be open after tea. They said no, Mademoiselle Paul was too upset, she was being looked after by relatives. I asked what had happened, and they told me there

had been an accident, that poor Monsieur Paul's body had been found
by some fishermen three miles up the coast, drowned."

Miss Clay had quite lost colour as she told her tale. She was obviously deeply shocked. The Marquise, at sight of her, gained courage.

"How perfectly terrible," she said. "Does anybody know when it
happened?"

"I couldn't go into details at the *pharmacie* because of the children,"
said Miss Clay, "but I think they found the body yesterday. Terribly
injured, they said. He must have hit some rocks before falling into the
sea. It's so dreadful I can't bear to think of it. And his poor sister,
whatever will she do without him?"

The Marquise put up her hand for silence and made a warning face.
The children were coming into the room.

They went down to the terrace for déjeuner, and the Marquise ate
better than she had done for two days. For some reason her appetite
had returned. Why this should be so she could not tell. She wondered
if it could possibly be that part of the burden of her secret was now
lifted. He was dead. He had been found. These things were known.
After déjeuner she told Miss Clay to ask the manager if he knew anything of the sad accident. Miss Clay was to say that the Marquise was
most concerned and grieved. While Miss Clay went about this business
the Marquise took the children upstairs.

Presently the telephone rang. The sound that she had dreaded. Her
heart missed a beat. She took off the receiver and listened.

It was the manager. He said Miss Clay had just been to him. He said
it was most gracious of Madame la Marquise to show concern at the
unfortunate accident that had befallen Monsieur Paul. He would
have spoken of it when the accident was discovered yesterday, but he
did not wish to distress the clientele. A drowning disaster was never
very pleasant at a seaside resort, it made people feel uncomfortable.
Yes, of course, the police had been called in directly the body was
found. It was assumed that he had fallen from the cliffs somewhere
along the coast. It seemed he was very fond of photographing the sea
views. And of course, with his disability, he could easily slip. His sister
had often warned him to be careful. It was very sad. He was such a
good fellow. Everyone liked him. He had no enemies. And such an
artist, too, in his way. Madame la Marquise had been pleased with the
studies Monsieur Paul had done of herself and the children? The

manager was go glad. He would make a point of letting Mademoiselle Paul know this, and also of the concern shown by Madame la Marquise. Yes, indeed, she would be deeply grateful for flowers, and for a note of sympathy. The poor woman was quite brokenhearted. No, the day of the funeral had not yet been decided . . .

When he had finished speaking, the Marquise called to Miss Clay and told her she must order a taxi and drive to the town seven miles inland, where the shops were larger, and where she seemed to remember there was an excellent florist. Miss Clay was to order flowers, lilies for choice, and to spare no expense, and the Marquise would write a note to go with them; and then if Miss Clay gave them to the manager when she returned he would see that they reached Mademoiselle Paul.

The Marquise wrote the note for Miss Clay to take with her to pin on the flowers. "In deepest sympathy at your great loss." She gave Miss Clay some money, and the governess went off to find a taxi.

Later the Marquise took the children to the beach.

"Is your chill better, Maman?" asked Céleste.

"Yes, chérie, now Maman can bathe again."

And she entered the warm yielding water with the children, and splashed with them.

Tomorrow Edouard would arrive, tomorrow Edouard would come in his car and drive them away, and the white dusty roads would lengthen the distance between her and the hotel. She would not see it any more, nor the headland, nor the town, and the holiday would be blotted out like something that had never been.

"When I die," thought the Marquise as she stared out across the sea, "I shall be punished. I don't fool myself. I am guilty of taking life. When I die, God will accuse me. Until then, I will be a good wife to Edouard, and a good mother to Céleste and Hélène. I will try to be a good woman from now. I will try and atone for what I have done by being kinder to everyone, to relations, friends, servants."

She slept well for the first time in three days.

Her husband arrived the next morning while she was still having her breakfast. She was so glad to see him that she sprang from her bed and flung her arms round his neck. The Marquis was touched at this reception.

"I believe my girl has missed me after all," he said.

"Missed you? But of course I've missed you. That's why I rang up. I wanted you to come so much."

"And you are quite determined to leave today after lunch?"

"Oh yes, yes . . . I couldn't bear to stay. Our packing is done, there are only the last things to put in the suitcases."

He sat on the balcony drinking coffee, laughing with the children, while she dressed and stripped the room of her personal possessions. The room that had been hers for a whole month became bare once more, and quite impersonal. In a fever of hurry she cleared the dressing table, mantelpiece, the table by her bed. It was finished with. The *femme de chambre* would come in presently with clean sheets and make all fresh for the next visitor. And she, the Marquise, would have gone.

"Listen, Edouard," she said, "why must we stay for déjeuner? Wouldn't it be more fun to lunch somewhere on the way? There is always something a little dreary in lunching at a hotel when one has already paid the bill. Tipping, everything, has been done. I cannot bear a sense of anticlimax."

"Just as you like," he said. She had given him such a welcome that he was prepared to gratify every whim. Poor little girl. She had been really lonely without him. He must make up to her for it.

The Marquise was making up her mouth in front of the mirror in the bathroom when the telephone rang.

"Answer it, will you?" she called to her husband. "It is probably the concierge about the luggage."

The Marquis did so, and in a few moments he shouted through to his wife.

"It's for you, dear. It's a Mademoiselle Paul who has called to see you, and asks if she may thank you for her flowers before you go."

The Marquise did not answer at once, and when his wife came into the bedroom it seemed to him that the lipstick had not enhanced her appearance. It made her look almost haggard, older. How very strange. She must have changed the colour. It was not becoming.

"Well," he asked, "what shall I say? You probably don't want to be bothered with her now, whoever she is. Would you like me to go down and get rid of her?"

The Marquise seemed uncertain, troubled. "No," she said, "no, I think I had better see her. The fact is, it's a very tragic thing. She and her brother kept a little shop in the town—I had some photographs done of myself and the children—and then a dreadful thing happened, the brother was drowned. I thought it only right to send flowers."

"How thoughtful of you," said her husband, "a very kind gesture. But do you need to bother now? Why, we are ready to go."

"Tell her that," said his wife, "tell her that we are leaving almost immediately."

The Marquis turned to the telephone again, and after a word or two put his hand over the receiver and whispered to his wife.

"She is very insistent," he said. "She says she has some prints belonging to you that she wants to give to you personally."

A feeling of panic came over the Marquise. Prints? What prints?

"But everything is paid for," she whispered back. "I don't know what she can mean."

The Marquis shrugged his shoulders.

"Well, what am I to say? She sounds as if she is crying."

The Marquise went back into the bathroom, dabbed more powder on her nose.

"Tell her to come up," she said, "but repeat that we are leaving in five minutes. Meanwhile, you go down, take the children to the car. Take Miss Clay with you. I will see the woman alone."

When he had gone she looked about the room. Nothing remained but her gloves, her handbag. One last effort, and then the closing door, the *ascenseur*, the farewell bow to the manager, and freedom.

There was a knock at the door. The Marquise waited by the entrance to the balcony, her hands clasped in front of her.

"*Entrez,*" she said.

Mademoiselle Paul opened the door. Her face was blotched and ravaged from weeping; her old-fashioned mourning dress was long, nearly touching the ground. She hesitated, then lurched forward, her limp grotesque, as though each movement must be agony.

"Madame la Marquise . . ." she began, then her mouth worked, she began to cry.

"Please don't," said the Marquise gently. "I am so dreadfully sorry for what has happened."

Mademoiselle Paul took her handkerchief and blew her nose.

"He was all I had in the world," she said. "He was so good to me. What am I to do now? How am I to live?"

"You have relatives?"

"They are poor folk, Madame la Marquise. I cannot expect them to support me. Nor can I keep the shop alone, without my brother. I haven't the strength. My health has always been my trouble."

The Marquise was fumbling in her bag. She took out a twenty-thousand-franc note.

"I know this is not much," she said, "but perhaps it will help just a little. I am afraid my husband has not many contacts in this part of the country, but I will ask him, perhaps he will be able to make some suggestions."

Mademoiselle Paul took the notes. It was strange. She did not thank the Marquise. "This will keep me until the end of the month," she said. "It will help to pay the funeral expenses."

She opened her bag. She took out three prints.

"I have more, similar to these, back in the shop," she said. "It seemed to me that perhaps, going away suddenly as you are doing, you had forgotten all about them. I found them amongst my poor brother's other prints and negatives in the cellar, where he used to develop them."

She handed the prints to the Marquise. The Marquise went cold when she saw them. Yes, she had forgotten. Or rather, she had not been aware of their existence. They were three views of her taken in the bracken. Careless, abandoned, half sleeping, with her head against his coat for a pillow, she had heard the click-click of the camera, and it had added a sort of zest to the afternoon. Some he had shown her. But not these.

She took the photographs and put them in her bag.

"You say you have others?" she asked, her voice without expression.

"Yes, Madame la Marquise."

She forced herself to meet the woman's eyes. They were swollen still with weeping, but the glint was unmistakable.

"What do you want me to do?" asked the Marquise.

Mademoiselle Paul looked about her in the hotel bedroom. Tissue paper strewn on the floor, odds and ends thrown into the wastepaper basket, the tumbled, unmade bed.

"I have lost my brother," she said, "my supporter, my reason for being alive. Madame la Marquise has had an enjoyable holiday and now returns home. I take it that Madame la Marquise would not desire her husband or her family to see these prints?"

"You are right," said the Marquise, "I do not even wish to see them myself."

"In which case," said Mademoiselle Paul, "twenty thousand francs is really very little return for a holiday that Madame la Marquise so much enjoyed."

The Marquise looked in her bag again. She had two *mille* notes and a few hundred francs.

"This is all I have," she said; "you are welcome to these as well."

Mademoiselle Paul blew her nose once more.

"I think it would be more satisfactory for both of us if we came to a more permanent arrangement," she said. "Now my poor brother has gone the future is very uncertain. I might not even wish to live in a neighbourhood that holds such sad memories. I cannot but ask myself how my brother met his death. The afternoon before he disappeared he went out to the headland and came back very distressed. I knew something had upset him, but I did not ask him what. Perhaps he had hoped to meet a friend, and the friend had not appeared. The next day he went again, and that night he did not return. The police were informed, and then three days later his body was found. I have said nothing of possible suicide to the police, but have accepted it, as they have done, as accidental. But my brother was a very sensitive soul, Madame la Marquise. Unhappy, he would have been capable of anything. If I make myself wretched thinking over these things, I might go to the police, I might suggest he did away with himself after an unhappy love affair. I might even give them leave to search through his effects for photographs."

In agony the Marquise heard her husband's footsteps outside the door.

"Are you coming, dearest?" he called, bursting it open and entering the room. "The luggage is all in, the children are clamouring to be off."

He said good morning to Mademoiselle Paul. She curtseyed.

"I will give you my address," said the Marquise, "both in Paris and in the country." She sought in her bag feverishly for cards. "I shall expect to hear from you in a few weeks' time."

"Possibly before that, Madame la Marquise," said Mademoiselle

Paul. "If I leave here, and find myself in your neighbourhood, I would come and pay my humble respects to you and Miss, and the little children. I have friends not so very far away. I have friends in Paris too. I have always wanted to see Paris."

The Marquise turned with a terrible bright smile to her husband.

"I have told Mademoiselle Paul," she said, "that if there is anything I can do for her at any time she has only to let me know."

"Of course," said her husband. "I am so sorry to hear of your tragedy. The manager here has been telling me all about it."

Mademoiselle Paul curtseyed again, looking from him back to the Marquise.

"He was all I had in the world, Monsieur le Marquis," she said. "Madame la Marquise knows what he meant to me. It is good to know that I may write to her, and that she will write to me, and when that happens I shall not feel alone and isolated. Life can be very hard for someone who is alone in the world. May I wish you a pleasant journey, Madame la Marquise, and happy memories of your holidays, and above all no regrets?"

Once more Mademoiselle Paul curtseyed, then turned and limped from the room.

"Poor woman," said the Marquis, "and what an appearance. I understand from the manager that the brother was crippled too?"

"Yes . . ." She fastened her handbag. Took her gloves. Reached for her dark glasses.

"Curious thing, but it often runs in families," said the Marquis as they walked along the corridor. He paused and rang the bell for the *ascenseur*. "You have never met Richard du Boulay, have you, an old friend of mine? He was crippled, much as this unfortunate little photographer seems to have been, but for all that, a charming, perfectly normal girl fell in love with him, and they got married. A son was born, and he turned out to be a hopeless clubfoot like his father. You can't fight that sort of thing. It's a taint in the blood that passes on."

They stepped into the *ascenseur* and the doors closed upon them.

"Sure you won't change your mind and stay for lunch? You look pale. We've got a long drive before us, you know."

"I'd rather go."

They were waiting in the hall to see her off. The manager, the receptionist, the concierge, the maître d'hôtel.

"Come again, Madame la Marquise. There will always be a welcome for you here. It has been such a pleasure looking after you. The hotel will not be the same once you have gone."

"Good-bye . . . Good-bye . . ."

The Marquise climbed into the car beside her husband. They turned out of the hotel grounds on to the road. Behind her lay the headland, the hot sands, and the sea. Before her lay the long straight road to home and safety. Safety . . . ?

Monte Verità

Tʜᴇʏ ᴛᴏʟᴅ ᴍᴇ afterwards they had found nothing. No trace of anyone, living or dead. Maddened by anger, and I believe by fear, they had succeeded at last in breaking into those forbidden walls, dreaded and shunned through countless years—to be met by silence. Frustrated, bewildered, frightened, driven to fury at the sight of those empty cells, that bare court, the valley people resorted to the primitive methods that have served so many peasants through so many centuries: fire and destruction.

It was the only answer, I suppose, to something they did not understand. Then, their anger spent, they must have realised that nothing of any purpose had been destroyed. The smouldering and blackened walls that met their eyes in the starry, frozen dawn had cheated them in the end.

Search parties were sent out, of course. The more experienced climbers amongst them, undaunted by the bare rock of the mountain summit, covered the whole ridge, from north to south, from east to west, with no result.

And that is the end of the story. Nothing more is known.

Two men from the village helped me to carry Victor's body to the valley, and he was buried at the foot of Monte Verità. I think I envied him, at peace there. He had kept his dream.

As to myself, my old life claimed me again. The second war churned up the world once more. Today, approaching seventy, I have few illusions; yet often I think of Monte Verità and wonder what could have been the final answer.

I have three theories, but none of them may be true.

The first, and the most fantastic, is that Victor was right, after all, to hold to his belief that the inhabitants of Monte Verità *had* reached some strange state of immortality which gave them power when the hour of need arrived, so that, like the prophets of old, they vanished into the heavens. The ancient Greeks believed this of their gods, the Jews believed it of Elijah, the Christians of their Founder. Throughout the long history of religious superstition and credulity runs this ever-recurrent conviction that some persons attain such holiness and power that death can be overcome. This faith is strong in Eastern countries, and in Africa; it is only to our sophisticated Western eyes that the disappearance of things tangible, of persons of flesh and blood, seems impossible.

Religious teachers disagree when they try to show the difference between good and evil: what is a miracle to one becomes black magic to another. The good prophets have been stoned, but so have the witch doctors. Blasphemy in one age becomes holy utterance in the next, and this day's heresy is tomorrow's credo.

I am no great thinker, and never have been. But this I do know, from my old climbing days: that in the mountains we come closest to whatever Being it is that rules our destiny. The great utterances of old were given from the mountaintops: it was always to the hills that the prophets climbed. The saints, the messiahs, were gathered to their fathers in the clouds. It is credible to me, in my more solemn moods, that the hand of magic reached down that night to Monte Verità and plucked those souls to safety.

Remember, I myself saw the full moon shining upon that mountain. I also, at midday, saw the sun. What I saw and heard and felt was not of this world. I think of the rock face, with the moon upon it; I hear the chanting from the forbidden walls; I see the crevasse, cupped like a chalice between the twin peaks of the mountain; I hear the laughter; I see the bare bronzed arms outstretched to the sun.

When I remember these things, I believe in immortality. . . .

Then—and this is perhaps because my climbing days are over, and the magic of the mountains loses its grip over old memories, as it does over old limbs—I remind myself that the eyes I looked into that last day on Monte Verità were the eyes of a living, breathing person, and the hands I touched were flesh.

Even the spoken words belonged to a human being. "Please do not concern yourself with us. We know what we must do." And then that final, tragic word, "Let Victor keep his dream."

So my second theory comes into being, and I see nightfall, and the stars, and the courage of that soul which chose the wisest way for itself and for the others; and while I returned to Victor, and the people from the valley gathered themselves together for the assault, the little band of believers, the last company of those seekers after Truth, climbed to that crevasse, between the peaks, and so were lost.

My third theory is one that comes to me in moods more cynical, more lonely, when, having dined well with friends who mean little to me, I take myself home to my apartment in New York. Looking from the window at the fantastic light and colour of my glittering fairy-world of fact that holds no tenderness, no quietude, I long suddenly for peace, for understanding. Then, I tell myself, perhaps the inhabitants of Monte Verità had long prepared themselves against departure, and when the moment came it found them ready, neither for immortality nor for death, but for the world of men and women. In stealth, in secret, they came down into the valley unobserved, and, mingling with the people, went their separate ways. I wonder, looking down from my apartment into the hub and hustle of my world, if some of them wander there, in the crowded streets and subways, and whether, if I went out and searched the passing faces, I should find such a one and have my answer.

Sometimes, when travelling, I have fancied to myself, in coming upon a stranger, that there is something exceptional in the turn of a head, in the expression of an eye, that is at once compelling and strange. I want to speak, and hold such a person instantly in conversation, but—possibly it is my fancy—it is as though some instinct warns them. A momentary pause, a hesitation, and they are gone. It might be in a train, or in some crowded thoroughfare, and for one brief moment I am aware of someone with more than earthly beauty and human grace, and I want to stretch out my hand and say, swiftly, softly, "Were you among those I saw on Monte Verità?" But there is never time. They vanish, they are gone, and I am alone again, with my third theory still unproven.

As I grow older—nearly seventy, as I have said, and memory shortens with the lengthening years—the story of Monte Verità becomes more dim to me, and more improbable, and because of this I have a great urge to write it down before memory fails me altogether. It may be that someone reading it will have the love of mountains that I had once, and so bring his own understanding to the tale, his own interpretation.

One word of warning. There are many mountain peaks in Europe, and countless numbers may bear the name of Monte Verità. They can be found in Switzerland, in France, in Spain, in Italy, in the Tyrol. I prefer to give no precise locality to mine. In these days, after two world wars, no mountain seems inaccessible. All can be climbed. None, with due caution, need be dangerous. My Monte Verità was never shunned because of difficulties of height, of ice and snow. The track leading to the summit could be followed by anyone of sure and certain step, even in late autumn. No common danger kept the climber back, but awe and fear.

I have little doubt that today my Monte Verità has been plotted upon the map with all the others. There may be resting camps near the summit, even an hotel in the little village on the eastern slopes, and the tourist lifted to the twin peaks by electric cable. Even so, I like to think there can be no final desecration, that at midnight, when the full moon rises, the mountain face is still inviolate, unchanged, and that in winter, when snow and ice, great wind and drifting cloud make the climb impassable to man, the rock face of Monte Verità, her

twin peaks lifted to the sun, stares down in silence and compassion
upon a blinded world.

We were boys together, Victor and I. We were both at Marlborough,
and went up to Cambridge the same year. In those days I was his
greatest friend, and if we did not see so much of each other after we
left the 'Varsity it was only because we moved in rather different
worlds: my work took me much abroad, while he was busily employed
running his own estate up in Shropshire. When we saw each other,
we resumed our friendship without any sense of having grown apart.

My work was absorbing, so was his; but we had money enough,
and leisure too, to indulge in our favourite pastime, which was climbing. The modern expert, with his equipment and his scientific training,
would think our expeditions amateur in the extreme—I am talking of
the idyllic days before the first world war—and, looking back on them,
I suppose they were just that. Certainly there was nothing professional
about the two young men who used to cling with hands and feet to
those projecting rocks in Cumberland and Wales, and later, when some
experience was gained, tried the more hazardous ascents in southern
Europe.

In time we became less foolhardy and more weather-wise, and learnt
to treat our mountains with respect—not as an enemy to be conquered,
but as an ally to be won. We used to climb, Victor and I, from no
desire for danger or because we wanted to add mountain peaks to our
repertoire of achievement. We climbed from desire, because we loved
the thing we won.

The moods of a mountain can be more varying, more swiftly changing, than any woman's, bringing joy, and fear, and also great repose.
The urge to climb will never be explained. In olden days, perhaps, it
was a wish to reach the stars. Today, anyone so minded can buy a
seat on a plane and feel himself master of the skies. Even so, he will
not have rock under his feet, or air upon his face; nor will he know
the silence that comes only on the hills.

The best hours of my life were spent, when I was young, upon the
mountains. That urge to spill all energy, all thought, to be as nothing,
blotted against the sky—we called it mountain fever, Victor and I. He
used to recover from the experience more quickly than I did. He would
look about him, methodical, careful, planning the descent, while I was

lost in wonder, locked in a dream I could not understand. Endurance had been tested, the summit was ours, but something indefinable waited to be won. Always it was denied me, the experience I desired, and something seemed to tell me the fault was in myself. But they were good days. The finest I have known . . .

One summer, shortly after I returned to London from a business trip to Canada, a letter arrived from Victor, written in tremendous spirits. He was engaged to be married. He was, in fact, to be married very soon. She was the loveliest girl he had ever seen, and would I be his best man? I wrote back, as one does on these occasions, expressing myself delighted and wishing him all the happiness in the world. A confirmed bachelor myself, I considered him yet another good friend lost, the best of all, bogged down in domesticity.

The bride-to-be was Welsh and lived just over the border from Victor's place in Shropshire. "And would you believe it," said Victor in a second letter, "she had never as much as set foot on Snowdon! I am going to take her education in hand." I could imagine nothing I should dislike more than trailing an inexperienced girl after me on any mountain.

A third letter announced Victor's arrival in London, and hers too, in all the bustle and preparation of the wedding. I invited both of them to luncheon. I don't know what I expected. Someone small, I think, and dark and stocky, with handsome eyes. Certainly not the beauty that came forward, putting out her hand to me and saying, "I am Anna."

In those days, before World War I, young women did not use make-up. Anna was free of lipstick, and her gold hair was rolled in great coils over her ears. I remember staring at her, at her incredible beauty, and Victor laughed, very pleased, and said, "What did I tell you?" We sat down to lunch, and the three of us were soon at ease and chatting comfortably. A certain reserve was part of her charm, but because she knew I was Victor's greatest friend I felt myself accepted, and liked into the bargain.

Victor certainly was lucky, I said to myself, and any doubt I might have felt about the marriage went on sight of her. Inevitably, with Victor and myself, the conversation turned to mountains, and to climbing, before lunch was halfway through.

"So you are going to marry a man whose hobby is climbing mountains," I said to her, "and you've never even gone up your own Snowdon."

"No," she said, "no, I never have."

Some hesitation in her voice made me wonder. A little frown had come between those two very perfect eyes.

"Why?" I asked. "It's almost criminal to be Welsh, and know nothing of your highest mountain."

Victor interrupted. "Anna is scared," he said. "Every time I suggest an expedition she thinks out an excuse."

She turned to him swiftly. "No, Victor," she said, "it's not that. You just don't understand. I'm not afraid of climbing."

"What is it, then?" he said.

He put out his hand and held hers on the table. I could see how devoted he was to her, and how happy they were likely to become. She looked across at me, feeling me, as it were, with her eyes, and suddenly I knew instinctively what she was going to say.

"Mountains are very demanding," she said. "You have to give everything. It's wiser, for someone like myself, to keep away."

I understood what she meant, at least I thought then that I did; but because Victor was in love with her, and she was in love with him, it seemed to me that nothing could be better than the fact that they might share the same hobby, once her initial awe was overcome.

"But that's splendid," I said, "you've got just the right approach to mountain climbing. Of course you have to give everything, but together you can achieve that. Victor won't let you attempt anything beyond you. He's more cautious than I am."

Anna smiled, and then withdrew her hand from Victor's on the table.

"You are both very obstinate," she said, "and you neither of you understand. I was born in the hills. I know what I mean."

And then some mutual friend of Victor's and my own came up to the table to be introduced, and there was no more talk of mountains.

They were married about six weeks later, and I have never seen a lovelier bride than Anna. Victor was pale with nerves, I remember well, and I thought what a responsibility lay on his shoulders, to make this girl happy for all time.

I saw much of her during the six weeks of their engagement, and, though Victor never realised it for one instant, came to love her as much as he did. It was not her natural charm, nor yet her beauty, but a strange blending of both, a kind of inner radiance, that drew me to her. My only fear for their future was that Victor might be a little too boisterous, too lighthearted and cheerful—his was a very open, simple nature—and that she might withdraw into herself because of it. Certainly they made a handsome pair as they drove off after the reception —given by an elderly aunt of Anna's, for her parents were dead—and I sentimentally looked forward to staying with them in Shropshire, and being godfather to the first child.

Business took me away shortly after the wedding, and it was not until the following December that I heard from Victor, asking me down for Christmas. I accepted gladly.

They had then been married about eight months. Victor looked fit and very happy, and Anna, it seemed to me, more beautiful than ever. It was hard to take my eyes off her. They gave me a great welcome, and I settled down to a peaceful week in Victor's fine old home, which I knew well from previous visits. The marriage was most definitely a success, that I could tell from the first. And if there appeared to be no heir on the way, there was plenty of time for that.

We walked about the estate, shot a little, read in the evenings, and were a most contented trio.

I noticed that Victor had adapted himself to Anna's quieter personality, though quiet, perhaps, is hardly the right definition for her gift of stillness. This stillness—for there is no other word for it—came from some depth within her and put a spell upon the whole house. It had always been a pleasant place in which to stay, with its lofty rambling rooms and mullioned windows; but now the peaceful atmosphere was somehow intensified and deepened, and it was as though every room had become impregnated with a strange brooding silence, to my mind quite remarkable, and much more than merely restful, as it had been before.

It is odd, but looking back to that Christmas week, I can recollect nothing of the traditional festivity itself. I don't remember what we ate or drank, or whether we set foot inside the church, which surely we must have done, with Victor as the local squire. I can only remember the quite indescribable peace of the evenings, when the shutters had been fastened and we sat before the fire in the great hall. My business trip must have tired me more than I realised, for sitting there, in

Victor's and Anna's home, I had no desire to do anything but relax and give myself up to this blessed, healing silence.

The other change that had come upon the house, which I did not fully take in until I had been there a few days, was that it was much barer than it had been before. The multiple odds and ends and the collection of furniture handed down from Victor's forebearers seemed to have disappeared. The big rooms were now sparse and the great hall, where we sat, had nothing in it but a long refectory table and the chairs before the open fire. It seemed very right that it should be so, yet, thinking about it, it was an odd change for a woman to make. The usual habit of a bride is to buy new curtains and carpets, to bring the feminine touch into a bachelor house. I ventured to remark upon it to Victor.

"Oh yes," he said, looking about him vaguely, "we have cleared out a lot of stuff. It was Anna's idea. She doesn't believe in possessions, you know. No, we didn't have a sale, or anything like that. We gave them all away."

The spare room allotted to me was the one I had always used in the past, and this was pretty much as it had been before. And I had the same old comforts—cans of hot water, early tea, biscuits by my bed, cigarette box filled, all the touches of a thoughtful hostess.

Yet once, passing down the long corridor to the stairhead, I noticed that the door of Anna's room, which was usually closed, was open; and as I knew it to have been Victor's mother's room in former days, with a fine old four-poster bed and several pieces of heavy solid furniture, all in keeping with the style of the house, ordinary curiosity made me glance over my shoulder as I passed the open door. The room was bare of furniture. There were no curtains to the windows, and no carpet on the floor. The wooden boards were plain. There was a table and a chair, and a long trestle bed with no covering upon it but a blanket. The windows were wide open to the dusk, which was then falling. I turned away and walked down the stairs, and as I did so came face to face with Victor, who was ascending. He must have seen me glance into the room and I did not wish to appear furtive in any way.

"Forgive the trespass," I said, "but I happened to notice the room looked very different from your mother's day."

"Yes," he said briefly, "Anna hates frills. Are you ready for dinner? She sent me to find you."

And we went downstairs together without further conversation. Somehow I could not forget that bare sparse bedroom, comparing it with the soft luxury of my own, and I felt oddly inferior that Anna should consider me as someone who could not dispense with ease and elegance, which she, for some reason, did so well without.

That evening I watched her as we sat beside the fire. Victor had been called from the hall on some business, and she and I were alone for a few moments. As usual I felt the still, soothing peace of her presence come upon me with the silence; I was wrapped about with it, enfolded, as it were, and it was unlike anything I knew in my ordinary humdrum life; this stillness came out of her, yet from another world. I wanted to tell her about it but could not find the words. At last I said, "You have done something to this house. I don't understand it."

"Don't you?" she said. "I think you do. We are both in search of the same thing, after all."

For some reason I felt afraid. The stillness was with us just the same, but intensified, almost overpowering.

"I am not aware," I said, "that I am in search of anything."

My words fell foolishly on the air and were lost. My eyes, which had drifted to the fire, were drawn, as if compelled, to hers.

"Aren't you?" she said.

I remember being swept by a feeling of profound distress. I saw myself, for the first time, as a very worthless, very trivial human being, travelling here and there about the world to no purpose, doing unnecessary business with other human beings as worthless as myself, and to no other end but that we should be fed and clothed and housed in adequate comfort until death.

I thought of my own small house in Westminster, chosen after long deliberation and furnished with great care. I saw my books, my pictures, my collection of china, and the two good servants who waited upon me and kept the house spotless always, in preparation for my return. Up to this moment my house and all it held had given me great pleasure. Now I was not sure that it had any value.

"What would you suggest?" I heard myself saying to Anna. "Should I sell everything I have and give up my work? What then?"

Thinking back on the brief conversation that passed between us, I realise nothing that she said warranted this sudden question on my part. She implied that I was in search of something, and instead of answering her directly, yes or no, I asked her if I must give up all I had. The significance of this did not strike me at the time. All I knew then was that I was profoundly moved, and whereas a few moments before I had been at peace, I was now troubled.

"Your answer may not be the same as mine," she said, "and anyway, I am not certain of my own as yet. One day I shall know."

"Surely," I thought to myself in looking upon her, "she has the answer now, with her beauty, her serenity, her understanding. What more can she possibly achieve, unless it is that up to the present she lacks children, and so feels unfulfilled?"

Victor came back into the hall, and it seemed to me his presence brought solidity and warmth to the atmosphere; there was something familiar and comfortable about his old smoking jacket worn with his evening trousers.

"It's freezing hard," he said. "I went outside to see. The thermometer is down to thirty. Lovely night, though. Full moon." He drew up his chair before the fire and smiled affectionately at Anna. "Almost as cold as the night we spent on Snowdon," he said. "Heavens above, I shan't forget that in a hurry." And turning to me with a laugh, he added, "I never told you, did I, that Anna condescended to come climbing with me after all?"

"No," I said, astonished. "I thought she had set herself against it."

I looked across at Anna, and I noticed that her eyes had grown strangely blank, without expression. I felt instinctively that the subject brought up by Victor was one she would not have chosen. Victor, insensitive to this, went prattling on.

"She's a dark horse," he said. "She knows just as much about climbing mountains as you or I. In fact, she was ahead of me the whole time, and I lost her."

He continued, half laughing, half serious, giving me every detail of the climb, which seemed hazardous in the extreme, as they had left it much too late in the year.

It seemed that the weather, which had promised well in the morning for their start, had turned by midafternoon, bringing thunder and lightning and finally a blizzard; so that darkness overtook them in the descent, and they were forced to spend the night in the open.

"The thing I shall never understand," said Victor, "is how I came to miss her. One moment she was by my side, and the next she had gone.

I can tell you I had a very bad three hours, in pitch darkness and half a gale."

Anna never said a word while he told the story. It was as though she withdrew herself completely. She sat in her chair, motionless. I felt uneasy, anxious. I wanted Victor to stop.

"Anyway," I said, to hasten him, "you got down all right, and none the worse for it."

"Yes," he said ruefully, "at about five in the morning, thoroughly wet and thoroughly frightened. Anna came up to me out of the mist not even damp, surprised that I was angry. Said she had been sheltered by a piece of rock. It was a wonder she had not broken her neck. Next time we go mountain climbing, I've told her that she can be the guide."

"Perhaps," I said, with a glance at Anna, "there won't be a next time. Once was enough."

"Not a bit of it," said Victor cheerfully, "we are all set, you know, to go off next summer. The Alps, or the Dolomites, or the Pyrenees, we haven't decided yet on the objective. You had better come with us and we'll have a proper expedition."

I shook my head regretfully.

"I only wish I could," I said, "but it's impossible. I must be in New York by May and shan't be home again until September."

"Oh, that's a long way ahead," said Victor, "anything may happen by May. We'll talk of it again, nearer the time."

Still Anna said no word, and I wondered why Victor saw nothing strange in her reticence. Suddenly she said good night and went upstairs. It was obvious to me that all this chatter of mountain climbing had been unwelcome to her. I felt an urge at attack Victor on the subject.

"Look here," I said, "do think twice about this holiday in the mountains. I am pretty sure Anna isn't for it."

"Not for it?" said Victor, surprised. "Why, it was her idea entirely."

I stared at him.

"Are you sure?" I asked.

"Of course I'm sure. I tell you, old fellow, she's crazy about mountains. She has a fetish about them. It's her Welsh blood, I suppose. I was being lighthearted just now about that night on Snowdon, but between ourselves, I was quite amazed at her courage and her endurance. I don't mind admitting that what with the blizzard, and being fright-

ened for her, I was dead beat by morning; but she came out of that
mist like a spirit from another world. I've never seen her like it. She
went down that blasted mountain as if she had spent the night on
Olympus, while I limped behind her like a child. She is a very remarkable person: you realise that, don't you?"

"Yes," I said slowly, "I do agree. Anna is very remarkable."

Shortly afterwards we went upstairs to bed, and as I undressed and
put on my pyjamas, which had been left to warm for me before the
fire, and noticed the Thermos flask of hot milk on the bedside table,
in case I should be wakeful, and padded about the thick-carpeted room
in my soft slippers, I thought once again of that strange bare room
where Anna slept, and of the narrow trestle bed. In a futile, unnecessary
gesture, I threw aside the heavy satin quilt that lay on top of my
blankets, and before getting into bed opened my windows wide.

I was restless, though, and could not sleep. My fire sank low and the
cold air penetrated the room. I heard my old worn travelling clock
race round the hours through the night. At four I could stand it no
longer and remembered the Thermos of milk with gratitude. Before
drinking it I decided to pamper myself still further and close the
window.

I climbed out of bed and, shivering, went across the room to do so.
Victor was right. A white frost covered the ground. The moon was
full. I stood for a moment by the open window, and from the trees in
shadow I saw a figure come and stand below me on the lawn. Not
furtive, as a trespasser, not creeping, as a thief. Whoever it was stood
motionless, as though in meditation, with face uplifted to the moon.

Then I perceived that it was Anna. She wore a dressing gown, with a
cord about it, and her hair was loose on her shoulders. She made no
sound as she stood there on the frosty lawn, and I saw, with a shock of
horror, that her feet were bare. I stood watching, my hand on the
curtain, and suddenly I felt that I was looking upon something intimate
and secret, which concerned me not. So I shut my window and returned to bed. Instinct told me that I must say nothing of what I had
seen to Victor, or to Anna herself; and because of this I was filled with
disquiet, almost with apprehension.

Next morning the sun shone and we were out about the grounds
with the dogs, Anna and Victor both so normal and cheerful that I
told myself I had been overwrought the previous night. If Anna chose

to walk barefoot in the small hours it was her business, and I had behaved ill in spying upon her. The rest of my visit passed without incident; we were all three happy and content, and I was very loath to leave them.

I saw them again for a brief moment, some months later, before I left for America. I had gone into the Map House, in St. James's, to buy myself some half-dozen books to read on that long thrash across the Atlantic—a journey one took with certain qualms in those days, the *Titanic* tragedy still fresh in memory—and there were Victor and Anna, poring over maps, which they had spread out over every available space.

There was no chance of a real meeting. I had engagements for the rest of the day, and so had they, so it was hail and farewell.

"You find us," said Victor, "getting busy about the summer holiday. The itinerary is planned. Change your mind and join us."

"Impossible," I said. "All being well, I should be home by September. I'll get in touch with you directly I return. Well, where are you making for?"

"Anna's choice," said Victor. "She's been thinking this out for weeks, and she's hit on a spot that looks completely inaccessible. Anyway, it's somewhere you and I have never climbed."

He pointed down to the large-scale map in front of them. I followed his finger to a point that Anna had already marked with a tiny cross.

"Monte Verità," I read.

I looked up and saw that Anna's eyes were upon me.

"Completely unknown territory, as far as I'm concerned," I said. "Be sure and have advice first, before setting forth. Get hold of local guides, and so on. What made you choose that particular ridge of mountains?"

Anna smiled, and I felt a sense of shame, of inferiority, beside her.

"The Mountain of Truth," she said. "Come with us, do."

I shook my head and went off upon my journey.

During the months that followed I thought of them both, and envied them too. They were climbing, and I was hemmed in, not by the mountains that I loved but by hard business. Often I wished I had the courage to throw my work aside, turn my back on the civilised world and its dubious delights, and go seeking after truth with my two friends. Only convention deterred me, the sense that I was making a successful career for myself, which it would be folly to cut short. The pattern of my life was set. It was too late to change.

I returned to England in September, and I was surprised, in going through the great pile of letters that awaited me, to have nothing from Victor. He had promised to write and give me news of all they had seen and done. They were not on the telephone, so I could not get in touch with them direct, but I made a note to write to Victor as soon as I had sorted out my business mail.

A couple of days later, coming out of my club, I ran into a man, a mutual friend of ours, who detained me a moment to ask some question about my journey, and then, just as I was going down the steps, called over his shoulder, "I say, what a tragedy about poor Victor. Are you going to see him?"

"What do you mean? What tragedy?" I asked. "Has there been an accident?"

"He's terribly ill in a nursing home here in London," came the answer. "Nervous breakdown. You know his wife has left him?"

"Good God, no," I exclaimed.

"Oh yes. That's the cause of all the trouble. He's gone quite to pieces .You know he was devoted to her."

I was stunned. I stood staring at the fellow, my face blank.

"Do you mean," I said, "that she has gone off with somebody else?"

"I don't know. I assume so. No one can get anything out of Victor. Anyway, there he has been for several weeks with this breakdown."

I asked for the address of the nursing home, and at once, without further delay, jumped into a cab and was driven there.

At first I was told, on making enquiry, that Victor was seeing no visitors, but I took out my card and scribbled a line across the back. Surely he would not refuse to see me? A nurse came, and I was taken upstairs to a room on the first floor.

I was horrified, when she opened the door, to see the haggard face that looked up at me from the chair beside the gas fire, so frail he was, so altered.

"My dear old boy," I said, going towards him, "I only heard five minutes ago that you were here."

The nurse closed the door and left us together.

To my distress Victor's eyes filled with tears.

"It's all right," I said, "don't mind me. You know I shall understand."

He seemed unable to speak. He just sat there, hunched in his dressing gown, the tears running down his cheeks. I had never felt more helpless. He pointed to a chair, and I drew it up beside him. I waited. If he did not want to tell me what had happened I would not press him. I only wanted to comfort him, to be of some assistance.

At last he spoke, and I hardly recognised his voice.

"Anna's gone," he said. "Did you know that? She's gone."

I nodded. I put my hand on his knee, as though he were a small boy again and not a man past thirty, of my own age.

"I know," I said gently, "but it will be all right. She will come back again. You are sure to get her back."

He shook his head. I had never seen such despair, and such complete conviction.

"Oh no," he said, "she will never come back. I know her too well. She's found what she wants."

It was pitiful to see how completely he had given in to what had happened. Victor, usually so strong, so well balanced.

"Who is it?" I said. "Where did she meet this other fellow?"

Victor stared at me, bewildered.

"What do you mean?" he said. "She hasn't met anyone. It's not that at all. If it were, that would be easy. . . ."

He paused, spreading out his hands in a hopeless gesture. And suddenly he broke down again, but this time not with weakness but with a more fearful sort of stifled rage, the impotent, useless rage of a man who fights against something stronger than himself. "It was the mountain that got her," he said, "that goddamned mountain, Monte Verità. There's a sect there, a closed order, they shut themselves up for life—there on that mountain. I never dreamed there could be such a thing. I never knew. And she's there. On that damned mountain. On Monte Verità . . ."

I sat there with him in the nursing home all afternoon, and little by little had the whole story from him.

The journey itself, Victor said, had been pleasant and uneventful. Eventually they reached the centre from which they proposed to explore the terrain immediately below Monte Verità, and here they met with difficulties. The country was unknown to Victor, and the people seemed morose and unfriendly, very different, he said, from the sort of folk who had welcomed us in the past. They spoke in a patois hard to understand, and they lacked intelligence.

"At least, that's how they struck me," said Victor. "They were very rough and somehow undeveloped, the sort of people who might have stepped out of a former century. You know how, when we climbed together, the people could not do enough to help us, and we always managed to find guides. Here, it was different. When Anna and I tried to find out the best approach to Monte Verità, they would not tell us. They just stared at us in a stupid sort of way, and shrugged their shoulders. They had no guides, one fellow said; the mountain was—savage, unexplored."

Victor paused, and looked at me with that same expression of despair.

"You see," he said, "that's when I made my mistake. I should have realised the expedition was a failure—to that particular spot, at any rate—and suggested to Anna that we turn back and tackle something else, something nearer to civilisation anyhow, where the people were more helpful and the country more familiar. But you know how it is. You get a stubborn feeling inside you, on the mountains, and any opposition somehow rouses you.

"And Monte Verità itself . . ." He broke off and stared in front of him. It was as though he was looking upon it again in his own mind. "I've never been one for lyrical description, you know that," he said. "On our finest climbs I was always the practical one and you the poet. For sheer beauty, I have never seen anything like Monte Verità. We have climbed many higher peaks, you and I, and far more dangerous ones, too; but this was somehow . . . sublime."

After a few moments' silence he continued talking. "I said to Anna, 'What shall we do?' and she answered me without hesitation, 'We must go on.' I did not argue, I knew perfectly well that would be her wish. The place had put a spell on both of us."

They left the valley, and began the ascent.

"It was a wonderful day," said Victor, "hardly a breath of wind, and not a cloud in the sky. Scorching sun—you know how it can be—but the air clean and cold. I chaffed Anna about that other climb, up Snowdon, and made her promise not to leave me behind this time.

She was wearing an open shirt and a brief kilted skirt, and her hair was loose. She looked . . . quite beautiful."

As he talked, slowly, quietly, I had the impression that it must surely be an accident that had happened, but that his mind, unhinged by tragedy, balked at Anna's death. It must be so. Anna had fallen. He had seen her fall and had been powerless to help her. He had then returned, broken in mind and spirit, telling himself she still lived on Monte Verità.

"We came to a village an hour before sundown," said Victor. "The climb had taken us all day. We were still about three hours from the peak itself, or so I judged. The village consisted of some dozen dwellings or so, huddled together. And as we walked towards the first one, a curious thing happened."

He paused and stared in front of him.

"Anna was a little ahead of me," he said, "moving swiftly with those long strides of hers—you know how she does. I saw two or three men, with some children and goats, come on to the track from a piece of pasture land to the right of us. Anna raised her hand in salute, and at sight of her the men started, as if terrified, and, snatching up the children, ran to the nearest group of hovels, as if all the fiends in hell were after them. I heard them bolt the doors and shutter the windows. It was the most extraordinary thing. The goats went scattering down the track, equally scared."

Victor said he had made some joke to Anna about a charming welcome, and that she seemed upset; she did not know what she could have done to frighten them. Victor went to the first hut and knocked upon the door.

Nothing happened at all, but he could hear whispers inside and a child crying. Then he lost patience and began to shout. This had effect, and after a moment one of the shutters was removed and a man's face appeared at the gap and stared at him. Victor, by way of encouragement, nodded and smiled. Slowly the man withdrew the whole of the shutter and Victor spoke to him. At first the man shook his head, then he seemed to change his mind and came and unbolted the door. He stood in the entrance, peering nervously about him, and, ignoring Victor, looked at Anna. He shook his head violently and, speaking very quickly and quite unintelligibly, pointed towards the summit of Monte Verità. Then from the shadows of the small room came an elderly

man, leaning on two sticks, who motioned aside the terrified children
and moved past them to the door. He, at least, spoke a language that
was not entirely patois.

"Who is that woman?" he asked. "What does she want with us?"

Victor explained that Anna was his wife, that they had come from
the valley to climb the mountain, that they were tourists on holiday,
and they would be glad of shelter for the night. He said the old man
stared away from him to Anna.

"She is your wife?" he said. "She is not from Monte Verità?"

"She is my wife," repeated Victor. "We come from England. We are
in this country on holiday. We have never been here before."

The old man turned to the younger and they muttered together for
a few moments. Then the younger man went back inside the house,
and there was further talk from the interior. A woman appeared, even
more frightened than the younger man. She was literally trembling,
Victor said, as she looked out of the doorway towards Anna. It was
Anna who disturbed them.

"She is my wife," said Victor again; "we come from the valley."

Finally the old man made a gesture of consent, of understanding.

"I believe you," he said. "You are welcome to come inside. If you
are from the valley, that is all right. We have to be careful."

Victor beckoned to Anna, and slowly she came up the track and
stood beside Victor, on the threshold of the house. Even now the
woman looked at her with timidity, and she and the children backed
away.

The old man motioned his visitors inside. The living-room was bare
but clean, and there was a fire burning.

"We have food," said Victor, unshouldering his pack, "and mattresses too. We don't want to be a nuisance. But if we could eat here,
and sleep on the floor, it will do very well indeed."

The old man nodded. "I am satisfied," he said. "I believe you."

Then he withdrew with his family.

Victor said he and Anna were both puzzled at their reception, and
could not understand why the fact of their being married and coming
from the valley should have gained them admittance after that first odd
show of terror. They ate, and unrolled their packs, and then the old
man appeared again with milk for them, and cheese. The woman re-

mained behind, but the younger man, out of curiosity, accompanied the elder.

Victor thanked the old fellow for his hospitality, and said that now they would sleep, and in the morning, soon after sunrise, they would climb to the summit of the mountain.

"Is the way easy?" he asked.

"It is not difficult," came the reply. "I would offer to send someone with you, but no one cares to go."

His manner was diffident, and Victor said he glanced again at Anna.

"Your wife will be all right in the house here," he said. "We will take care of her."

"My wife will climb with me," said Victor. "She won't want to stay behind."

A look of anxiety came into the old man's face.

"It is better that your wife does not go up Monte Verità," he said. "It will be dangerous."

"Why is it dangerous for me to go up Monte Verità?" asked Anna.

The old man looked at her, his anxiety deepening.

"For girls," he said, "for women, it is dangerous."

"But how?" asked Anna. "Why? You told my husband the path is easy."

"It is not the path that is dangerous," he answered; "my son can set you on the path. It is because of the . . ." and Victor said he used a word that neither he nor Anna understood, but that it sounded like *sacerdotessa*, or *sacerdozio*.

"That's priestess, or priesthood," said Victor. "It can't be that. I wonder what on earth he means?"

The old man, anxious and distressed, looked from one to the other of them.

"It is safe for you to climb Monte Verità, and to descend again," he repeated to Victor, "but not for your wife. They have great power, the *sacerdotesse*. Here in the village we are always in fear for our young girls, for our women."

Victor said the whole thing sounded like an African travel tale, where a tribe of wild men pounced out of the jungle and carried off the female population into captivity.

"I don't know what he's talking about," he said to Anna, "but I suppose they are riddled with some sort of superstition, which will appeal to you, with your Welsh blood."

He laughed, he told me, making light of it, and then, being confoundedly sleepy, arranged their mattresses in front of the fire. Bidding the old man good evening, he and Anna settled themselves for the night.

He slept soundly, in the profound sleep that comes after climbing, and woke suddenly, just before daybreak, to the sound of a cock crowing in the village outside.

He turned over on his side to see if Anna was awake.

The mattress was thrown back, and bare. Anna had gone. . . .

No one was yet astir in the house, Victor said, and the only sound was the cock crowing. He got up and put on his shoes and coat, went to the door and stepped outside.

It was the cold, still moment that comes just before sunrise. The last few stars were paling in the sky. Clouds hid the valley, some thousands of feet below. Only here, near the summit of the mountain, was it clear.

At first Victor felt no misgiving. He knew by this time that Anna was capable of looking after herself, and was as sure-footed as he—more so, possibly. She would take no foolish risks, and anyway, the old man had told them that the climb was not dangerous. He felt hurt, though, that she had not waited for him. It was breaking the promise that they should always climb together. And he had no idea how much of a start she had in front of him. The only thing he could do was to follow her as swiftly as he could.

He went back into the room to collect their rations for the day—she had not thought of that. Their packs they could fetch later, for the descent, and they would probably have to accept hospitality here for another night.

His movements must have roused his host, for suddenly the old man appeared from the inner room and stood beside him. His eye fell on Anna's empty mattress, then he searched Victor's eyes, almost in accusation.

"My wife has gone on ahead," Victor said. "I am going to follow her."

The old man looked very grave. He went to the open door and stood there, staring away from the village, up the mountain.

"It was wrong to let her go," he said; "you should not have permitted it." He appeared very distressed, Victor said, and shook his head to and fro, murmuring to himself.

"It's all right," said Victor. "I shall soon catch her up, and we shall probably be back again, soon after midday."

He put his hand on the old fellow's arm, to reassure him.

"I fear very much that it will be too late," said the old man. "She will go to them, and once she is with them she will not come back."

Once again he used the word *sacerdotesse*, the power of the *sacerdotesse*, and his manner, his state of apprehension, now communicated itself to Victor, so that he too felt a sense of urgency, and of fear.

"Do you mean that there are living people at the top of Monte Verità?" he said. "People who may attack her, and harm her bodily?"

The old man began to talk rapidly, and it was difficult to make any sense out of the torrent of words that now sprang from him. No, he said, the *sacerdotesse* would not hurt her, they hurt no one; it was that they would take her to become one of them. Anna would go to them, she could not help herself, the power was so strong. Twenty, thirty years ago, the old man said, his daughter had gone to them: he had never seen her again. Other young women from the village, and from down below, in the valley, were called by the *sacerdotesse*. Once they were called they had to go, no one could keep them back. No one saw them again. Never, never. It had been so for many years, in his father's time, his father's father's time, before that, even.

It was not known now when the *sacerdotesse* first came to Monte Verità. No man living had set eyes upon them. They lived there, enclosed, behind their walls, but with power, he kept insisting, with magic. "Some say they have this from God, some from the devil," he said, "but we do not know, we cannot tell. It is rumoured that the *sacerdotesse* on Monte Verità never grow old, they stay forever young and beautiful, and that it is from the moon they draw their power. It is the moon they worship, and the sun."

Victor gathered little from this wild talk. It must all be legend, superstition.

The old man shook his head and looked towards the mountain track. "I saw it in her eyes last night," he said, "I was afraid of it. She had the eyes they have, when they are called. I have seen it before. With my own daughter, with others."

By now the rest of the family had wakened and had come by turn into the room. They seemed to sense what had happened. The younger man and the woman, even the children, looked at Victor with anxiety and a strange sort of compassion. He said the atmosphere filled him not so much with alarm as with anger and irritation. It made him think of cats, and broomsticks, and sixteenth-century witchcraft.

The mist was breaking slowly down in the valley, and the clouds were going. The soft glow in the sky, beyond the range of mountains to the eastward, heralded the rising sun.

The old man said something to the younger, and pointed with his stick.

"My son will put you on the track," he said; "he will come part of the way only. Further he does not care to go."

Victor said he set off with all their eyes upon him; and not only from this first hut, but from the other dwellings in the little village, he was aware of faces looking from drawn shutters, and faces peering from half-opened doors. The whole village was astir now and intent upon watching him, held by a fearful fascination.

His guide made no attempt to talk to him. He walked ahead, his shoulders bent, his eyes on the ground. Victor felt that he went only on command of the old man, his father.

The track was rough and stony, broken in many places, and was, Victor judged, part of an old watercourse that would be impassable when the rains came. Now, in full summer, it was easy enough to climb. Verdure, thorn, and scrub they left behind them, after climbing steadily for an hour, and the summit of the mountain pierced the sky directly above their heads, split into two like a divided hand. From the depths of the valley, and from the village even, this division could not be seen; the two peaks seemed as one.

The sun had risen with them as they climbed, and now shone in full upon the southeastern face, turning it to coral. Great banks of clouds, soft and rolling, hid the world below. Victor's guide stopped suddenly and pointed ahead, where a jutting lip of rock wound in a razor's edge and curved southward out of sight.

"Monte Verità," he said, and then repeated it again, "Monte Verità."

Then he turned swiftly and began scrambling back along the way that they had come.

Victor called to him, but the man did not answer; he did not even

bother to turn his head. In a moment he was out of sight. There was
nothing for it but to go on alone, round the lip of the escarpment,
Victor said, and trust that he would find Anna waiting for him on the
further side.

It took him another half hour to encircle the projecting shoulder of
the mountain, and with every step he took his anxiety deepened, because now, on the southward side, there was no gradual incline—the
mountain face was sheer. Soon further progress would be impossible.

"Then," Victor said, "I came out through a sort of gully-way, over a
ridge about three hundred feet only from the summit; and I saw it, the
monastery, built out of the rock between the two peaks, absolutely
bare and naked; a steep rock wall enclosing it, a drop of a thousand feet
beneath the wall to the next ridge, and above, nothing but the sky and
the twin peaks of Monte Verità."

It was true, then. Victor had not lost his mind. The place existed.
There had been no accident. He sat there, in his chair by the gas fire,
in the nursing home; and this had happened, it was not fantasy, born
out of tragedy.

He seemed calm, now that he had told me so much. A great part of
the strain had gone, his hands no longer trembled. He looked more like
the old Victor, and his voice was steady.

"It must have been centuries old," he said after a moment or two.
"God knows how long it must have taken to build, hewn out of the
rock face like that. I have never seen anything more stark and savage,
nor, in a strange way, more beautiful. It seemed to hang there, sus-
pended, between the mountain and the sky. There were many long
narrow slits, for light and air. No real windows, in the sense we know
them. There was a tower, looking west, with a sheer drop below. The
great wall encircled the whole place, making it impregnable, like a
fortress. I could see no way of entrance. There was no sign of life. No
sign of anyone. I stood there staring at the place, and the narrow
window slits stared back at me. There was nothing I could do but wait
there until Anna showed herself. Because now, you see, I was convinced the old man had been right, and I knew what must have happened. The inhabitants had seen Anna from behind those slit windows,
and had called to her. She was with them now, inside. She must see
me standing outside the wall, and presently would come out to me.
So I waited there, all day. . . ."

His words were simple. Just a plain statement of fact. Any husband might have waited thus for a wife who had, during their holiday, ventured forth one morning to call upon friends. He sat down, and later ate his lunch, and watched the rolling banks of cloud that hid the world below move, and disperse, and form again; and the sun, in all its summer strength, beat down upon the unprotected face of Monte Verità, on the tower and the narrow window slits, and the great encircling wall, whence came no movement and no sound.

"I sat there all the day," said Victor, "but she did not come. The force of the sun was blinding, scorching, and I had to go back to the gully-way for shelter. There, lying under the shadow of a projecting rock, I could still watch that tower and those window slits. You and I in the past have known silence on the mountains, but nothing like the silence beneath those twin peaks of Monte Verità.

"The hours dragged by, and I went on waiting. Gradually it grew cooler, and then, as my anxiety increased, time raced instead. The sun went too fast into the west. The colour of the rock face was changing. There was no longer any glare. I began to panic then. I went to the wall and shouted. I felt along the wall with my hands, but there was no entrance, there was nothing. My voice echoed back to me, again and again. I looked up, and all I could see were those blind slits of windows. I began to doubt everything, the old man's story, all that he had said. This place was uninhabited, no one had lived there for a thousand years. It was something built long ago in time, and now deserted. And Anna had never come to it at all. She had fallen, on that narrow lip-way where the track ended and the man had left me. She must have fallen into the sheer depths where the southern shoulder of the mountain ridge began. And this is what had happened to the other women who had come this way, the old man's daughter, the girls from the valley; they had all fallen, none of them had ever reached the ultimate rock face, here between the peaks."

The suspense would have been easier to bear if the first strain and sign of breakdown had come back into Victor's voice. As it was, sitting there in the London nursing home, the room impersonal and plain, the routine bottles of medicines and pills on the table by his side, and the sound of traffic coming from Wigmore Street, he spoke in a steady, monotonous tone, like a clock ticking; it would have been more natural had he turned suddenly, and screamed.

"Yet I dared not go back," he said, "unless she came. I was compelled to go on waiting there, beneath the wall. The clouds banked up towards me and turned grey. All the warning evening shadows that I knew too well crept into the sky. One moment the rock face, and the wall, and the slit windows were golden; then suddenly, the sun was gone. There was no dusk at all. It was cold, and it was night."

Victor told me that he stayed there against the wall until daybreak. He did not sleep. He paced up and down to keep warm. When dawn came he was chilled and numb, faint, too, from want of food. He had brought with him only the rations for their midday meal.

Sense told him that to wait now, through another day, was madness. He must return to the village for food and drink, and if possible enlist the help of the men there to form a search party. Reluctantly, when the sun rose, he left the rock face. Silence enwrapped it still. He was certain now there was no life behind the walls.

He went back, round the shoulder of the mountain, to the track; and so down into the morning mist, and to the village.

Victor said they were waiting there for him. It was as though he was expected. The old man was standing at the entrance of his home, and gathered about him were neighbours, mostly men and children.

Victor's first question was, "Has my wife returned?" Somehow, as he descended from the summit, hope had come to him again—that she had never climbed the mountain track, that she had walked another way, and had come back to the village by a different path. When he saw their faces his hope went.

"She will not come back," said the old man; "we told you she would not come back. She has gone to them, on Monte Verità."

Victor had wisdom enough to ask for food and drink before entering into argument. They gave him these. They stood beside him, watching him with compassion. Victor said the greatest agony was the sight of Anna's pack, her mattress, her drinking bottle, her knife; the little personal possessions she had not taken with her.

When he had eaten they continued to stand there, waiting for him to speak. He told the old man everything. How he had waited all day, and through the night. How there was never a sound, or a sign of life, from those slit windows on the rock face of Monte Verità. Now and again the old man translated what Victor said to the neighbours.

When Victor had finished the old man spoke.

"It is as I said. Your wife is there. She is with them."

Victor, his nerves to pieces, shouted aloud.

"How can she be there? There is no one alive in that place. It's dead, it's empty. It's been dead for centuries."

The old man leant forward and put his hand on Victor's shoulder. "It is not dead. That is what many have said before. They went and waited, as you waited. Twenty-five years ago I did the same. This man here, my neighbour, waited three months, day after day, night after night, many years ago, when his wife was called. She never came back. No one who is called to Monte Verità returns."

She had fallen, then. She had died. It was that after all. Victor told them this, he insisted upon it, he begged that they would go now, with him, and search the mountain for her body.

Gently, compassionately, the old man shook his head. "In the past we did that too," he said. "There are those among us who climb with great skill, who know the mountain, every inch of it, and who have descended the southern side even, to the edge of the great glacier, beyond which no one can live. There are no bodies. Our women never fell. They were not there. They are in Monte Verità, with the *sacerdotesse*."

It was hopeless, Victor said. It was no use to try argument. He knew that he must go down to the valley, and if he could not get help there go further yet, back to some part of the country that was familiar to him, where he could find guides who would be willing to return with him.

"My wife's body is somewhere on this mountain," he said. "I must find it. If your people won't help me, I will get others."

The old man looked over his shoulder and spoke a name. From the little crowd of silent spectators came a child, a small girl of about nine years old. He laid his hand upon her head.

"This child," he said to Victor, "has seen and spoken with the *sacerdotesse*. Other children, in the past, have seen them too. Only to children, and then rarely, do they show themselves. She will tell you what she saw."

The child began her recitation in a high singsong voice, her eyes fixed upon Victor; and he could tell, he said, that it was a tale she had repeated so many times, to the same listeners, that it was now a chant, a lesson learnt by heart. And it was all in patois. Not one word could Victor understand.

When she had finished the old man acted as interpreter; and from force of habit he too declaimed as the child had done, his tone taking that same singsong quality.

"I was with my companions on Monte Verità. A storm came, and my companions ran away. I walked, and lost myself, and came to the place where the wall is, and the windows. I cried; I was afraid. She came out of the wall, the tall and splendid one, and another with her, also young and beautiful. They comforted me and I wanted to go inside the walls with them, when I heard the singing from the tower, but they told me it was forbidden. When I was thirteen years old I could return to live with them. They wore white raiment to the knees, their arms and legs were bare, the hair close to the head. They were more beautiful than the people of this world. They led me back from Monte Verità, down the track where I could find my way. Then they went from me. I have told all I know."

The old man watched Victor's face when he had finished his recital. Victor said the faith that must have been put in the child's statement astounded him. It was obvious, he thought, that the child had fallen asleep, and dreamt, and translated her dream into reality.

"I am sorry," he told his interpreter, "but I can't believe the child's tale. It is imagination."

Once again the child was called and spoken to, and she at once ran out of the house and disappeared.

"They gave her a circlet of stones on Monte Verità," said the old man. "Her parents keep it locked up, in case of evil. She has gone to ask for it, to show you."

In a few moments the child returned, and she put into Victor's hand a girdle, small enough to encompass a narrow waist, or else to hang about the neck. The stones, which looked like quartz, were cut and shaped by hand, fitting into one another in hollowed grooves. The craftsmanship was fine, even exquisitely done. It was not the rude handiwork of peasants, done of a winter's evening, to pass the time. In silence Victor handed the circlet back to the child.

"She may have found it on the mountainside," he said.

"We do not work thus," answered the old man, "nor the people in the valley, nor even in the cities of this country, where I have been.

The child was given the circlet, as she has told us, by those who inhabit Monte Verità."

Victor knew then that further argument was useless. Their obstinacy was too strong, and their superstition proof against all worldly sense. He asked if he might remain in the house another day and night.

"You are welcome to stay," said the old man, "until you know the truth."

One by one the neighbours dispersed, the routine of the quiet day was resumed. It was as though nothing had happened. Victor went out again, this time towards the northern shoulder of the mountain. He had not gone far before he realised that this ridge was unclimbable, at any rate without skilled help and equipment. If Anna had gone that way she had found certain death.

He went back to the village, which, situated as it was on the eastern slopes, had already lost the sun. He went into the living-room, and saw that there was a meal prepared for him, and his mattress lay on the floor before the hearth.

He was too exhausted to eat. He flung himself down on the mattress and slept. Next morning he rose early, and climbed once more to Monte Verità, and sat there all the day. He waited, watching the slit windows, while the hot sun scorched the rock face through the long hours and then sank down into the western sky; and nothing stirred, and no one came.

He thought of that other man from the village who some years ago had waited there three months, day after day, night after night; and Victor wondered what limitation time would put to his endurance, and whether he would equal the other in fortitude.

On the third day, at that moment of midday when the sun was strongest, he could bear the heat no longer and went to lie in the gully-way, in the shadow and blessed coolness of the projecting rock. Worn with the strain of watching, and with the despair that now filled his entire being, Victor slept.

He awoke with a start. The hands of his watch pointed to five o'clock, and it was already cold inside the gully. He climbed out and looked towards the rock face, golden now in the setting sun. Then he saw her. She was standing beneath the wall, but on a ledge only a few feet in circumference, and below her the rock face fell away sheer, a thousand feet or more.

She waited there, looking towards him, and he ran towards her, shouting, "Anna . . . Anna . . ." And he said that he heard himself sobbing, and he thought his heart would burst.

When he drew closer he saw that he could not reach her. The great drop to the depths below divided them. She was a bare twelve feet away from him, and he could not touch her.

"I stood where I was, staring at her," said Victor. "I did not speak. Something seemed to choke my voice. I felt the tears running down my face. I was crying. I had made up my mind that she was dead, you see, that she had fallen. And she was there, she was alive. Ordinary words wouldn't come. I tried to say, 'What has happened? Where have you been?'—but it wasn't any use. Because as I looked at her I knew in one moment, with terrible blinding certainty, that it was all true, what the old man had said, and the child; it wasn't imagination, it wasn't superstition. Though I saw no one but Anna, the whole place suddenly became alive. From behind those window slits above me there were God knows how many eyes, watching, looking down on me. I could feel the nearness of them, beyond those walls. And it was uncanny, and horrible, and real."

Now the strain had come back into Victor's voice, now his hands trembled once again. He reached out for a glass of water and drank thirstily.

"She was not wearing her own clothes," he said. "She had a kind of shirt, like a tunic, to her knees, and round her waist a circlet of stones, like the one the child had shown me. Nothing on her feet, and her arms bare. What frightened me most was that her hair was cut quite short, as short as yours or mine. It altered her strangely, made her look younger, but in some way terribly austere. Then she spoke to me. She said quite naturally, as if nothing had happened, 'I want you to go back home, Victor darling. You mustn't worry about me any more.' "

Victor told me he could hardly credit it, at first, that she could stand there and say this to him. It reminded him of those so-called psychic messages that mediums give out to relatives at a spiritualistic séance. He could hardly trust himself to answer. He thought that perhaps she had been hypnotised and was speaking under suggestion.

"Why do you want me to go home?" he said, very gently, not wanting to damage her mind, which these people might have destroyed.

"It's the only thing to do," she answered. And then, Victor said, she smiled, normally, happily, as if they were at home discussing plans. "I'm all right, darling," she said. "This isn't madness, or hypnotism, or any of the things you imagine it to be. They have frightened you in the village, and it's understandable. This thing is so much stronger than most people. But I must have always known it existed, somewhere; and I've been waiting all these years. When men go into monasteries, and women shut themselves up in convents, their relatives suffer very much, I know, but in time they come to bear it. I want you to do the same, Victor, please. I want you, if you can, to understand."

She stood there, quite calm, quite peaceful, smiling down at him.

"You mean," he said, "you want to stay in this place always?"

"Yes," she said, "there can be no other life for me, any more, ever. You must believe this. I want you to go home, and live as you have always done, and look after the house and the estate, and if you fall in love with anyone to marry and be happy. Bless you for your love and kindness and devotion, darling, which I shall never forget. If I were dead, you would want to think of me at peace, in Paradise. This place, to me, is Paradise. And I would rather jump now, to those rocks hundreds of feet below me, than go back to the world from Monte Verità."

Victor said he went on staring at her as she spoke, and he said there was a radiance about her there had never been before, even in their most contented days.

"You and I," he said to me, "have both read of transfiguration in the Bible. That is the only word I can use to describe her face. It was not hysteria, it was not emotion; it was just that. Something—out of this world of ours—had put its hand upon her. To plead with her was useless, to attempt force impossible. Anna, rather than go back to the world, would throw herself off the rock face. I should achieve nothing."

He said the feeling of utter helplessness was overwhelming, the knowledge that there was nothing he could do. It was as if he and she were standing on a dockway, and she was about to set foot on a ship, bound to an unknown destination, and the last few minutes were passing by before the ship's siren blew, warning him the gangways would be withdrawn and she must go.

He asked her if she had all she needed, if she would be given sufficient food, enough covering, and whether there were any facilities should she fall ill. He wanted to know if there was anything she wanted that he could send to her. And she smiled back at him, saying she had everything, within those walls, that she would ever need.

He said to her, "I shall return every year, at this time, to ask you to come back. I shall never forget."

She said, "It will be harder for you if you do that. Like putting flowers on a grave. I would rather you stayed away."

"I can't stay away," he said, "with the knowledge you are here, behind these walls."

"I won't be able to come to you again," she said; "this is the last time you will see me. Remember, though, that I shall go on looking like this, always. That is part of the belief. Carry me with you."

Then, Victor said, she asked him to go. She could not return inside the walls until he had gone. The sun was low in the sky and already the rock face was in shadow.

Victor looked at Anna a long time; then he turned his back on her, standing by the ledge, and walked away from the wall towards the gully, without looking over his shoulder. When he came to the gully he waited there a few minutes, then looked out again towards the rock face. Anna was no longer standing on the ledge. There was nothing there but the wall and the slit windows, and above, not yet in shadow, the twin peaks of Monte Verità.

I managed to spare half an hour or so, every day, to go and visit Victor in the nursing home. Each day he appeared stronger, more himself. I spoke to the doctor attending him, to the matron and the nurses. They told me there was no question of a deranged mind; he came to them suffering from severe shock and nervous collapse. It had already done him immense good to see me and to talk to me. In a fortnight he was well enough to leave the nursing home, and he came to stay with me in Westminster.

During those autumn evenings we went over all that had happened again and again. I questioned him more closely than I had done before. He denied that there had ever been anything abnormal about Anna. Theirs had been a normal, happy marriage. Her dislike of possessions and her spartan way of living were, he agreed, unusual; but they had not struck him as peculiar—it was Anna. I told him of the night I had seen her standing with bare feet in the garden, on the frosted lawn. Yes, he said, that was the sort of thing she did. But she had a fastidiousness, a certain personal reticence, that he respected. He never intruded upon it.

I asked him how much he knew of her life before he married her. He told me there was very little to know. Her parents had died when she was young, and she had been brought up in Wales by an aunt. There was no peculiar background, no skeletons in the cupboard. Her upbringing had been entirely ordinary in every way.

"It's no use," said Victor, "you can't explain Anna. She is just herself, unique. You can't explain her any more than you can explain the sudden phenomenon of a musician, born to ordinary parents, or a poet, or a saint. There is no accounting for them. They just appear. It was my great fortune, praise God, to find her, just as it is my own personal hell, now, to have lost her. Somehow I shall continue living, as she expected me to do. And once a year I shall go back to Monte Verità."

His acquiescence to the total break-up of his life astounded me. I felt that I could not have overcome my own despair, had the tragedy been mine. It seemed to me monstrous that an unknown sect, on a mountainside, could, in the space of a few days, have such power over a woman, a woman of intelligence and personality. It was understandable that ignorant peasant girls could be emotionally misled and their relatives, blinded by superstition, do nothing about it. I told Victor this. I told him that it should be possible, through the ordinary channels of our embassy, to approach the government of that country, to have a nation-wide enquiry, to get the press on to it, the backing of our own government. I told him I was prepared, myself, to set all this in motion. We were living in the twentieth century, not in the Middle Ages. A place like Monte Verità should not be permitted to exist. I would arouse the whole country with the story, create an international situation.

"But why," said Victor quietly, "to what end?"

"To get Anna back," I said, "and to free the rest. To prevent the break-up of other people's lives."

"We don't," said Victor, "go about destroying monasteries or convents. There are hundreds of them, all over the world."

"That is different," I argued. "They are organised bodies of religious people. They have existed for centuries."

"I think, very probably, Monte Verità has too."

"How do they live, how do they eat, what happens when they fall ill, when they die?"

"I don't know. I try not to think about it. All I cling to is that Anna said she had found what she was searching for, that she was happy. I'm not going to destroy that happiness."

Then he looked at me, in a way half puzzled, half wise, and said, "It's odd, your talking in this way. Because by rights you should understand Anna's feelings more than I do. You were always the one with mountain fever. You were the one, in old climbing days, to have your head in the clouds and quote to me—

> "*The world is too much with us; late and soon,*
> *Getting and spending, we lay waste our powers.*"

I remember getting up and going over to the window and looking out over the foggy street, down to the embankment. I said nothing. His words had moved me very much. I could not answer them. And I knew, in the depths of my heart, why I hated the story of Monte Verità and wanted the place to be destroyed. It was because Anna had found her Truth, and I had not. . . .

That conversation between Victor and myself made, if not a division in our friendship, at least a turning point. We had reached a halfway mark in both our lives. He went back to his home in Shropshire, and later wrote to me that he intended making over the property to a young nephew, still at school, and during the next few years intended having the lad to stay with him in the holidays, to get him acquainted with the place. After that, he did not know. He would not commit himself to plans. My own future, at this time, was full with change. My work necessitated living in America for a period of two years.

Then, as it turned out, the whole tenor of the world became disrupted. The following year was 1914.

Victor was one of the first to join up. Perhaps he thought this would be his answer. Perhaps he thought he might be killed. I did not follow his example until my period in America was over. It was certainly not my answer, and I disliked every moment of my army years. I saw nothing of Victor during the whole of the war; we fought on different fronts, and did not even meet on leave. I did hear from him, once. And this is what he said:

*In spite of everything, I have managed to get to Monte Verità each
year, as I promised to do. I stayed a night with the old man in the
village, and climbed on to the mountaintop the following day. It
looked exactly the same. Quite dead, and silent. I left a letter for
Anna beneath the wall and sat there, all the day, looking at the place,
feeling her near. I knew she would not come to me. The next day I
went again, and was overjoyed to find a letter from her in return. If
you can call it a letter. It was cut on flat stone, and I suppose this is the
only method they have of communication. She said she was well, and
strong, and very happy. She gave me her blessing, and you also. She
told me never to be anxious for her. That was all. It was, as I told you
at the nursing home, like a spirit message from the dead. With this I
have to be content, and am. If I survive this war, I shall probably go
out and live somewhere in that country, so that I can be near her,
even if I never see her again, or hear nothing of her but a few words
scrawled on a stone once a year.*

Good luck to yourself, old fellow. I wonder where you are.

Victor

When the Armistice came, and I got myself demobilised and set
about the restoration of my normal life, one of the first things I did
was to enquire for Victor. I wrote to him, in Shropshire. I had a
courteous reply from the nephew. He had taken over the house and the
estate. Victor had been wounded, but not badly. He had now left
England and was somewhere abroad, either in Italy or Spain, the
nephew was not sure which. But he believed his uncle had decided to
live out there for good. If he had news of him, he would let me know.
No further news came. As to myself, I decided I disliked post-war London and the people who lived there. I cut myself loose from home ties
too, and went to America.

I did not see Victor again for nearly twenty years.

It was not chance that brought us together again. I am sure of that.
These things are predestined. I have a theory that each man's life is
like a pack of cards, and those we meet and sometimes love are shuffled
with us. We find ourselves in the same suit, held by the hand of Fate.
The game is played, we are discarded, and pass on. What combination
of events brought me to Europe again at the age of fifty-five, two or

three years before the second world war, does not matter to this story. It so happened that I came.

I was flying from one capital city to another—the names of both are immaterial—and the aeroplane in which I travelled made a forced landing, luckily without loss of life, in desolate mountainous country. For two days the crew and passengers, myself amongst them, held no contact with the outer world. We camped in the partially wrecked machine and waited for rescue. This adventure made headlines in the world press at the time, even taking precedence, for a few days, over the simmering European situation.

Hardship, for those forty-eight hours, was not acute. Luckily there were no women or children passengers travelling, so we men put the best face on it we could, and waited for rescue. We were confident that help would reach us before long. Our wireless had functioned until the moment of the forced landing, and the operator had given our position. It was all a matter of patience, and of keeping warm.

For my part, with my mission in Europe accomplished and no ties strong enough back in the States to believe myself anxiously awaited, this sudden plunging into the sort of country that years ago I had most passionately loved was a strange experience. I had become so much a man of cities, and a creature of comfort. The high pulse of American living, the pace, the vitality, the whole breathless energy of the New World had combined to make me forget the ties that still bound me to the Old.

Now, looking about me in the desolation and the splendour, I knew what I had lacked all these years. I forgot my fellow travellers, forgot the grey fuselage of the crippled plane—an anachronism, surely, amid the wilderness of centuries—and forgot, too, my grey hair, my heavy frame, and all the burden of my five-and-fifty years. I was a boy again, hopeful, eager, seeking an answer to eternity. Surely it was there, waiting, beyond the further peaks. I stood there, incongruous in my city clothes, and the mountain fever raced back into my blood.

I wanted to get away from the wrecked plane and the pinched faces of my companions; I wanted to forget the waste of the years between. What I would have given to be young again, a boy, and, reckless of the consequences, set forth towards those peaks and climb to glory. I knew how it would feel, up there on the higher mountains. The air keener and still more cold, the silence deeper. The strange burning quality of ice, the penetrating strength of the sun, and that moment when the heart misses a beat as the foot, momentarily slipping on the narrow ledge, seeks safety; the hand's clutch to the rope.

I gazed up at them, the mountains that I loved, and felt a traitor. I had betrayed them for baser things, for comfort, ease, security. When rescue came to me and to my fellow travellers, I would make amends for the time that had been lost. There was no pressing hurry to return to the States. I would take a vacation, here in Europe, and go climbing once again. I would buy proper clothes, equipment, set myself to it. This decision taken, I felt lighthearted, irresponsible. Nothing seemed to matter any more. I returned to my little party, sheltering beside the plane, and laughed and joked through the remaining hours.

Help reached us on the second day. We had been certain of rescue when we had sighted an aeroplane, at dawn, hundreds of feet above us. The search party consisted of true mountaineers and guides, rough fellows but likeable. They had brought clothing, kit, and food for us, and were astonished, they admitted, that we were all in condition to make use of them. They had thought to find none of us alive.

They helped us down to the valley in easy stages, and it took us until the following day. We spent the night encamped on the north side of the great ridge of mountains that had seemed to us, beside the useless plane, so remote and so inaccessible. At daybreak we set forth again, a splendid clear day, and the whole of the valley below our camp lay plain to the eye. Eastward the mountain range ran sheer, and as far as I could judge impassable, to a snow-capped peak, or possibly two, that pierced the dazzling sky like the knuckles on a closed hand.

I said to the leader of the rescue expedition, just as we were starting out on the descent, "I used to climb much, in old days, when I was young. I don't know this country at all. Do many expeditions come this way?"

He shook his head. He told me conditions were difficult. He and his companions came from some distance away. The people in the valley to the eastward there were backward and ignorant; there were few facilities for tourists or for strangers. If I cared about climbing he could take me to other places, where I should find good sport. It was already rather late in the year, though, for expeditions.

I went on looking at that eastward ridge, remote and strangely beautiful.

"What do they call them," I said, "those twin peaks, to the east?"

He answered, "Monte Verità."

I knew then what had brought me back to Europe. . . .

We parted, my fellow travellers and I, at a little town some twenty miles from the spot where the aeroplane had crashed. Transport took them on to the nearest railway line, and to civilisation. I remained behind. I booked a room at the small hotel and deposited my luggage there. I bought myself strong boots, a pair of breeches, a jerkin, and a couple of shirts. Then I turned my back upon the town and climbed.

It was, as the guide had told me, late in the year for expeditions. Somehow I did not care. I was alone, and on the mountains once again. I had forgotten how healing solitude could be. The old strength came back to my legs and to my lungs, and the cold air bit into the whole of me. I could have shouted with delight at fifty-five. Gone were the turmoil and the stress, the anxious stir of many millions; gone were the lights, and the vapid city smells. I had been mad to endure it for so long.

In a mood of exaltation I came to the valley that lies at the eastern foot of Monte Verità. It had not changed much, it seemed to me, from the description Victor gave of it, those many years ago before the war. The little town was small and primitive, the people dull and dour. There was a rough sort of inn—one could not grace it by the name of hotel—where I proposed to stay the night.

I was received with indifference, though not discourtesy. After supper I asked if the track was still passable to the summit of Monte Verità. My informant behind his bar—for bar and café were in one, and I ate there, being the only visitor—regarded me without interest as he drank the glass of wine I offered him.

"It is passable, I believe, as far as the village. Beyond that I do not know," he said.

"Is there much coming and going between your people in the valley here and those in the village on the mountain?" I asked.

"Sometimes. Perhaps. Not at this time of year," he answered.

"Do you ever have tourists here?"

"Few tourists. They go north. It is better in the north."

"Is there any place in the village where I could sleep tomorrow night?"

"I do not know."

I paused a moment, watching his heavy sullen face, then I said to him, "And the *sacerdotesse*, do they still live on the rock face on the summit of Monte Verità?"

He started. He turned his eyes full upon me, and leant over the bar. "Who are you, then? What do you know of them?"

"Then they do exist still?" I said.

He watched me, suspicious. Much had happened to his country in the past twenty years, violence, revolution, hostility between father and son, and even this remote corner must have had its share. It may have been this that made reserve.

"There are stories," he said slowly. "I prefer not to mix myself up in such matters. It is dangerous. One day there will be trouble."

"Trouble for whom?"

"For those in the village, for those who may live on Monte Verità— I know nothing of them—for us here in the valley. I do not know. If I do not know, no harm can come to me."

He finished his wine, and cleaned his glass, and wiped the bar with a cloth. He was anxious to be rid of me.

"At what time do you wish for your breakfast in the morning?" he said.

I told him seven, and went up to my room.

I opened the double windows and stood out on the narrow balcony. The little town was quiet. Few lights winked in the darkness. The night was clear and cold. The moon had risen and would be full tomorrow or the day after. It shone upon the dark mountain mass in front of me. I felt oddly moved, as though I had stepped back into the past. This room, where I should pass the night, might have been the same one where Victor and Anna slept, all those years ago, in the summer of 1913. Anna herself might have stood here, on the balcony, gazing up at Monte Verità, while Victor, unconscious of the tragedy so few hours distant, called to her from within.

And now, in their footsteps, I had come to Monte Verità.

The next morning I took my breakfast in the café-bar, and my landlord of the night before was absent. My coffee and bread were brought me by a girl, perhaps his daughter. Her manner was quiet and courteous, and she wished me a pleasant day.

"I am going to climb," I said, "the weather seems set fair. Tell me, have you ever been to Monte Verità?"

Her eyes flickered away from mine instantly.

"No," she said, "no, I have never been away from the valley."

My manner was matter-of-fact, and casual. I said something about friends of mine having been here, some while ago—I did not say how long—and that they had climbed to the summit, and had found the rock face there, between the peaks, and had been much interested to learn about the sect who lived enclosed within the walls.

"Are they still there, do you know?" I asked, lighting a cigarette, elaborately at ease.

She glanced over her shoulder nervously, as though conscious that she might be overheard.

"It is said so," she answered. "My father does not discuss it before me. It is a forbidden subject to young people."

I went on smoking my cigarette.

"I live in America," I said, "and I find that there, as in most places, when the young people get together there is nothing they like discussing so well as forbidden subjects."

She smiled faintly but said nothing.

"I dare say you and your young friends often whisper together about what happens on Monte Verità," I said.

I felt slightly ashamed of my duplicity, but I felt that this method of attack was the most likely one to produce information.

"Yes," she said, "that is true. But we say nothing out loud. But just lately . . ." Once again she glanced over her shoulder, and then resumed, her voice pitched lower, "A girl I knew quite well, she was to marry shortly, she went away one day, she has not come back, and they are saying she has been called to Monte Verità."

"No one saw her go?"

"No. She went by night. She left no word, nothing."

"Could she not have gone somewhere quite different, to a large town, to one of the tourist centres?"

"It is believed not. Besides, just before, she had acted strangely. She had been heard talking in her sleep about Monte Verità."

I waited a moment, then continued my enquiry, still nonchalant, still casual.

"What is the fascination in Monte Verità?" I asked. "The life there must be unbearably harsh, and even cruel?"

"Not to those who are called," she said, shaking her head. "They stay young always, they never grow old."

"If nobody has ever seen them, how can you know?"

"It has always been so. That is the belief. That is why here, in the valley, they are hated and feared, and also envied. They have the secret of life, on Monte Verità."

She looked out of the window towards the mountain. There was a wistful expression in her eyes.

"And you?" I said. "Do you think you will ever be called?"

"I am not worthy," she said. "Also, I am afraid."

She took away my coffee and offered me some fruit.

"And now," she said, her voice still lower, "since this last disappearance, there is likely to be trouble. The people are angry, here in the valley. Some of the men have climbed to the village and are trying to rouse them there, to get force of numbers, and then they will attack the rock. Our men will go wild. They will try to kill those who live there. Then there will be more trouble, we shall get the army here, there will be enquiries, punishment, shooting; it will all end badly. So it is not pleasant at the moment. Everyone goes about afraid. Everybody is whispering in secret."

A footstep outside sent her swiftly behind the bar. She busied herself there, her head low, as her father came into the room.

He glanced at both of us, suspiciously. I put out my cigarette and rose from the table.

"So you are still intent to climb?" he asked me.

"Yes," I said. "I shall be back in a day or two."

"It would be imprudent to stay there longer," he said.

"You mean the weather will break?"

"The weather will break, yes. Also, it might not be safe."

"In what way might it not be safe?"

"There may be disturbance. Things are unsettled just now. Men are out of temper. When they are out of temper, they lose their heads. And strangers, foreigners, can come to harm at such a time. It would be better if you gave up your idea of climbing Monte Verità and turned northwards. There is no trouble there."

"Thank you. But I have set my heart on climbing Monte Verità."

He shrugged his shoulders. He looked away from me.

"As you will," he said, "it is not my affair."

I walked out of the inn, down to the street, and, crossing the little bridge above the mountain stream, I set my face to the track through the valley that led me to the eastern face of Monte Verità.

At first the sounds from the valley were distinct. The barking of dogs, the tinkle of cowbells, the voices of men calling to one another, all these rose clearly to me in the still air. Then the blue smoke from the houses merged and became one misty haze, and the houses themselves took on a toy-town quality. The track wound above me and away, ever deeper into the heart of the mountain itself, until by midday the valley was lost in the depths and I had no other thought in my mind but to climb upwards, higher, always higher, win my way beyond that first ridge to the left, leave it behind me and gain the second, forget both in turn to achieve the third, steeper yet and overshadowed. My progress was slow, with untuned muscles and imperfect wind, but exhilaration of spirit kept me going and I was in no way tired, rather the reverse. I could have gone on for ever.

It was with a shock of surprise that I came finally upon the village, for I had pictured it at least another hour away. I must have climbed at a great pace, for it was barely four o'clock. The village wore a forlorn, almost deserted appearance, and I judged that today there were few remaining inhabitants. Some of the dwellings were boarded up, others fallen in and partly destroyed. Smoke came from only two or three of them, and I saw no one working in the pasture land around. A few cows, lean-looking and unkempt, grazed by the side of the track, the jangling bells around their necks sounding hollow somehow in the still air. The place had a sombre, depressing effect, after the stimulation of the climb. If this was where I must spend the night I did not think much of it.

I went to the door of the first dwelling that had a thin wisp of smoke coming from the roof and knocked upon the door. It was opened, after some time, by a lad of about fourteen, who after one look at me called over his shoulder to somebody within. A man of about my own age, stupid-looking and heavy, came to the door. He said something to me in patois; then, staring a moment, and realising his mistake, he broke, even more haltingly than I, into the language of the country.

"You are the doctor from the valley?" he said to me.

"No," I replied, "I am a stranger on vacation, climbing in the district. I want a bed for the night, if you can give me one."

His face fell. He did not reply directly to my request.

"We have someone here very sick," he said, "I do not know what to do. They said a doctor would come from the valley. You met no one?"

"I'm afraid not. No one climbed from the valley except myself. Who is ill? A child?"

The man shook his head. "No, no, we have no children here."

He went on looking at me, in a dazed, helpless sort of way, and I felt sorry for his trouble, but I did not see what I could do. I had no sort of medicines upon me but a first-aid packet and a small bottle of aspirin. The aspirin might be of use, if there was fever. I undid it from my pack and gave a handful to the man.

"These may help," I said, "if you care to try them."

He beckoned me inside. "Please to give them yourself," he said.

I had some reluctance to step within and be faced with the grim spectacle of a dying relative, but plain humanity told me I could hardly do otherwise. I followed him into the living-room. There was a trestle bed against the wall and lying upon it, covered with two blankets, was a man, his eyes closed. He was pale and unshaven, and his features had that sharp pointed look about them that comes upon the face when near to death. I went close to the bed and gazed down upon him. He opened his eyes. For a moment we stared at one another, unbelieving. Then he put out his hand to me, and smiled. It was Victor. . . .

"Thank God," he said.

I was too much moved to speak. I saw him beckon to the fellow, who stood apart, and speak to him in the patois, and he must have told him we were friends, for some sort of light broke in the man's face and he withdrew. I went on standing by the trestle bed, with Victor's hand in mine.

"How long have you been like this?" I asked at length.

"Nearly five days," he said. "Touch of pleurisy; I've had it before. Rather worse this time. I'm getting old."

Once again he smiled, and although I guessed him to be desperately ill he was little changed, he was the same Victor still.

"You seem to have prospered," he said to me, still smiling; "you have all the sleek appearance of success."

I asked him why he had never written, and what he had been doing with himself for twenty years.

"I cut myself adrift," he said. "I gather you did the same, but in a

different way. I haven't been back to England since I left. What is it
that you're holding there?"

I showed him the bottle of aspirin.

"I'm afraid that's no use to you," I said. "The best thing I can suggest
is for me to stay here tonight, and then first thing in the morning get
the chap here, and one or two others, to help me carry you down to
the valley."

He shook his head. "Waste of time," he said. "I'm done for. I know
that."

"Nonsense. You need a doctor, proper nursing. That's impossible in
this place." I looked around the primitive living-room, dark and airless.

"Never mind about me," he said. "Someone else is more important."

"Who?"

"Anna," he said, and then as I answered nothing, at a loss for words,
he added, "She's still here, you know, on Monte Verità."

"You mean," I said, "that she's in that place, enclosed, she's never
left it?"

"That's why I'm here," said Victor. "I come every year, and have
done, since the beginning. I wrote and told you, surely, after the war?
I live in a little fishing port all the year round, very isolated and quiet,
and then come here once in twelve months. I left it later this year, because I had been ill."

It was incredible. What an existence, all these years, without friends,
without interests, enduring the long months until the time came for
this hopeless annual pilgrimage.

"Have you ever seen her?" I asked.

"Never."

"Do you write to her?"

"I bring a letter every year. I take it up with me and leave it beneath
the wall, and then return the following day."

"The letter gets taken?"

"Always. And in its place there is a slab of stone with writing
scrawled upon it. Never more than a few words. I take the stones away
with me. I have them all down on the coast, where I live."

It was heart-rending, his faith in her, his fidelity through the years.

"I've tried to study it," he said, "this religion, belief. It's very ancient,
way back before Christianity. There are old books that hint at it. I've
picked them up from time to time, and I've spoken to people, scholars,

who have made a study of mysticism and the old rites of ancient Gaul,
and the Druids; there's a strong link between all mountain folk of those
times. In every instance that I have read there is this insistence on the
power of the moon and the belief that the followers stay young and
beautiful."

"You talk, Victor, as if you believe that too," I said.

"I do," he answered. "The children believe it, here in the village, the
few that remain."

Talking to me had tired him. He reached out for a pitcher of water
that stood beside the bed.

"Look here," I said, "these aspirin can't hurt you, they can only help,
if you have fever. And you might get some sleep."

I made him swallow three, and drew the blankets closer round him.

"Are there any women in the house?" I asked.

"No," he said, "I've been puzzled about that, since I've been here
this time. The village is pretty much deserted. All the women and
children have shifted to the valley. There are about twenty men and
boys left, all told."

"Do you know when the women and children went?"

"I gather they left a few days before I came. This fellow here—he's
the son of the old man who used to live here, who died many years
ago—is such a fool that he never knows anything. He just looks vague
if you question him. But he's competent, in his own way. He'll give you
food, and find bedding for you, and the little chap is bright enough."

Victor closed his eyes, and I hoped that he might sleep. I thought I
knew why the women and children had left the village. It was since the
girl from the valley had disappeared. They had been warned that trouble might come to Monte Verità. I did not dare tell Victor this. I
wished I could persuade him to be carried down into the valley.

By this time it was quite dark, and I was hungry. I went through a
sort of recess to the back. There was no one there but the boy. I asked
him for something to eat and drink, and he understood. He brought
me bread, and meat, and cheese, and I ate it in the living-room, with
the boy watching me. Victor's eyes were still closed and I believed he
slept.

"Will he get better?" asked the boy. He did not speak in patois.

"I think so," I answered, "if I can get help to carry him to a doctor
in the valley."

"I will help you," said the boy, "and two of my companions. We should go tomorrow. After that, it will be difficult."

"Why?"

"There will be coming and going the day after. Men from the valley, much excitement, and my companions and I will join them."

"What is going to happen?"

He hesitated. He looked at me with quick bright eyes.

"I do not know," he said. He slipped away, back to the recess.

Victor's voice came from the trestle bed.

"What did the boy say?" he asked. "Who is coming from the valley?"

"I don't know," I said casually, "some expedition, perhaps. But he has offered to help take you down the mountain tomorrow."

"No expeditions ever come here," said Victor, "there must be some mistake." He called to the boy, and when the lad reappeared spoke to him in the patois. The boy was ill at ease, and diffident; he seemed reluctant now to answer questions. Several times I heard the words Monte Verità repeated, both by him and Victor. Presently he went back to the inner room and left us alone.

"Did you understand any of that?" asked Victor.

"No," I replied.

"I don't like it," he said, "there's something queer. I've felt it since I've lain here these last few days. The men look furtive, odd. He tells me there's been some disturbance in the valley, and the people there are very angry. Did you hear anything about it?"

I did not know what to say. He was watching me closely.

"The fellow in the inn was not very forthcoming," I said, "but he did advise against coming to Monte Verità."

"What reason did he give?"

"No particular reason. He just said there might be trouble."

Victor was silent. I could feel him thinking there beside me.

"Have any of the women disappeared from the valley?" he said.

It was useless to lie. "I heard something about a missing girl," I told him, "but I don't know if it's true."

"It will be true. That is it, then."

He said nothing for a long while, and I could not see his face—it was in shadow. The room was lit by a single lamp, giving a pallid glow.

"You must climb tomorrow and warn Anna at Monte Verità," he said at last.

I think I had expected this. I asked him how it could be done.

"I can sketch the track for you," he said, "you can't go wrong. It's straight up the old watercourse, heading south all the while. The rains haven't made it impassable yet. If you leave before dawn you'll have all day before you."

"What happens when I get there?"

"You must leave a letter, as I do, and then come away. They won't fetch it while you are there. I will write also. I shall tell Anna that I am ill here, and that you've suddenly appeared, after over twenty years. You know, I was thinking, just now, while you were talking to the boy, it's like a miracle. I have a strange sort of feeling Anna brought you here."

His eyes were shining with that old boyish faith that I remembered.

"Perhaps," I said. "Either Anna, or what you used to call my mountain fever."

"Isn't that the same thing?" he said to me.

We looked at one another in the silence of that small dark room, and then I turned away and called the boy to bring me bedding and a pillow. I would sleep the night on the floor by Victor's bed.

He was restless in the night, and breathed with difficulty. Several times I got up to him and gave him more aspirin and water. He sweated much, which might be a good thing or a bad, I did not know. The night seemed endless, and for myself, I barely slept at all. We were both awake when the first darkness paled.

"You should start now," he said, and, going to him, I saw with apprehension that his skin had gone clammy cold. He was worse, I was certain, and much weaker.

"Tell Anna," he said, "that if the valley people come she and the others will be in great danger. I am sure of it."

"I will write all that," I said.

"She knows how much I love her. I tell her that always in my letters, but you could say so, once again. Wait in the gully. You may have to wait two hours, or even three, or longer still. Then go back to the wall and look for the answer on the slab of stone. It will be there."

I touched his cold hand and went out into the chill morning air. Then, as I looked about me, I had my first misgiving. There was cloud everywhere. Not only beneath me, masking the track from the valley where I had come the night before, but here in the silent village, wreathing in mist the roofs of the huts, and also above me, where the path wound through scrub and disappeared upon the mountainside.

Softly, silently, the clouds touched my face and drifted past, never dissolving, never clearing. The moisture clung to my hair and to my hands, and I could taste it on my tongue. I looked this way and that, in the half light, wondering what I should do. All the old instinct of self-preservation told me to return. To set forth, in breaking weather, was madness, to my remembered mountain lore. Yet to stay there, in the village, with Victor's eyes upon me, hopeful, patient, was more than I could stand. He was dying, we both knew it. And I carried in my breast pocket his last letter to his wife.

I turned to the south, and still the clouds came travelling past, slowly, relentlessly, down from the summit of Monte Verità.

I began to climb. . . .

Victor had told me that I should reach the summit in two hours. Less than that, with the rising sun behind me. I had also a guide, the rough sketch map that he had drawn.

In the first hour after leaving the village I realised my error. I should never see the sun that day. The clouds drove past me, vapour in my face, clammy and cold. They hid the winding watercourse up which I had climbed five minutes since, down which already came the mountain springs, loosening the earth and stones.

By the time the contour changed and I was free of roots and scrub and feeling my way upon bare rock, it was past midday. I was defeated. Worse still, I was lost. I turned back and could not find the watercourse that had brought me so far. I approached another, but it ran northeast and had already broken for the season; a torrent of water washed away down the mountainside. One false move, and the current would have borne me away, tearing my hands to pieces as I sought for a grip among the stones.

Gone was my exultation of the day before. I was no longer in the thrall of mountain fever but held instead by the equally well-remembered sense of fear. It had happened in the past, many a time, the coming of cloud. Nothing renders a man so helpless, unless he can recognise every inch of the way by which he has come, and so descend. But I had been young in those days, trained, and climbing fit. Now I

was a middle-aged city dweller, alone on a mountain I had never
climbed before, and I was scared.

I sat down under the lea of a great boulder, away from the drifting
cloud, and ate my lunch—the remainder of sandwiches packed at the
valley inn—and waited. Then, still waiting, I got up and stamped about
for warmth. The air was not penetrating yet but seeping cold, the moist
chill cold that always comes with cloud.

I had this one hope, that with the coming of darkness, and with a
fall in temperature, the cloud would lift. I remembered it would be
full moon, a great point to my advantage, for cloud rarely lingers at
these times, but tends to break up and dissolve. I welcomed, therefore,
the coming of a sharper cold into the atmosphere. The air was per-
ceptibly keener, and looking out towards the south, from which direction the cloud had drifted all the day, I could now see some ten
feet ahead. Below me it was still as thick as ever. A wall of impenetrable mist hid the descent. I went on waiting. Above me, always to the
south, the distance that I could see increased from a dozen feet to
fifteen, from fifteen to twenty. The cloud was cloud no longer, but
vapour only, thin, and vanishing; and suddenly the whole contour of
the mountain came into view, not the summit as yet, but the great
jutting shoulder, leaning south, and beyond it my first glimpse of the
sky.

I looked at my watch again. It was a quarter to six. Night had fallen
on Monte Verità.

Vapour came again, obscuring that clear patch of sky that I had seen,
and then it drifted, and the sky was there once more. I left my place of
shelter where I had been all day. For the second time I was faced with a
decision. To climb, or to descend. Above me, the way was clear. There
was the shoulder of the mountain, described by Victor; I could even
see the ridge along it running to the south, which was the way I should
have taken twelve hours before. In two or three hours the moon
would have risen and would give me all the light I needed to reach the
rock face of Monte Verità. I looked east, to the descent. The whole of
it was hidden in the same wall of cloud. Until the cloud dissolved I
should still be in the same position I had been all day, uncertain of
direction, helpless in visibility that was never more than three feet.

I decided to go on, and to climb to the summit of the mountain with
my message.

Now the cloud was beneath me my spirits revived. I studied the rough map drawn by Victor, and set out towards the southern shoulder. I was hungry, and would have given much to have back the sandwiches I had eaten at midday. A roll of bread was all that remained to me. That, and a packet of cigarettes. Cigarettes were not helpful to the wind, but at least they staved off the desire for food.

Now I could see the twin peaks themselves, clear and stark against the sky. And a new excitement came to me as I looked up at them, for I knew that when I had rounded the shoulder and had come to the southern face of the mountain, I should have reached my journey's end.

I went on climbing; and I saw how the ridge narrowed and how the rock steepened, becoming more sheer as the southern slopes opened up to view, and then, over my shoulder, rose the first tip of the moon's great face, out of the misty vapour to the east. The sight of it stirred me to a new sense of isolation. It was as though I walked alone on the earth's rim, the universe below me and above. No one trod this empty discus but myself, and it spun its way through space to ultimate darkness.

As the moon rose, the man who climbed with it shrank to insignificance. I was no longer aware of personal identity. This shell in which I had my being moved forward without feeling, drawn to the summit of the mountain by some nameless force which seemed to hold suction from the moon itself. I was impelled, like the flow and ebb of tide upon water. I could not disobey the law that urged me on, any more than I could cease to breathe. This was not mountain fever in my blood, but mountain magic. It was not nervous energy that drove me, but the tug of the full moon.

The rock narrowed and closed above my head, making an arch, a gully, so that I had to stoop and feel my way; then I emerged from darkness into light, and there before me, silver-white, were the twin peaks and the rock face of Monte Verità.

For the first time in my life I looked on beauty bare. My mission was forgotten, my anxiety for Victor, my own fear of cloud that had clamped me through the day. This indeed was journey's end. This was fulfilment. Time did not matter. I had no thought of it. I stood there staring at the rock face under the moon.

How long I remained motionless I do not know, nor do I remember when the change came to the tower and the walls; but suddenly the figures were there that had not been before. They stood one behind the other on the walls, silhouetted against the sky, and they might have been stone images, carved from the rock itself, so still they were, so motionless.

I was too distant from them to see their faces or their shape. One stood alone, within the open tower; this one alone was shrouded in a garment reaching from head to foot. Suddenly there came to my mind old tales of ancient days, of Druids, of slaughter, and of sacrifice. These people worshipped the moon, and the moon was full. Some victim was going to be flung to the depths below, and I would witness the act.

I had known fear in my life before, but never terror. Now it came upon me in full measure. I knelt down in the shadow of the gully, for surely they must see me standing there in the moon's path. I saw them raise their arms above their heads, and slowly a murmur came from them, low and indistinct at first, then swelling louder, breaking upon the silence that hitherto had been profound. The sound echoed from the rock face, rose and fell upon the air, and I saw them one and all turn to the full moon. There was no sacrifice. No act of slaughter. This was their song of praise.

I hid there in the shadows, with all the ignorance and shame of one who stumbles into a place of worship alien to his knowledge, while the chanting rang in my ears, unearthly, terrifying, yet beautiful in a way impossible to bear. I clasped my hands over my head, I shut my eyes, I bent low until my forehead touched the ground.

Then slowly, very slowly, the great hymn of praise faded in strength. It sank lower to a murmur, to a sigh. It hushed and died away. Silence came back to Monte Verità.

Still I dared not move. My hands covered my head. My face was to the ground. I am not ashamed of my terror. I was lost between two worlds. My own was gone, and I was not of theirs. I longed for the sanctuary of the drifting cloud again.

I waited, still upon my knees. Then furtive, creeping, I lifted up my head and looked towards the rock face. The walls and the tower were bare. The figures had vanished. And a cloud, dark and ragged, hid the moon.

I stood up, but I did not move. I kept my eyes fixed upon the tower and the walls. Nothing stirred, now that the moon was masked. They might never have been, the figures and the chanting. Perhaps my own fear and imagination had created them.

I waited until the cloud that hid the moon's face passed away. Then I took courage and felt for the letters in my pocket. I do not know what Victor had written, but my own ran thus:

Dear Anna,

Some strange providence brought me to the village on Monte Verità. I found Victor there. He is desperately ill, and I think dying. If you have a message to send him, leave it beneath the wall. I will carry it to him. I must warn you also that I believe your community to be in danger. The people from the valley are frightened and angry because one of their women has disappeared. They are likely to come to Monte Verità, and do damage.

In parting, I want to tell you that Victor has never stopped loving you and thinking about you.

And I signed my name at the bottom of the page.

I started walking towards the wall. As I drew close I could see the slit windows, described to me long ago by Victor, and it came to me that there might be eyes behind them, watching, that beyond each narrow opening there could be a figure, waiting.

I stooped and put the letters on the ground beneath the wall. As I did so, the wall before me swung back suddenly and opened. Arms stretched forth from the yawning gap and seized me, and I was flung to the ground, with hands about my throat.

The last thing I heard, before losing consciousness, was the sound of a boy, laughing.

I awoke with violence, jerked back into reality from some great depth of slumber, and I knew that a moment before I had not been alone. Someone had been beside me, kneeling, peering down into my sleeping face.

I sat up and looked about me, cold and numb. I was in a cell about ten foot long, and the daylight, ghostly pale, filtered through the narrow slit in the stone wall. I glanced at my watch. The hands pointed to a quarter to five. I must have lain unconscious for a little over four hours, and this was the false light that comes before dawn.

My first feeling now, on waking, was one of anger. I had been fooled.

The people in the village below Monte Verità had lied to me, and to Victor too. The rough hands that had seized me, and the boy's laugh that I heard, these had belonged to the villagers themselves. That man and his son had preceded me up the mountain track, and had lain in wait for me. They knew a way of entry through the walls. They had fooled Victor through the years, and thought to fool me too. God alone knew their motive. It could not be robbery. We neither of us had anything but the clothes we wore. This cell into which they had thrust me was quite bare. No sign of human habitation, not even a board on which to lie. A strange thing, though—they had not bound me. And there was no door to the cell. The entry was open, a long slit, like the window, but large enough to permit the passage of a single form.

I sat waiting for the light to strengthen and for the feeling, too, to come back to my shoulders, arms, and legs. My sense of caution told me this was wise. If I ventured through the opening now, I might in the dim light stumble, and fall, and be lost in some labyrinth of passageway or stair.

My anger grew with the daylight, yet with it also a feeling of despair. I longed more than anything to get hold of the fellow and his son, threaten them both, fight them if necessary—I would not be thrown to the ground a second time unawares. But what if they had gone away and left me in this place, without means of exit? Supposing this, then, was the trick they played on strangers, and had done so through countless years, the old man before them, and others before him, luring the women from the valley too, and once inside these walls leaving the victims to starvation and death? The uneasiness mounting in me would turn to panic if I thought too far ahead, and to calm myself I felt in my pocket for my cigarette case. The first few puff's steadied me; the smell and the taste of the smoke belonged to the world I knew.

Then I saw the frescoes. The growing light betrayed them to me. They covered the walls of the cell, and were drawn upon the ceiling too. Not the rough primitive efforts of uncultured peasants, nor yet the saintly scrawling of religious artists, deeply moved by faith. These frescoes had life and vigour, colour and intensity, and whether they told a story or not, I did not know, but the motif was clearly worship of the moon. Some figures knelt, others stood; one and all had their arms up, raised to the full moon traced upon the ceiling. Yet in some strange fashion the eyes of the worshippers, drawn with uncanny skill, looked down upon me, not upwards to the moon. I smoked my cigarette and looked away, but all the time I felt their eyes fasten on me, as the day-light grew, and it was like being back outside the walls again, aware of silent watchers from behind the slit windows.

I got up, stamping on my cigarette, and it seemed to me that any-thing would be better than to remain there in the cell, alone with those figures on the painted walls. I moved to the opening, and as I did so I heard the laughter once again. Softer this time, as though subdued, but mocking and youthful still. That damned boy . . .

I plunged through the opening, cursing him and shouting. He might have a knife upon him, but I didn't care. And there he was, flattened against the wall, waiting for me. I could see the gleam of his eyes, and I saw his close-cropped hair. I struck at his face, and missed. I heard him laughing as he slipped to one side. Then he wasn't alone any more; there was another just behind, and a third. They threw themselves upon me and I was borne to the ground as though I had no strength at all, and the first one knelt with his knee on my chest and his hands about my throat, and he was smiling at me.

I lay fighting for breath, and he relaxed his grip, and the three of them watched me, with that same mocking smile upon their lips. I saw then that none of them was the boy from the village, nor was the father there, and they did not have the faces of village people or of the valley people: their faces were like the painted frescoes on the wall.

Their eyes were heavy-lidded, slanting, without mercy, like the eyes I had seen once long ago on an Egyptian tomb, and on a vase long hid-den and forgotten under the dust and rubble of a buried city. Each wore a tunic to his knees, with bare arms, bare legs, and hair cropped close to the head, and there was a strange austere beauty about them, and a devilish grace as well. I tried to raise myself from the ground, but the one who had his hand upon my throat pressed me back, and I knew I was no match for him or his companions, and if they wanted to they could throw me from the walls down to the depths below Monte Verità. This was the end, then. It was only a matter of time, and Victor would die alone, back in the hut on the mountainside.

"Go ahead," I said, "have done with it," resigned, caring no longer. I expected the laughter again, mocking and youthful, and the sudden seizing of my body with their hands, and the savage thrusting of me through the slit window to darkness and to death. I closed my eyes, and with nerves taut braced myself for horror. Nothing happened. I felt the boy touch my lips. I opened my eyes, and he was smiling still, and he had a cup in his hands, with milk in it, and he was urging me to drink, but he did not speak. I shook my head, but his companions came and knelt behind me, supporting my shoulders and my back, and I began to drink, foolishly, gratefully, like a child. The fear went as they held me, and the horror too, and it was as though strength passed from their hands to mine, and not only to my hands but to the whole of me.

When I had finished drinking the first one took the cup from me and put it on the ground, then he placed his two hands on my heart, his fingers touching, and the feeling that came to me was something I had never experienced in my life before. It was as if the peace of God came upon me, quiet and strong, and, with the touch of hands, took from me all anxiety and fear, all the fatigue and terror of the preceding night; and my memory of the cloud and mist on the mountain, and Victor dying on his lonely bed, became suddenly things of no importance. They shrank into insignificance beside this feeling of strength and beauty that I knew now. If Victor died it would not matter. His body would be a shell lying there in the peasant hut, but his heart would be beating here, as mine was beating, and his mind would come to us too.

I say "to us" because it seemed to me, sitting there in the narrow cell, that I had been accepted by my companions and made one of them. "This," I thought to myself, still wondering but bewildered, happy, "this is what I always hoped that death would be. The negation of all pain and all distress, and the centre of life flowing, not from the quibbling brain, but from the heart."

The boy took his hands from me, still smiling, but the feeling of strength, of power, was with me still. He rose to his feet and I did the same, and I followed him and the two others through the gap in the cell. There was no honeycomb of twisting corridors, no dark cloisters, but a great open court on to which the cells all gave, and the fourth side of the court led upwards to the twin peaks of Monte Verità, ice-capped, beautiful, caught now in the rose light of the rising sun. Steps cut in the ice led to the summit, and now I knew the reason for the silence within the walls and in the court as well, for there were the other ones, ranged upon the steps, dressed in those same tunics, with bare arms and legs, girdles about the waist, and the hair cropped close to the head.

We passed through the court and up the steps beside them. There was no sound: they did not speak to me or to one another, but they smiled as the first three had done; and their smile was neither courteous nor tender, as we know it in the world, but had a strange exulting quality, as if wisdom and triumph and passion were all blended into one. They were ageless, they were sexless, they were neither male nor female, old nor young, but the beauty of their faces, and of their bodies too, was more stirring and exciting than anything I had ever seen or known, and with a sudden longing I wanted to be one of them, to be dressed as they were dressed, to love as they must love, to laugh and worship and be silent.

I looked down at my coat and shirt, my climbing breeches, my thick socks and shoes, and suddenly I hated and despised them. They were like grave clothes covering the dead, and I flung them off, in haste to have them gone, throwing them over my shoulder down to the court below; and I stood naked under the sun. I was without embarrassment or shame. I was quite unconscious how I looked and I did not care. All I knew was that I wanted to have done with the trappings of the world, and my clothes seemed to symbolise the self I had once been.

We climbed the steps and reached the summit, and now the whole world lay before us, without mist or cloud, the lesser peaks stretching away into infinity, and far below, concerning us not at all, hazy and green and still, were the valleys and the streams and the little sleeping towns. Then, turning from the world below, I saw that the twin peaks of Monte Verità were divided by a great crevasse, narrow yet impassable, and standing on the summit, gazing downwards, I realised with wonder, and with awe as well, that my eyes could not penetrate the depths. The ice-blue walls of the crevasse descended smooth and hard without a break to some great bottomless chasm, hidden forever in the mountain heart. The sun that rose to bathe the peaks at midday would never touch the depths of that crevasse, nor would the rays of the full moon come to it, but it seemed to me, between the peaks, that the shape of it was like a chalice held between two hands.

Someone was standing there, dressed in white from head to foot, on the very brink of the chasm, and although I could not see her features, for the cowl of the white robe concealed them, the tall upright figure, with head thrown back and arms outstretched, caught at my heart with sudden tense excitement.

I knew it was Anna. I knew that no one else would stand in just that way. I forgot Victor, I forgot my mission, I forgot time and place and all the years between. I remembered only the stillness of her presence, the beauty of her face, and that quiet voice saying to me, "We are both in search of the same thing, after all." I knew then that I had loved her always, and that though she had met Victor first, and chosen him, and married him, the ties and ceremony of marriage concerned neither of us, and never had. Our minds had met and crossed and understood from the first moment when Victor introduced us in my club, and that queer, inexplicable bond of the heart breaking, through every barrier, every restraint, had kept us close to one another always, in spite of silence, absence, and long years of separation.

The mistake was mine from the beginning in letting her go alone to find her mountain. Had I gone with them, she and Victor, when they asked me that day in the Map House long ago, intuition would have told me what was in her mind and the spell would have come upon me as well. I would not have slept on in the hut, as Victor had slept, but would have wakened and gone with her, and the years that I had wasted and thrown away, futile and misspent, would have been our years, Anna's and mine, shared here on the mountain, cut off from the world.

Once again I looked about me and at the faces of those who stood beside me, and I guessed dimly, with a sort of hunger near to pain, what ecstasy of love they knew that I had never known. Their silence was not a vow, condemning them to darkness, but a peace that the mountain gave to them, merging their minds in tune. There was no need for speech, when a smile, a glance, conveyed a message and a thought; while laughter, triumphant always, sprang from the heart's centre, never to be suppressed. This was no closed order, gloomy, sepulchral, denying all that instinct gave the heart. Here Life was fulfilled, clamouring, intense, and the great heat of the sun seeped into the veins, becoming part of the blood stream, part of the living flesh; and the frozen air, merging with the direct rays of the sun, cleansed the body and the lungs, bringing power and strength—the power I had felt when the fingers touched my heart.

In the space of so short a while my values had all changed, and the self who had climbed the mountain through the mist, fearful, anxious and angry too, but a little while ago, seemed to exist no more. I was grey-haired, past middle age, a madman to the world's eyes if they could see me now, a laughingstock, a fool; and I stood naked with the rest of them on Monte Verità and held up my arms to the sun. It rose now in the sky and shone upon us, and the blistering of my skin was pain and pleasure blended, and the heat drove through my heart and through my lungs.

I kept my eyes fixed on Anna, loving her with such intensity that I heard myself calling aloud, "Anna . . . Anna . . ." And she knew that I was there, for she lifted her hand in signal. None of them minded, none of them cared. They laughed with me, they understood.

Then from the midst of us came a girl, walking. She was dressed in a simple village frock, with stockings and shoes, and her hair hung loose on her shoulders. I thought her hands were folded together, as though in prayer, but they were not. She held them to her heart, the fingers touching.

She went to the brink of the crevasse, where Anna stood. Last night, beneath the moon, I should have been gripped by fear, but not now. I had been accepted. I was one of them. For one instant, in its space of time above us in the sky, the sun's ray touched the lip of the crevasse, and the blue ice shone. We knelt with one accord, our faces to the sun, and I heard the hymn of praise.

"This," I thought, "was how men worshipped in the beginning, how they will worship in the end. Here is no creed, no saviour, and no deity. Only the sun, which gives us light and life. This is how it has always been, from the beginning of time."

The sun's ray lifted and passed on, and then the girl, rising to her feet, threw off her stockings and her shoes and her dress also, and Anna, with a knife in her hand, cut off her hair, cropping it close above the ears. The girl stood before her, her hands upon her heart.

"Now she is free," I thought. "She won't go back to the valley again. Her parents will mourn her, and her young man too, and they'll never discover what she has found here on Monte Verità. In the valley there would have been feasting and celebration, and then dancing at the wedding, and afterwards the turmoil of a brief romance turning to humdrum married life, the cares of her house, the cares of children, anxiety, fret, illness, trouble, the day-by-day routine of growing old. Now she is spared all that. Here, nothing once felt is lost. Love and beauty don't die or fade away. Living's hard, because Nature's hard, and

Nature has no mercy; but it was this she wanted in the valley, it was for this she came. She will know everything here that she never knew before and would not have discovered, below there in the world. Passion and joy and laughter, the heat of the sun, the tug of the moon, love without emotion, sleep with no waking dream. And that's why they hate it, in the valley, that's why they're afraid of Monte Verità. Because here on the summit is something they don't possess and never will, so they are angry and envious and unhappy."

Then Anna turned, and the girl who had thrown her sex away with her past life and her village clothes followed barefoot, bare-armed, cropped-haired like the others; and she was radiant, smiling, and I knew that nothing would ever matter to her again.

They descended to the court, leaving me alone on the summit, and I felt like an outcast before the gates of heaven. My brief moment had come and gone. They belonged here, and I did not. I was a stranger from the world below.

I put on my clothes again, restored to a sanity I did not want, and remembering Victor and my mission, I too went down the steps to the court and, looking upwards, I saw that Anna was waiting for me in the tower above.

The others flattened themselves against the wall to let me pass, and I saw that Anna alone amongst them wore the long white robe and the cowl. The tower was lofty, open to the sky, and characteristically, with that same gesture I remembered when she used to sit on the low stool before the fire in the great hall, Anna sat down now, on the topmost step of the tower, one knee raised and elbow on that knee. Today was yesterday, today was six-and-twenty years ago, and we were alone once more in the manor house in Shropshire; and the peace she had brought to me then she brought me now. I wanted to kneel beside her and take her hand. Instead I went and stood beside the wall, my arms folded.

"So you found it at last," she said. "It took a little time."

The voice was soft and still and quite unchanged.

"Did you bring me here?" I asked. "Did you call me when the aircraft crashed?"

She laughed, and I had never been away from her. Time stood still on Monte Verità.

"I wanted you to come long before that," she said, "but you shut your mind away from me. It was like clamping down a receiver. It always took two to make a telephone call. Does it still?"

"It does," I answered, "and our more modern inventions need valves for contact. Not the mind, though."

"Your mind has been a box for so many years," she said. "It was a pity—we could have shared so much. Victor had to tell me his thoughts in letters, which wouldn't have been necessary with you."

It was then, I think, that the first hope came to me. I must feel my way towards it, though, with care.

"You've read his letter," I asked, "and mine as well? You know that he's dying?"

"Yes," she said, "he's been ill for many weeks. That's why I wanted you to be here at this time, so that you could be with him when he died. And it will be all right for him, now, when you go back to him and tell him that you've spoken to me. He'll be happy then."

"Why not come yourself?"

"Better this way," she said. "Then he can keep his dream."

His dream? What did she mean? They were not, then, all-powerful here on Monte Verità? She understood the danger in which they stood.

"Anna," I said, "I'll do what you want me to do. I'll return to Victor and be with him at the last. But time is very short. More important still is the fact that you and the others here are in great danger. Tomorrow, tonight even, the people from the valley are going to climb here to Monte Verità, and they'll break into this place and kill you. It's imperative that you get away before they come. If you have no means of saving yourselves, then you must allow me to do something to help you. We are not so far from civilisation as to make that impossible. I can get down to the valley, find a telephone, get through to the police, to the army, to some authority in charge . . ."

My words trailed off, because although my plans were not clear in my own mind I wanted her to have confidence in me, to feel that she could trust me.

"The point is," I told her, "that life is going to be impossible for you here, from now on. If I can prevent the attack this time, which is doubtful, it will happen next week, next month. Your days of security are numbered. You've lived here shut away so long that you don't understand the state of the world as it is now. Even this country here is torn in two with suspicion, and the people in the valley aren't superstitious peasants any longer; they're armed with modern weapons, and they've got murder in their hearts. You won't stand a chance, you and the rest, here on Monte Verità."

She did not answer. She sat there on the step, listening, a remote and silent figure in her white robe and cowl.

"Anna," I said, "Victor's dying. He may be already dead. When you leave here he can't help you, but I can. I've loved you always. No need to tell you that, you must have guessed it. You destroyed two men, you know, when you came to live on Monte Verità six-and-twenty years ago. But that doesn't matter any more. I've found you again. And there are still places far away, inaccessible to civilisation, where we could live, you and I—and the others with you here, if they wished to come with us. I have money enough to arrange all that; you won't have to worry about anything."

I saw myself discussing practicalities with consuls, embassies, going into the question of passports, papers, clothing.

I saw too, in my mind's eye, the map of the world. I ranged in thought from a ridge of mountains in South America to the Himalayas, from the Himalayas to Africa. Or the northern wastes of Canada were still vast and unexplored, and stretches of Greenland. And there were islands, innumerable, countless islands, where no man ever trod, visited only by sea birds, washed by the lonely sea. Mountain or island, scrubby wilderness or desert, impenetrable forest or Arctic waste, I did not care which she chose; but I had been without sight of her for so long, and now all I wanted was to be with her always.

This was now possible, because Victor, who would have claimed her, was going to die. I was blunt. I was truthful. I told her this as well. And then I waited, to hear what she would say.

She laughed, that warm, much-loved and well-remembered laugh, and I wanted to go to her and put my arms round her, because the laugh held so much life in it, and so much joy and promise.

"Well?" I said.

Then she got up from the step and came and stood beside me, very still.

"There was once a man," she said, "who went to the booking office at Waterloo and said to the clerk eagerly, hopefully, 'I want a ticket to Paradise. A single ticket. No return.' And when the clerk told him there was no such place the man picked up the inkwell and threw it in the clerk's face. The police were summoned, and took the man away and put him in prison. Isn't that what you're asking of me now, a ticket to Paradise? This is the mountain of truth, which is very different."

I felt hurt, irritated even. She hadn't taken a word of my plans seriously and was making fun of me.

"What do you propose, then?" I asked. "To wait here, behind these walls, for the people to come and break them down?"

"Don't worry about us," she said. "We know what we shall do."

She spoke with indifference, as if the matter was of no importance, and in agony I saw the future that I had begun to plan for us both slip away from me.

"Then you do possess some secret?" I asked, almost in accusation. "You can work some miracle, and save yourself and the others too? What about me? Can't you take me with you?"

"You wouldn't want to come," she said. She put her hand on my arm. "It takes time, you know, to build a Monte Verità. It isn't just doing without clothes and worshipping the sun."

"I realise that," I told her. "I'm prepared to begin all over again, to learn new values, to start from the beginning. I know that nothing I've done in the world is any use. Talent, hard work, success, all those things are meaningless. But if I could be with you . . ."

"How? With me?" she said.

And I did not know what to answer, because it would be too sudden and too direct, but I knew in my heart that what I wanted was everything that could be between a woman and a man; not at first, of course, but later, when we had found our other mountain, or our wilderness, or wherever it was we might go to hide ourselves from the world. There was no need to rehearse all that now. The point was that I was prepared to follow her anywhere, if she would let me.

"I love you, and have always loved you. Isn't that enough?" I asked.

"No," she said, "not on Monte Verità."

And she threw back her cowl and I saw her face.

I gazed at her in horror. . . . I could not move, I could not speak. It was as though all feeling had been frozen. My heart was cold. . . . One side of her face was eaten quite away, ravaged, terrible. The disease had come upon her brow, her cheek, her throat, blotching, searing the skin. The eyes that I had loved were blackened, sunk deep into the sockets.

"You see," she said, "it isn't Paradise."

I think I turned away. I don't remember. I know I leant against the rock of the tower and stared down into the depths below, and saw nothing but the great bank of cloud that hid the world.

"It happened to others," Anna said, "but they died. If I survived longer, it was because I was hardier than they. Leprosy can come to anyone, even to the supposed immortals of Monte Verità. It hasn't really mattered, you know. I regret nothing. Long ago I remember telling you that those who go to the mountains must give everything. That's all there is to it. I no longer suffer, so there's no need to suffer for me."

I said nothing. I felt the tears run down my face. I didn't bother to wipe them away.

"There are no illusions and no dreams on Monte Verità," she said. "They belong to the world, and you belong there too. If I've destroyed the fantasy you made of me, forgive me. You've lost the Anna you knew once, and found another one instead. Which you will remember longer rather depends upon yourself. Now go back to your world of men and women and build yourself a Monte Verità."

Somewhere there was scrub and grass and stunted trees; somewhere there was earth and stones and the sound of running water. Deep in the valley there were homes, where men lived with their women, reared their children. They had firelight, curling smoke, and lighted windows. Somewhere there were roads, there were railways, there were cities. So many cities, so many streets. And all with crowded buildings, lighted windows. They were there, beneath the cloud, beneath Monte Verità.

"Don't be anxious or afraid," said Anna, "and as for the valley people, they can't harm us. One thing only . . ." She paused, and although I did not look at her I think she smiled. "Let Victor keep his dream," she said.

Then she took my hand, and we went down the steps of the tower together, and through the court and to the walls of the rock face. They stood there watching us, those others, with their bare arms and legs, their close-cropped hair, and I saw too the little village girl, the proselyte, who had renounced the world and was now one of them. I saw her turn and look at Anna, and I saw the expression in her eyes; there was no horror there, no fear and no revulsion. One and all they looked at Anna with triumph, with exultation, with all knowledge and all understanding. And I knew that what she felt and what she endured they felt also, and shared with her, and accepted. She was not alone.

They turned their eyes to me, and their expression changed; instead of love and knowledge, I read compassion.

Anna did not say good-bye. She put her hand an instant on my shoulder. Then the wall opened, and she was gone from me. The sun was no longer overhead. It had started its journey in the western sky. The great white banks of cloud rolled upward from the world below. I turned my back on Monte Verità.

It was evening when I came to the village. The moon had not yet risen. Presently, within two hours or less, it would top the eastern ridge of the further mountains and give light to the whole sky. They were waiting, the people from the valley. There must have been three hundred or more, waiting there in groups beside the huts. All of them were armed, some with rifles, with grenades, others, more primitive, with picks and axes. They had kindled fires, on the village track between the huts, and had brought provisions too. They stood or sat before the fires, eating and drinking, smoking and talking. Some of them had dogs held tightly on a leash.

The owner of the first hut stood by the door with his son. They too were armed. The boy had a pick and a knife thrust in his belt. The man watched me with his sullen, stupid face.

"Your friend is dead," he said. "He has been dead these many hours."

I pushed past him and went into the living-room of the hut. Candles had been lit. One at the head of the bed, one at the foot. I bent over Victor and took his hand. The man had lied to me. Victor was breathing still. When he felt me touch his hand, he opened his eyes.

"Did you see her?" he asked.

"Yes," I answered.

"Something told me you would," he said. "Lying here, I felt that it would happen. She's my wife, and I've loved her all these years, but you only have been allowed to see her. Too late, isn't it, to be jealous now?"

The candlelight was dim. He could not see the shadows by the door, nor hear the movement and the whispering without.

"Did you give her my letter?" he said.

"She has it," I answered. "She told you not to worry, not to be anxious. She is all right. Everything is well with her."

Victor smiled. He let go my hand.

"So it's true," he said, "all the dreams I had of Monte Verità. She is happy and contented and she will never grow old, never lose her beauty. Tell me, her hair, her eyes, her smile—were they still the same?"

"Just the same," I said. "Anna will always be the most beautiful woman you or I have ever known."

He did not answer. And as I waited there beside him, I heard the sudden blowing of a horn, echoed by a second and a third. I heard the restless movement of the men outside in the village as they shouldered their weapons, kicked out the fires, and gathered together for the climb. I heard the dogs barking and the men laughing, ready now, excited. When they had gone I went and stood alone in the deserted village, and I watched the full moon rising from the dark valley.

The Apple Tree

It was three months after she died that he first noticed the apple tree. He had known of its existence, of course, with the others, standing upon the lawn in front of the house, sloping upwards to the field beyond. Never before, though, had he been aware of this particular tree looking in any way different from its fellows, except that it was the third one on the left, a little apart from the rest and leaning more closely to the terrace.

It was a fine clear morning in early spring, and he was shaving by the open window. As he leant out to sniff the air, the lather on his face, the razor in his hand, his eye fell upon the apple tree. It was a trick of light, perhaps, something to do with the sun coming up over the woods, that happened to catch the tree at this particular moment; but the likeness was unmistakable.

He put his razor down on the window ledge and stared. The tree was scraggy and of a depressing thinness, possessing none of the gnarled solidity of its companions. Its few branches, growing high up on the trunk like narrow shoulders on a tall body, spread themselves in martyred resignation, as though chilled by the fresh morning air. The roll of wire circling the tree, and reaching to about halfway up the truck from the base, looked like a grey tweed skirt covering lean limbs; while the topmost branch, sticking up into the air above the ones below, yet sagging slightly, could have been a drooping head poked forward in an attitude of weariness.

How often he had seen Midge stand like this, dejected. No matter where it was, whether in the garden, or in the house, or even shopping in the town, she would take upon herself this same stooping posture, suggesting that life treated her hardly, that she had been singled out from her fellows to carry some impossible burden, but in spite of it would endure to the end without complaint. "Midge, you look worn out, for heaven's sake sit down and take a rest!" But the words would be received with the inevitable shrug of the shoulder, the inevitable sigh, "Someone has got to keep things going," and, straightening herself, she would embark upon the dreary routine of unnecessary tasks she forced herself to do, day in, day out, through the interminable changeless years.

He went on staring at the apple tree. That martyred bent position, the stooping top, the weary branches, the few withered leaves that had not blown away with the wind and rain of the past winter and now shivered in the spring breeze like wispy hair; all of it protested soundlessly to the owner of the garden looking upon it, "I am like this because of you, because of your neglect."

He turned away from the window and went on shaving. It would not do to let his imagination run away with him and start building fancies in his mind just when he was settling at long last to freedom. He bathed and dressed and went down to breakfast. Eggs and bacon were waiting for him on the hot plate, and he carried the dish to the single place laid for him at the dining table. *The Times*, folded smooth and new, was ready for him to read. When Midge was alive he had handed it to her first, from long custom, and when she gave it back to him after breakfast, to take with him to the study, the pages were always in the wrong order and folded crookedly, so that part of the pleasure of reading it was spoilt. The news, too, would be stale to him after she had read the worst of it aloud, which was a morning habit she used to take upon herself, always adding some derogatory remark of her own about what she read. The birth of a daughter to mutual friends would bring a click of the tongue, a little jerk of the head. "Poor things, another girl," or if a son, "A boy can't be much fun to educate these days." He used to think it psychological, because they themselves were childless, that she should so grudge the entry of new life into the world; but as time passed it became thus with all bright or joyous things, as though there was some fundamental blight upon good cheer.

"It says here that more people went on holiday this year than ever before. Let's hope they enjoyed themselves, that's all." But no hope lay in her words, only disparagement. Then, having finished breakfast, she would push back her chair and sigh and say, "Oh well . . ." leaving the sentence unfinished; but the sigh, the shrug of the shoulders, the slope of her long, thin back as she stooped to clear the dishes from the serving table—thus sparing work for the daily maid—were all part of her long-term reproach, directed at him, that had marred their existence over a span of years.

Silent, punctilious, he would open the door for her to pass through to the kitchen quarters, and she would labour past him, stooping under the weight of the laden tray that there was no need for her to carry, and presently, through the half-open door, he would hear the swish of the running water from the pantry tap. He would return to his chair and sit down again, the crumpled *Times*, a smear of marmalade upon it, lying against the toast rack; and once again, with monotonous insistence, the question hammered at his mind, "What have I done?"

It was not as though she nagged. Nagging wives, like mothers-in-law, were chestnut jokes for music halls. He could not remember Midge ever losing her temper or quarrelling. It was just that the undercurrent of reproach, mingled with suffering nobly borne, spoilt the atmosphere of his home and drove him to a sense of furtiveness and guilt.

Perhaps it would be raining and he, seeking sanctuary within his study, electric fire aglow, his after-breakfast pipe filling the small room with smoke, would settle down before his desk in a pretence of writing letters, but in reality to hide, to feel the snug security of four safe walls that were his alone. Then the door would open and Midge, struggling into a raincoat, her wide-brimmed felt hat pulled low over her brow, would pause and wrinkle her nose in distaste.

"Phew! What a fug."

He said nothing, but moved slightly in his chair, covering with his arm the novel he had chosen from a shelf in idleness.

"Aren't you going into the town?" she asked him.

"I had not thought of doing so."

"Oh! Oh well, it doesn't matter." She turned away again towards the door.

"Why, is there anything you want done?"

"It's only the fish for lunch. They don't deliver on Wednesdays. Still, I can go myself if you are busy. I only thought . . ."

She was out of the room without finishing her sentence.

"It's all right, Midge," he called, "I'll get the car and go and fetch it presently. No sense in getting wet."

Thinking she had not heard, he went out into the hall. She was standing by the open front door, the mizzling rain driving in upon her. She had a long flat basket over her arm and was drawing on a pair of gardening gloves.

"I'm bound to get wet in any case," she said, "so it doesn't make much odds. Look at those flowers, they all need staking. I'll go for the fish when I've finished seeing to them."

Argument was useless. She had made up her mind. He shut the front door after her and sat down again in the study. Somehow the room no longer felt so snug, and a little later, raising his head to the window, he saw her hurry past, her raincoat not buttoned properly and flapping, little drips of water forming on the brim of her hat and the garden basket filled with limp Michaelmas daisies already dead. His conscience pricking him, he bent down and turned out one bar of the electric fire.

Or yet again it would be spring, it would be summer. Strolling out hatless into the garden, his hands in his pockets, with no other purpose in his mind but to feel the sun upon his back and stare out upon the woods and fields and the slow winding river, he would hear, from the bedrooms above, the high-pitched whine of the Hoover slow down suddenly, gasp, and die. Midge called down to him as he stood there on the terrace.

"Were you going to do anything?" she said.

He was not. It was the smell of spring, of early summer, that had driven him out into the garden. It was the delicious knowledge that, being retired now, no longer working in the City, time was a thing of no account, he could waste it as he pleased.

"No," he said, "not on such a lovely day. Why?"

"Oh, never mind," she answered, "it's only that the wretched drain under the kitchen window has gone wrong again. Completely plugged up and choked. No one ever sees to it, that's why. I'll have a go at it myself this afternoon."

Her face vanished from the window. Once more there was a gasp, a rising groan of sound, and the Hoover warmed to its task again. What foolishness that such an interruption could damp the brightness of the day. Not the demand, nor the task itself—clearing a drain was in its own way a schoolboy piece of folly, playing with mud—but that wan face of hers looking out upon the sunlit terrace, the hand that went up wearily to push back a strand of falling hair, and the inevitable sigh before she turned from the window, the unspoken "I wish I had the time to stand and do nothing in the sun. Oh well . . ."

He had ventured to ask once why so much cleaning of the house was necessary. Why there must be the incessant turning out of rooms. Why chairs must be lifted to stand upon other chairs, rugs rolled up and ornaments huddled together on a sheet of newspaper. And why, in particular, the sides of the upstairs corridor, on which no one ever trod, must be polished laboriously by hand, Midge and the daily woman taking it in turns to crawl upon their knees the whole endless length of it, like slaves of bygone days.

Midge had stared at him, not understanding.

"You'd be the first to complain," she said, "if the house was like a pigsty. You like your comforts."

So they lived in different worlds, their minds not meeting. Had it been always so? He did not remember. They had been married nearly twenty-five years and were two people who, from force of habit, lived under the same roof.

When he had been in business, it seemed different. He had not noticed it so much. He came home to eat, to sleep, and to go up by train again in the morning. But when he retired he became aware of her forcibly, and day by day his sense of her resentment, of her disapproval, grew stronger.

Finally, in that last year before she died, he felt himself engulfed in it, so that he was led into every sort of petty deception to get away from her, making a pretence of going up to London to have his hair cut, to see the dentist, to lunch with an old business friend; and in reality he would be sitting by his club window, anonymous, at peace.

It was mercifully swift, the illness that took her from him. Influenza, followed by pneumonia, and she was dead within a week. He hardly knew how it happened, except that as usual she was overtired and caught a cold, and would not stay in bed. One evening, coming home by the late train from London, having sneaked into a cinema during the afternoon, finding release amongst the crowd of warm friendly people enjoying themselves—for it was a bitter December day—he found her bent over the furnace in the cellar, poking and thrusting at the lumps of coke.

She looked up at him, white with fatigue, her face drawn.

"Why, Midge, what on earth are you doing?" he said.

"It's the furnace," she said, "we've had trouble with it all day, it won't stay alight. We shall have to get the men to see it tomorrow. I really cannot manage this sort of thing myself."

There was a streak of coal dust on her cheek. She let the stubby poker fall on the cellar floor. She began to cough, and as she did so winced with pain.

"You ought to be in bed," he said, "I never heard of such nonsense. What the dickens does it matter about the furnace?"

"I thought you would be home early," she said, "and then you might have known how to deal with it. It's been bitter all day, I can't think what you found to do with yourself in London."

She climbed the cellar stairs slowly, her back bent, and when she reached the top she stood shivering and half closed her eyes.

"If you don't mind terribly," she said, "I'll get your supper right away, to have it done with. I don't want anything myself."

"To hell with my supper," he said, "I can forage for myself. You go up to bed. I'll bring you a hot drink."

"I tell you, I don't want anything," she said. "I can fill my hot-water bottle myself. I only ask one thing of you. And that is to remember to turn out the lights everywhere, before you come up." She turned into the hall, her shoulders sagging.

"Surely a glass of hot milk?" he began uncertainly, starting to take off his overcoat; and as he did so the torn half of the ten-and-sixpenny seat at the cinema fell from his pocket on to the floor. She saw it. She said nothing. She coughed again and began to drag herself upstairs.

The next morning her temperature was a hundred and three. The doctor came and said she had pneumonia. She asked if she might go to a private ward in the cottage hospital, because having a nurse in the house would make too much work. This was on the Tuesday morning. She went there right away, and they told him on the Friday evening that she was not likely to live through the night. He stood inside the room, after they told him, looking down at her in the high impersonal hospital bed, and his heart was wrung with pity, because surely they had given her too many pillows, she was propped too high, there could be no rest for her that way. He had brought some flowers, but there seemed no purpose now in giving them to the nurse to arrange, because Midge was too ill to look at them. In a sort of delicacy he put them on a table beside the screen, when the nurse was bending down to her.

"Is there anything she needs?" he said. "I mean, I can easily . . ." He did not finish the sentence, he left it in the air, hoping the nurse would understand his intention, that he was ready to go off in the car, drive somewhere, fetch what was required.

The nurse shook her head. "We will telephone you," she said, "if there is any change."

What possible change could there be? he wondered as he found himself outside the hospital. The white pinched face upon the pillows would not alter now, it belonged to no one.

Midge died in the early hours of Saturday morning.

He was not a religious man, he had no profound belief in immortality, but when the funeral was over, and Midge was buried, it distressed him to think of her poor lonely body lying in that brand-new coffin with the brass handles: it seemed such a churlish thing to permit. Death should be different. It should be like bidding farewell to someone at a station before a long journey, but without the strain. There was something of indecency in this haste to bury underground the thing that but for ill-chance would be a living, breathing person. In his distress he fancied he could hear Midge saying with a sigh, "Oh well . . ." as they lowered the coffin into the open grave.

He hoped with fervour that after all there might be a future in some unseen Paradise and that poor Midge, unaware of what they were doing to her mortal remains, walked somewhere in green fields. But who with? he wondered. Her parents had died in India many years ago; she would not have much in common with them now if they met her at the gates of Heaven. He had a sudden picture of her waiting her turn in a queue, rather far back, as was always her fate in queues, with that large shopping bag of woven straw which she took everywhere, and on her face that patient martyred look. As she passed through the turnstile into Paradise she looked at him reproachfully.

These pictures, of the coffin and the queue, remained with him for about a week, fading a little day by day. Then he forgot her. Freedom was his, and the sunny empty house, the bright crisp winter. The routine he followed belonged to him alone. He never thought of Midge until the morning he looked out upon the apple tree.

Later that day he was taking a stroll round the garden, and he found himself drawn to the tree through curiosity. It had been stupid fancy after all. There was nothing singular about it. An apple tree like any other apple tree. He remembered then that it had always been a poorer tree than its fellows, was in fact more than half dead, and at one time there had been talk of chopping it down, but the talk came to nothing. Well, it would be something for him to do over the week end. Axing a tree was healthy exercise, and apple wood smelt good. It would be a treat to have it burning on the fire.

Unfortunately wet weather set in for nearly a week after that day, and he was unable to accomplish the task he had set himself. No sense in pottering out of doors this weather, and getting a chill into the bargain. He still noticed the tree from his bedroom window. It began to irritate him, humped there, straggling and thin, under the rain. The weather was not cold, and the rain that fell upon the garden was soft and gentle. None of the other trees wore this aspect of dejection. There was one young tree—only planted a few years back, he recalled quite well—growing to the right of the old one and standing straight and firm, the lithe young branches lifted to the sky, positively looking as if it enjoyed the rain. He peered through the window at it, and smiled. Now why the devil should he suddenly remember that incident, years back, during

the war, with the girl who came to work on the land for a few months
at the neighbouring farm? He did not suppose he had thought of her
in months. Besides, there was nothing to it. At week ends he had
helped them at the farm himself—war work of a sort—and she was
always there, cheerful and pretty and smiling; she had dark curling
hair, crisp and boyish, and a skin like a very young apple.

He looked forward to seeing her, Saturdays and Sundays; it was an
antidote to the inevitable news bulletins put on throughout the day by
Midge, and to ceaseless war talk. He liked looking at the child—she
was scarcely more than that, nineteen or so—in her slim breeches and
gay shirts; and when she smiled it was as though she embraced the
world.

He never knew how it happened, and it was such a little thing; but
one afternoon he was in the shed doing something to the tractor,
bending over the engine, and she was beside him, close to his shoulder,
and they were laughing together; and he turned round, to take a bit of
waste to clean a plug, and suddenly she was in his arms and he was
kissing her. It was a happy thing, spontaneous and free, and the girl so
warm and jolly, with her fresh young mouth. Then they went on with
the work of the tractor, but united now, in a kind of intimacy that
brought gaiety to them both, and peace as well. When it was time for
the girl to go and feed the pigs he followed her from the shed, his hand
on her shoulder, a careless gesture that meant nothing really, a half
caress; and as they came out into the yard he saw Midge standing there,
staring at them.

"I've got to go in to a Red Cross meeting," she said. "I can't get the
car to start. I called you. You didn't seem to hear."

Her face was frozen. She was looking at the girl. At once guilt covered
him. The girl said good evening cheerfully to Midge, and crossed the
yard to the pigs.

He went with Midge to the car and managed to start it with the
handle. Midge thanked him, her voice without expression. He found
himself unable to meet her eyes. This, then, was adultery. This was sin.
This was the second page in a Sunday newspaper—"Husband Intimate with Land Girl in Shed. Wife Witnesses Act." His hands were
shaking when he got back to the house and he had to pour himself a
drink. Nothing was ever said. Midge never mentioned the matter. Some
craven instinct kept him from the farm the next week end, and then he

heard that the girl's mother had been taken ill and she had been called back home.

He never saw her again. Why, he wondered, should he remember her suddenly, on such a day, watching the rain falling on the apple trees? He must certainly make a point of cutting down the old dead tree, if only for the sake of bringing more sunshine to the little sturdy one; it hadn't a fair chance, growing there so close to the other.

On Friday afternoon he went round to the vegetable garden to find Willis, the jobbing gardener, who came three days a week, to pay him his wages. He wanted, too, to look in the tool shed and see if the axe and saw were in good condition. Willis kept everything neat and tidy there—this was Midge's training—and the axe and saw were hanging in their accustomed place upon the wall.

He paid Willis his money, and was turning away when the man suddenly said to him, "Funny thing, sir, isn't it, about the old apple tree?"

The remark was so unexpected that it came as a shock. He felt himself change colour.

"Apple tree? What apple tree?" he said.

"Why, the one at the far end, near the terrace," answered Willis. "Been barren as long as I've worked here, and that's some years now. Never an apple from her, nor as much as a sprig of blossom. We were going to chop her up that cold winter, if you remember, and we never did. Well, she's taken on a new lease now. Haven't you noticed?" The gardener watched him, smiling, a knowing look in his eye.

What did the fellow mean? It was not possible that he had been struck also by that fantastic freak resemblance—no, it was out of the question, indecent, blasphemous; besides, he had put it out of his own mind now, he had not thought of it again.

"I've noticed nothing," he said, on the defensive.

Willis laughed. "Come round to the terrace, sir," he said, "I'll show you."

They went together to the sloping lawn, and when they came to the apple tree Willis put his hand up and pulled down a branch within reach. It creaked a little as he did so, as though stiff and unyielding, and Willis brushed away some of the dry lichen and revealed the spiky twigs. "Look there, sir," he said, "she's growing buds. Look at them, feel them for yourself. There's life here yet, and plenty of it. Never known such a thing before. See this branch too." He released the first, and leant up to reach another.

Willis was right. There were buds in plenty, but so small and brown that it seemed to him they scarcely deserved the name; they were more like blemishes upon the twig, dusty, and dry. He put his hands in his pockets. He felt a queer distaste to touch them.

"I don't think they'll amount to much," he said.

"I don't know, sir," said Willis, "I've got hopes. She's stood the winter, and if we get no more bad frosts there's no knowing what we'll see. It would be some joke to watch the old tree blossom. She'll bear fruit yet." He patted the trunk with his open hand, in a gesture at once familiar and affectionate.

The owner of the apple tree turned away. For some reason he felt irritated with Willis. Anyone would think the damned tree lived. And now his plan to axe the tree over the week end would come to nothing.

"It's taking the light from the young tree," he said. "Surely it would be more to the point if we did away with this one, and gave the little one more room?"

He moved across to the young tree and touched a limb. No lichen here. The branches smooth. Buds upon every twig, curling tight. He let go the branch and it sprang away from him, resilient.

"Do away with her, sir," said Willis, "while there's still life in her? Oh no, sir, I wouldn't do that. She's doing no harm to the young tree. I'd give the old tree one more chance. If she doesn't bear fruit, we'll have her down next winter."

"All right, Willis," he said, and walked swiftly away. Somehow he did not want to discuss the matter any more.

That night, when he went to bed, he opened the window wide as usual and drew back the curtains; he could not bear to wake up in the morning and find the room close. It was full moon, and the light shone down upon the terrace and the lawn above it, ghostly pale and still. No wind blew. A hush upon the place. He leant out, loving the silence. The moon shone full upon the little apple tree, the young one. There was a radiance about it in this light that gave it a fairy-tale quality. Small and lithe and slim, the young tree might have been a dancer, her arms upheld, poised ready on her toes for flight. Such a careless, happy grace about it. Brave young tree. Away to the left stood the other one, half of it in shadow still. Even the moonlight could not give it beauty. What in heaven's name was the matter with the thing that it had to stand there, humped and stooping, instead of looking upwards to the light? It marred the still quiet night, it spoilt the setting. He had been a fool to give way to Willis and agree to spare the tree. Those ridiculous buds would never blossom, and even if they did . . .

His thoughts wandered, and for the second time that week he found himself remembering the land girl and her joyous smile. He wondered what had happened to her. Married, probably, with a young family. Made some chap happy, no doubt. Oh well . . . He smiled. Was he going to make use of that expression now? Poor Midge! Then he caught his breath and stood quite still, his hand upon the curtain. The apple tree, the one on the left, was no longer in shadow. The moon shone upon the withered branches, and they looked like skeleton's arms raised in supplication. Frozen arms, stiff and numb with pain. There was no wind, and the other trees were motionless; but there, in those topmost branches, something shivered and stirred, a breeze that came from nowhere and died away again. Suddenly a branch fell from the apple tree to the ground below. It was the near branch, with the small dark buds upon it, which he would not touch. No rustle, no breath of movement came from the other trees. He went on staring at the branch as it lay there on the grass, under the moon. It stretched across the shadow of the young tree close to it, pointing as though in accusation.

For the first time in his life that he could remember he drew the curtains over the window to shut out the light of the moon.

Willis was supposed to keep to the vegetable garden. He had never shown his face much round the front when Midge was alive. That was because Midge attended to the flowers. She even used to mow the grass, pushing the wretched machine up and down the slope, her back bent low over the handles.

It had been one of the tasks she set herself, like keeping the bed-rooms swept and polished. Now Midge was no longer there to attend to the front garden and to tell him where he should work, Willis was always coming through to the front. The gardener liked the change. It made him feel responsible.

"I can't understand how that branch came to fall, sir," he said on the Monday.

"What branch?"

"Why, the branch on the apple tree. The one we were looking at before I left."

"It was rotten, I suppose. I told you the tree was dead."

"Nothing rotten about it, sir. Why, look at it. Broke clean off."

Once again the owner was obliged to follow his man up the slope above the terrace. Willis picked up the branch. The lichen upon it was wet, bedraggled-looking, like matted hair.

"You didn't come again to test the branch, over the week end, and loosen it in some fashion, did you, sir?" asked the gardener.

"I most certainly did not," replied the owner, irritated. "As a matter of fact, I heard the branch fall during the night. I was opening the bedroom window at the time."

"Funny. It was a still night too."

"These things often happen to old trees. Why you bother about this one I can't imagine. Anyone would think . . ."

He broke off; he did not know how to finish the sentence.

"Anyone would think that the tree was valuable," he said.

The gardener shook his head. "It's not the value," he said. "I don't reckon for a moment that this tree is worth any money at all. It's just that after all this time, when we thought her dead, she's alive and kicking, as you might say. Freak of nature, I call it. We'll hope no other branches fall before she blossoms."

Later, when the owner set off for his afternoon walk, he saw the man cutting away the grass below the tree and placing new wire around the base of the trunk. It was quite ridiculous. He did not pay the fellow a fat wage to tinker about with a half-dead tree. He ought to be in the kitchen garden, growing vegetables. It was too much effort, though, to argue with him.

He returned home about half-past five. Tea was a discarded meal since Midge had died, and he was looking forward to his armchair by the fire, his pipe, his whisky-and-soda, and silence.

The fire had not long been lit and the chimney was smoking. There was a queer, rather sickly smell about the living-room. He threw open the windows and went upstairs to change his heavy shoes. When he came down again the smoke still clung about the room and the smell was as strong as ever. Impossible to name it. Sweetish, strange. He called to the woman out in the kitchen.

"There's a funny smell in the house," he said. "What is it?"

The woman came out into the hall from the back.

"What sort of a smell, sir?" she said, on the defensive.

"It's in the living-room," he said. "The room was full of smoke just now. Have you been burning something?"

Her face cleared. "It must be the logs," she said. "Willis cut them up specially, sir, he said you would like them."

"What logs are those?"

"He said it was apple wood, sir, from a branch he had sawed up. Apple wood burns well, I've always heard. Some people fancy it very much. I don't notice any smell myself, but I've got a slight cold."

Together they looked at the fire. Willis had cut the logs small. The woman, thinking to please him, had piled several on top of one another, to make a good fire to last. There was no great blaze. The smoke that came from them was thin and poor. Greenish in colour. Was it possible she did not notice that sickly rancid smell?

"The logs are wet," he said abruptly. "Willis should have known better. Look at them. Quite useless on my fire."

The woman's face took on a set, rather sulky expression. "I'm very sorry," she said. "I didn't notice anything wrong with them when I came to light the fire. They seemed to start well. I've always understood apple wood was very good for burning, and Willis said the same. He told me to be sure and see that you had these on the fire this evening, he had made a special job of cutting them for you. I thought you knew about it and had given orders."

"Oh, all right," he answered abruptly. "I dare say they'll burn in time. It's not your fault."

He turned his back on her and poked at the fire, trying to separate the logs. While she remained in the house there was nothing he could do. To remove the damp smouldering logs and throw them somewhere round the back and then light the fire afresh with dry sticks would arouse comment. He would have to go through the kitchen to the back passage where the kindling wood was kept, and she would stare at him, and come forward and say, "Let me do it, sir. Has the fire gone out then?" No, he must wait until after supper, when she had cleared away and washed up and gone off for the night. Meanwhile, he would endure the smell of the apple wood as best he could.

He poured out his drink, lit his pipe, and stared at the fire. It gave out no heat at all, and with the central heating off in the house the living-room struck chill. Now and again a thin wisp of the greenish smoke puffed from the logs, and with it seemed to come that sweet, sickly smell, unlike any sort of wood smoke that he knew. That interfering fool of a gardener . . . Why saw up the logs? He must have known they were damp. Riddled with damp. He leant forward, staring more closely. Was it damp, though, that oozed there in a thin trickle from the pale logs? No, it was sap, unpleasant, slimy.

He seized the poker, and in a fit of irritation thrust it between the logs, trying to stir them to flame, to change that green smoke into a normal blaze. The effort was useless. The logs would not burn. And all the while the trickle of sap ran on to the grate and the sweet smell filled the room, turning his stomach. He took his glass and his book and went and turned on the electric fire in the study and sat in there instead.

It was idiotic. It reminded him of the old days, how he would make a pretence of writing letters, and go and sit in the study because of Midge in the living-room. She had a habit of yawning in the evenings, when her day's work was done; a habit of which she was quite unconscious. She would settle herself on the sofa with her knitting, the click-click of the needles going fast and furious; and suddenly they would start, those shattering yawns, rising from the depths of her, a prolonged "Ah . . . Ah . . . Hi-oh!" followed by the inevitable sigh. Then there would be silence except for the knitting needles, but as he sat behind his book, waiting, he knew that within a few minutes another yawn would come, another sigh.

A hopeless sort of anger used to stir within him, a longing to throw down his book and say, "Look, if you are so tired, wouldn't it be better if you went to bed?"

Instead, he controlled himself, and after a little while, when he could bear it no longer, he would get up and leave the living-room, and take refuge in the study. Now he was doing the same thing all over again because of the apple logs. Because of the damned sickly smell of the smouldering wood.

He went on sitting in his chair by the desk, waiting for supper. It was nearly nine o'clock before the daily woman had cleared up, turned down his bed, and gone for the night.

He returned to the living-room, which he had not entered since leaving it earlier in the evening. The fire was out. It had made some effort to burn, because the logs were thinner than they had been before, and had sunk low into the basket grate. The ash was meagre, yet the sickly smell clung to the dying embers. He went out into the kitchen and found an empty scuttle and brought it back into the living-room. Then he lifted the logs into it, and the ashes too. There must have been some damp residue in the scuttle, or the logs were still not dry, because as they settled there they seemed to turn darker than before, with a kind of scum upon them. He carried the scuttle down to the cellar, opened the door of the central heating furnace, and threw the lot inside.

He remembered then, too late, that the central heating had been given up now for two or three weeks, owing to the spring weather, and that unless he relit it now the logs would remain there, untouched, until the following winter. He found paper, matches, and a can of paraffin, and, setting the whole alight, closed the door of the furnace and listen to the roar of flames. That would settle it. He waited a moment and then went up the steps, back to the kitchen passage, to lay and relight the fire in the living-room. The business took time, he had to find kindling and coal, but with patience he got the new fire started, and finally settled himself down in his armchair before it.

He had been reading perhaps for twenty minutes before he became aware of the banging door. He put down his book and listened. Nothing at first. Then, yes, there it was again. A rattle, a slam of an unfastened door in the kitchen quarters. He got up and went along to shut it. It was the door at the top of the cellar stairs. He could have sworn he had fastened it. The catch must have worked loose in some way. He switched on the light at the head of the stairs, and bent to examine the catch. There seemed nothing wrong with it. He was about to close the door firmly when he noticed the smell again. The sweet, sickly smell of smouldering apple wood. It was creeping up from the cellar, finding its way to the passage above.

Suddenly, for no reason, he was seized with a kind of fear, a feeling of panic almost. What if the smell filled the whole house through the night, came up from the kitchen quarters to the floor above, and while he slept found its way into his bedroom, choking him, stifling him, so that he could not breathe? The thought was ridiculous, insane—and yet . . .

Once more he forced himself to descend the steps into the cellar.

No sound came from the furnace, no roar of flames. Wisps of smoke, thin and green, oozed their way from the fastened furnace door; it was this that he had noticed from the passage above.

He went to the furnace and threw open the door. The paper had all burnt away, and the few shavings with them. But the logs, the apple logs, had not burnt at all. They lay there as they had done when he threw them in, one charred limb above another, black and huddled, like the bones of someone darkened and dead by fire. Nausea rose in him. He thrust his handkerchief into his mouth, choking. Then scarcely knowing what he did, he ran up the steps to find the empty scuttle, and with a shovel and tongs tried to pitch the logs back into it, scraping for them through the narrow door of the furnace. He was retching in his belly all the while. At last the scuttle was filled, and he carried it up the steps and through the kitchen to the back door.

He opened the door. Tonight there was no moon and it was raining. Turning up the collar of his coat, he peered about him in the darkness, wondering where he should throw the logs. Too wet and dark to stagger all the way to the kitchen garden and chuck them on the rubbish heap, but in the field behind the garage the grass was thick and long and they might lie there hidden. He crunched his way over the gravel drive and, coming to the fence beside the field, threw his burden on to the concealing grass. There they could rot and perish, grow sodden with rain, and in the end become part of the mouldy earth; he did not care. The responsibility was his no longer. They were out of his house, and it did not matter what became of them.

He returned to the house, and this time made sure the cellar door was fast. The air was clear again, the smell had gone.

He went back to the living-room to warm himself before the fire, but his hands and feet, wet with the rain, and his stomach, still queasy from the pungent apple smoke, combined together to chill his whole person, and he sat there, shuddering.

He slept badly when he went to bed that night, and awoke in the morning feeling out of sorts. He had a headache, and an ill-tasting tongue. He stayed indoors. His liver was thoroughly upset. To relieve his feelings he spoke sharply to the daily woman.

"I've caught a bad chill," he said to her, "trying to get warm last night. So much for apple wood. The smell of it has affected my insides as well. You can tell Willis, when he comes tomorrow."

She looked at him in disbelief.

"I'm sure I'm very sorry," she said. "I told my sister about the wood last night, when I got home, and that you had not fancied it. She said it was most unusual. Apple wood is considered quite a luxury to burn, and burns well, what's more."

"This lot didn't, that's all I know," he said to her, "and I never want to see any more of it. As for the smell . . . I can taste it still, it's completely turned me up."

Her mouth tightened. "I'm sorry," she said. And then, as she left the dining-room, her eye fell on the empty whisky bottle on the sideboard. She hesitated a moment, then put it on her tray.

"You've finished with this, sir?" she said.

Of course he had finished with it. It was obvious. The bottle was empty. He realised the implication, though. She wanted to suggest that the idea of apple-wood smoke upsetting him was all my eye, he had done himself too well. Damned impertinence.

"Yes," he said, "you can bring another in its place."

That would teach her to mind her own business.

He was quite sick for several days, queasy and giddy, and finally rang up the doctor to come and have a look at him. The story of the apple wood sounded nonsense, when he told it, and the doctor, after examining him, appeared unimpressed.

"Just a chill on the liver," he said, "damp feet, and possibly something you've eaten combined. I hardly think wood smoke has much to do with it. You ought to take more exercise, if you're inclined to have a liver. Play golf. I don't know how I should keep fit without my weekend golf." He laughed, packing up his bag. "I'll make you up some medicine," he said, "and once this rain has cleared off, I should get out and into the air. It's mild enough, and all we want now is a bit of sunshine to bring everything on. Your garden is farther ahead than mine. Your fruit trees are ready to blossom." And then, before leaving the room, he added, "You mustn't forget, you had a bad shock a few months ago. It takes time to get over these things. You're still missing your wife, you know. Best thing is to get out and about and see people. Well, take care of yourself."

His patient dressed and went downstairs. The fellow meant well, of course, but his visit had been a waste of time. "You're still missing your wife, you know." How little the doctor understood. Poor Midge

. . . At least he himself had the honesty to admit that he did not miss her at all, that now she was gone he could breathe, he was free, and that apart from the upset liver he had not felt so well for years.

During the few days he had spent in bed the daily woman had taken the opportunity to spring-clean the living-room. An unnecessary piece of work, but he supposed it was part of the legacy Midge had left behind her. The room looked scrubbed and straight and much too tidy. His own personal litter cleared, books and papers neatly stacked. It was an infernal nuisance, really, having anyone to do for him at all. It would not take much for him to sack her and fend for himself as best he could. Only the bother, the tie of cooking and washing up, prevented him. The ideal life, of course, was that led by a man out East, or in the South Seas, who took a native wife. No problem there. Silence, good service, perfect waiting, excellent cooking, no need for conversation; and then, if you wanted something more than that, there she was, young, warm, a companion for the dark hours. No criticism ever, the obedience of an animal to its master, and the lighthearted laughter of a child. Yes, they had wisdom all right, those fellows who broke away from convention. Good luck to them.

He strolled over to the window and looked out up the sloping lawn. The rain was stopping and tomorrow it would be fine; he would be able to get out, as the doctor had suggested. The man was right, too, about the fruit trees. The little one near the steps was in flower already, and a blackbird had perched himself on one of the branches, which swayed slightly under his weight.

The raindrops glistened and the opening buds were very curled and pink, but when the sun broke through tomorrow they would turn white and soft against the blue of the sky. He must find his old camera, and put a film in it, and photograph the little tree. The others would be in flower, too, during the week. As for the old one, there on the left, it looked as dead as ever; or else the so-called buds were so brown they did not show up from this distance. Perhaps the shedding of the branch had been its finish. And a good job too.

He turned away from the window and set about rearranging the room to his taste, spreading his things about. He liked pottering, opening drawers, taking things out and putting them back again. There was a red pencil in one of the side tables that must have slipped down behind a pile of books and been found during the turn-out. He sharpened it, gave it a sleek fine point. He found a new film in another drawer, and kept it out to put in his camera in the morning. There were a number of papers and old photographs in the drawer, heaped in a jumble, and snapshots too, dozens of them. Midge used to look after these things at one time and put them in albums; then during the war she must have lost interest, or had too many other things to do.

All this junk could really be cleared away. It would have made a fine fire the other night, and might have got even the apple logs to burn. There was little sense in keeping any of it. This appalling photo of Midge, for instance, taken heaven knows how many years ago, not long after their marriage, judging from the style of it. Did she really wear her hair that way? That fluffy mop, much too thick and bushy for her face, which was long and narrow even then. The low neck, pointing to a V, and the dangling earrings, and the smile, too eager, making her mouth seem larger than it was. In the left-hand corner she had written, "To my own darling Buzz, from his loving Midge." He had completely forgotten his old nickname. It had been dropped years back, and he seemed to remember he had never cared for it: he had found it ridiculous and embarrassing and had chided her for using it in front of people.

He tore the photograph in half and threw it on the fire. He watched it curl up upon itself and burn, and the last to go was that vivid smile. My own darling Buzz . . . Suddenly he remembered the evening dress in the photograph. It was green, not her colour ever, turning her sallow; and she had bought it for some special occasion, some big dinner party with friends who were celebrating their wedding anniversary. The idea of the dinner had been to invite all those friends and neighbours who had been married roughly around the same time, which was the reason Midge and he had gone.

There was a lot of champagne, and one or two speeches, and much conviviality, laughter, and joking—some of the joking rather broad— and he remembered that when the evening was over, and they were climbing into the car to drive away, his host, with a gust of laughter, said, "Try paying your addresses in a top hat, old boy, they say it never fails!" He had been aware of Midge beside him, in that green evening frock, sitting very straight and still, and on her face that same smile which she had worn in the photograph just destroyed, eager yet uncertain, doubtful of the meaning of the words that her host, slightly intoxicated, had let fall upon the evening air, yet wishing to seem advanced, anxious to please, and more than either of these things desperately anxious to attract.

When he had put the car away in the garage and gone into the house he had found her waiting there in the living-room for no reason at all. Her coat was thrown off to show the evening dress, and the smile, rather uncertain, was on her face.

He yawned and, settling himself down in a chair, picked up a book. She waited a little while, then slowly took up her coat and went upstairs. It must have been shortly afterwards that she had that photograph taken. "My own darling Buzz, from his loving Midge." He threw a great handful of dry sticks on to the fire. They crackled and split and turned the photograph to ashes. No damp green logs tonight. . .

It was fine and warm the following day. The sun shone, and the birds sang. He had a sudden impulse to go to London. It was a day for sauntering along Bond Street, watching the passing crowds. A day for calling in at his tailor's, for having a haircut, for eating a dozen oysters at his favourite bar. The chill had left him. The pleasant hours stretched before him. He might even look in at a matinee.

The day passed without incident, peaceful, untiring, just as he had planned, making a change from day-by-day country routine. He drove home about seven o'clock, looking forward to his drink and to his dinner. It was so warm he did not need his overcoat, not even now, with the sun gone down. He waved a hand to the farmer, who happened to be passing the gate as he turned into the drive.

"Lovely day," he shouted.

The man nodded, smiled. "Can do with plenty of these from now on," he shouted back. Decent fellow. They had always been very matey since those war days, when he had driven the tractor.

He put away the car and had a drink, and while waiting for supper took a stroll around the garden. What a difference those hours of sunshine had made to everything. Several daffodils were out, narcissi too, and the green hedgerows fresh and sprouting. As for the apple trees, the buds had burst, and they were all of them in flower. He went to his little favourite and touched the blossom. It felt soft to his hand and he gently shook a bough. It was firm, well set, and would not fall. The scent was scarcely perceptible as yet, but in a day or two, with a little more sun, perhaps a shower or two, it would come from the open flower and softly fill the air, never pungent, never strong, a modest scent. A scent which you would have to find for yourself, as the bees did. Once found, it stayed with you, it lingered always, alluring, comforting, and sweet. He patted the little tree and went down the steps into the house.

Next morning, at breakfast, there came a knock on the dining-room door, and the daily woman said that Willis was outside and wanted to have a word with him. He asked Willis to step in.

The gardener looked aggrieved. Was it trouble, then?

"I'm sorry to bother you, sir," he said, "but I had a few words with Mr. Jackson this morning. He's been complaining."

Jackson was the farmer who owned the neighbouring fields.

"What's he complaining about?"

"Says I've been throwing wood over the fence into his field, and the young foal out there, with the mare, tripped over it and went lame. I've never thrown wood over the fence in my life, sir. Quite nasty he was, sir. Spoke of the value of the foal, and it might spoil his chances to sell it."

"I hope you told him, then, it wasn't true."

"I did, sir. But the point is, someone has been throwing wood over the fence. He showed me the very spot. Just behind the garage. I went with Mr. Jackson, and there they were. Logs had been tipped there, sir. I thought it best to come to you about it before I spoke in the kitchen, otherwise you know how it is, there would be unpleasantness."

He felt the gardener's eye upon him. No way out, of course. And it was Willis' fault in the first place.

"No need to say anything in the kitchen, Willis," he said. "I threw the logs there myself. You brought them into the house, without my asking you to do so, with the result that they put out my fire, filled the room with smoke, and ruined an evening. I chucked them over the fence in a devil of a temper, and if they have damaged Jackson's foal you can apologise for me, and tell him I'll pay him compensation. All I ask is that you don't bring any more logs like those into the house again."

"No, sir. I understood they had not been a success. I didn't think, though, that you would go so far as to throw them out."

"Well, I did. And there's an end to it."

"Yes, sir." He made as if to go, but before he left the dining-room he paused and said, "I can't understand about the logs not burning, all the same. I took a small piece back to the wife, and it burnt lovely in our kitchen, bright as anything."

"It did not burn here."

"Anyway, the old tree is making up for one spoilt branch, sir. Have you seen her this morning?"

"No."

"It's yesterday's sun that has done it, sir, and the warm night. Quite a treat she is, with all the blossom. You should go out and take a look at her directly."

Willis left the room, and he continued his breakfast.

Presently he went out on to the terrace. At first he did not go up on to the lawn; he made a pretence of seeing to other things, of getting the heavy garden seat out, now that the weather was set fair. And then, fetching a pair of clippers, he did a bit of pruning to the few roses under the windows. Yet, finally, something drew him to the tree.

It was just as Willis said. Whether it was the sun, the warmth, the mild still night, he could not tell; but the small brown buds had unfolded themselves, had ripened into flower, and now spread themselves above his head into a fantastic cloud of white, moist blossom. It grew thickest at the top of the tree, the flowers so clustered together that they looked like wad upon wad of soggy cotton wool, and all of it, from the topmost branches to those nearer to the ground, had this same pallid colour of sickly white.

It did not resemble a tree at all; it might have been a flapping tent left out in the rain by campers who had gone away, or else a mop, a giant mop, whose streaky surface had been caught somehow by the sun, and so turned bleached. The blossom was too thick, too great a burden for the long thin trunk, and the moisture clinging to it made it heavier still. Already, as if the effort had been too much, the lower flowers, those nearest the ground, were turning brown; yet there had been no rain.

Well, there it was. Willis had been proved right. The tree had blossomed. But instead of blossoming to life, to beauty, it had somehow, deep in nature, gone awry and turned a freak. A freak which did not know its texture or its shape, but thought to please. Almost as though it said, self-conscious, with a smirk, "Look. All this is for you."

Suddenly he heard a step behind him. It was Willis.

"Fine sight, sir, isn't it?"

"Sorry, I don't admire it. The blossom is far too thick."

The gardener stared at him and said nothing. It struck him that Willis must think him very difficult, very hard, and possibly eccentric. He would go and discuss him in the kitchen with the daily woman.

He forced himself to smile at Willis.

"Look here," he said, "I don't mean to damp you. But all this blossom doesn't interest me. I prefer it small and light and colourful, like the little tree. But you take some of it back home to your wife. Cut as much of it as you like, I don't mind at all. I'd like you to have it."

He waved his arm generously. He wanted Willis to go now, and fetch a ladder, and carry the stuff away.

The man shook his head. He looked quite shocked.

"No, thank you, sir, I wouldn't dream of it. It would spoil the tree. I want to wait for the fruit. That's what I'm banking on, the fruit."

There was no more to be said.

"All right, Willis. Don't bother, then."

He went back to the terrace. But when he sat down there in the sun, looking up the sloping lawn, he could not see the little tree at all, standing modest and demure above the steps, her soft flowers lifting to the sky. She was dwarfed and hidden by the freak, with its great cloud of sagging petals, already wilting, dingy white, on to the grass beneath. And whichever way he turned his chair, this way or that upon the terrace, it seemed to him that he could not escape the tree, that it stood there above him, reproachful, anxious, desirous of the admiration that he could not give.

That summer he took a longer holiday than he had done for many years—a bare ten days with his old mother in Norfolk, instead of the customary month that he used to spend with Midge, and the rest of August and the whole of September in Switzerland and Italy.

He took his car, and so was free to motor from place to place as the mood inclined. He cared little for sight-seeing or excursions, and was not much of a climber. What he liked most was to come upon a little town in the cool of the evening, pick out a small but comfortable hotel, and then stay there, if it pleased him, for two or three days at a time, doing nothing, mooching.

He liked sitting about in the sun all morning, at some café or restaurant, with a glass of wine in front of him, watching the people; so many gay young creatures seemed to travel nowadays. He enjoyed the chatter of conversation around him, as long as he did not have to join in; and now and again a smile would come his way, a word or two of greeting from some guest in the same hotel, but nothing to commit him, merely a sense of being in the swim, of being a man of leisure on his own, abroad.

The difficulty in the old days, on holiday anywhere with Midge, would be her habit of striking up acquaintance with people, some other couple who struck her as looking "nice" or, as she put it, "our sort." It would start with conversation over coffee, and then pass on to mutual planning of shared days, car drives in foursomes—he could not bear it, the holiday would be ruined.

Now, thank heaven, there was no need for this. He did what he liked, in his own time. There was no Midge to say, "Well, shall we be moving?" when he was still sitting contentedly over his wine, no Midge to plan a visit to some old church that did not interest him.

He put on weight during his holiday, and he did not mind. There was no one to suggest a good long walk to keep fit after the rich food, thus spoiling the pleasant somnolence that comes with coffee and dessert; no one to glance, surprised, at the sudden wearing of a jaunty shirt, a flamboyant tie.

Strolling through the little towns and villages, hatless, smoking a cigar, receiving smiles from the jolly young folk around him, he felt himself a dog. This was the life, no worries, no cares. No "We have to be back on the fifteenth because of that committee meeting at the hospital"; no "We can't possibly leave the house shut up for longer than a fortnight, something might happen." Instead, the bright lights of a little country fair, in a village whose name he did not even bother to find out; the tinkle of music, boys and girls laughing, and he himself, after a bottle of the local wine, bowing to a young thing with a gay handkerchief round her head and sweeping her off to dance under the hot tent. No matter if her steps did not harmonize with his—it was years since he had danced—this was the thing, this was it. He released her when the music stopped, and off she ran, giggling, back to her young friends, laughing at him no doubt. What of it? He had had his fun.

He left Italy when the weather turned, at the end of September, and was back home the first week in October. No problem to it. A telegram to the daily woman, with the probable date of arrival, and that was all. Even a brief holiday with Midge and the return meant complications. Written instructions about groceries, milk, and bread; airing of beds, lighting of fires, reminders about the delivery of the morning papers. The whole business turned into a chore.

He turned into the drive on a mellow October evening and there was smoke coming from the chimneys, the front door open, and his pleasant home awaiting him. No rushing through to the back regions to learn of possible plumbing disasters, breakages, water shortages, food difficulties; the daily woman knew better than to bother him with these. Merely, "Good evening, sir. I hope you had a good holiday. Supper at the usual time?" And then silence. He could have his drink, light his pipe, and relax; the small pile of letters did not matter. No feverish tearing of them open, and then the start of the telephoning, the hearing of those endless one-sided conversations between women friends. "Well? How are things? Really? My dear . . . And what did you say to that? . . . She did? . . . I can't possibly on Wednesday . . ."

He stretched himself contentedly, stiff after his drive, and gazed comfortably around the cheerful, empty living-room. He was hungry after his journey up from Dover, and the chop seemed rather meagre after foreign fare. But there it was, it wouldn't hurt him to return to plainer food. A sardine on toast followed the chop, and then he looked about him for dessert.

There was a plate of apples on the sideboard. He fetched them and put them down in front of him on the dining-room table. Poor-looking things. Small and wizened, dullish brown in colour. He bit into one, but as soon as the taste of it was on his tongue he spat it out. The thing was rotten. He tried another. It was just the same. He looked more closely at the pile of apples. The skins were leathery and rough and hard; you would expect the insides to be sour. On the contrary, they were pulpy-soft, and the cores were yellow. Filthy-tasting things.

A stray piece stuck to his tooth and he pulled it out. Stringy, beastly . . .

He rang the bell, and the woman came through from the kitchen. "Have we any other dessert?" he said.

"I am afraid not, sir. I remembered how fond you were of apples, and Willis brought in these from the garden. He said they were especially good, and just ripe for eating."

"Well, he's quite wrong. They're uneatable."

"I'm very sorry, sir. I wouldn't have put them through had I known. There's a lot more outside too. Willis brought in a great basketful."

"All the same sort?"

"Yes, sir. The small brown ones. No other kind at all."

"Never mind, it can't be helped. I'll look for myself in the morning."

He got up from the table and went through to the living-room. He had a glass of port to take away the taste of the apples, but it seemed to make no difference, not even a biscuit with it. The pulpy rotten tang clung to his tongue and the roof of his mouth, and in the end he was obliged to go up to the bathroom and clean his teeth. The maddening thing was that he could have done with a good clean apple, after that rather indifferent supper: something with a smooth clear skin, the inside not too sweet, a little sharp in flavour. He knew the kind. Good biting texture. You had to pick them, of course, at just the right moment.

He dreamt that night he was back again in Italy, dancing under the tent in the little cobbled square. He woke with the tinkling music in his ear, but he could not recall the face of the peasant girl or remember the feel of her tripping against his feet. He tried to recapture the memory, lying awake, over his morning tea, but it eluded him.

He got up out of bed and went over to the window, to glance at the weather. Fine enough, with a slight nip in the air.

Then he saw the tree. The sight of it came as a shock, it was so unexpected. Now he realised at once where the apples had come from the night before. The tree was laden, bowed down, under her burden of fruit. They clustered, small and brown, on every branch, diminishing in size as they reached the top, so that those on the high boughs, not grown yet to full size, looked like nuts. They weighed heavy on the tree, and because of this it seemed bent and twisted out of shape, the lower branches nearly sweeping the ground; and on the grass, at the foot of the tree, were more and yet more apples, windfalls, the first-grown, pushed off by their clamouring brothers and sisters. The ground was covered with them, many split open and rotting where the wasps had been. Never in his life had he seen a tree so laden with fruit. It was a miracle that it had not fallen under the weight.

He went out before breakfast—curiosity was too great—and stood beside the tree, staring at it. There was no mistake about it, these were the same apples that had been put in the dining-room last night. Hardly bigger than tangerines, and many of them smaller than that, they grew so close together on the branches that to pick one you would be forced to pick a dozen.

There was something monstrous in the sight, something distasteful; yet it was pitiful, too, that the months had brought this agony upon the tree, for agony it was, there could be no other word for it. The tree was tortured by fruit, groaning under the weight of it, and the frightful part about it was that not one of the fruit was eatable. Every apple was rotten through and through. He trod them underfoot, the windfalls on the grass, there was no escaping them; and in a moment they were mush and slime, clinging about his heels—he had to clean the mess off with wisps of grass.

It would have been far better if the tree had died, stark and bare, before this ever happened. What use was it to him or anyone, this load of rotting fruit, littering up the place, fouling the ground? And the tree itself, humped, as it were, in pain and yet, he could almost swear, triumphant, gloating.

Just as in spring, when the mass of fluffy blossom, colourless and sodden, dragged the reluctant eye away from the other trees, so it did now. Impossible to avoid seeing the tree, with its burden of fruit. Every window in the front part of the house looked out upon it. And he knew how it would be. The fruit would cling there until it was picked, staying upon the branches through October and November, and it never would be picked, because nobody could eat it. He could see himself being bothered with the tree throughout the autumn. Whenever he came out on to the terrace there it would be, sagging and loathsome.

It was extraordinary, the dislike he had taken to the tree. It was a perpetual reminder of the fact that he . . . well, he was blessed if he knew what . . . a perpetual reminder of all the things he most detested, and always had, he could not put a name to them. He decided then and there that Willis should pick the fruit and take it away, sell it, get rid of it, anything, as long as he did not have to eat it, and as long as he was not forced to watch the tree drooping there, day after day, throughout the autumn.

He turned his back upon it and was relieved to see that none of the other trees had so degraded themselves to excess. They carried a fair crop, nothing out of the way, and as he might have known, the young tree, to the right of the old one, made a brave little show on its own, with a light load of medium-sized, rosy-looking apples, not too dark in colour, but freshly reddened where the sun had ripened them. He would pick one now, and take it in, to eat with breakfast. He made his choice, and the apple fell at the first touch into his hand. It looked so good that he bit into it with appetite. That was it, juicy, sweet-smelling, sharp, the dew upon it still. He did not look back at the old tree. He went indoors, hungry, to breakfast.

It took the gardener nearly a week to strip the tree, and it was plain he did it under protest.

"I don't care what you do with them," said his employer. "You can sell them and keep the money, or you can take them home and feed them to your pigs. I can't stand the sight of them, and that's all there is to it. Find a long ladder, and start on the job right away."

It seemed to him that Willis, from sheer obstinacy, spun out the time. He would watch the man from the windows act as though in slow motion. First the placing of the ladder. Then the laborious climb, and the descent to steady it again. After that the performance of plucking off the fruit, dropping them, one by one, into the basket. Day after day it was the same. Willis was always there on the sloping lawn with his ladder under the tree, the branches creaking and groaning, and beneath him on the grass baskets, pails, basins, any receptacle that would hold the apples.

At last the job was finished. The ladder was removed, the baskets and pails also, and the tree was stripped bare. He looked out at it, the evening of that day, in satisfaction. No more rotting fruit to offend his eye. Every single apple gone.

Yet the tree, instead of seeming lighter from the loss of its burden, looked, if it were possible, more dejected than ever. The branches still sagged, and the leaves, withering now to the cold autumnal evening, folded upon themselves and shivered. "Is this my reward?" it seemed to say. "After all I've done for you?"

As the light faded, the shadow of the tree cast a blight upon the dank night. Winter would soon come. And the short, dull days.

He had never cared much for the fall of the year. In the old days, when he went up to London every day to the office, it had meant that early start by train on a nippy morning. And then, before three o'clock in the afternoon, the clerks were turning on the lights, and as often as not there would be fog in the air, murky and dismal, and a slow chugging journey home, daily breaders like himself sitting five abreast in a carriage, some of them with colds in their heads. Then the long evening followed, with Midge opposite him before the living-room fire, and he listening, or feigning to listen, to the account of her days and the things that had gone wrong.

If she had not shouldered any actual household disaster, she would pick upon some current event to cast a gloom. "I see fares are going up again. What about your season ticket?" or "This business in South Africa looks nasty, quite a long bit about it on the six o'clock news," or yet again, "Three more cases of polio over at the isolation hospital. I don't know, I'm sure, what the medical world thinks it's doing. . . ."

Now, at least, he was spared the role of listener, but the memory of those long evenings was with him still, and when the lights were lit and the curtains were drawn he would be reminded of the click-click of the needles, the aimless chatter, and the "Hi-oh" of the yawns. He began to drop in, sometimes before supper, sometimes afterwards, at the Green Man, the old public house a quarter of a mile away on the main road. Nobody bothered him there. He would sit in a corner, having said good evening to genial Mrs. Hill, the proprietress, and then, with a cigarette and a whisky-and-soda, watch the local inhabitants stroll in to have a pint, to throw a dart, to gossip.

In a sense it made a continuation of his summer holiday. It bore resemblance, admittedly slight, to the carefree atmosphere of the cafés and the restaurants; and there was a kind of warmth about the bright smoke-filled bar, crowded with workingmen who did not bother him, which he found pleasant, comforting. These visits cut into the length of the dark winter evenings, making them more tolerable.

A cold in the head, caught in mid-December, put a stop to this for more than a week. He was obliged to keep to the house. And it was odd, he thought to himself, how much he missed the Green Man, and how sick to death he became of sitting about in the living-room or in the study, with nothing to do but read or listen to the wireless. The cold and the boredom made him morose and irritable, and the enforced inactivity turned his liver sluggish. He needed exercise. Whatever the weather, he decided towards the end of yet another cold grim day, he would go out tomorrow. The sky had been heavy from mid-afternoon and threatened snow, but no matter, he could not stand the house for a further twenty-four hours without a break.

The final edge to his irritation came with the fruit tart at supper. He was in that final stage of a bad cold when the taste is not yet fully returned, appetite is poor, but there is a certain emptiness within that needs ministration of a particular kind. A bird might have done it. Half a partridge, roasted to perfection, followed by a cheese soufflé. As well ask for the moon. The daily woman, not gifted with imagination, produced plaice, of all fish the most tasteless, the most dry. When she had borne the remains of this away—he had left most of it upon his plate—she returned with a tart, and because hunger was far from being satisfied, he helped himself to it liberally.

One taste was enough. Choking, spluttering, he spat out the contents of his spoon upon the plate. He got up and rang the bell.

The woman appeared, a query on her face, at the unexpected summons.

"What the devil is this stuff?"

"Jam tart, sir."

"What sort of jam?"

"Apple jam, sir. Made from my own bottling."

He threw down his napkin on the table.

"I guessed as much. You've been using some of those apples that I complained to you about months ago. I told you and Willis quite distinctly that I would not have any of those apples in the house."

The woman's face became tight and drawn.

"You said, sir, not to cook the apples, or to bring them in for dessert. You said nothing about not making jam. I thought they would taste all right as jam. And I made some myself, to try. It was perfectly all right. So I made several bottles of jam from the apples Willis gave me. We always made jam here, Madam and myself."

"Well, I'm sorry for your trouble, but I can't eat it. Those apples disagreed with me in the autumn, and whether they are made into jam or whatever you like, they will do so again. Take the tart away, and don't let me see it, or the jam, again. I'll have some coffee in the living-room."

He went out of the room, trembling. It was fantastic that such a small incident should make him feel so angry. God! What fools people were. She knew, Willis knew, that he disliked the apples, loathed the taste and the smell of them, but in their cheese-paring way they decided that it would save money if he was given homemade jam, jam made from the apples he particularly detested.

He swallowed down a stiff whisky and lit a cigarette.

In a moment or two she appeared with the coffee. She did not retire immediately on putting down the tray.

"Could I have a word with you, sir?"

"What is it?"

"I think it would be for the best if I gave in my notice."

Now this, on top of the other. What a day, what an evening.

"What reason? Because I can't eat apple tart?"

"It's not just that, sir. Somehow I feel things are very different from what they were. I have meant to speak several times."

"I don't give much trouble, do I?"

"No, sir. Only in the old days, when Madam was alive, I felt my work was appreciated. Now it's as though it didn't matter one way or the other. Nothing's ever said, and although I try to do my best I can't be sure. I think I'd be happier if I went where there was a lady again who took notice of what I did."

"You are the best judge of that, of course. I'm sorry if you haven't liked it here lately."

"You were away so much too, sir, this summer. When Madam was alive it was never for more than a fortnight. Everything seems so changed. I don't know where I am, or Willis either."

"So Willis is fed-up too?"

"That's not for me to say, of course. I know he was upset about the apples, but that's some time ago. Perhaps he'll be speaking to you himself."

"Perhaps he will. I had no idea I was causing so much concern to you both. All right, that's quite enough. Good night."

She went out of the room. He stared moodily about him. Good riddance to them both, if that was how they felt. Things weren't the same. Everything so changed. Damned nonsense. As for Willis being upset about the apples, what infernal impudence. Hadn't he a right to do what he liked with his own tree? To hell with his cold and with the weather. He couldn't stand sitting about in front of the fire thinking about Willis and the cook. He would go down to the Green Man and forget the whole thing.

He put on his overcoat and muffler and his old cap and walked briskly down the road, and in twenty minutes he was sitting in his usual corner in the Green Man, with Mrs. Hill pouring out his whisky and expressing her delight to see him back. One or two of the habitués smiled at him, asked after his health.

"Had a cold, sir? Same everywhere. Everyone's got one."

"That's right."

"Well, it's the time of year, isn't it?"

"Got to expect it. It's when it's on the chest it's nasty."

"No worse than being stuffed up, like, in the head."

"That's right. One's as bad as the other. Nothing to it."

Likeable fellows. Friendly. Not harping at one, not bothering.

"Another whisky, please."

"There you are, sir. Do you good. Keep out the cold."

Mrs. Hill beamed behind the bar. Large, comfortable old soul. Through a haze of smoke he heard the chatter, the deep laughter, the click of the darts, the jocular roar at a bull's eye.

". . . and if it comes on to snow, I don't know how we shall manage," Mrs. Hill was saying, "them being so late delivering the coal. If we had a load of logs it would help us out, but what do you think they're asking? Two pounds a load. I mean to say . . ."

He leant forward and his voice sounded far away, even to himself. "I'll let you have some logs," he said.

Mrs. Hill turned round. She had not been talking to him.

"Excuse me?" she said.

"I'll let you have some logs," he repeated. "Got an old tree, up at home, needed sawing down for months. Do it for you tomorrow."

He nodded, smiling.

"Oh no, sir. I couldn't think of putting you to the trouble. The coal will turn up, never fear."

"No trouble at all. A pleasure. Like to do it for you; the exercise, you know, do me good. Putting on weight. You count on me."

He got down from his seat and reached rather carefully for his coat. "It's apple wood," he said. "Do you mind apple wood?"

"Why, no," she answered, "any wood will do. But can you spare it, sir?"

He nodded mysteriously. It was a bargain, it was a secret.

"I'll bring it down to you in my trailer tomorrow night," he said.

"Careful, sir," she said, "mind the step . . ."

He walked home through the cold crisp night, smiling to himself. He did not remember undressing or getting into bed, but when he woke the next morning the first thought that came to his mind was the promise he had made about the tree.

It was not one of Willis' days, he realised with satisfaction. There would be no interfering with his plan. The sky was heavy and snow had fallen in the night. More to come. But as yet nothing to worry about, nothing to hamper him.

He went through to the kitchen garden, after breakfast, to the tool shed. He took down the saw, the wedges, and the axe. He might need all of them. He ran his thumb along the edges. They would do. As he shouldered his tools and walked back to the front garden he laughed to himself, thinking that he must resemble an executioner of old days setting forth to behead some wretched victim in the Tower.

He laid his tools down beneath the apple tree. It would be an act of mercy, really. Never had he seen anything so wretched, so utterly woebegone, as the apple tree. There couldn't be any life left in it. Not a leaf remained. Twisted, ugly, bent, it ruined the appearance of the lawn. Once it was out of the way, the whole setting of the garden would change.

A snowflake fell on to his hand, then another. He glanced down past the terrace to the dining-room window. He could see the woman laying his lunch. He went down the steps and into the house. "Look," he said, "if you like to leave my lunch ready in the oven, I think I'll fend for myself today. I may be busy, and I don't want to be pinned down for time. Also, it's going to snow. You had better go off early today and get home, in case it becomes really bad. I can manage perfectly well. And I prefer it."

Perhaps she thought his decision came through offence at her giving notice the night before. Whatever she thought, he did not mind. He wanted to be alone. He wanted no face peering from the window.

She went off at about twelve-thirty, and as soon as she had gone he went to the oven and got his lunch. He meant to get it over, so that he could give up the whole short afternoon to the felling of the tree.

No more snow had fallen, apart from a few flakes that did not lie. He took off his coat, rolled up his sleeves, and seized the saw. With his left hand he ripped away the wire at the base of the tree. Then he placed the saw about a foot from the bottom and began to work it, backwards, forwards.

For the first dozen strokes all went smoothly. The saw bit into the wood, the teeth took hold. Then after a few moments the saw began to bind. He had been afraid of that.

He tried to work it free, but the opening that he had made was not yet large enough, and the tree gripped upon the saw and held it fast. He drove in the first wedge, with no result. He drove in the second, and the opening gaped a little wider, but still not wide enough to release the saw.

He pulled and tugged at the saw, to no avail. He began to lose his temper. He took up his axe and started hacking at the tree, pieces of the trunk flying outwards, scattering on the grass.

That was more like it. That was the answer.

Up and down went the heavy axe, splitting and tearing at the tree. Off came the pealing bark, the great white strips of under-wood, raw and stringy. Hack at it, blast at it, gouge at the tough tissue, throw the axe away, claw at the rubbery flesh with the bare hands. Not far enough yet, go on, go on.

There goes the saw, and the wedge, released. Now up with the axe again. Down there, heavy, where the stringy threads cling so steadfast. Now she's groaning, now she's splitting, now she's rocking and swaying, hanging there upon one bleeding strip. Boot her, then. That's it, kick her, kick her again, one final blow, she's over, she's falling . . . she's down . . . damn her, blast her . . . she's down, splitting the air with sound, and all her branches spread about her on the ground.

He stood back, wiping the sweat from his forehead, from his chin.

The wreckage surrounded him on either side, and below him, at his feet, gaped the torn, white, jagged stump of the axed tree.

It began snowing.

His first task, after felling the apple tree, was to hack off the branches and the smaller boughs, and so to grade the wood in stacks, which made it easier to drag away.

The small stuff, bundled and roped, would do for kindling; Mrs. Hill would no doubt be glad of that as well. He brought the car, with the trailer attached, to the garden gate, hard by the terrace. This chopping up of the branches was simple work; much of it could be done with a hook. The fatigue came with bending and tying the bundles, and then heaving them down past the terrace and through the gate up on to the trailer. The thicker branches he disposed of with the axe, then split them into three or four lengths, which he could also rope and drag, one by one, to the trailer.

He was fighting all the while against time. The light, what there was of it, would be gone by half-past four, and the snow went on falling. The ground was already covered, and when he paused for a moment in his work, and wiped the sweat away from his face, the thin frozen flakes fell upon his lips and made their way, insidious and soft, down his collar to his neck and body. If he lifted his eyes to the sky he was blinded at once. The flakes came thicker, faster, swirling about his head, and it was as though the heaven had turned itself into a canopy of snow, ever descending, coming nearer, closer, stifling the earth. The snow fell upon the torn boughs and the hacked branches, hampering his work. If he rested but an instant to draw breath and renew his strength, it seemed to throw a protective cover, soft and white, over the pile of wood.

He could not wear gloves. If he did so he had no grip upon his hook or his axe, nor could he tie the rope and drag the branches. His fingers were numb with cold, soon they would be too stiff to bend. He had a pain now, under the heart, from the strain of dragging the stuff on to the trailer; and the work never seemed to lessen. Whenever he returned to the fallen tree the pile of wood would appear as high as ever, long boughs, short boughs, a heap of kindling there, nearly covered with the snow, which he had forgotten: all must be roped and fastened and carried or pulled away.

It was after half-past four, and almost dark, when he had disposed of all the branches, and nothing now remained but to drag the trunk, already hacked into three lengths, over the terrace to the waiting trailer.

He was very nearly at the point of exhaustion. Only his will to be rid of the tree kept him to the task. His breath came slowly, painfully, and all the while the snow fell into his mouth and into his eyes and he could barely see.

He took his rope and slid it under the cold slippery trunk, knotting it fiercely. How hard and unyielding was the naked wood, and the bark was rough, hurting his numb hands.

"That's the end of you," he muttered, "that's your finish."

Staggering to his feet, he bore the weight of the heavy trunk over his shoulder, and began to drag it slowly down over the slope to the terrace and to the garden gate. It followed him, bump . . . bump . . . down the steps of the terrace. Heavy and lifeless, the last bare limbs of the apple tree dragged in his wake through the wet snow.

It was over. His task was done. He stood panting, one hand upon the trailer. Now nothing more remained but to take the stuff down to the Green Man before the snow made the drive impossible. He had chains for the car, he had thought of that already.

He went into the house to change the clothes that were clinging to him and to have a drink. Never mind about his fire, never mind about drawing curtains, seeing what there might be for supper, all the chores the daily woman usually did—that would come later. He must have his drink and get the wood away.

His mind was numb and weary, like his hands and his whole body. For a moment he thought of leaving the job until the following day, flopping down into the armchair, and closing his eyes. No, it would not do. Tomorrow there would be more snow, tomorrow the drive would be two or three feet deep. He knew the signs. And there would be the trailer, stuck outside the garden gate, with the pile of wood inside it, frozen white. He must make the effort and do the job tonight.

He finished his drink, changed, and went out to start the car. It was still snowing, but now that darkness had fallen a colder, cleaner feeling had come into the air, and it was freezing. The dizzy, swirling flakes came more slowly now, with precision.

The engine started and he began to drive downhill, the trailer in tow. He drove slowly, and very carefully, because of the heavy load.

And it was an added strain, after the hard work of the afternoon, peering through the falling snow, wiping the windscreen. Never had the lights of the Green Man shone more cheerfully as he pulled up into the little yard.

He blinked as he stood within the doorway, smiling to himself. "Well, I've brought your wood," he said.

Mrs. Hill stared at him from behind the bar, one or two fellows turned and looked at him, and a hush fell upon the dart players.

"You never . . ." began Mrs. Hill, but he jerked his head at the door and laughed at her.

"Go and see," he said, "but don't ask me to unload it tonight."

He moved to his favourite corner, chuckling to himself, and there they all were, exclaiming and talking and laughing by the door, and he was quite a hero, the fellows crowding round with questions, and Mrs. Hill pouring out his whisky and thanking him and laughing and shaking her head. "You'll drink on the house tonight," she said.

"Not a bit of it," he said, "this is my party. Rounds one and two to me. Come on, you chaps."

It was festive, warm, jolly, and good luck to them all, he kept saying, good luck to Mrs. Hill, and to himself, and to the whole world. When was Christmas? Next week, the week after? Well, here's to it, and a merry Christmas. Never mind the snow, never mind the weather. For the first time he was one of them, not isolated in his corner. For the first time he drank with them, he laughed with them, he even threw a dart with them, and there they all were in that warm, stuffy, smoke-filled bar, and he felt they liked him, he belonged, he was no longer "the gentleman" from the house up the road.

The hours passed, and some of them went home, and others took their place, and he was still sitting there, hazy, comfortable, the warmth and the smoke blending together. Nothing of what he heard or saw made very much sense, but somehow it did not seem to matter, for there was jolly, fat, easygoing Mrs. Hill to minister to his needs, her face glowing at him over the bar.

Another face swung into his view, that of one of the labourers from the farm, with whom, in the old war days, he had shared the driving of the tractor. He leant forward, touching the fellow on the shoulder.

"What happened to the little girl?" he said.

The man lowered his tankard. "Beg pardon, sir?" he said.

"You remember. The little land girl. She used to milk the cows, feed the pigs, up at the farm. Pretty girl, dark curly hair, always smiling."

Mrs. Hill turned round from serving another customer.

"Does the gentleman mean May, I wonder?" she asked.

"Yes, that's it, that was the name, young May," he said.

"Why, didn't you ever hear about it, sir?" said Mrs. Hill, filling up his glass. "We were all very much shocked at the time, everyone was talking of it, weren't they, Fred?"

"That's right, Mrs. Hill."

The man wiped his mouth with the back of his hand.

"Killed," he said, "thrown from the back of some chap's motor bike. Going to be married very shortly. About four years ago, now. Dreadful thing, eh? Nice kid too."

"We all sent a wreath, from just around," said Mrs. Hill. "Her mother wrote back, very touched, and sent a cutting from the local paper, didn't she, Fred? Quite a big funeral they had, ever so many floral tributes. Poor May. We were all fond of May."

"That's right," said Fred.

"And fancy you never hearing about it, sir!" said Mrs. Hill.

"No," he said, "no, nobody ever told me. I'm sorry about it. Very sorry."

He stared in front of him at his half-filled glass.

The conversation went on around him, but he was no longer part of the company. He was on his own again, silent, in his corner. Dead. That poor, pretty girl was dead. Thrown off a motor bike. Been dead for three or four years. Some careless, bloody fellow, taking a corner too fast, the girl behind him, clinging on to his belt, laughing probably in his ear, and then crash . . . finish. No more curling hair blowing about her face, no more laughter.

May, that was the name; he remembered clearly now. He could see her smiling over her shoulder when they called to her. "Coming," she sang out, and put a clattering pail down in the yard and went off, whistling, with big clumping boots. He had put his arm about her and kissed her for one brief, fleeting moment. May, the land girl, with the laughing eyes.

"Going, sir?" said Mrs. Hill.

"Yes. Yes, I think I'll be going now."

He stumbled to the entrance and opened the door. It had frozen hard during the past hour and it was no longer snowing. The heavy pall had gone from the sky and the stars shone.

"Want a hand with the car, sir?" said someone.

"No, thank you," he said, "I can manage."

He unhitched the trailer and let it fall. Some of the wood lurched forward heavily. That would do tomorrow. Tomorrow, if he felt like it, he would come down again and help to unload the wood. Not tonight. He had done enough. Now he was really tired; now he was spent.

It took him some time to start the car, and before he was halfway up the side road leading to his house he realised that he had made a mistake to bring it at all. The snow was heavy all about him, and the track he had made earlier in the evening was now covered. The car lurched and slithered, and suddenly the right wheel dipped and the whole body plunged sideways. He had got into a drift.

He climbed out and looked about him. The car was deep in the drift, impossible to move without two or three men to help him, and even then, if he went for assistance, what hope was there of trying to continue further, with the snow just as thick ahead? Better leave it. Try again in the morning, when he was fresh. No sense in hanging about now, spending half the night pushing and shoving at the car, all to no purpose. No harm would come to it here on the side road; nobody else would be coming this way tonight.

He started walking up the road towards his own drive. It was bad luck that he had got the car into the drift. In the centre of the road the going was not bad and the snow did not come above his ankles. He thrust his hands deep in the pockets of his overcoat and ploughed on up the hill, the countryside a great white waste on either side of him.

He remembered that he had sent the daily woman home at midday and that the house would strike cheerless and cold on his return. The fire would have gone out, and in all probability the furnace too. The windows, uncurtained, would stare bleakly down at him, letting in the night. Supper to get into the bargain. Well, it was his own fault. No one to blame but himself. This was the moment when there should be someone waiting, someone to come running through from the living-room to the hall, opening the front door, flooding the hall with light. "Are you all right, darling? I was getting anxious."

He paused for breath at the top of the hill and saw his home, shrouded by trees, at the end of the short drive. It looked dark and forbidding without a light in any window. There was more friendliness in the open, under the bright stars, standing on the crisp white snow, than in the sombre house.

He had left the side gate open, and he went through that way to the terrace, shutting the gate behind him. What a hush had fallen upon the garden—there was no sound at all. It was as though some spirit had come and put a spell upon the place, leaving it white and still.

He walked softly over the snow towards the apple trees.

Now the young one stood alone, above the steps, dwarfed no longer; and with her branches spread, glistening white, she belonged to the spirit world, a world of fantasy and ghosts. He wanted to stand beside the little tree and touch the branches, to make certain she was still alive, that the snow had not harmed her, so that in the spring she would blossom once again.

She was almost within his reach when he stumbled and fell, his foot twisted underneath him, caught in some obstacle hidden by the snow. He tried to move his foot, but it was jammed, and he knew suddenly, by the sharpness of the pain biting his ankle, that what had trapped him was the jagged split stump of the old apple tree he had felled that afternoon.

He leant forward on his elbows, in an attempt to drag himself along the ground, but such was his position, in falling, that his leg was bent backwards, away from his foot, and every effort that he made only succeeded in imprisoning the foot still more firmly in the grip of the trunk. He felt for the ground under the snow, but wherever he felt his hands touched the small broken twigs from the apple tree that had scattered there when the tree fell and then were covered by the falling snow. He shouted for help, knowing in his heart no one could hear.

"Let me go," he shouted, "let me go," as though the thing that held him there in its mercy had the power to release him, and as he shouted tears of frustration and of fear ran down his face. He would have to lie there all night, held fast in the clutch of the old apple tree. There was no hope, no escape, until they came to find him in the morning, and supposing it was then too late, that when they came he was dead, lying stiffly in the frozen snow?"

Once more he struggled to release his foot, swearing and sobbing as he did so. It was no use. He could not move. Exhausted, he laid his head upon his arms and wept. He sank deeper, ever deeper into the snow, and when a stray piece of brushwood, cold and wet, touched his lips, it was like a hand, hesitant and timid, feeling its way towards him in the darkness.

The Old Man

Dɪᴅ ɪ ʜᴇᴀʀ you asking about the old man? I thought so. You're a newcomer to the district, here on holiday. We get plenty these days, during the summer months. Somehow they always find their way eventually over the cliffs down to this beach, and then they pause and look from the sea back to the lake. Just as you did.

It's a lovely spot, isn't it? Quiet and remote. You can't wonder at the old man choosing to live here.

I don't remember when he first came. Nobody can. Many years ago, it must have been. He was here when I arrived, long before the war. Perhaps he came to escape from civilisation, much as I did myself. Or maybe, where he lived before, the folks around made things too hot for him. It's hard to say. I had the feeling, from the very first, that he had done something, or something had been done to him, that gave him a grudge against the world. I remember the first time I set eyes on him I said to myself, "I bet that old fellow is one hell of a character."

Yes, he was living here beside the lake, along of his missus. Funny sort of lash-up they had, exposed to all the weather, but they didn't seem to mind.

I had been warned about him by one of the fellows from the farm, who advised me, with a grin, to give the old man who lived down by the lake a wide berth—he didn't care for strangers. So I went warily, and I didn't stay to pass the time of day. Nor would it have been any use if I had, not knowing a word of his lingo. The first time I saw him he was standing by the edge of the lake, looking out to sea, and from tact I avoided the piece of planking over the stream, which meant passing close to him, and crossed to the other side of the lake by the beach instead. Then, with an awkward feeling that I was trespassing and had no business to be there, I bobbed down behind a clump of gorse, took out my spyglass, and had a peep at him.

He was a big fellow, broad and strong—he's aged, of course, lately; I'm speaking of several years back—but even now you can see what he must have been once. Such power and drive behind him, and that fine head, which he carried like a king. There's an idea in that, too. No, I'm not joking. Who knows what royal blood he carries inside him, harking back to some remote ancestor? And now and again, surging in him—not through his own fault—it gets the better of him and drives him fighting mad. I didn't think about that at the time. I just looked at him, and ducked behind the gorse when I saw him turn, and I wondered to myself what went on in his mind, whether he knew I was there, watching him.

If he should decide to come up the lake after me I should look pretty foolish. He must have thought better of it, though, or perhaps he did not care. He went on staring out to sea, watching the gulls and the incoming tide, and presently he ambled off his side of the lake, heading for the missus and home and maybe supper.

I didn't catch a glimpse of her that first day. She just wasn't around. Living as they do, close in by the left bank of the lake, with no proper track to the place, I hardly had the nerve to venture close and come upon her face to face. When I did see her, though, I was disappointed. She wasn't much to look at after all. What I mean is, she hadn't got anything like his character. A placid, mild-tempered creature, I judged her.

They had both come back from fishing when I saw them, and were making their way up from the beach to the lake. He was in front, of course. She tagged along behind. Neither of them took the slightest notice of me, and I was glad, because the old man might have paused, and waited, and told her to get on back home, and then come down towards the rocks where I was sitting. You ask what I would have said, had he done so? I'm damned if I know. Maybe I would have got up, whistling and seeming unconcerned, and then, with a nod and a smile—useless, really, but instinctive, if you know what I mean—said good day and pottered off. I don't think he would have done anything. He'd just have stared after me, with those strange narrow eyes of his, and let me go.

After that, winter and summer, I was always down on the beach or the rocks, and they went on living their curious, remote existence, sometimes fishing in the lake, sometimes at sea. Occasionally I'd come across them in the harbour on the estuary, taking a look at the yachts anchored there, and the shipping. I used to wonder which of them made the suggestion. Perhaps suddenly he would be lured by the thought of the bustle and life of the harbour, and all the things he had either wantonly given up or never known, and he would say to her, "Today we are going into town." And she, happy to do whatever pleased him best, followed along.

You see, one thing that stood out—and you couldn't help noticing it—was that the pair of them were devoted to one another. I've seen her greet him when he came back from a day's fishing and had left her back home, and towards evening she'd come down the lake and on to the beach and down to the sea to wait for him. She'd see him coming from a long way off, and I would see him too, rounding the corner of the bay. He'd come straight in to the beach, and she would go to meet him, and they would embrace each other, not caring a damn who saw them. It was touching, if you know what I mean. You felt there was something lovable about the old man, if that's how things were between them. He might be a devil to outsiders, but he was all the world to her. It gave me a warm feeling for him when I saw them together like that.

You asked if they had any family. I was coming to that. It's about the family I really wanted to tell you. Because there was a tragedy, you see. And nobody knows anything about it except me. I suppose I could have told someone, but if I had, I don't know . . . They might have taken the old man away, and she'd have broken her heart without him, and anyway, when all's said and done, it wasn't my business. I know the evidence against the old man was strong, but I hadn't positive proof, it might have been some sort of accident, and anyway, nobody made any enquiries at the time the boy disappeared, so who was I to turn busybody and informer?

I'll try and explain what happened. But you must understand that all this took place over quite a time, and sometimes I was away from home or busy, and didn't go near the lake. Nobody seemed to take any interest in the couple living there but myself, so that it was only what I observed with my own eyes that makes this story, nothing that I heard from anybody else, no scraps of gossip or tales told about them behind their backs.

Yes, they weren't always alone, as they are now. They had four kids. Three girls and a boy. They brought up the four of them in that ramshackle old place by the lake, and it was always a wonder to me how they did it. God, I've known days when the rain lashed the lake into little waves that burst and broke on the muddy shore near by their place, and turned the marsh into a swamp, and the wind driving straight in. You'd have thought anyone with a grain of sense would have taken his missus and his kids out of it and gone off somewhere where they could get some creature comforts at least. Not the old man. If he could stick it, I guess he decided she could too, and the kids as well. Maybe he wanted to bring them up the hard way.

Mark you, they were attractive youngsters. Especially the youngest girl. I never knew her name, but I called her Tiny, she had so much go to her. Chip off the old block, in spite of her size. I can see her now, as a little thing, the first to venture paddling in the lake on a fine morning, way ahead of her sisters and the brother.

The brother I nicknamed Boy. He was the eldest and, between you and me, a bit of a fool. He hadn't the looks of his sisters and was a clumsy sort of fellow. The girls would play around on their own, and go fishing, and he'd hang about in the background, not knowing what to do with himself. If he possibly could he'd stay around home, near his mother. Proper mother's boy. That's why I gave him the name. Not that she seemed to fuss over him any more than she did the others. She treated the four alike, as far as I could tell. Her thoughts were always for the old man rather than for them. But Boy was just a great baby, and I have an idea he was simple.

Like their parents, the youngsters kept themselves to themselves. Been dinned into them, I dare say, by the old man. They never came down to the beach on their own and played; and it must have been a temptation, I thought, in full summer, when people came walking over the cliffs down to the beach to bathe and picnic. I suppose, for those strange reasons best known to himself, the old man had warned them to have no truck with strangers.

They were used to me pottering, day in, day out, fetching driftwood and that. And often I would pause and watch the kids playing by the lake. I didn't talk to them, though. They might have gone back and told the old man. They used to look up when I passed by, then glance away again, sort of shy. All but Tiny. Tiny would toss her head and do a somersault, just to show off.

I sometimes watched them go off, the six of them—the old man, the missus, Boy, and the three girls, for a day's fishing out to sea. The old man, of course, in charge; Tiny eager to help, close to her dad; the missus looking about her to see if the weather was going to keep fine; the two other girls alongside; and Boy, poor simple Boy, always the last to leave home. I never knew what sport they had. They used to stay out late, and I'd have left the beach by the time they came back again. But I guess they did well. They must have lived almost entirely on what they caught. Well, fish is said to be full of vitamins, isn't it? Perhaps the old man was a food faddist in his way.

Time passed, and the youngsters began to grow up. Tiny lost something of her individuality then, it seemed to me. She grew more like her sisters. They were a nice-looking trio, all the same. Quiet, you know, well behaved.

As for Boy, he was enormous. Almost as big as the old man, but with what a difference! He had none of his father's looks, or strength, or personality; he was nothing but a great clumsy lout. And the trouble was, I believe the old man was ashamed of him. He didn't pull his weight in the home, I'm certain of that. And out fishing he was perfectly useless. The girls would work away like beetles, with Boy, always in the background, making a mess of things. If his mother was there he just stayed by her side.

I could see it rattled the old man to have such an oaf of a son. Irritated him, too, because Boy was so big. It probably didn't make sense to his intolerant mind. Strength and stupidity didn't go together. In any normal family, of course, Boy would have left home by now and gone out to work. I used to wonder if they argued about it back in the evenings, the missus and the old man, or if it was something never admitted between them but tacitly understood—Boy was no good.

Well, they did leave home at last. At least, the girls did.

I'll tell you how it happened.

It was a day in late autumn, and I happened to be over doing some shopping in the little town overlooking the harbour, three miles from this place, and suddenly I saw the old man, the missus, the three girls, and Boy all making their way up to Pont—that's at the head of a creek going eastward from the harbour. There are a few cottages at Pont, and a farm and a church up behind. The family looked washed and spruced up, and so did the old man and the missus, and I wondered if they were going visiting. If they were, it was an unusual thing for them to do. But it's possible they had friends or acquaintances up there of whom I knew nothing. Anyway, that was the last I saw of them, on the fine Saturday afternoon, making for Pont.

It blew hard over the week end, a proper easterly gale. I kept indoors and didn't go out at all. I knew the seas would be breaking good and hard on the beach. I wondered if the old man and the family had been able to get back. They would have been wise to stay with their friends up Pont, if they had friends there.

It was Tuesday before the wind dropped and I went down to the beach again. Seaweed, driftwood, tar, and oil all over the place. It's always the same after an easterly blow. I looked up the lake, towards the old man's shack, and I saw him there, with the missus, just by the edge of the lake. But there was no sign of the youngsters.

I thought it a bit funny, and waited around in case they should appear. They never did. I walked right round the lake, and from the opposite bank I had a good view of their place, and even took out my old spyglass to have a closer look. They just weren't there. The old man was pottering about as he often did when he wasn't fishing, and the missus had settled herself down to bask in the sun. There was only one explanation. They had left the family with friends in Pont. They had sent the family for a holiday.

I can't help admitting I was relieved, because for one frightful moment I thought maybe they had started off back home on the Saturday night and got struck by the gale; and, well—that the old man and his missus had got back safely, but not the kids. It couldn't be that, though. I should have heard. Someone would have said something. The old man wouldn't be pottering there in his usual unconcerned fashion and the missus basking in the sun. No, that must have been it. They had left the family with friends. Or maybe the girls and Boy had gone up-country, gone to find themselves jobs at last.

Somehow it left a gap. I felt sad. So long now I had been used to seeing them all around, Tiny and the others. I had a strange sort of feeling that they had gone for good. Silly, wasn't it? To mind, I mean. There was the old man, and his missus, and the four youngsters, and I'd more or less watched them grow up, and now for no reason they had gone.

I wished then I knew even a word or two of his language so that I could have called out to him, neighbour-like, and said, "I see you and the missus are on your own. Nothing wrong, I hope?"

But there, it wasn't any use. He'd have looked at me with his strange eyes and told me to go to hell.

I never saw the girls again. No, never. They just didn't come back. Once I thought I saw Tiny, somewhere up the estuary, with a group of friends, but I couldn't be sure. If it was, she'd grown, she looked different. I tell you what I think. I think the old man and the missus took them with a definite end in view, that last week end, and either settled them with friends they knew or told them to shift for themselves.

I know it sounds hard, not what you'd do for your own son and daughters, but you have to remember the old man was a tough customer, a law unto himself. No doubt he thought it would be for the best, and so it probably was, and if only I could know for certain what happened to the girls, especially Tiny, I wouldn't worry.

But I do worry sometimes, because of what happened to Boy.

You see, Boy was fool enough to come back. He came back about three weeks after that final week end. I had walked down through the woods—not my usual way, but down to the lake by the stream that feeds it from a higher level. I rounded the lake by the marshes to the north, some distance from the old man's place, and the first thing I saw was Boy.

He wasn't doing anything. He was just standing by the marsh. He looked dazed. He was too far off for me to hail him; besides, I didn't have the nerve. But I watched him as he stood there in his clumsy loutish way, and I saw him staring at the far end of the lake. He was staring in the direction of the old man.

The old man, and the missus with him, took not the slightest notice of Boy. They were close to the beach, by the plank bridge, and were either just going out to fish or coming back. And here was Boy, with his dazed stupid face, but not only stupid—frightened.

I wanted to say, "Is anything the matter?" but I didn't know how to say it. I stood there, like Boy, staring at the old man.

Then what we both must have feared would happen, happened. The old man lifted his head and saw Boy.

He must have said a word to his missus, because she didn't move, she stayed where she was, by the bridge, but the old man turned like a flash of lightning and came down the other side of the lake towards the marshes, towards Boy. He looked terrible. I shall never forget his appearance. That magnificent head I had always admired now angry, evil; and he was cursing Boy as he came. I tell you, I heard him.

Boy, bewildered, scared, looked hopelessly about him for cover. There was none. Only the thin reeds that grew beside the marsh. But the poor fellow was so dumb he went in there, and crouched, and believed himself safe—it was a horrible sight.

I was just getting my own courage up to interfere when the old man stopped suddenly in his tracks, pulled up short as it were, and then, still cursing, muttering, turned back again and returned to the bridge. Boy watched him from his cover of reeds, then, poor clot that he was, came out on to the marsh again, with some idea, I suppose, of striking for home.

I looked about me. There was no one to call. No one to give any help. And if I went and tried to get someone from the farm they would tell me not to interfere, that the old man was best left alone when he got in one of his rages, and anyway, that Boy was old enough to take care of himself. He was as big as the old man. He could give as good as he got. I knew different. Boy was no fighter. He didn't know how.

I waited quite a time beside the lake, but nothing happened. It began to grow dark. It was no use my waiting there. The old man and the missus left the bridge and went on home. Boy was still standing there on the marsh by the lake's edge.

I called to him softly. "It's no use. He won't let you in. Go back to Pont, or wherever it is you've been. Go to some place, anywhere, but get out of here."

He looked up, that same queer dazed expression on his face, and I could tell he hadn't understood a word I said.

I felt powerless to do any more. I went home myself. But I thought about Boy all evening, and in the morning I went down to the lake again, and I took a great stick with me to give me courage. Not that it would have been much good. Not against the old man.

Well . . . I suppose they had come to some sort of agreement during the night. There was Boy, by his mother's side, and the old man was pottering on his own.

I must say, it was a great relief. Because, after all, what could I have said or done? If the old man didn't want Boy home, it was really his affair. And if Boy was too stupid to go, that was Boy's affair.

But I blamed the mother a good deal. After all, it was up to her to tell Boy he was in the way, and the old man was in one of his moods, and Boy had best get out while the going was good. But I never did think she had great intelligence. She did not seem to show much spirit at any time.

However, what arrangement they had come to worked for a time. Boy stuck close to his mother—I suppose he helped her at home, I don't know—and the old man left them alone and was more and more by himself.

He took to sitting down by the bridge, humped, staring out to sea, with a queer brooding look on him. He seemed strange, and lonely. I didn't like it. I don't know what his thoughts were, but I'm sure they were evil. It suddenly seemed a very long time since he and the missus and the whole family had gone fishing, a happy, contented party. Now everything had changed for him. He was thrust out in the cold, and the missus and Boy stayed together.

I felt sorry for him, but I felt frightened too. Because I felt it could not go on like this indefinitely; something would happen.

One day I went down to the beach for driftwood—it had been blowing in the night—and when I glanced towards the lake I saw that Boy wasn't with his mother. He was back where I had seen him that first day, on the edge of the marsh. He was as big as his father. If he'd known how to use his strength he'd have been a match for him any day, but he hadn't the brains. There he was, back on the marsh, a great big frightened foolish fellow, and there was the old man, outside his home, staring down towards his son with murder in his eyes.

I said to myself, "He's going to kill him." But I didn't know how or when or where, whether by night, when they were sleeping, or by day, when they were fishing. The mother was useless, she would not prevent it. It was no use appealing to the mother. If only Boy would use one little grain of sense, and go . . .

I watched and waited until nightfall. Nothing happened.

It rained in the night. It was grey, and cold, and dim. December was everywhere, trees all bare and bleak. I couldn't get down to the lake until late afternoon, and then the skies had cleared and the sun was shining in that watery way it does in winter, a burst of it, just before setting below the sea.

I saw the old man, and the missus too. They were close together, by the old shack, and they saw me coming, for they looked towards me. Boy wasn't there. He wasn't on the marsh, either. Nor by the side of the lake.

I crossed the bridge and went along the right bank of the lake, and I had my spyglass with me, but I couldn't see Boy. Yet all the time I was aware of the old man watching me.

Then I saw him. I scrambled down the bank, and crossed the marsh, and went to the thing I saw lying there behind the reeds.

He was dead. There was a great gash on his body. Dried blood on his back. But he had lain there all night. His body was sodden with the rain.

Maybe you'll think I'm a fool, but I began to cry like an idiot, and I shouted across to the old man, "You murderer, you bloody goddamned murderer." He did not answer. He did not move. He stood there outside his shack with the missus, watching me.

You'll want to know what I did. I went back and got a spade, and I dug a grave for Boy, in the reeds behind the marsh, and I said one of my own prayers for him, being uncertain of his religion. When I had finished I looked across the lake to the old man.

And do you know what I saw?

I saw him lower his great head and bend towards her and embrace her. And she lifted her head to him and embraced him too. It was both a requiem and a benediction. An atonement and a giving of praise. In their strange way they knew they had done evil, but now it was over, because I had buried Boy and he was gone. They were free to be together again, and there was no longer a third to divide them.

They came out into the middle of the lake, and suddenly I saw the old man stretch his neck and beat his wings, and he took off from the water, full of power, and she followed him. I watched the two swans fly out to sea right into the face of the setting sun, and I tell you, it was one of the most beautiful sights I ever saw in my life: the two swans flying there, alone, in winter.

The Split Second

MRS. ELLIS was methodical and tidy. She disliked disorder. Unanswered letters, unpaid bills, the litter and rummage of a slovenly writing desk were things that she abhorred.

Today, more than usual, she was in what her late husband used to call her "clearing" mood.

She had wakened to this mood; it remained with her throughout breakfast and lasted the whole morning.

Besides, it was the first of the month, and as she ripped off the page of her daily calendar and saw the bright clean 1 staring at her, it seemed to symbolise a new start to her day.

The hours ahead of her must somehow seem untarnished like the date; she must let nothing slide.

First she checked the linen. The smooth white sheets lying in rows upon their shelves, pillow slips beside, and one set still in its pristine newness from the shop, tied with blue ribbon, waiting for a guest that never came.

Next, the store cupboard. The stock of homemade jam pleased her, the labels, and the date in her own handwriting.

There were also bottled fruit, and tomatoes, and chutney to her own recipe. She was sparing of these, keeping them in reserve for the holidays when Susan should be home, and even then, when she brought them down and put them proudly on the table, the luxury of the treat was spoilt by a little stab of disappointment; it would mean a gap upon the store-cupboard shelf.

When she had closed the store cupboard and hidden the key (she could never be quite certain of Grace, her cook), Mrs. Ellis went into the drawing-room and settled herself at her desk.

She was determined to be ruthless. The pigeonholes were searched, and those old envelopes that she had kept because they were not torn and could be used again (to tradesmen, not to friends) were thrown away. She would buy fresh buff envelopes of a cheap quality instead.

Here were some receipts of two years back. Unnecessary to keep them now. Those of a year ago were filed, and tied with tape.

A little drawer, stiff to open, she found crammed with old counter-foils from her chequebook. This was wasting space.

Instead, she wrote in her clear handwriting, "Letters to Keep." In the future, the drawer would be used for this purpose.

She permitted herself the luxury of filling her blotter with new sheets of paper. The pen tray was dusted. A new pencil sharpened. And steeling her heart, she threw the stub of the little old one, with worn rubber at the base, into the wastepaper basket.

She straightened the magazines on the side table, pulled the books to the front on the shelf beside the fire—Grace had an infuriating habit of pushing them all to the back—and filled the flower vases with clean water. Then with a bare ten minutes before Grace popped her head round the door and said, "Lunch is in," Mrs. Ellis sat down, a little breathless, before the fire, and smiled in satisfaction. Her morning had been very full indeed. Happy, well spent.

She looked about her drawing-room (Grace insisted on calling it the lounge and Mrs. Ellis was forever correcting her) and thought how comfortable it was, and bright, and how wise they had been not to move when poor Wilfred suggested it a few months before he died. They had so nearly taken that house in the country, because of his health, and his fad that vegetables should be picked fresh every morning and brought to the table, and then luckily—well, hardly luckily, it was most terribly sad and a fearful shock to her—but before they had signed the lease, Wilfred had a heart attack and died. Mrs. Ellis was able to stay on in the home she knew and loved, and where she had first gone as a bride ten years before.

People were inclined to say the locality was going downhill, that it had become worse than surburban. Nonsense. The blocks of flats that were going up at the top end of the road could not be seen from her windows, and the houses, solid like her own, standing in a little circle of front garden, were quite unspoilt.

Besides, she liked the life. Her mornings, shopping in the town, her basket over her arm. The tradesmen knew her, treated her well.

Morning coffee at eleven, at the Cosy Café opposite the bookshop, was a small pleasure she allowed herself on cold mornings—she could not get Grace to make good coffee—and in the summer, the Cosy Café sold ice cream.

Childishly, she would hurry back with this in a paper bag and eat it for lunch; it saved thinking of a sweet.

She believed in a brisk walk in the afternoons, and the heath was so close to hand, it was just as good as the country; and in the evenings she read, or sewed, or wrote to Susan.

Life, if she thought deeply about it, which she did not because to think deeply made her uncomfortable, was really built round Susan. Susan was nine years old, and her only child.

Because of Wilfred's ill-health and, it must be confessed, his irritability, Susan had been sent to boarding school at an early age. Mrs. Ellis had passed many sleepless nights before making this decision, but in the end she knew it would be for Susan's good. The child was healthy and high-spirited, and it was impossible to keep her quiet and subdued in one room, with Wilfred fractious in another. It meant sending her down to the kitchen with Grace, and that, Mrs. Ellis decided, did not do.

Reluctantly, the school was chosen, some thirty miles away. It was easily reached within an hour and a half by a Green Line bus; the children seemed happy and well cared for, the principal was grey-haired and sympathetic, and as the prospectus described it, the place was a "home from home."

Mrs. Ellis left Susan, on the opening day of her first term, in agony of mind, but constant telephone calls between herself and the head-mistress during the first week reassured her that Susan had settled placidly to her new existence.

When her husband died, Mrs. Ellis thought Susan would want to return home and go to a day school, but to her surprise and disappoint-ment the suggestion was received with dismay, and even tears.

"But I love my school," said the child; "we have such fun, and I have lots of friends."

"You would make other friends at a day school," said her mother, "and think, we would be together in the evenings."

"Yes," answered Susan doubtfully, "but what would we do?"

Mrs. Ellis was hurt, but she did not permit Susan to see this.

"Perhaps you are right," she said. "You are contented and happy where you are. Anyway, we shall always have the holidays."

The holidays were like brightly coloured beads on a frame and stood out with significance in Mrs. Ellis' engagement diary, throwing the weeks between into obscurity.

How leaden was February, in spite of its twenty-eight days; how blue and interminable was March, for all that morning coffee at the Cosy Café, the choosing of library books, the visit with friends to the local cinema, or sometimes, more dashing, a matinee "in town."

Then April came, and danced its flowery way across the calendar. Easter, and daffodils, and Susan with glowing cheeks whipped by a spring wind, hugging her once again; honey for tea, scones baked by Grace ("You've been and grown again"), those afternoon walks across the heath, sunny and gay because of the figure running on ahead. May was quiet, and June pleasant because of wide-flung windows, and the snapdragons in the front garden; June was leisurely.

Besides, there was the school play on Parents' Day, and Susan, with bright eyes, surely much the best of the pixies, and although she did not speak, her actions were so good.

July dragged until the twenty-fourth, and then the weeks spun them-selves into a sequence of glory until the last week in September. Susan at the sea . . . Susan on a farm . . . Susan on Dartmoor . . . Susan just at home, licking an ice cream, leaning out of a window.

"She swims quite well for her age," thus casually, to a neighbor on the beach; "she insists on going in, even when it's cold."

"I don't mind saying," this to Grace, "that I hated going through that field of bullocks, but Susan did not mind a scrap. She has a way with animals."

Bare scratched legs in sandals, summer frocks outgrown, a sun hat, faded, lying on the floor. October did not bear thinking about. . . . But, after all, there was always plenty to do about the house. Forget November, and the rain, and the fogs that turned white upon the heath. Draw the curtains, poke the fire, settle to something. The *Weekly Home Companion*. Fashions for Young Folk. Not that pink, but the green with the smocked top, and a wide sash would be just the thing for Susan at parties in the Christmas holidays. December . . . Christmas . . .

This was the best, this was the height of home enjoyment.

As soon as Mrs. Ellis saw the first small trees standing outside the florist and those orange boxes of dates in the grocer's window, her heart would give a little leap of excitement.

Susan would be home in three weeks now. Then the laughter and the chatter. The nods between herself and Grace. The smiles of mystery. The furtiveness of wrappings.

All over in one day like the bursting of a swollen balloon; paper ribbon, cracker novelties, even presents, chosen with care, thrown aside. But no matter. It was worth it.

Mrs. Ellis, looking down upon a sleeping Susan tucked in with a doll in her arms, turned down the light and crept off to her own bed, sapped, exhausted.

The egg cosy, Susan's handiwork at school, hastily stitched, stood on her bedside table.

Mrs. Ellis never ate boiled eggs, but, as she said to Grace, there is such a gleam in the hen's eye; it's very cleverly done.

The fever, the pace of the New Year. The Circus, the Pantomime. Mrs. Ellis watched Susan, never the performers.

"You should have seen her laugh when the seal blew the trumpet; I have never known a child with such a gift for enjoyment."

And how she stood out at parties, in the green frock, with her fair hair and blue eyes. Other children were so stumpy. Ill-made little bodies, or big shapeless mouths.

"She said, 'Thank you for a lovely time,' when we left, which was more than most of them did. And she won at Musical Chairs."

There were bad moments, too, of course. The restless night, the high spot of colour, the sore throat, the temperature of 102.

Shaking hands on the telephone. The doctor's reassuring voice. And his very footsteps on the stairs, a steady, reliable man.

"We had better take a swab, in case."

A swab? That meant diphtheria, scarlet fever?

A little figure being carried down in blankets, an ambulance, hospital . . . ?

Thank God, it proved to be a relaxed throat. Lots of them about. Too many parties, keep her quiet for a few days. Yes, Doctor, yes.

The relief from dread anxiety, and on and on without a stop, the reading to Susan from her *Playbook Annual*, story after story, terrible and trite, "and so Nicky Nod *did* lose his treasure after all, which just served him right, didn't it, children?"

"All things pass," thought Mrs. Ellis, "pleasure and pain, and happiness and suffering, and I suppose my friends would say my life is a dull one, rather uneventful, but I am grateful for it, and contented, and although sometimes I feel I did not do my utmost for poor Wilfred—his was a difficult nature, luckily Susan has not inherited it—at least I believe I have succeeded in making a happy home for Susan." She looked about her, that first day of the month, and noticed with affection and appreciation those bits and pieces of furniture, the pictures on the walls, the ornaments on the mantelpiece, all the things she had gathered about her during ten years of marriage, and which meant herself, her home.

The sofa and two chairs, part of an original suite, were worn but comfortable. The pouf by the fire, she had covered it herself. The fire irons, not quite so polished as they should be, she must speak to Grace. The rather melancholy portrait of Wilfred in that dark corner behind the bookshelf, he looked at least distinguished. And was, thought Mrs. Ellis to herself, hastily. The flower picture showed more to advantage over the mantelpiece; the green foliage harmonised so well with the green coat of the Staffordshire figure who stood with his lady beside the clock.

"I could do with new covers," thought Mrs. Ellis, "and curtains too, but they must wait. Susan has grown so enormously the last few months. Her clothes are more important. The child is tall for her age."

Grace looked round the door. "Lunch is in," she said.

"If she would open the door outright," thought Mrs. Ellis, "and come right into the room, I have mentioned it a hundred times. It's the sudden thrust of the head that is so disconcerting, and if I have anyone to lunch . . ."

She sat down to guinea fowl and apple charlotte, and she wondered if they were remembering to give Susan extra milk at school this term, and the Minidex tonic; the matron was inclined to be forgetful.

Suddenly, for no reason, she laid her spoon down on the plate, swept with a wave of such intense melancholy as to be almost unbearable. Her heart was heavy. Her throat tightened. She could not continue her lunch.

"Something is wrong with Susan," she thought; "this is a warning that she wants me."

She rang for coffee and went into the drawing-room. She crossed to the window and stood looking at the back of the house opposite. From an open window sagged an ugly red curtain, and a lavatory brush hung from a nail.

"The district *is* losing class," thought Mrs. Ellis. "I shall have lodginghouses for neighbours soon."

She drank her coffee, but the feeling of uneasiness, of apprehension, did not leave her. At last she went to the telephone and rang up the school.

The secretary answered. Surprised, and a little impatient, surely. Susan was perfectly all right. She had just eaten a good lunch. No, she had no sign of a cold. No one was ill in the school. Did Mrs. Ellis want to speak to Susan? The child was outside with the others, playing, but could be called in if necessary.

"No," said Mrs. Ellis, "it was just a foolish notion on my part that Susan might not be well. I am so sorry to have bothered you."

She hung up the receiver, and then went to her bedroom to put on her outdoor clothes. A good walk would do her good.

She gazed in satisfaction upon the photograph of Susan on the dressing table. The photographer had caught the expression in her eyes to perfection. Such a lovely light on the hair too.

Mrs. Ellis hesitated. Was it really a walk she needed? Or was this vague feeling of distress a sign that she was overtired, that she had better rest?

She looked with inclination at the downy quilt upon her bed. Her hot-water bottle, hanging by the washstand, would take only a moment to fill.

She could loosen her girdle, throw off her shoes, and lie down for an hour on the bed, warm with the bottle under the downy quilt. No. She decided to be firm with herself. She went to the wardrobe and got out her camel coat, wound a scarf round her head, pulled on a pair of gauntlet gloves, and walked downstairs.

She went into the drawing-room and made up the fire, and put the guard in front of it. Grace was apt to be forgetful of the fire. She opened the window at the top so that the room should not strike stuffy when she came back.

She folded the daily papers ready to read when she returned, and replaced the marker in her library book.

"I'm going out for a little while. I shan't be long," she called down to the basement to Grace.

"All right, ma'am," came the answer.

Mrs. Ellis caught the whiff of cigarette, and frowned. Grace could do as she liked in the basement, but there was something not quite right about a maidservant smoking.

She shut the front door behind her, and went down the steps, and into the road, and turned left towards the heath.

It was a dull, grey day. Mild for the time of year, almost to oppression. Later, there would be fog, perhaps, rolling up from London the way it did, in a great wall, stifling the clean air.

Mrs. Ellis made her "short round," as she always called it. Eastward, to the Viaduct ponds, and then back, circling, to the Vale of Health.

It was not an inviting afternoon, and she did not enjoy her walk. She kept wishing she was home again, in bed with a hot-water bottle, or sitting in the drawing-room beside the fire, soon to shut out the muggy, murky sky, and draw the curtains.

She walked swiftly past nurses pushing prams, two or three of them in groups chatting together, their charges running ahead. Dogs barked beside the ponds. Solitary men in mackintoshes stared into vacancy. An old woman on a seat threw crumbs to chirping sparrows. The sky took on a darker, olive tone. Mrs. Ellis quickened her steps. The fairground by the Vale of Health looked sombre, the merry-go-round shrouded in its winter wrappings of canvas, and two lean cats stalked each other in and out of the palings.

A milkman, whistling, clanked his tray of bottles and, lifting them to his cart, urged the pony to a trot.

"I must," thought Mrs. Ellis inconsequently, "get Susan a bicycle for her birthday. Nine is a good age for a first bicycle."

She saw herself choosing one, asking advice, feeling the handle bars. The colour red perhaps. Or a good blue. A little basket on the front and a leather bag, for tools, strapped to the back of the seat. The brakes must be good, but not too gripping, otherwise Susan would topple headfirst over the handle bars and graze her face.

Hoops were out of fashion, which was a pity. When she had been a child there had been no fun like a good springy hoop, struck smartly with a little stick, bowling its way ahead of you. Quite an art to it too. Susan would have been good with a hoop.

Mrs. Ellis came to the junction of two roads, and crossed to the opposite side; the second road was her own, and her house the last one on the corner.

As she did so she saw the laundry van swinging down towards her, much too fast. She saw it swerve, heard the screech of its brakes. She saw the look of surprise on the face of the laundry boy.

"I shall speak to the driver next time he calls," she said to herself. "One of these days there will be an accident."

She thought of Susan on the bicycle, and shuddered.

Perhaps a note to the manager of the laundry would do more good.

"If you could possibly give a word of warning to your driver, I should be grateful. He takes his corners much to fast."

And she would ask to remain anonymous. Otherwise the man might complain about carrying the heavy basket down the steps each time.

She had arrived at her own gate. She pushed it open, and noticed with annoyance that it was nearly off its hinges. The men calling for the laundry must have wrenched at it in some way and done the damage. The note to the manager would be stronger still. She would write immediately after tea. While it was on her mind.

She took out her key and put it in the Yale lock of the front door. It stuck. She could not turn it. How very irritating.

She rang the bell. This would mean bringing Grace up from the basement, which she did not like.

Better to call down, perhaps, and explain the situation.

She leant over the steps and called down to the kitchen.

"Grace, it's only me," she said, "my key has jammed in the door; could you come up and let me in?"

She paused. There was no sound from below. Grace must have gone out. This was sheer deceit. It was an agreed bargain between them that when Mrs. Ellis was out Grace must stay in. The house must not be left. But sometimes Mrs. Ellis suspected that Grace did not keep to the bargain. Here was proof.

She called once again, rather more sharply this time.

"Grace?"

There was a sound of a window opening below, and a man thrust his head out of the kitchen. He was in his shirt sleeves. And he had not shaved.

"What are you bawling your head off about?" he said.

Mrs. Ellis was too stunned to answer. So this was what happened when her back was turned. Grace, respectable, well over thirty, had a man in the house. Mrs. Ellis swallowed, but kept her temper.

"Perhaps you will have the goodness to ask Grace to come upstairs and let me in," she said.

The sarcasm was wasted, of course. The man blinked at her, bewildered.

"Who's Grace?" he said.

This was too much. So Grace had the nerve to pass under another name. Something fanciful, no doubt. Shirley, or Marlene.

She was pretty sure now what must have happened. Grace had slipped out to the public house down the road to buy this man beer. The man was left to loll in the kitchen. He might even have been poking his fingers in the larder. Now she knew why there was so little left on the joint two days ago.

"If Grace is out," said Mrs. Ellis, and her voice was icy, "kindly let me in yourself. I prefer not to use the back entrance."

That would put him in his place. Mrs. Ellis trembled with rage. She was angry seldom; she was a mild, even-tempered woman. But this reception, from a lout in shirt sleeves, at her own kitchen window, was rather more than she could bear.

It was going to be unpleasant, the interview with Grace. Grace would give notice in all probability. But some things could not be allowed to slide, and this was one of them.

She heard shuffling footsteps coming along the hall. The man had mounted from the basement. He opened the front door and stood there, staring at her.

"Who is it you want?" he said.

Mrs. Ellis heard the furious yapping of a little dog from the drawing-room. Callers . . . This was the end. How perfectly frightful, how really overwhelmingly embarrassing. Someone had called, and Grace had let them in, or, worse still, this man in his shirt sleeves had done so. What would people think?

"Who is in the drawing-room, do you know?" she murmured swiftly.

"I think Mr. and Mrs. Bolton are in, but I'm not sure," he said. "I can hear the dog yapping. Was it them you wanted to see?"

Mrs. Ellis did not know a Mr. and Mrs. Bolton. She turned impatiently towards the drawing-room, first whipping off her coat and putting her gloves in her pocket.

"You had better go down to the basement again," she said to the man, who was still staring at her; "tell Grace not to bring tea until I ring. These people may not stay."

The man appeared bewildered.

"All right," he said, "I'm going down. But if you want Mr. and Mrs. Bolton again, ring twice."

He shuffled off down the basement stairs. He was drunk, no doubt. He meant to be insulting. If he proved difficult, later in the evening, after dark, it would mean ringing for the police.

Mrs. Ellis slipped into the lobby to hang up her coat. No time to go upstairs if callers were in the drawing-room. She fumbled for the switch and turned it, but the bulb had gone. Another pinprick. Now she could not see herself in the mirror.

She stumbled over something, and bent to see what it was. It was a man's boot. And here was another, and a pair of shoes, and beside them a suitcase and an old rug. If Grace had allowed that man to put his things in her lobby, then Grace would go tonight. Crisis had come. High crisis.

Mrs. Ellis opened the drawing-room door, forcing a smile of welcome, not too warm, upon her lips. A little dog rushed towards her, barking furiously.

"Quiet, Judy," said a man, grey-haired, with horn spectacles, sitting before the fire. He was clicking a typewriter.

Something had happened to the room. It was covered with books and papers; odds and ends of junk littered the floor. A parrot, in a cage, hopped on its perch and screeched a welcome.

Mrs. Ellis tried to speak, but her voice would not come. Grace had gone raving mad. She had let that man into the house, and this one too, and they had brought the most terrible disorder; they had turned the room upside down; they had deliberately, maliciously, set themselves to destroy her things.

No. Worse! It was part of a great thieving plot. She had heard of such things. Gangs went about breaking into houses. Grace, perhaps, was not at fault. She was lying in the basement, gagged and bound. Mrs. Ellis felt her heart beating much too fast. She also felt a little faint.

"I must keep calm," she said to herself, "whatever happens, I must keep calm. If I can get to the telephone, to the police, it is the only hope. This man must not see that I am planning what to do."

The little dog kept sniffing at her heels.

"Excuse me," said the intruder, pushing his horn spectacles on to his forehead, "but do you want anything? My wife is upstairs."

The diabolic cunning of the plot. The cool bluff of his sitting there, the typewriter on his knees. They must have brought all this stuff in through the door to the back garden; the french window was ajar. Mrs. Ellis glanced swiftly at the mantelpiece. It was as she feared. The Staffordshire figures had been removed, and the flower picture too. There must be a car, a van, waiting down the road. . . . Her mind worked quickly. It might be that the man had not guessed her identity. Two could play at bluff. Memories of amateur theatricals flashed through her mind. Somehow she must detain these people until the police arrived. How fast they had worked. Her desk was gone, the bookshelves too, nor could she see her armchair.

But she kept her eyes steadily on the stranger. He must not notice her brief glance round the room.

"Your wife is upstairs?" said Mrs. Ellis, her voice strained, yet calm.

"Yes," said the man, "if you've come for an appointment, she always makes them. You'll find her in the studio. Room in the front."

Steadily, softly, Mrs. Ellis left the drawing-room, but the wretched little dog had followed her, sniffing at her heels.

One thing was certain. The man had not realised who she was. They believed the householder out of the way for the afternoon, and that she, standing now in the hall, listening, her heart beating, was some caller to be fobbed off with a lie about appointments.

She stood silently by the drawing-room door. The man had resumed typing on his machine. She marvelled at the coolness of it, the drawn-out continuity of the bluff.

There had been nothing in the papers very recently about large-scale house robberies. This was something new, something outstanding. It was extraordinary that they should pick on her house. But they must know she was a widow, on her own, with one maidservant. The telephone had already been removed from the stand in the hall. There was a loaf of bread on it instead, and something that looked like meat wrapped up in newspaper. So they had brought provisions. . . . There was a chance that the telephone in her bedroom had not yet been taken away, nor the wires cut. The man had said his wife was upstairs. It may have been part of his bluff, or it might be true that he worked with a woman accomplice. This woman, even now, was probably turning out Mrs. Ellis' wardrobe, seizing her fur coat, ramming the single string of cultured pearls into a pocket.

Mrs. Ellis thought she could hear footsteps in her bedroom.

Her anger overcame her fear. She had not the strength to do battle with the man, but she could face the woman. And if the worst came to the worst, she would run to the window, put her head out, and scream. The people next door would hear. Or someone might be passing in the street.

Stealthily, Mrs. Ellis crept upstairs. The little dog led the way with confidence. She paused outside her bedroom door. There was certainly movement from within. The little dog waited, his eyes fixed upon her with intelligence.

At that moment the door of Susan's small bedroom opened, and a fat elderly woman looked out, blowzy, and red in the face. She had a tabby cat under her arm. As soon as the dog saw the cat it started a furious yapping.

"Now that's torn it," said the woman. "What do you want to bring the dog upstairs for? They always fight when they meet. Do you know if the post's been yet? Oh, sorry. I thought you were Mrs. Bolton."

She brought an empty milk bottle from under her other arm and put it down on the landing.

"I'm blowed if I can manage the stairs today," she said, "somebody else will have to take it down for me. Is it foggy out?"

"No," said Mrs. Ellis, shocked into a natural answer, and then, feeling the woman's eyes upon her, hesitated between entering her bedroom door and withdrawing down the stairs. This evil-looking old woman was part of the gang and might call the man from below.

"Got an appointment?" said the other. "She won't see you if you haven't booked an appointment."

A tremour of a smile appeared on Mrs. Ellis' lips.

"Thank you," she said, "yes, I have an appointment."

She was amazed at her own steadiness, and that she could carry off the situation with such aplomb. An actress on the London stage could not have played her part better.

The elderly woman winked and, drawing nearer, plucked Mrs. Ellis by the sleeve.

"Is she going to do you straight or fancy?" she whispered. "It's the fancy ones that get the men. You know what I mean!"

She nudged Mrs. Ellis and winked again.

"I see by your ring you're married," she said. "You'd be surprised, even the quietest husbands like their pictures fancy. Take a tip from an old pro. Get her to do you fancy."

She lurched back into Susan's room, the cat under her arm, and shut the door.

"It's possible," thought Mrs. Ellis, the faint feeling coming over her once again, "that a group of lunatics have escaped from an asylum, and in their terrible, insane fashion, they have broken into my house not to thieve, not to destroy my belongings, but because in some crazed, deluded fashion they believe themselves to be at home."

The publicity would be frightful once it became known. Headlines in the papers. Her photograph taken. So bad for Susan. Susan . . . That horrible, disgusting old woman in Susan's bedroom.

Emboldened, fortified, Mrs. Ellis opened her own bedroom door. One glance revealed the worst. The room was bare, was stripped.

There were several lights at various points of the room, flexes attached, and a camera on a tripod. A divan was pushed against the wall. A young woman, with a crop of thick fuzzy hair, was kneeling on the floor, sorting papers.

"Who is it?" she said. "I don't see anyone without an appointment. You've no right to come in here."

Mrs. Ellis, calm, resolute, did not answer. She had made certain that the telephone, though it had been moved like the rest of her things, was still in the room.

She went to it and lifted the receiver.

"Leave my telephone alone," cried the shock-haired girl, and she began to struggle to her knees.

"I want the police," said Mrs. Ellis firmly to the exchange, "I want them to come at once to 17 Elmhurst Road. I am in great danger. Please report this message to the police at once."

The girl was beside her now, taking the receiver from her.

"Who's sent you here?" said the girl, her face sallow, colourless, against the fuzzy hair. "If you think you can come in snooping, you're mistaken. You won't find anything. Nor the police, neither. I have a trade license for the work I do."

Her voice had risen, and the dog, alarmed, joined her with high-pitched barks. The girl opened the door and called down the stairs.

"Harry?" she shouted. "Come here and throw this woman out."

Mrs. Ellis remained quite calm. She stood with her back to the wall, her hands folded. The exchange had taken her message. It would not be long now before the police arrived.

She heard the drawing-room door open from below, and the man's voice called up, petulant, irritated.

"What's the matter?" he shouted. "You know I'm busy. Can't you deal with the woman? She probably wants a special pose."

The girl's eyes narrowed. She looked closely at Mrs. Ellis.

"What did my husband say to you?" she said.

"Ah!" thought Mrs. Ellis triumphantly. "They are getting frightened. It's not such an easy game as they think."

"I had no conversation with your husband," said Mrs. Ellis quietly; "he merely told me I should find you upstairs. In this room. Don't try any bluff with me. It's too late. I can see what you have been doing."

She gestured at the room. The girl stared at her.

"You can't put any phony business over on me," she said; "this studio is decent, respectable, everyone knows that. I take camera studies of children. Plenty of clients can testify to that. You've got no proof of anything else. Show me a negative, and then I might believe you."

Mrs. Ellis wondered how long it would be before the police came. She must continue to play for time. Later, she might even feel sorry, perhaps, for this wretched, deluded girl who had wrought such havoc in the bedroom, believing herself to be a photographer; but this moment, now, she must be calm, calm.

"Well?" said the girl. "What are you going to say when the police come? What's your story?"

It did not do to antagonize lunatics. Mrs. Ellis knew that. They must be humoured. She must humour this girl until the police came.

"I shall tell them that I live here," she said gently; "that is all they will need to know. Nothing further."

The girl looked at her, puzzled, and lit a cigarette.

"Then it is a pose you want?" she said. "That call was just a bluff? Why don't you come clean and say why you're here?"

The sound of their voices had attracted the attention of the old woman in Susan's room. She tapped on the door, which was already open, and stood on the threshold.

"Anything wrong, dear?" she said slyly to the girl.

"Push on out of it," said the girl impatiently, "this is none of your business. I don't interfere with you, and you don't interfere with me."

"I'm not interfering, dear," said the woman, "I only wanted to know if I could help. Difficult client, eh? Wants something outsize?"

"Oh, shut your mouth," said the girl.

The girl's husband, Bolton or whatever his name was, the spectacled man from the drawing-room, came upstairs and into the bedroom.

"Just what's going on?" he said.

The girl shrugged her shoulders and glanced at Mrs. Ellis.

"I don't know," she said, "but I think it's blackmail."

"Has she got any negatives?" said the man swiftly.

"Not that I know of. Never seen her before."

"She might have got them from another client," said the elderly woman, watching.

The three of them stared at Mrs. Ellis. She was not afraid. She had
the situation well in hand.

"I think we've all become a little overwrought," she said, "and much
the best thing to do would be to go downstairs, sit quietly by the fire,
and have a little chat, and you can talk to me about your work. Tell
me, are you all three photographers?"

As she spoke, half of her mind was wondering where they had
managed to hide her things. They must have bundled her bed into
Susan's room; the wardrobe was in two parts, of course, and could be
taken to pieces very soon; but her clothes . . . her ornaments . . . these
must have been concealed in a lorry. Somewhere, there was a lorry
filled with all her things. It might be parked down another road, or
might have been driven off already by yet another accomplice. The
police were good at tracing stolen goods, she knew that, and everything
was insured; but such a mess had been made of the house; insurance
would never cover that, nor would her fire policy, unless there was
some clause, some proviso against damage by lunatics; surely the insurance people would not call that an act of God. . . . Her mind ran
on and on, taking in the mess, the disorder, these people had created,
and how many days and weeks would it take for her and Grace to get
everything straight again?

Poor Grace. She had forgotten Grace. Grace must be shut up somewhere in the basement with that dreadful man in shirt sleeves, another
of the gang, not a follower at all.

"Well," said Mrs. Ellis with the other half of her mind, the half that
was acting so famously, "shall we do as I suggest and go downstairs?"

She turned, and led the way, and to her surprise they followed her,
the man and his wife, not the horrible old woman. She remained above,
leaning over the banisters.

"Call me if you want me," she said.

Mrs. Ellis could not bear to think of her fingering Susan's things in
the little bedroom.

"Won't you join us?" she said, steeling herself to courtesy. "It's far
more cheerful down below."

The old woman smirked. "That's for Mr. and Mrs. Bolton to say,"
she said, "I don't push myself."

"If I can get all three of them pinned into the drawing-room,"
thought Mrs. Ellis, "and somehow lock the door, and make a tremen-

dous effort at conversation, I might possibly keep their attention until the police arrive. There is, of course, the door into the garden, but then they will have to climb the fence, fall over that potting shed next door. The old woman, at least, would never do it."

"Now," said Mrs. Ellis, her heart turning over inside at the havoc of the drawing-room, "shall we sit down and recover ourselves, and you shall tell me all about this photography."

But she had scarcely finished speaking before there was a ring at the front door, and a knock, authoritative, loud.

The relief sent her dizzy. She steadied herself against the door. It was the police. The man looked at the girl, a question in his eye.

"Better have 'em in," he said, "she's got no proof."

He crossed the hall and opened the front door.

"Come in, officer," he said. "There's two of you, I see."

"We had a telephone call," Mrs. Ellis heard the constable say, "some trouble going on, I understand."

"I think there must be some mistake," said Bolton. "The fact is, we've had a caller and I think she got hysterical."

Mrs. Ellis walked out into the hall. She did not recognise the constable, nor the young policeman from the beat. It was unfortunate, but it did not really matter. Both were stout, well-built men.

"I am not hysterical," she said firmly, "I am perfectly all right. I put the telephone call through to the exchange."

The constable took out a notebook and a pencil.

"What's the trouble?" he said. "But give me first your name and address."

Mrs. Ellis smiled patiently. She hoped he was not going to be a stupid man.

"It's hardly necessary," she said, "but my name is Mrs. Wilfred Ellis of this address."

"Lodge here?" asked the constable.

Mrs. Ellis frowned. "No," she said, "this is my house, I live here." And then because she saw a look flash from Bolton to his wife, she knew the time had come to be explicit. "I must speak to you alone, Constable," she said, "the matter is terribly urgent; I don't think you quite understand."

"If you have any charge to bring, Mrs. Ellis," said the officer, "you can bring it at the police station at the proper time. We were informed that somebody lodging here at Number 17 was in danger. Are you, or are you not, the person who gave that information to the exchange?"

Mrs. Ellis began to lose control.

"Of course I am that person," she said. "I returned home to find that my house had been broken into by thieves, these people here, dangerous thieves, lunatics, I don't know what they are, and my things carried away, the whole of my house turned upside down, the most terrible disorder everywhere."

She talked so rapidly, her words fell over themselves.

The man from the basement had now joined them in the hall. He stared at the two policemen, his eyes goggling.

"I saw her come to the door," he said; "I thought she was balmy. Wouldn't have let her in if I had known."

The constable, a little nettled, turned to the interruption.

"Who are you?" he said.

"Name of Upshaw," said the man, "William Upshaw. Me and my missus has the basement flat here."

"That man is lying," said Mrs. Ellis, "he does not live here; he belongs to this gang of thieves. Nobody lives in the basement except my maid—perhaps I should say cook-general—Grace Jackson, and if you will search the premises you will probably find her gagged and bound somewhere, and by that ruffian."

She had now lost all restraint. She could hear her voice, usually low and quiet, rising to a hysterical pitch.

"Balmy," said the man from the basement, "you can see the straw in her hair."

"Quiet, please," said the constable, and turned an ear to the young policeman, who murmured something in his ear.

"Yes, yes," he said, "I've got the directory here. It's all in order."

He consulted another book. Mrs. Ellis watched him feverishly. Never had she seen such a stupid man. Why had they sent out such a slow-witted fool from the police station?

The constable now turned to the man in the horn spectacles.

"Are you Henry Bolton?" he asked.

"Yes, officer," replied the man eagerly, "and this is my wife. We have the ground floor here. This is my wife. She uses an upstairs room for a studio. Camera portraits, you know."

There was a shuffle down the stairs, and the old evil woman came to the foot of the banisters.

"My name's Baxter," she said, "Billie Baxter they used to call me in my old stage days. Used to be in the profession, you know. I have the first-floor back here at Number 17. I can witness this woman came as a sort of Paul Pry, and up to no good. I saw her looking through the keyhole of Mrs. Bolton's studio."

"Then she doesn't lodge here?" asked the constable. "I didn't think she did; the name isn't in the directory."

"We have never seen her before, officer," said Bolton. "Mr. Upshaw let her into the house through some error; she walked into our living-room, and then forced her way into my wife's studio, threatened her, and in hysterical fashion rang for the police."

The constable looked at Mrs. Ellis.

"Anything to say?" he said.

Mrs. Ellis swallowed. If only she could keep calm, if only her heart would not beat so dreadfully fast, and the terrible desire to cry would not rise in her throat.

"Constable," she said, "there has been some terrible mistake. You are new to the district, perhaps, and the young policeman too—I don't seem to recognise him—but if you would kindly get through to your headquarters, they must know all about me; I have lived here for years. My maid Grace has been with me a very long time; I am a widow; my husband, Wilfred Ellis, has been dead two years; I have a little girl of nine at school. I went out for a walk on the heath this afternoon, and during my absence these people have broken into my house, seized or destroyed my belongings—I don't know which—the whole place is up-side down; if you would please get through immediately to your head-quarters . . ."

"There, there," said the constable, putting his notebook away, "that's all right; we can go into all that quietly down at the station. Now, do any of you want to charge Mrs. Ellis with trespassing?"

There was silence. Nobody said anything.

"We don't wish to be unkind," said Bolton diffidently; "I think my wife and myself are quite willing to let the matter pass."

"I think it should be clearly understood," interposed the shock-haired girl, "that anything this woman says about us at the police station is completely untrue."

"Quite," said the officer. "You will both be called, if needed, but I very much doubt the necessity. Now, Mrs. Ellis"—he turned to her, not harshly in any way, but with authority—"we have a car outside, and we can run you down to the station, and you can tell your story there. Have you a coat?"

Mrs. Ellis turned blindly to the lobby. She knew the police station well; it was barely five minutes away. It was best to go there direct. See someone in authority, not this fool, this hopeless, useless fool. But in the meantime, these people were getting away with their criminal story. By the time she and an additional police force returned, they would have fled. She groped for her coat in the dark lobby, stumbling again over the boots, the suitcases.

"Constable," she said softly, "here, one minute."

He moved towards her.

"Yes?" he said.

"They've taken away the electric bulb," she said rapidly in a low whisper; "it was perfectly all right this afternoon, and these boots, and this pile of suitcases, all these have been brought in, and thrown here; the suitcases are probably filled with my ornaments. I must ask you most urgently to leave the policeman in charge here until we return, to see that these people don't escape."

"That's all right, Mrs. Ellis," said the officer. "Now, are you ready to come along?"

She saw a look pass between the constable and the young policeman. The young policeman was trying to hide his smile.

Mrs. Ellis felt certain that the constable was *not* going to remain in the house. And a new suspicion flashed into her mind. Could this officer and his subordinate be genuine members of the police force? Or were they, after all, members of the gang? This would explain their strange faces, their obvious mishandling of the situation. In which case they were now going to take her away to some lair, drug her, kill her possibly.

"I'm not going with you," she said swiftly.

"Now, Mrs. Ellis," said the constable, "don't give any trouble. You shall have a cup of tea down at the station, and no one is going to hurt you."

He seized her arm. She tried to shake it off. The young policeman moved closer.

"Help," she shouted, "help . . . help . . ."

There must be someone. Those people from next door, she barely knew them, but no matter, if she raised her voice loud enough . . .

"Poor thing," said the man in shirt sleeves, "seems sad, don't it? I wonder how she got like it."

Mrs. Ellis saw his bulbous eyes fixed on her with pity, and she nearly choked.

"You rogue," she said, "how dare you, how dare you!" But she was being bundled down the steps, and through the front garden, and into the car, and there was another policeman at the wheel of the car; and she was thrust at the back, the constable keeping a steady hold upon her arm.

The car turned downhill, past the stretch of heath; she tried to see out of the windows the direction, but the bulk of the constable prevented her.

After twisting and turning, the car stopped, to her great surprise, in front of the police station.

Then these men were genuine, after all. They were not members of the gang. Stupefied for a moment, but relieved, thankful, Mrs. Ellis stumbled from the car. The constable, still holding her arm, led her inside.

The hall was not unfamiliar; she remembered coming once before, years ago, when the ginger cat was lost; there was somebody in charge always, sitting at a sort of desk, everything very official, very brisk. She supposed she would stop here in the hall, but the constable led her on to an inner room, and here was another officer seated at a large desk, a more superior type altogether, thank heaven, and he looked intelligent.

She was determined to get her word in before the constable spoke.

"There has been great confusion," she began. "I am Mrs. Ellis, of 17 Elmhurst Road, and my house has been broken into, robbery is going on at this moment on a huge scale; I believe the thieves to be very desperate and extraordinarily cunning; they have completely taken in the constable here, and the other policeman . . ."

To her indignation this superior officer did not look at her. He raised his eyebrows at the constable, and the constable, who had taken off his hat, coughed and approached the desk. A policewoman, appearing from nowhere, stood beside Mrs. Ellis and held her arm.

The constable and the superior officer were talking together in low tones. Mrs. Ellis could not hear what they were saying. Her legs trembled with emotion. She felt her head swim.

Thankfully, she accepted the chair dragged forward by the police-woman, and in a few moments, too, she was given a cup of tea. She did not want it though. Precious time was being lost.

"I must insist that you hear what I have to say," she said, and the policewoman tightened her grip on Mrs. Ellis' arm. The superior offi-cer behind the desk motioned Mrs. Ellis forward, and she was assisted to another chair, the policewoman remaining beside her all the while.

"Now," he said, "what is it you want to tell me?"

Mrs. Ellis gripped her hands together. She had a premonition that this man, in spite of his superior face, was going to prove as great a fool as the constable.

"My name is Ellis," she said, "Mrs. Wilfred Ellis, of 17 Elmhurst Road. I am in the telephone book. I am in the directory. I am very well known in the district, and have lived at Elmhurst Road for ten years. I am a widow, and I have one little girl of nine years at present at school. I employ one maidservant, Grace Jackson, who cooks for me and does general work. This afternoon I went for a short walk on the heath, round by the Viaduct and the Vale of Health ponds, and when I returned home I found my house had been broken into; my maid had disappeared; the rooms were already stripped of my belongings, and the thieves were in possession of my home, putting up a stupendous act of bluff that deceived even the constable here. I put the call through to the exchange, which frightened the thieves, and I endeavoured to keep them pinned in my drawing-room until help arrived."

Mrs. Ellis paused for breath. She saw that the officer was paying attention to her story, and kept his eyes fixed upon her.

"Thank you," he said, "that is very helpful, Mrs. Ellis. Now, have you anything you can show me to prove your identity?"

She stared at him. Prove her identity? Well, of course. But not here, not actually on her person. She had come away without her handbag, and her calling cards were in the writing desk, and her passport—she and Wilfred had been to Dieppe once—was, if she remembered rightly, in the left-hand pigeonhole of the small writing desk in her bedroom.

But she suddenly remembered the havoc of the house. Nothing would be found. . . .

"It's very unfortunate," she said to the officer, "but I did not take my handbag with me when I went out for my walk this afternoon. I left it in the chest of drawers in the bedroom. My calling cards are in the desk in the drawing-room, and there is a passport—rather out of date; my husband and I did not travel much—in a pigeonhole in a small desk in my bedroom. But everything has been upset, taken by these thieves. The house is in utter chaos."

The officer made a note on a pad beside him.

"You can't produce your identity card or your ration book?" he asked.

"I have explained," said Mrs. Ellis, governing her temper, "my calling cards are in my writing desk. I don't know what you mean by ration book."

The officer went on writing on his pad. He glanced at the police-woman, who began feeling Mrs. Ellis' pockets, touching her in a familiar way. Mrs. Ellis tried to think which of her friends could be telephoned to, who could vouch for her, who could come at once by car and make these idiots, these stone-witted fools, see sense.

"I must keep calm," she told herself again, "I must keep calm."

The Collins were abroad; they would have been the best, but Netta Draycott should be at home; she was usually at home about this time because of the children.

"I have asked you," said Mrs. Ellis, "to verify my name and address in the telephone book, or the district directory. If you refuse to do that, ask the postmaster, or the manager of my bank, a branch of which is in the High Street, and where I cashed a cheque on Saturday. Finally, would you care to ring up Mrs. Draycott, a friend of mine, 21 Charlton Court, the block of flats in Charlton Avenue, who will vouch for me?"

She sat back in the chair, exhausted. No nightmare, she told herself, could ever have the horror, the frustrated hopelessness, of her present plight. Little incident piled on little incident. If she had only remembered to bring her handbag, there was a calling-card case in her handbag. And all the while those thieves, those devils, breaking up her home, getting away with her precious things, her belongings . . .

"Now, Mrs. Ellis," said the officer, "we have checked up on your

statements, you know, and they won't do. You are not in the telephone book, nor in the directory."

"I assure you I am," said Mrs. Ellis with indignation; "give me the
books and I'll show you."

The constable, still standing, placed the books before her. She ran
her finger down the name of Ellis to the position on the left-hand page
where she knew it would be. The name Ellis was repeated, but not
hers. And none with her address or number. She looked in the directory
and saw that beside 17 Elmhurst Road were the names of Bolton, of
Upshaw, of Baxter. . . . She pushed both books away from her. She
stared at the officer.

"There is something wrong with these books," she said, "they are not
up to date, they are false, they are not the books I have at home."

The officer did not answer. He closed the books.

"Now, Mrs. Ellis," he said, "I can see you are tired, and a rest would
do you good. We will try to find your friends for you. If you will go
along now, we will get in touch with them as soon as possible. I will
send a doctor along to you, and he may chat with you a little and give
you a sedative, and then, after some rest, you will feel better in the
morning and we may have news for you."

The policewoman helped Mrs. Ellis to her feet.

"Come along now," she said.

"But my house?" said Mrs. Ellis. "Those thieves, and my maid Grace,
Grace may be lying in the basement; surely you are going to do something about the house; you won't permit them to get away with this
monstrous crime; even now we have wasted a precious half hour——"

"That's all right, Mrs. Ellis," said the officer, "you can leave everything in our hands."

The policewoman led her away, still talking, still protesting, and
now she was being taken down a corridor, and the policewoman kept
saying:

"Now, don't fuss, take it calmly; no one's going to hurt you," and
she was in a little room with a bed; heavens . . . it was a cell, a cell
where they put the prisoners, and the policewoman was helping her
off with her coat, unpinning the scarf that was still tied round her hair,
and because Mrs. Ellis felt so faint the policewoman made her lie
down on the bed, covered her with the coarse grey blanket, placed
the little hard pillow under her head.

Mrs. Ellis seized the woman's hands. Her face, after all, was not unkind.

"I beg of you," she said, "ring up Hampstead 4072, the number of my friend Mrs. Draycott, at Charlton Court, and ask her to come here. The officer won't listen to me. He won't hear my story."

"Yes, yes, that will be all right," said the policewoman.

Now somebody else was coming into the room, the cell. Clean-shaven, alert, he carried a case in his hands. He said good evening to the policewoman, and opened his case. He took out a stethoscope and a thermometer. He smiled at Mrs. Ellis.

"Feeling a little upset, I hear," he said. "Well, we'll soon put that to rights. Now, will you give me your wrist?"

Mrs. Ellis sat up on the hard narrow bed, pulling the blanket close.

"Doctor," she said, "there is nothing whatever the matter with me. I admit I have been through a terrible experience, quite enough to unnerve anyone; my house has been broken into; no one here will listen to my story, but I am Mrs. Ellis, Mrs. Wilfred Ellis, of 17 Elmhurst Road; if you can possibly persuade the authorities here . . ."

He was not listening to her. With the assistance of the policewoman he was taking her temperature, under her arm, not in the mouth, treating her like a child; and now he was feeling her pulse, dragging down the pupils of her eyes, listening to her chest. . . . Mrs. Ellis went on talking.

"I realise this is a matter of routine. You are obliged to do this. But I want to warn you that my whole treatment, since I have been brought here, since the police came to my house before that, has been infamous, scandalous. I don't personally know our M.P., but I sincerely believe that when he hears my story he will take the matter up, and someone is going to answer for the consequences. Unfortunately I am a widow, no immediate relatives, my little daughter is away at school; my closest friends, a Mr. and Mrs. Collins, are abroad, but my bank manager . . ."

He was dabbing her arm with spirit; he was inserting a needle, and with a whimper of pain Mrs. Ellis fell back on to the hard pillow. The doctor went on holding her arm, her wrist, and Mrs. Ellis, her head going round and round, felt a strange numb sensation as the injection worked into her blood stream. Tears ran down her cheeks. She could not fight. She was too weak.

"How is that?" said the doctor. "Better, eh?"

Her throat was parched, her mouth without saliva. It was one of those drugs that paralysed you, made you helpless.

But the emotion bubbling within her was eased, was still. The anger, the fear and frustration that had keyed her nerves to a point of contraction seemed to die away.

She had explained things badly. The folly of coming out without her handbag had caused half the trouble. And the terrible, wicked cunning of those thieves. "Be still," she said to her mind, "be still. Rest now."

"Now," said the doctor, letting go her wrist, "supposing you tell me your story again. You say your name is Mrs. Ellis?"

Mrs. Ellis sighed and closed her eyes. Must she go into it all again? Had not they got the whole thing written down in their notebooks? What was the use, when the inefficiency of the whole establishment was so palpable? Those telephone books, directories, with wrong names, wrong addresses. Small wonder there were burglaries, murders, every sort of crime, with a police force that was obviously rotten to the core. What was the name of the Member? It was on the tip of her tongue. A nice man, sandy-haired, always looked so trustworthy on a poster. Hampstead was a safe seat, of course. He would take up her case . . .

"Mrs. Ellis," said the doctor, "do you think you can remember now your real address?"

Mrs. Ellis opened her eyes. Wearily, patiently, she fixed them upon the doctor.

"I live at 17 Elmhurst Road," she said mechanically. "I am a widow, my husband has been dead two years. I have a little girl of nine at school. I went for a short walk on the heath this afternoon after lunch, and when I returned——"

He interrupted her.

"Yes," he said, "we know that. We know what happened after your walk. What we want you to tell us is what happened before."

"I had lunch," said Mrs. Ellis; "I remember perfectly well what I ate. Guinea fowl and apple charlotte, followed by coffee. Then I nearly decided to take a nap upstairs on my bed, because I was not feeling very well, but decided the air would do me good."

As soon as she said this, she regretted it. The doctor looked at her keenly.

"Ah!" he said. "You weren't feeling very well. Can you tell me what the trouble was?"

Mrs. Ellis knew what he was after. He and the rest of the police force at the station wanted to certify her as insane. They would make out she had suffered from some brain storm, that her whole story was fabrication.

"There was nothing much the matter," she said quickly. "I was rather tired from sorting things during the morning. I tidied the linen, cleared out my desk in the drawing-room—all that took time."

"Can you describe your house, Mrs. Ellis?" he said. "The furniture, for instance, of your bedroom, your drawing-room?"

"Very easily," she answered, "but you must remember that the thieves who broke into the house this afternoon have done what I begin to fear is irreparable damage. Everything had been seized, hidden away. The rooms were strewn with rubbish, and there was a young woman upstairs in my bedroom pretending to be a photographer."

"Yes," he said, "don't worry about that. Just tell me about your furniture, how the various things were placed, and so on."

He was more sympathetic then she had thought. Mrs. Ellis launched into a description of every room in her house. She named the ornaments, the pictures, the position of the chairs and tables.

"And you say your cook is called Grace Jackson?"

"Yes, Doctor, she has been with me several years. She was in the kitchen when I left this afternoon; I remember most distinctly calling down to the basement and saying that I was going for a short walk and would not be long. I am extremely worried about her, Doctor. Those thieves will have got hold of her, perhaps kidnapped her."

"We'll see to that," said the doctor. "Now, Mrs. Ellis, you have been very helpful, and you have given such a clear account of your home that I think we shan't be long in tracing it, and your relations. You must stay here tonight, and I hope in the morning we shall have news for you. Now, you say your small daughter is at school? Can you remember the address?"

"Of course," said Mrs. Ellis, "and the telephone number too. The school is High Close, Bishops' Lane, Hatchworth, and the telephone number is Hatchworth 202. But I don't understand what you mean about tracing my home. I have told you, I come from 17 Elmhurst Road."

"There is nothing to worry about," said the doctor; "you are not ill, and you are not lying, I quite realise that. You are suffering from a temporary loss of memory that often happens to all sorts of people, and it quickly passes. We've had many cases before."

He smiled. He stood up, his case in his hand.

"But it isn't true," said Mrs. Ellis, trying to raise herself from the pillow. "My memory is perfectly all right. I have given you every detail I can think of; I have told you my name, where I live, a description of my home, the address of my daughter at school . . ."

"All right," he said, "now, don't worry. Just try to relax and have a little sleep. We shall find your friends for you."

He murmured something to the policewoman and left the cell. The policewoman came over to the bed and tucked in the blanket.

"Now, cheer up," she said, "do as the doctor said. Get a little rest. Everything will be all right, you'll see."

Rest . . . But how? Relax . . . But to what purpose? Even now her house was being looted, sacked, every room stripped. The thieves getting clear away with their booty, leaving no trace behind them. They would take Grace with them; poor Grace could not come down to the police station to give witness to her identity. But the people next door, the Furbers, surely they would be good enough; it would not be too much trouble . . . Mrs. Ellis supposed she should have called, been more friendly, had them to tea, but after all, people did not expect that unless they lived in the country; it was out of date if the police officer had not got hold of Netta Draycott; then the Furbers must be got in touch with at once. . . .

Mrs. Ellis plucked at the policewoman's sleeve.

"The Furbers," she said, "next door, at number 19, they will vouch for me. They are not friends of mine, but they know me well by sight. We have been neighbours for quite six years. The Furbers."

"Yes," said the policewoman, "try to get some sleep."

Oh, Susan, my Susan, if this had happened in the holidays, how much more fearful; what would we have done? Coming back from an afternoon walk to find those devils in the house, and then, who knows, that dreadful photographer woman and her husband taking a fancy to Susan, so pretty, so fair, and wanting to kidnap her. Then what fear, what terror . . . At least the child was safe, knew nothing of what was happening, and if only the story could be kept out of the newspapers, she need never know. So shameful, so degrading, a night spent in a prison cell through such crass stupidity, through such appalling blunders . . .

"You've had a good sleep then," said the policewoman, handing her a cup of tea.

"I don't know what you mean," said Mrs. Ellis, "I haven't slept at all."

"Oh yes, you have." The woman smiled. "They all say that."

Mrs. Ellis blinked, sat up on the narrow bed. She had been speaking to the policewoman only a moment before. Her head ached abominably. She sipped at the tea, tasteless, unrefreshing. She yearned for her bed at home, for Grace coming in noiselessly, drawing the curtains.

"You're to have a wash," said the policewoman, "and I'll give you a comb through, and then you are to see the doctor again."

Mrs. Ellis suffered the indignity of washing under supervision, of having her hair combed; then her scarf and coat and gloves were given to her again, and she was taken out of the cell, along the corridor, back through the hall to the room where they had questioned her the night before. This time a different officer sat at the desk, but she recognised the police constable, and the doctor too.

The last came towards her with that same bland smile on his face.

"How are you feeling today?" he said. "A little more like your true self?"

"On the contrary," said Mrs. Ellis, "I am feeling very unwell indeed, and shall continue to do so until I know what has happened at home. Is anyone here prepared to tell me what has happened at 17 Elmhurst Road since last night? Has anything at all been done to safeguard my property?"

The doctor did not answer, but guided her towards the chair at the desk.

"Now," he said, "the officer here wants to show you a picture in a newspaper."

Mrs. Ellis sat down in the chair. The officer handed her a copy of *The News of the World*—a paper Grace took on Sundays; Mrs. Ellis never looked at it—and there was a photograph of a woman with a scarf round her head, and chubby cheeks, wearing some sort of light-coloured coat. The photograph had a red circle round it, and underneath was written:

"Missing from Home, Ada Lewis, aged 36, widow, of 105 Albert Buildings, Kentish Town."

Mrs. Ellis handed the paper back across the desk.

"I'm afraid I can't help you," she said. "I don't know this woman."

"The name Ada Lewis conveys nothing to you?" said the officer. "Nor Albert Court Buildings?"

"No," said Mrs. Ellis, "certainly not."

Suddenly she knew the purpose of the interrogation. The police thought that she was this missing woman, this Ada Lewis from Albert Buildings. Simply because she wore a light-coloured coat and had a scarf round her hair. She rose from the chair.

"This is absolutely preposterous," she said. "I have told you my name is Ellis, Mrs. Wilfred Ellis, of 17 Elmhurst Road, and you persist in disbelieving me. My detention here is an outrage; I demand to see a lawyer, my own lawyer. . . ." But wait, she hadn't needed the services of a lawyer since Wilfred died, and the firm had moved or been taken over by somebody else; better not give the name; they would think she was lying once again; it was safer to give the name of the bank manager. . . .

"One moment," said the officer, and she was interrupted once again, because somebody else came into the room, a seedy, common-looking man in a checked shabby suit, holding his trilby hat in his hand.

"Can you identify this woman as your sister, Ada Lewis?" asked the officer.

A flush of fury swept Mrs. Ellis as the man stepped forward and peered into her face.

"No, sir," he said, "this isn't Ada. Ada isn't so stout, and this woman's teeth seem to be her own. Ada wore dentures. Never seen this woman before."

"Thank you," said the officer, "that's all. You can go. We will let you know if we find your sister."

The seedy-looking man left the room. Mrs. Ellis turned in triumph to the officer behind the desk.

"Now," she said, "perhaps you will believe me?"

The officer considered her a moment, and then, glancing at the doctor, looked down at some notes on his desk.

"Much as I would like to believe you," he said, "it would save us all a great deal of trouble if I could, unfortunately I can't. Your facts have been proved wrong in every particular. So far."

"What do you mean?" said Mrs. Ellis.

"First, your address. You do not live at 17 Elmhurst Road because the house is occupied by various tenants who have lived there for some time and who are known to us. Number 17 is an apartment house, and the floors are let separately. You are not one of the tenants."

Mrs. Ellis gripped the sides of her chair. The obstinate, proud, and completely unmoved face of the officer stared back at her.

"You are mistaken," said Mrs. Ellis quietly. "Number 17 is not a lodginghouse. It is a private house. My own."

The officer glanced down again at his notes.

"There are no people called Furber living at number 19," he went on. "Number 19 is also a lodginghouse. You are not in the directory under the name of Ellis, nor in the telephone book. There is no Ellis on the register of the branch of the bank you mentioned to us last night. Nor can we trace anyone of the name of Grace Jackson in the district."

Mrs. Ellis looked up at the doctor, at the police constable, at the policewoman, who was still standing by her side.

"Is there some conspiracy?" she said. "Why are you all against me? I don't understand what I have done. . . ."

Her voice faltered. She must not break down. She must be firm with them, be brave, for Susan's sake.

"You rang up my friend at Charlton Court?" she asked. "Mrs. Draycott, that big block of flats?"

"Mrs. Draycott is not living at Charlton Court, Mrs. Ellis," said the police officer, "for the simple reason that Charlton Court no longer exists. It was destroyed by a fire bomb."

Mrs. Ellis stared at him in horror. A fire bomb? But how perfectly terrible! When? How? In the night? Disaster upon disaster . . . Who could have done it, anarchists, strikers, unemployed, gangs of people, possibly those who had broken into her house? Poor Netta and her husband and children; Mrs. Ellis felt her head reeling. . . .

"Forgive me," she said, summoning her strength, her dignity, "I had no idea there had been such a fearful outrage. No doubt part of the same plot, those people in my house . . ."

Then she stopped, because she realised they were lying to her; everything was lies; they were not policemen; they had seized the building; they were spies; the government was to be overthrown; but then why bother with her, with a simple harmless individual like herself; why were they not getting on with the civil war, bringing machine guns into the street, marching to Buckingham Palace; why sit here, pretending to her?

A policeman came into the room and clicked his heels and stood before the desk.

"Checked up on all the nursing homes," he said, "and the mental homes, sir, in the district, and within a radius of five miles. Nobody missing."

"Thank you," said the officer. Ignoring Mrs. Ellis, he looked across at the doctor.

"We can't keep her here," he said; "you'll have to persuade them to take her at Moreton Hill. The matron *must* find a room. Say it's a temporary measure. Case of amnesia."

"I'll do what I can," said the doctor.

Moreton Hill. Mrs. Ellis knew at once what they meant by Moreton Hill. It was a well-known mental home somewhere near Highgate, very badly run, she always heard, a dreadful place.

"Moreton Hill?" she said. "You can't possibly take me there. It has a shocking reputation. The nurses are always leaving. I refuse to go to Moreton Hill. I demand to see a lawyer—no, my doctor, Dr. Godber; he lives in Parkwell Gardens."

The officer stared at her thoughtfully.

"She must be a local woman," he said; "she gets the names right every time. But Godber went to Portsmouth, didn't he? I remember Godber."

"If he's at Portsmouth," said Mrs. Ellis, "he would only have gone for a few days. He's most conscientious. But his secretary knows me. I took Susan there last holidays."

Nobody listened to her though, and the officer was consulting his notes again.

"By the way," he said, "you gave me the name of that school correctly. Wrong telephone number, but right school. Co-educational. We got through to them last night."

"I'm afraid then," said Mrs. Ellis, "that you got the wrong school.

High Close is most certainly not co-educational, and I should never have sent Susan there if it had been."

"High Close," repeated the officer, reading from his notes, "is a co-educational school, run by a Mr. Foster and his wife."

"It is run by a Miss Slater," said Mrs. Ellis, "a Miss Hilda Slater."

"You mean it *was* run by a Miss Slater," said the officer; "a Miss Slater had the school and then retired, and it was taken over by Mr. and Mrs. Foster. They have no pupil there of the name of Susan Ellis."

Mrs. Ellis sat very still in her chair. She looked at each face in turn. None was harsh. None was unfriendly. And the policewoman smiled encouragement. They all watched her steadily. At last she said:

"You are not deliberately trying to mislead me? You do realise that I am anxious, most desperately anxious, to know what has happened? If all that you are saying is some kind of a game, some kind of torture, would you tell me so that I know, so that I can understand?"

The doctor took her hand, and the officer leant forward in his chair.

"We are trying to help you," he said; "we are doing everything we can to find your friends."

Mrs. Ellis held tight to the doctor's hand. It had suddenly become a refuge.

"I don't understand," she said, "what has happened. If I am suffering from loss of memory, why do I remember everything so clearly? My address, my name, people, the school . . . Where is Susan; where is my little girl?"

She looked round her in blind panic. She tried to rise from the chair.

"If Susan is not at High Close, where is she?" said Mrs. Ellis.

Someone was patting her on the shoulder. Someone was giving her a glass of water.

"If Miss Slater had retired to give place to a Mr. and Mrs. Foster, I should have heard, they would have told me," she kept repeating; "I only telephoned the school yesterday. Susan was quite well, and playing in the grounds."

"Are you suggesting that Miss Slater answered you herself?" inquired the officer.

"No, the secretary answered. I telephoned because I had . . . what seemed to me a premonition that Susan might not be well. The secretary assured me that the child had eaten a good lunch and was playing. I am not making this up. It happened yesterday. I tell you, the secretary would have told me if Miss Slater was making changes in the school."

Mrs. Ellis searched the doubtful faces fixed upon her. And momentarily her attention was caught by the large 2 on the calendar standing on the desk.

"I *know* it was yesterday," she said, "because today is the second of the month, isn't it? And I distinctly remember tearing off the page in my calendar, and because it was the first of the month I decided to tidy my desk, sort out my papers, during the morning."

The police officer relaxed and smiled.

"You are certainly very convincing," he said, "and we can all tell from your appearance, the fact that you have no money on you, that your shoes are polished, and other little signs, that you do definitely belong somewhere in this district; you have not wandered from any great distance. But you do not come from 17 Elmhurst Road, Mrs. Ellis, that is quite certain. For some reason, which we hope to discover, that address has become fixed in your mind, and other addresses too. I promise you everything will be done to clear your mind and to get you well again; and you need have no fear about going to Moreton Hill; I know it well, and they will look after you there."

Mrs. Ellis saw herself shut up behind those grey forbidding walls, grimly situated, frowning down upon the further ponds the far side of the heath. She had skirted those walls many times, pitying the inmates within.

The man who came with the groceries had a wife who became insane. Mrs. Ellis remembered Grace coming to her one morning full of the story, "and he says they've taken her to Moreton Hill."

Once inside, she would never get out. These men at the police station would not bother with her any more.

And now there was this new, hideous misunderstanding about Susan, and the talk of a Mr. and Mrs. Foster taking over the school.

Mrs. Ellis leant forward, clasping her hands together.

"I do assure you," she said, "that I don't want to make trouble. I have always been a very quiet, peaceable sort of person, not easily excited, never quarrelsome, and if I have really lost my memory I will do what the doctor tells me, take any drugs or medicines that will help. But I am worried, desperately worried, about my little girl and what you have told me about the school and Miss Slater's having retired. Would you do just one thing for me? Telephone the school and ask them where you can get in touch with Miss Slater. It is just possible that she has taken the house down the road and removed there with some of the children, Susan amongst them; and whoever answered the telephone was new to the work and gave you vague information."

She spoke clearly, without any sort of hysteria or emotion; they must see that she was in deadly earnest, and this request of hers was not wild fancy.

The police officer glanced at the doctor, then he seemed to make up his mind.

"Very well," he said, "we will do that. We will try to contact this Miss Slater, but it may take time. Meanwhile, I think it is best if you wait in another room while we put through the enquiry."

Mrs. Ellis stood up, this time without the help of the policewoman. She was determined to show that she was well, mentally and bodily, and quite capable of managing her affairs without the assistance of anybody, if it could be permitted.

She wished she had a hat instead of the scarf, which she knew instinctively was unbecoming, and her hands were lost without her handbag. At least she had gloves. But gloves were not enough.

She nodded briskly to the police officer and the doctor—at all costs she must show civility—and followed the policewoman to a waiting room. This time she was spared the indignity of a cell. Another cup of tea was brought to her.

"It's all they think about," she said to herself, "cups of tea. Instead of getting on with their job."

Suddenly she remembered poor Netta Draycott and the terrible tragedy of the fire bomb. Possibly she and her family had escaped and were now with friends, but there was no immediate means of finding out.

"Is it all in the morning papers about the disaster?" she asked the policewoman.

"What disaster?" said the woman.

"The fire at Charlton Court the officer spoke to me about."

The policewoman stared at her with a puzzled expression.

"I don't remember him saying anything about a fire," she said.

"Oh yes, he did," said Mrs. Ellis. "He told me that Charlton Court had been destroyed by fire, by some bomb. I was aghast to hear it because I have friends living there. It must surely be in all the morning papers."

The woman's face cleared.

"Oh, that," she said. "I think the officer was referring to some fire bomb during the war."

"No, no," said Mrs. Ellis impatiently. "Charlton Court was built a long time after the war. I remember the block being built when my husband and I first came to Hampstead. No, this accident apparently happened last night, the most dreadful thing."

The policewoman shrugged her shoulders.

"I think you're mistaken," she said; "there's been no talk of any accident or disaster here."

An ignorant, silly sort of girl, thought Mrs. Ellis. It was a wonder she had passed her test into the force. She thought they only employed very intelligent women.

She sipped her tea in silence. No use carrying on any sort of conversation with her.

It seemed a long while before the door opened, but when it did it was to reveal the doctor, who stood on the threshold with a smile on his face.

"Well," he said, "I think we're a little nearer home. We were able to contact Miss Slater."

Mrs. Ellis rose to her feet, her eyes shining.

"Oh, Doctor, thank heaven . . . Have you news of my daughter?"

"Steady a moment now. You mustn't get excited or we shall have all last night's trouble over again, and that would never do. I take it, when you refer to your daughter, you mean someone who is called, or was called, Susan Ellis?"

"Yes, yes, of course," said Mrs. Ellis swiftly. "Is she all right, is she with Miss Slater?"

"No, she is not with Miss Slater, but she is perfectly well, and I have spoken to her on the telephone myself, and I have her present address here in my notebook."

The doctor patted his breast pocket and smiled again.

"Not with Miss Slater?" Mrs. Ellis stared in bewilderment. "Then the school *has* been handed over; you spoke to these people called Foster. Is it next door? Have they moved far? What has happened?"

The doctor took her hand and led her to the seat once more.

"Now," he said, "I want you to think quite calmly and quite clearly and not be agitated in any way, and your trouble will be cleared up, and your mind will be free again. You remember last night you gave us the name of your maid, Grace Jackson?"

"Yes, Doctor."

"Now, take your time. Tell us a little about Grace Jackson."

"Have you found her? Is she at home? Is she all right?"

"Never mind for the moment. Describe Grace Jackson."

Mrs. Ellis was horribly afraid poor Grace had been found murdered, and they were going to ask her to identify the body.

"She is a big girl," she said, "at least not really a girl, about my own age, but you know how one is inclined to talk of a servant as a girl; she has a large bust, rather thick ankles, brownish hair, grey eyes, and she would be wearing, let me see, I think she may not have changed into her cap and apron when those thieves arrived; she was still probably in her overalls; she is inclined to change rather late in the afternoon; I have often spoken about it; it looks so bad to open the front door in overalls, slovenly, like a boardinghouse; Grace has good teeth and a pleasant expression, though of course if anything has happened to her she would hardly——"

Mrs. Ellis broke off. Murdered, battered. Grace would not be smiling.

The doctor did not seem to notice this. He was looking closely at Mrs. Ellis.

"You know," he said, "you have given a very accurate description of yourself."

"Myself?" said Mrs. Ellis.

"Yes. Figure, colouring, and so on. We think, you know, it is just possible that your amnesia has taken the form of mistaken identity and that you are really Grace Jackson, believing yourself to be a Mrs. Ellis, and now we are doing our best to trace the relatives of Grace Jackson."

This was too much. Mrs. Ellis swallowed. Outraged pride rose in her.

"Doctor," she said rapidly, "you have gone a little too far. I bear no sort of resemblance to my maid, Grace Jackson, and if and when you ever find trace of the unfortunate girl, she would be the first to agree with me. Grace has been in my employment seven years; she came

originally from Scotland; her parents were Scottish, I believe—in fact,
I know it, because she used to go for her holiday to Aberdeen. Grace
is a good, hard-working, and I like to think honest girl; we have had
our little ups and downs, but nothing serious; she is inclined to be
obstinate; I am obstinate myself—who is not?—but . . ."

If only the doctor would not look at her in that smiling, patronising
way.

"You see," he said, "you do know a very great deal about Grace
Jackson."

Mrs. Ellis could have hit him. He was so self-assured, so confident.

"I must keep my temper," she told herself. "I must, I must . . ."

Aloud she said: "Doctor, I know about Grace Jackson because, as
I have told you, she has been in my employment for seven years. If she
is found ill or in any way hurt, I shall hold the police force here responsible, because in spite of my entreaties, I do not believe they kept
a watch on my house last night. Now perhaps you will be good enough
to tell me where I can find my child. She, at least, will recognise me."

Mrs. Ellis considered she had been very restrained, very calm. In
spite of terrible provocation she had not lost control of herself.

"You insist that your age is thirty-five?" said the doctor, switching
the subject. "And that Grace Jackson was approximately the same?"

"I was thirty-five in August last," said Mrs. Ellis; "I believe Grace to
be a year younger, I am not sure."

"You certainly don't look more," said the doctor, smiling.

Surely, at such a moment, he was not going to attempt to appease
her by gallantry?

"But," he continued, "following upon the telephone conversation
I have just had, Grace Jackson should be, today, at least fifty-five or
fifty-six."

"There are probably," said Mrs. Ellis icily, "several persons of the
name of Grace Jackson employed as domestic servants. If you propose
tracing every one of them, it will take you and the police force a con-
siderable time. I am sorry to insist, but I must know the whereabouts
of my daughter Susan before anything else."

He was relenting; she could see it in his eye.

"As a matter of fact," he said, "it happens, very conveniently, that
Miss Slater was able to put us in touch with the lady; we have spoken
to her on the telephone, and she is only a short distance away, in St.

John's Wood. She is not sure, but she thinks she would remember Grace Jackson if she saw her."

For a moment Mrs. Ellis was speechless. What in the world was Susan doing in St. John's Wood? And how monstrous to drag the child to the telephone and question her about Grace. Of course she would be bewildered and say she "thought" she would remember Grace, though goodness only knows it was only two months since Grace was waving her good-bye from the doorstep when she left for school.

Then she suddenly remembered the Zoo. Perhaps, if these changes at school were all being decided upon in a great hurry, one of the junior mistresses had taken a party of children up to London to the Zoo, to be out of the way. The Zoo or Madame Tussaud's.

"Do you know where she spoke from?" asked Mrs. Ellis sharply. "I mean, somebody was in charge, somebody was looking after her?"

"She spoke from 2a Halifax Avenue," said the doctor, "and I don't think you will find she needs any looking after. She sounded very capable, and I heard her turn from the telephone and call to a little boy named Keith to keep quiet and not make so much noise, because she couldn't hear herself speak."

A tremour of a smile appeared on Mrs. Ellis' lips. How clever of Susan to have shown herself so quick and lively. It was just like her, though. She was so advanced for her age. Such a little companion. But Keith . . . It sounded very much as though the school *had* suddenly become co-educational; this was a mixed party being taken to the Zoo or Madame Tussaud's. They were all having lunch, perhaps, at Halifax Avenue, relations of Miss Slater's, or these Fosters, but really the whole thing was most inexcusable, that changes should come about like this, and the children be taken backwards and forwards from High Close to London without any attempt to notify the parents. Mrs. Ellis would write very strongly to Miss Slater about it, and if the school had changed hands and was to be co-educational, she would remove Susan at the end of the term.

"Doctor," she said, "I am ready to go to Halifax Avenue at once, if the authorities here will only permit me to do so."

"Very well," said the doctor. "I am afraid I can't accompany you, but we have arranged for that, and Sister Henderson, who knows all about the matter, will go with you."

He nodded to the policewoman, who opened the door of the wait-

ing room and admitted a severe middle-aged woman in nurse's uniform. Mrs. Ellis said nothing, but her mouth tightened. She was very
sure that Sister Henderson had been summoned from Moreton Hill.

"Now, Sister," said the doctor cheerfully, "this is the lady, and you
know where to take her and what to do; and I think you will only be a
few minutes at Halifax Avenue, and then we hope things will be
straightened out."

"Yes, Doctor," said the nurse.

She looked across at Mrs. Ellis with a quick professional eye.

"If only I had a hat," thought Mrs. Ellis, "if only I had not come
out with nothing but this wretched scarf, and I can feel bits and pieces
of hair straggling at the back of my neck. No powder compact on me,
no comb, nothing. Of course I must look terrible to them, ungroomed,
common . . ."

She straightened her shoulders, resisted an impulse to put her hands
in her pockets. She walked stiffly towards the open door. The doctor,
the Sister, and the policewoman conducted her down the steps of the
police station to a waiting car.

A uniformed chauffeur was to drive, she was thankful to see, and
she climbed into the car, followed by the Sister.

The awful thought flashed through her mind that there might be
some charge for the night's lodging in the cell and for the cups of tea;
also, should she have tipped the policewoman? But anyway, she had
no money. It was impossible. She nodded brightly to the policewoman
as a sort of sop, to show she had no ill feeling. She felt rather different
towards the doctor. She bowed rather formally, coldly. The car drove
away.

Mrs. Ellis wondered if she was expected to make conversation with
the Sister, who sat stalwart and forbidding at her side. Better not,
perhaps. Anything she said might be taken as evidence of mental disturbance. She stared straight in front of her, her gloved hands primly
folded on her lap.

The traffic jams were very bad, worse than she had ever known.
There must be a Motor Exhibition on. So many American cars on the
road. A rally, perhaps . . .

She did not think much of Halifax Avenue when they came to it.
Houses very shabby, and quite a number with windows broken.

The car drew up at a small house that had 2a written on the pillar outside. Curious place to take a party of children for lunch. A good Lyons Café would have been so much better.

The Sister got out of the car and waited to help Mrs. Ellis.

"We shan't be long," she said to the chauffeur.

"That's what you think," said Mrs. Ellis to herself, "but I shall certainly stay with Susan as long as I please."

They walked through the piece of front garden to the front door. The Sister rang the bell. Mrs. Ellis saw a face looking at them from the front window and then quickly dart behind a curtain. Good heavens . . . It was Dorothy, Wilfred's younger sister, who was a schoolteacher in Birmingham; of course it was, it must be. . . . Everything became clearer; the Fosters must know Dorothy; people to do with education always knew each other, but how awkward, what a bore. Mrs. Ellis had never cared for Dorothy, had stopped writing to her in fact; Dorothy had been so unpleasant when poor Wilfred died, and had insisted that the writing bureau was hers, and rather a nice piece of jewellery that Mrs. Ellis had always understood had been given by Wilfred's mother to her, Mrs. Ellis; and in fact the whole afternoon after the funeral had been spent in most unpleasant argument and discussion, that Mrs. Ellis had been only too glad to send Dorothy away with the jewellery, and the bureau, and a very nice rug to which she had no right at all.

Dorothy was the last person Mrs. Ellis wanted to see, and especially in these very trying circumstances, with this Sister at her side, and herself looking so untidy, without a hat or a bag.

There was no time to compose herself because the door opened. No . . . no, it was not Dorothy after all, but . . . how strange, so very like her. That same thin nose and rather peeved expression. A little taller, perhaps, and the hair was lighter. The resemblance, though, was really quite extraordinary.

"Are you Mrs. Drew?" asked the Sister.

"Yes," answered the young woman, and then because a child was calling from an inner room she called back over her shoulder impatiently, "Oh, be quiet, Keith, do, for heaven's sake."

A little boy of about five appeared along the hall dragging a toy on wheels. "Dear little fellow," thought Mrs. Ellis, "what a tiresome nagging mother. But where are all the children; where is Susan?"

"This is the person I have brought along for you to identify," said the Sister.

"You had better come inside," said Mrs. Drew rather grudgingly. "I'm afraid everything's in a fearful mess. I've got no help, and you know how it is."

Mrs. Ellis, whose temper was beginning to rise again, stepped neatly over a broken toy on the door mat and, followed by the Sister, went into what she supposed was this Mrs. Drew's living-room. It was certainly a mess. Remains of breakfast not cleared away—or was it lunch? —and toys everywhere, and some material for cutting out spread on a table by the window.

Mrs. Drew laughed apologetically.

"What with Keith's toys and my material—I'm a dressmaker in my spare time—and trying to get a decent meal for my husband when he comes home in the evening, life isn't a bed of roses," she said.

Her voice was so like Dorothy's. Mrs. Ellis could hardly take her eyes off her. The same note of complaint.

"We don't want to take up your time," said the Sister civilly, "if you will just say whether this person is Grace Jackson or not."

The young woman, Mrs. Drew, stared at Mrs. Ellis thoughtfully.

"No," she said at length, "I'm sure she is not. I haven't seen Grace for years, not since I married; I used to look her up in Hampstead occasionally before then; but she had quite a different appearance from this person. She was stouter, darker, older too."

"Thank you," said the Sister, "then you are sure you have never seen this lady before?"

"No, never," said Mrs. Drew.

"Very well then," said the Sister, "we needn't detain you any longer."

She turned, as though to go, but Mrs. Ellis was not to be fobbed off with the nonsense that had just passed.

"Excuse me," she said to Mrs. Drew, "there has been a most unfortunate misunderstanding all round, but I understand you spoke to the doctor at the police station at Hampstead this morning, or someone did from this house, and that you have a party of school children here from High Close, my child amongst them. Can you tell me if she is still here; is anyone from the school in charge?"

The Sister was about to intervene, but Mrs. Drew did not notice this, because the little boy had come into the room, dragging his toy.

"Keith, I *told* you to stay outside," she nagged.

Mrs. Ellis smiled at the boy. She loved all children.

"What a pretty boy," she said, and she held out her hand to him. He took it, holding it tight.

"He doesn't usually take to strangers," said Mrs. Drew, "he's very shy. It makes me wild at times when he won't speak and hangs his head."

"I was shy myself as a child, I understand it," said Mrs. Ellis.

Keith looked up at her with confidence and trust. Her heart warmed to him. But she was forgetting Susan. . . .

"We were talking about the party from High Close," she said.

"Yes," said Mrs. Drew, "but that police officer was rather an idiot, I'm afraid, and got everything wrong. My name was Susan Ellis before I married, and I used to go to school at High Close, and that's where the mistake came in. There are no children from the school here."

"What a remarkable coincidence," said Mrs. Ellis, smiling, "because my name is Ellis, and my daughter is called Susan, and an even stranger coincidence is that you are so like a sister of my late husband's."

"Oh?" said Mrs. Drew. "Well, the name is common enough, isn't it? The butcher is Ellis, down the road."

Mrs. Ellis flushed. Not a very tactful remark. And she felt suddenly nervous, too, because the Sister was advancing and was leaning forward as though to take her by the arm and walk to the front door. Mrs. Ellis was determined not to leave the house. Or at any rate, not to leave it with the Sister.

"I've always found High Close such a homey sort of school," she said rapidly, "but I am rather distressed about the changes they are making there, and I am afraid it is going to be on rather a different tone in the future."

"I don't think they've changed it much," said Mrs. Drew; "most small children are horrible little beasts, anyway, and it does them good not to see too much of their parents and to be thoroughly well mixed up with every sort of type."

"I'm afraid I don't agree with you on that," said Mrs. Ellis. So peculiar. The tone, the expression might have been Dorothy's.

"Of course," said Mrs. Drew, "I can't help being grateful to old

Slaty. She's a funny old stick, but a heart of gold, and she did her best for me, I'll say that, and kept me in the holidays, even after my mother was killed in a street accident."

"How good of her," said Mrs. Ellis, "and what a dreadful thing for you."

Mrs. Drew laughed.

"I was pretty tough, I think," she said. "I don't remember much about it. But I do remember my mother was a very kind person, and pretty too. I think Keith takes after her."

The little boy had not relinquished Mrs. Ellis' hand.

"It's time we were getting along," said the Sister. "Come now, Mrs. Drew has told us all we need to know."

"I don't want to go," said Mrs. Ellis calmly, "and you have no right to make me go."

The Sister exchanged a glance with Mrs. Drew.

"I'm sorry," she said in a low tone, "I shall have to get the chauffeur. I wanted them to send another nurse with me, but they said it wouldn't be necessary."

"That's all right," said Mrs. Drew. "So many people are bats these days, one extra doesn't make much difference. But perhaps I had better remove Keith to the kitchen, or she may kidnap him."

Keith, protesting, was carried from the room.

Once again the Sister looked at Mrs. Ellis.

"Come along now," she said, "be reasonable."

"No," said Mrs. Ellis, and with a quickness that surprised herself she reached out to the table where Mrs. Drew had been cutting out material, and seized the pair of scissors.

"If you come near me, I shall stab you," she said.

The Sister turned and went quickly out of the room and down the steps, calling for the chauffeur. The next few moments passed quickly, but for all this Mrs. Ellis had time to realise that her tactics were brilliant, rivalling the heroes of detective fiction.

She crossed the room, opened the long french windows that gave on to a back yard. The window of the bedroom was open; she could hear the chauffeur calling.

"Tradesmen's entrance is ajar," he shouted; "she must have gone this way."

"Let them go on with their confusion," thought Mrs. Ellis, leaning against the bed. "Let them. Good luck to them in their running about. This will take down some of that Sister's weight. Not much running about for her at Moreton Hill. Cups of tea at all hours, and sweet biscuits, while the patients were given bread and water."

The movement went on for some time. Somebody used the telephone. There was more talk. And then, when Mrs. Ellis was nearly dozing off against the bed valance, she heard the car drive away.

Everything was silent. Mrs. Ellis listened. The only sound was the little boy playing in the hall below. She crept to the door and listened once again. The wheeled toy was being dragged backwards and forwards, up and down the hall.

And there was a new sound coming from the living-room. The sound of a sewing machine going at great speed. Mrs. Drew was at work.

The Sister and the chauffeur had gone.

An hour, two hours must have passed since they had left. Mrs. Ellis glanced at the clock on the mantelpiece. It was two o'clock. What an untidy, scattered sort of room, everything all over the place. Shoes in the middle of the floor, a coat flung down on a chair, and Keith's cot had not been made up; the blankets were rumpled, anyhow.

"Badly brought up," thought Mrs. Ellis, "and such rough, casual manners. But poor girl, if she had no mother . . ."

She took a last glance round the room, and she saw with a shrug of her shoulder that even Mrs. Drew's calendar had a printing error. It said 1952 instead of 1932. How careless . . .

She tiptoed to the head of the stairs. The door of the living-room was shut. The sound of the sewing machine came at breathless speed.

"They must be hard up," thought Mrs. Ellis, "if she has to do dressmaking. I wonder what her husband does for a living."

Softly she crept downstairs. She made no sound. And if she had, the sound of the sewing machine would have covered it.

As she passed the living-room door it opened. The boy stood there, staring at her. He said nothing. He smiled. Mrs. Ellis smiled back at him. She could not help herself. She had a feeling that he would not give her away.

"Shut the door, Keith, *do*," nagged his mother from within. The door slammed. The sound of the sewing machine became more distant, muffled. Mrs. Ellis let herself out of the house and slipped away.

. . . She turned northward, like an animal scenting direction, because northward was her home.

She was soon swallowed up in traffic, the buses swinging past her in the Finchley Road, and her feet began to ache, and she was tired, but she could not take a bus or summon a taxi because she had no money.

No one looked at her; no one bothered with her; they were all intent upon their business, either going from home or returning, and it seemed to Mrs. Ellis, as she toiled up the hill towards Hampstead, that for the first time in her life she was friendless and alone. She wanted her house, her home, the consolation of her own surroundings; she wanted to take up her normal, everyday life that had been interrupted in so brutal a fashion.

There was so much to straighten out, so much to do, and Mrs. Ellis did not know where to begin or whom to ask for help.

"I want everything to be as it was before that walk yesterday," thought Mrs. Ellis, her back aching, her feet throbbing. "I want my home. I want my little girl."

And here was the heath once again. This was where she had stood before crossing the road. She even remembered what she had been thinking about. She had been planning to buy a red bicycle for Susan. Something light, but strong, a good make.

The memory of the bicycle made her forget her troubles, her fatigue. As soon as all this muddle and confusion were over, she would buy a red bicycle for Susan.

Why, though, for the second time, that screech of brakes when she crossed the road, and the vacant face of the laundry boy looking down at her?

No Motive

MARY FARREN went into the gun room one morning about half-past eleven and took her husband's revolver and loaded it, then shot herself. The butler heard the sound of the gun from the pantry. He knew Sir John was out and would not be back until lunch time, and no one had any business to be in the gun room at that hour of the day.

He went to investigate, and there he saw Lady Farren lying on the floor, in her own pool of blood. She was dead.

Aghast, he called the housekeeper, and after consultation they agreed he must first telephone the doctor, then the police, and lastly Sir John himself, who was at a board meeting.

The butler told the doctor and the police, who arrived within a few minutes of each other, what had happened; his message on the telephone had been the same to each.

"Her ladyship has had an accident. She is lying in the gun room with a gunshot wound in her head. I fear she is dead."

The message summoning Sir John home was worded differently. It just said, would Sir John please return home at once, as her ladyship had met with an accident.

The doctor, therefore, had to break the news to the husband when he came.

It was a painful, wretched business. He had known John Farren for years; both he and Mary Farren were patients of his; a happier married couple did not exist, and they were both looking forward to the baby that was to be born to them in the spring. No difficulties were expected; Mary Farren was normal, healthy, and delighted at the prospect of being a mother.

The suicide, therefore, did not make sense. Because it was suicide. There was no doubt about it. Mary Farren had scribbled three words on a writing pad, which she had put on the desk in the gun room. The words were, "Forgive me, darling."

The gun had been put away unloaded, as always. Mary Farren had quite definitely taken out the gun, loaded it, then shot herself.

The police corroborated with the doctor that the wound had been self-inflicted. Mercifully, she must have died at once.

Sir John Farren was a broken man. In that half hour, talking to the doctors and the police, he aged about twenty years. "But why did she do it?" he kept asking in agony. "We were so happy. We loved each other; the baby was on its way. There was no motive, I tell you, absolutely no motive."

Neither the police nor the doctor had an answer for him.

The usual formalities were gone through, the official business of an inquest, with the expected verdict, "Suicide, with no evidence to show the state of mind of the deceased."

Sir John Farren talked to the doctor again and again, but neither of them could come to any conclusion.

"Yes, it is possible," said the doctor, "women can become temporarily deranged at such a time, but you would have noticed signs of it, and so would I. You tell me she was perfectly normal the night

before, perfectly normal at breakfast. As far as you know, there was
nothing on her mind at all?"

"Absolutely nothing," said Sir John. "We breakfasted together, as
we always did; we made plans for the afternoon; after I returned from
the board meeting I was going to take her for a drive. She was cheerful
and completely happy."

Lady Farren's cheerfulness was also corroborated by the servants.
The housemaid, who had gone to the bedroom at half-past ten,
found her ladyship examining shawls that had come by the parcel post.
Lady Farren, delighted with the work, had shown the shawls to her and
had said she would keep both pink and blue, for boy or girl.

At eleven a travelling salesman had called from a firm that made
garden furniture. Her ladyship had seen the man, chosen two large
garden seats from his catalogue. The butler knew this, because Lady
Farren had shown him the catalogue after the man had gone, when he
had come to enquire if there were any orders for the chauffeur, and
her ladyship had said, "No, I shan't be going out until after lunch,
when Sir John will be taking me for a drive."

The butler had gone from the room, leaving her ladyship drinking a
glass of milk. He was the last person to see Lady Farren alive.

"It comes to this," said Sir John, "between that time, which was
approximately twenty minutes past eleven, and eleven-thirty, when she
shot herself, Mary went off her head. It doesn't make sense. There
must have been something wrong. I've got to find out what it was. I
shall never rest until I do."

The doctor did his best to dissuade him, but it was no use. He himself was convinced that Mary Farren had succumbed to a sudden brain
storm, owing to her condition, and, not knowing what she was doing,
had made an end of herself.

Let it stay there. Let it rest. And Time only would help John Farren
to forget.

John Farren did not try to forget. He went to a private-detective
agency and interviewed a man called Black, recommended by the
firm as trustworthy and discreet. Sir John told him the story. Black
was a canny Scot. He didn't talk much, but he listened. It was his
private opinion that the doctor's theory was right, and a sudden brain
storm, owing to pregnancy, was the motive for the suicide. However, he
was thorough at his job, and he went down to the country and inter-

viewed the household. He asked many questions that the police had not asked, chatted with the doctor, checked up on the mail that had come for Lady Farren during the past few weeks, enquired about telephone calls and encounters with personal friends; and still there was no answer he could give to his client.

The one obvious solution that had come to his practised mind—that Lady Farren was expecting a child by a lover—did not work. Check and double check revealed no possibility of this. Husband and wife were devoted and had not been apart since their marriage three years previously. The servants all spoke of their great attachment for one another. There were no financial worries. Nor could the shrewd Black trace any infidelity on the part of Sir John. Servants, friends, neighbours, all spoke of his high integrity. Therefore, his wife had not shot herself through any fault of his that had come to light.

Temporarily Black was baffled. But not beaten. Once he took on a case, he liked to see it through to the end, and hardened though he was, he felt sorry to see Sir John's agony of mind.

"You know, sir," he said, "in cases of this sort we often have to go back in a person's life, rather further than the immediate past. I've been through every inch of your wife's desk, with your permission, and searched her papers and all correspondence, and I have found nothing to give the faintest clue to the trouble on her mind—if there was trouble.

"You have told me that you met Lady Farren—Miss Marsh, as she was then—while on a visit to Switzerland. She was living with an invalid aunt, Miss Vera Marsh, who had brought her up, her parents being dead."

"That is correct," said Sir John.

"They lived in Sierre and also in Lausanne, and you met both the Misses Marsh at the house of a mutual friend in Sierre. You struck up a friendship with the younger Miss Marsh, and by the end of your holiday you had fallen in love with her, and she with you, and you asked her to marry you."

"Yes."

"The elder Miss Marsh made no objection; in fact, she was delighted. It was arranged between you that you should make her an allowance to cover the expenses of a companion to take her niece's place, and within a couple of months or so you were married at Lausanne."

"Correct again."

"There was no question of the aunt coming to live with you in England?"

"No," said Sir John. "Mary wanted her to—she was much attached to her aunt—but the old lady refused. She had lived in Switzerland so long, she couldn't face the English climate or the English food. Incidentally, we have been out twice to see her since we married."

Black asked if Sir John had heard from his wife's aunt since the tragedy. Yes. He had written, of course, at once, and she had seen the news in the papers too. She was horrified. She could give no reason why Mary should have taken her life. A happy letter, written a week before, full of her happiness at the prospect of the future baby, had arrived in Sierre only a few days prior to the calamity. Miss Marsh had enclosed the letter for Sir John to read. And Sir John gave it to Black.

"I take it," said Black, "that the two ladies, when you met them first three years ago, were living very quietly?"

"They had this small villa, as I told you before," said Sir John, "and about twice a year they used to go down to Lausanne and take rooms in a pension. The old lady had some sort of trouble with her lungs, but not serious enough for a sanatorium or anything like that. Mary was a most devoted niece. It was one of the first things that drew me to her. Her gentleness and sweet temper to the old lady, who, like many elderly people, semi-invalid, was apt to be fractious at times."

"So your wife, the younger Miss Marsh, did not get about much? Not many friends her own age, and that sort of thing?"

"I suppose not. It did not seem to worry her. Hers was such a contented nature."

"And this had been her life since she was quite small?"

"Yes. Miss Marsh was Mary's only relative. She had adopted her when Mary's parents died. Mary was a child at the time."

"And how old was your wife when you married her?"

"Thirty-one."

"No history of a previous engagement or a love affair?"

"Absolutely none. I used to tease Mary about it. She said she had never seen anyone to give her the slightest flutter. And her aunt agreed. I remember Miss Marsh saying to me when we became engaged, 'It's rare to find anyone so unspoilt as Mary. She's got the prettiest face and is quite unaware of it, and the sweetest nature and doesn't realise that either. You're a very lucky man.' And I was."

Sir John sat staring at Black with such abject misery in his eyes that the tough Scot hardly liked to cross-question him further.

"So it really was a love match on both sides?" he said. "You are quite certain there was no pull in your title and position? I mean, the aunt might have told her niece that here was a chance she mustn't miss, another man like you might not come along. After all, ladies do think of these things."

Sir John shook his head.

"Miss Marsh might have had an eye to the main chance, I don't know," he said, "but certainly Mary had not.

"Right from the beginning it was I who sought out her, not the other way round. If Mary had been looking about for a husband, she would have shown signs of it when we first met. And you know what cats women can be. The friend at whose chalet I originally met the Marshes would have warned me that here was a girl, past thirty, in search of a husband. She said no such thing. She said, 'I want you to meet a perfect darling of a girl whom we all adore and feel rather sorry for because she leads such a lonely life.' "

"Yet she didn't appear lonely to you?"

"Not at all. She seemed perfectly content."

Black handed back Miss Marsh's letter to Sir John.

"You still want me to go on with this enquiry?" he said. "You don't think it would be simpler to decide, once and for all, that your doctor was right about Lady Farren, and she had some sort of a black-out which affected her mind and made her take her life?"

"No," said Sir John, "I tell you, somewhere there is a clue to this tragedy, and I shan't give up until I've found it. Or rather you find it for me. That's why I'm employing you."

Black rose from his chair.

"Very well," he said, "if that's the way you feel about it, I'll go right ahead with the case."

"What are you going to do?" asked Sir John.

"I shall fly to Switzerland tomorrow."

Black handed in his card at the Chalet Bon Repos at Sierre and was shown into a small salon that gave on to a balcony with a fine view across the Rhone Valley.

A woman, Miss Marsh's companion he supposed, led him through the salon on to the balcony. Black had time to notice that the room was furnished neatly, with good taste, but nothing out of the way, very much the room of an elderly English spinster living abroad who did not fling her money around.

There was a large picture of Lady Farren on the mantelpiece, taken recently, a duplicate of the one he had seen in Sir John's study. And another on a writing bureau of Lady Farren aged about twenty, he judged. A pretty, shy-looking girl, her hair worn rather longer than in the more recent portrait.

Black went on to the balcony and introduced himself to the elderly lady seated there in a wheeled chair as a friend of Sir John Farren's.

Miss Marsh had white hair, blue eyes, and a firm mouth. From the way she spoke to her companion, who immediately left them together, Black decided she was hard on those who served her. She seemed, however, genuinely pleased to see Black, and at once asked after Sir John with much concern and wanted to know if any light at all had been thrown on the tragedy.

"I'm sorry to say, none," answered Black. "In fact, I am here to ask you what you know about it. You knew Lady Farren better than any of us, even her husband. Sir John thinks you may have some ideas on the subject."

Miss Marsh looked surprised.

"But I wrote and told Sir John I was horrified and completely baffled," she said. "I enclosed Mary's last letter. Did he tell you?"

"Yes," said Black, "I saw the letter. And you have others?"

"I kept all her letters," said Miss Marsh. "She wrote me regularly, every week, after she married. If Sir John wants me to send him the letters I shall be pleased to do so. There is not one letter that isn't full of her affection for him, and her pride and delight in her new home. It was her one regret that I wouldn't stir myself to go and visit her. But you see, I am such an invalid."

"You look hearty enough," thought Black, "but perhaps you just didn't want to go."

"I gather you and your niece were much attached?" he said.

"I was deeply fond of Mary, and I like to think she was equally fond of me," was the swift reply. "Heaven knows I can be cantankerous at times, but Mary never seemed to mind. She was the sweetest-natured girl.

"You were sorry to lose her?"

"Of course I was sorry. I missed her terribly, and still do. But naturally her happiness came first."

"Sir John told me he made you an allowance to cover the cost of your present companion."

"Yes. It was generous of him. Will it continue, do you know?"

The inflection in her voice was sharp. Black decided that his original idea of Miss Marsh as someone who did not wholly disregard money was probably sound.

"Sir John didn't say. But I feel sure, if it was otherwise, you would have heard from him or from his lawyers," said Black.

Black looked at Miss Marsh's hands. They tapped the sides of the wheeled chair in a little nervous gesture.

"There was nothing in your niece's past that would account for her suicide?" he said.

She looked startled. "What on earth do you mean?"

"No previous engagement, or love affair gone wrong?"

"Good heavens, no."

Curious. She seemed relieved at the wording of his question.

"Sir John was Mary's only love. She led rather a solitary life with me, you know. Not many young people in the district. Even in Lausanne she never seemed to seek out people nearer her own age. It was not that she was particularly shy or reserved. Just self-contained."

"What about school friends?"

"I taught her lessons myself when she was small. She had a few terms in Lausanne when she was older, but as a day girl; we lived in a pension close by. I seem to remember one or two girls coming in for tea. But no especial friend."

"Have you any photographs of her at that age?"

"Yes. Several. I've got them all in an album somewhere. Would you care to see them?"

"I think I should. Sir John showed me several photographs, but I don't think he had any dating before their marriage."

Miss Marsh pointed to the bureau in the salon behind and told him to open the second drawer and bring back an album. He did so, and putting on spectacles, she opened the album, and he drew his seat beside her.

They went through the album at random. There were many snapshots, none of any particular interest. Lady Farren alone. Miss Marsh alone. Lady Farren and Miss Marsh in groups with other people. Snaps of the chalet. Snaps of Lausanne. Black turned the pages. No clue here.

"Is that the lot?" he said.

"I'm afraid it is," said Miss Marsh. "She was such a pretty girl, wasn't she? Those warm brown eyes. It is the most dreadful thing . . . Poor Sir John."

"You haven't any snaps of her when she was a child, I notice. These seem to start when she was around fifteen."

There was a pause, and then Miss Marsh replied, "No . . . no, I don't think I had a camera in those days."

Black had a well-trained ear. It was an easy matter for him to detect a falsehood. Miss Marsh was lying about something. About what?

"What a pity," he said. "I always think it's interesting to trace the child in the adult face. I'm a married man myself. My wife and I wouldn't be without the first albums of our youngster for the world."

"Yes, it was stupid of me, wasn't it?" said Miss Marsh.

She put the album down in front of her on the table.

"I expect you have the ordinary studio portraits?" said Black.

"No," said Miss Marsh, "or if I once had, I must have lost them. In the move, you know. We didn't come here until Mary was fifteen. We were in Lausanne before that."

"And you adopted Mary when she was five, I think Sir John said?"

"Yes. She would have been about five."

Again the momentary hesitation, the inflection in her voice.

"Have you any photographs of Lady Farren's parents?"

"No."

"Yet her father was your only brother, I understand?"

"My only brother, yes."

"What decided you to adopt Lady Farren as a child?"

"The mother was dead, and my brother did not know how to take care of her. She was a delicate child. We both of us felt it was the best solution."

"Of course your brother made you an allowance for the child's up-keep and education?"

"Naturally. I couldn't have managed otherwise." Then Miss Marsh made a mistake. But for this one mistake, Black might have let the whole thing go.

"You ask the most extraordinarily remote questions, Mr. Black," she said with a hard little laugh. "I don't see that the allowance paid to me by Mary's father can be of the slightest interest to you. What you want to know is why poor Mary killed herself, and so does her husband, and so do I."

"Anything even remotely connected with Lady Farren's past life is of interest to me," said Black. "You see, Sir John has employed me for that very purpose. Perhaps it is time that I explained to you I am not a personal friend of his. I am a private detective."

Miss Marsh turned grey. Her composure went. She became suddenly a very frightened old woman.

"What have you come to find out?" she said.

"Everything," said Black.

Now it was a favourite theory of the Scot's, which he often ex-pounded to the director of the agency for whom he worked, that there are very few people in this world who haven't got something to hide. Time and time again he had seen men and women in the witness box, under cross-examination, and one and all were afraid; not of the ques-tions put to them, which they must answer, and which might shed light on the particular case then under trial; but that in answering the ques-tions, they would, by some mishap, by some slip of the tongue, reveal some personal secret pertaining to themselves which would discredit them.

Black was certain that Miss Marsh found herself in this position now. She might know nothing of Mary Farren's suicide or of its cause. But Miss Marsh herself was guilty of something that she had long sought to hide.

"If Sir John has found out about the allowance and thinks I have been defrauding Mary all these years, he might have had the decency to tell me himself, and not employ a detective," she said.

"Oh, ho, here we go," thought Black. "Give the old lady enough rope and she'll hang herself."

"Sir John did not mention the word fraud," he replied to Miss

Marsh; "he merely thought the circumstances were rather strange."

Black was taking a chance, but he felt the result might be worth it.

"Of course they were strange," said Miss Marsh. "I tried to act for the best, and I believed I did. I can swear to you, Mr. Black, that I used very little money on myself, and that the most part of it went for Mary's upkeep, according to the agreement with the child's father. When Mary married, and as it happened married well, I did not think there was any harm in keeping the capital for myself. Sir John was rich, and Mary would not miss it."

"I take it," said Black, "that Lady Farren knew nothing of what was going on financially?"

"Nothing," said Miss Marsh. "She was never interested in money matters, and she believed herself entirely dependent on me. You don't think Sir John is going to prosecute me, Mr. Black? If he won a case against me, which he undoubtedly would, I should be destitute."

Black stroked his chin and pretended to consider.

"I don't think Sir John intends anything of the sort, Miss Marsh," he said. "But he would like to know the truth of what happened."

Miss Marsh sank back in her wheeled chair. No longer stiff and upright, she looked a tired old lady.

"Now that Mary is dead, it can't hurt her, the truth coming out," she said. "The fact is, Mr. Black, she wasn't my niece at all. I was paid a large sum of money to look after her. The money should have gone to her on her majority, but I kept it myself. Mary's father, with whom I signed the agreement, had died in the meantime. Living here in Switzerland, no one knew anything about the matter. It was so simple to keep it secret. I intended no harm."

It was always the way, thought Black. Temptation came to a man or a woman, and they gave way to it. They never "intended" harm.

"I see," he said. "Well, Miss Marsh, I don't want to go into the details of what you did or how you spent the money intended for Lady Farren. What does interest me is this. If she wasn't your niece, who was she?"

"She was the only daughter of a Mr. Henry Warner. That is all I ever knew. He never told me his address, or where he lived. All I knew was the address of his bankers, and the branch in London; four cheques were paid to me from that address. After I took Mary in my care, Mr. Warner went to Canada and died there five years later.

"The bank informed me of this, and as I never heard from them again, I believed myself safe to do—what I did—with her money."

Black noted the name Henry Warner, and Miss Marsh gave him the address of the bank.

"Mr. Warner was not a personal friend of yours?" he asked.

"Oh no. I only met him twice. The first time was when I answered his advertisement to a box number for someone to take charge, indefinitely, of a delicate girl. I was very poor at the time and had just lost a post as governess to an English family returning to England.

"I did not want to take a position in a school, and this advertisement came as a godsend, especially as the sum to be paid for the child's upkeep, which the father intended to accumulate, was so generous. I knew I should be able to live as I had, frankly, never lived before. You can hardly blame me."

Something of her former confidence was returning. She looked sharply at Black.

"I am not blaming you," he said. "Tell me more about Henry Warner."

"There is little to tell," she said. "He asked very few questions about myself or my background. The only point he made clear was that he wanted Mary to remain with me for good; he had no intention of having her back with him again, or corresponding with her. He planned to go to Canada, he told me, and cut himself off from all former connections. I was entirely free to bring up his daughter as I thought fit. In other words, he washed his hands of her."

"A callous sort of customer?" suggested Black.

"Not exactly callous," replied Miss Marsh. "He looked anxious and careworn, as though the responsibility of looking after the child had been too much for him. His wife apparently was dead. Then I enquired in what way his daughter was delicate, because I knew little of nursing and did not particularly relish an ailing child.

"He explained to me that she was not physically delicate, but that she had witnessed a terrible train accident a few months previously, and the shock of this had caused her to lose her memory.

"She was perfectly normal otherwise, perfectly sane. But she remembered nothing previous to the shock. She did not even know he was her father. This was the reason, he told me, why he wanted her to begin a new life in another country."

Black jotted down some notes. The case at last was beginning to show possibilities.

"So you were willing to take the risk of having this child—suffering from mental shock—on your hands for life?" he asked.

He had not intended his question to be cynical, but Miss Marsh saw a sting in it. She flushed.

"I am used to teaching and used to children," she said; "also, independence was dear to me. I accepted Mr. Warner's offer, on condition I took to the child and the child took to me. At our second meeting he brought Mary with him. It was impossible not to feel an affection for her at once. That pretty little face, those large eyes, and the soft, gentle manner. She seemed quite normal, but young for her age. I chatted with her and asked her if she would like to come and stay with me, and she said she would; she put her hand in mine in the most confiding way. I told Mr. Warner 'Yes,' and the bargain was struck. He left Mary with me that evening, and we neither of us ever saw him again. It was easy enough to tell the child she was my niece, as she remembered nothing of her past; she accepted anything I cared to tell her about herself as gospel truth. It was all too easy."

"And from that day she did not once recover her memory, Miss Marsh?"

"Never. Life began for her when her father handed her over to me at that hotel in Lausanne, and it really began for me too. I could not have loved her better had she been in truth my niece."

Black glanced through his notes and put them in his pocket.

"So beyond the fact that you knew she was the daughter of a Mr. Henry Warner, you were completely ignorant as to her background?" he asked.

"Completely," said Miss Marsh.

"She was merely a little girl of five years old who had lost her memory?"

"Fifteen," corrected Miss Marsh.

"How do you mean, fifteen?" said Black.

Miss Marsh flushed again.

"I forgot," she said. "I misled you earlier in the afternoon. I always told Mary, and everybody else, that I had adopted my niece when she was five. It made it so much easier for me, and easier for Mary too, because she remembered nothing of her life previous to the time she came to live with me. She was, in point of fact, fifteen. You will realise now why I have no snapshots or photographs of Mary as a child."

"Indeed, yes," said Black. "And I must thank you, Miss Marsh, for being so helpful. I don't think Sir John is likely to raise any questions about the money, and for the present, at any rate, I shall keep the whole story of what you have told me as entirely confidential. What I now have to find out is where Lady Farren—Mary Warner—was living for the first fifteen years of her life, and what that life was. It may have some bearing on the suicide."

Miss Marsh rang for her companion to show Black out. She had not quite recovered her equanimity.

"There is only one thing that has always puzzled me," she said. "I feel her father, Henry Warner, did not speak the truth. Mary showed no fear of trains at any time, and though I made several enquiries of many people, I could learn of no severe train accident that had happened in England, or anywhere else for that matter, during the months before Mary came to me."

Black returned to London, but he did not get in touch with Sir John Farren, because he thought it best to wait until he had more definite news to communicate.

It seemed to him unnecessary to reveal the truth about Miss Marsh and the adoption. It would only unsettle Sir John further, and it was hardly likely that this fact had suddenly come to light and driven his wife to suicide.

The more intriguing possibility was that Lady Farren had received a shock which, in the timing of a moment, had pierced the veil which had shrouded her memory for nineteen years.

It was Black's business to discover the nature of that shock. The first thing he did in London was to go to the branch of the bank where Henry Warner had kept an account. He saw the manager and explained his mission.

It appeared that Henry Warner had indeed gone to Canada, had married again when he was out there, and had subsequently died. The widow had written, closing the account in England. The manager did not know whether Henry Warner had left a second family in Canada, nor did he know the address of the widow. Henry Warner's first wife had died many years previously. Yes, the manager knew about the daughter of the first marriage. She had been adopted by a Miss Marsh in Switzerland. Cheques had been paid to Miss Marsh, and they ceased when Henry Warner married a second time. The only positive information that the bank manager could give Black which might be helpful was Henry Warner's old address. And the piece of news, which Henry Warner had certainly not told Miss March, that his profession was the Church, and that at the time Miss Marsh had adopted his daughter he was vicar of All Saints, in the parish of Long Common, Hampshire.

Black travelled down to Hampshire with a pleasurable feeling of anticipation. He always began to enjoy himself when the clues began to unravel. It reminded him of boyhood days of hide-and-seek. It was his interest in the unexpected that had called him to be a private detective in the first place, and he had never regretted his call.

He believed in keeping an open mind about his case, but it was difficult not to see the Reverend Henry Warner as the villain of this piece. The sudden handing over of a mentally sick daughter to a perfect stranger abroad, and then cutting himself loose from her and going to Canada seemed an extraordinarily heartless thing for a clergyman to do.

Black smelt scandal, and if the taint still lingered in Long Common after nineteen years, it would not be difficult to ferret out what the scandal had been.

Black put up at the local inn, describing himself as a writer on old churches in Hampshire, and with this same excuse he wrote a polite note to the present incumbent, asking if he might call.

His wish was granted, and the vicar, a young man, an enthusiast on architecture, showed him every corner of the church from nave to belfry, with a wealth of detail about fifteenth-century carving.

Black listened politely, disguising his own ignorance, and finally led the vicar round to talking of his predecessors.

Unfortunately the present vicar had been at Long Common for only six years, and he knew little about Warner, who had been succeeded by someone who had moved to Hull, but Warner had definitely held the living for twelve years, and his wife was buried in the churchyard.

Black saw the grave and noted the headstone. "Emily Mary, dearly beloved wife of Henry Warner who passed to rest safe in the arms of Jesus."

He also noted the date. The daughter Mary would have been ten years old at the time.

Yes, said the present vicar, he had heard that Warner had given up the living in a great hurry and gone to the Dominions, Canada, he believed. Some of the people in the village would remember him, especially the older ones. Possibly his own gardener would remember most. He had been gardener at the rectory for thirty years.

But as far as he, the vicar, knew, Warner had not been a historian or a collector; he had done no research work on the church.

If Mr. Black would care to come to the rectory, he, the present vicar, had many interesting books on Long Common history.

Mr. Black excused himself. He had got all he wanted out of the present incumbent. He felt that an evening at the bar of the inn where he was staying would prove more profitable, and it did.

He learnt no more about fifteenth-century carving, but a good deal about the Reverend Henry Warner.

The vicar had been respected in the parish, but never deeply liked because of his rigid views and his intolerance. He was not the sort of man to whom his parishioners went when they were in trouble; he was always more likely to condemn than to console. He never entered the bar of the inn, never mixed in friendly fashion with the humble.

He was known to have private means, and he was not dependent on his benefice. He liked to be invited to the few large houses in the neighbourhood, because he placed social values high; but he had not been particularly popular there either.

In short, the Reverend Henry Warner had been an intolerant, narrow-minded snob, which were three poor qualities for a vicar to hold. His wife, on the contrary, had been much loved by all, and it had been universally regretted when she died after an operation for cancer. She had been a most sweet-tempered lady, very thoughtful for others, most kindhearted, and her little girl took after her.

Had the child been much affected by her mother's death?

No one remembered. It was thought not. She went away to school and was only home during the holidays. One or two recollected her riding about on her bicycle, a pretty, friendly little thing. The gardener and his wife had acted as married couple for the Reverend Henry Warner, the same gardener that was up at the rectory now. Old Harris. No, he did not come down to the pub of an evening. He was a tee-

totaller. He lived up in one of the cottages near the church. No, his
wife was dead. He lived with a married daughter. He was a great rose
fancier and won prizes for his roses every year at the local show.

Black finished his pint and departed. The evening was yet young. He
dropped out of his disguise as a writer on old Hampshire churches and
slipped into the role of a collector of Hampshire roses. He found old
Harris smoking a pipe outside his cottage. There were roses growing up
his fence. Black stopped to admire them. The conversation was
launched.

It took him the better part of an hour to lead Harris from roses to
past vicars, from past vicars to Warner, from Warner to Mrs. Warner,
from Mrs. Warner to Mary Warner, but the picture unfolded, and
there was nothing very remarkable to see in it. The same tale was
repeated that he had heard in the village.

The Reverend Warner was a hard man, not given to being friendly-
like; very sparing, he was, with his praises. Took no interest in the
garden. Stuck-up sort of chap. But down on you like a ton of bricks if
anything was wrong. The lady was very different. Proper shame when
she died. Miss Mary was a nice child too. His wife had been very fond
of Miss Mary. Nothing stuck-up or proud about her.

"I suppose the Reverend Warner gave up the living because he was
lonely after Mrs. Warner died?" said Black, offering Harris some of his
own tobacco.

"No, it wasn't nothing to do with that. It was along of Miss Mary's
health, and her having to live abroad after being so ill with the rheumatic fever. They went off to Canada, and we never heard from them
no more."

"Rheumatic fever?" said Black. "That's a nasty thing to get."

"It wasn't anything to do with the beds here," said old Harris; "my
wife kept the place aired and looked after everything, just as she used
to when Mrs. Warner was living. It was at school Miss Mary caught it,
and I remember saying to my wife that the vicar ought to sue the
teachers up there for neglect. The child nearly died of it."

Black fingered the rose Harris had picked for him and placed it
neatly in his buttonhole.

"Why didn't the vicar sue the school?" he asked.

"He never told us if he did or not," said the gardener; "all we was
told was to pack up Miss Mary's things and send them off to the

address in Cornwall he gave us, and then to get his own things packed, and dust covers put over the furniture, and before we knew what was happening a great van came to pack the furniture and take it to store, or to be sold—we heard afterwards it was sold, and then that the vicar had given up the living and they was going off to Canada. My wife was most upset about Miss Mary; she never had a word from her or from the vicar, and we had served them all those years."

Black agreed that it was a poor return for what they had done. "So the school was in Cornwall?" he observed. "I'm not surprised at anyone catching rheumatic fever in Cornwall. A very damp county."

"Of no, sir," said old Harris. "Miss Mary went down to Cornwall for her convalescence. Place called Carnleath, I believe it was. She was at school at Hythe, in Kent."

"I have a daughter at school near Hythe," lied Black with ease. "I hope it's not the same place. What was the name of Miss Mary's school?"

"Couldn't tell you, sir," said old Harris, shaking his head, "it's too long ago. But I remember Miss Mary saying it was a lovely place, right on the sea, and she was very happy there, fond of the games and that."

"Ah," said Black, "can't be the same then. My daughter's school is inland. It's funny how people get hold of the wrong end of the stick. I heard Mr. Warner's name spoken down in the village this evening—queer, if you hear a name once in a day you hear it again—and someone was saying the reason they went to Canada was because the daughter had been badly injured in a train accident."

Old Harris laughed scornfully.

"Them fellows at the pub will say anything when they've a drop of beer inside them," he said. "Train accident indeed. Why, the whole village knew at the time it was rheumatic fever and that the vicar was almost out of his mind with the worry of it, being sent for so sudden up to the school and all. I've never seen a man so demented. To tell you the truth, neither the wife nor myself had ever thought him so fond of Miss Mary until that happened. He used to neglect her, we thought. She was so much her mother's girl. But his face was terrible when he came back from being sent for to the school, and he said to my wife that it was for God to punish the head teacher there for criminal negligence. Those were his words. Criminal negligence."

"Perhaps," said Black, "he had an uneasy conscience and blamed the school for neglect, when at heart he blamed himself."

"Could be," said old Harris, "could be. He'd always look for the fault in the other fellow."

Black considered the time had come to pass from the Warners to the roses once again. He lingered five more minutes, made a note of the blooms recommended for planting by an amateur like himself who wanted quick results, said good evening, and went back to the inn. He slept soundly and caught the first train back to London in the morning. He did not think he would secure any more information at Long Common. In the afternoon he took a train to Hythe. On this expedition he did not bother the local vicar, but addressed himself to the manageress of his hotel.

"I am looking around the coast for a suitable school for my daughter," he said, "and I understand that there are one or two in this part of the world that are very good indeed. I wonder if you happen to know the names of any you could recommend."

"Oh yes," said the manageress, "there are two very good schools in Hythe. There is Miss Braddock's, up at the top of the hill, and of course there is St. Bees, the big co-educational school right on the front. Here at the hotel we mostly get parents with children at St. Bees."

"Co-educational?" said Black. "Has it always been so?"

"Since it was first founded, thirty years ago," said the manageress. "Mr. and Mrs. Johnson are still the principals, though of course they are both elderly now. It's very well run and has an excellent tone. I know there is sometimes prejudice against a co-educational school, because people say it makes the girls masculine and the boys effeminate, but I've never seen a sign of that myself. The children always look very happy and just like other children, and they only take them up to fifteen anyway. Would you care for me to make an appointment for you to see either Mr. or Mrs. Johnson? I know them well."

Mr. Black wondered if she got a commission on pupils to whom she had recommended the school.

"Thank you very much," he said, "I would be pleased if you would." The appointment was made for eleven-thirty the next morning.

Black was surprised at St. Bees' being co-educational. He had not thought that the Reverend Henry Warner would have been open-minded on mixed tuition. St. Bees it must be, however, from the description given by old Harris, the gardener. St. Bees was certainly facing the sea, with a fine surround. The other school, Miss Braddock's, was tucked away behind the hill at the top of the town, with hardly any view at all, and no playing fields. Black had made sure of this by going to look at the outside before keeping his appointment at St. Bees.

A smell of shining linoleum, scrubbed floors, and varnish greeted him as he stood at the entrance, having mounted the school steps. A parlourmaid answered his bell and showed him into a large study on the right of the hall.

An elderly man with a bald head, horn spectacles, and an effusive smile rose to his feet and greeted him.

"Glad to meet you, Mr. Black," he said. "So you are looking for a school for your daughter? I hope you are going to leave St. Bees believing that you have found it."

Mr. Black summed him up in a word. "Salesman," he said to himself. Aloud he proceeded to spin a neat yarn about his daughter Phyllis, who was just reaching the awkward age.

"Awkward?" said Mr. Johnson. "Then St. Bees is the place for Phyllis. We have no awkward children here. All the odd spots get rubbed off. We pride ourselves on our happy, healthy boys and girls. Come and have a look at them."

He clapped Black upon the back and proceeded to lead him round the school. Black was not interested in schools, co-educational or otherwise; he was only interested in Mary Warner's rheumatic fever of nineteen years ago. But he was a patient man and allowed himself to be shown every classroom, every dormitory—the two wings were separated for the two sexes—the gymnasium, the swimming bath, the lecture hall, the playing fields, and finally the kitchen.

He then returned with a triumphant Mr. Johnson to the study.

"Well, Mr. Black?" said the principal, smiling behind his horn rims. "And are we to be allowed to have Phyllis?"

Black sat back and folded his hands, the picture of a fond father. "Yours is a delightful school," he said, "but I must tell you that we have to be very careful of Phyllis' health. She is not a strong child and gets colds very easily. I am only wondering whether the air might not be too strong for her."

Mr. Johnson laughed and, opening a drawer in his desk, took out a book.

"My dear Mr. Black," he said, "St. Bees has one of the best health records of any school in England. A child develops a cold. He or she is isolated at once. That cold does not spread. In the winter months noses and throats are sprayed as a matter of routine. In the summer months the children do exercises for the lungs in front of open windows. We have not had an influenza epidemic for five years. One case of measles two years ago. One case of whooping cough three years ago. I have here a list of illnesses contracted by the boys and girls over the years, and it is a list I am proud to show to every parent."

He handed the book to Mr. Black, who took it with evidence of pleasure. It was just the evidence he wanted.

"This is remarkable," he said, turning the pages, "and of course modern methods of hygiene have helped you to have such a good health record. It can't have been the same some years ago."

"It has always been the same," said Mr. Johnson, getting up and reaching for another volume on his shelf. "Choose any year you fancy. You won't catch me out."

Without hesitation Black chose the year that Mary Warner had been removed from the school by her father.

Mr. Johnson ran his hand along the volumes and produced the year in question. Black turned the pages in search of rhematic fever. There were cold cases, one broken leg, one German measles, one sprained ankle, one mastoid—but not the case he sought.

"Have you ever had a case of rheumatic fever?" he enquired. "My wife is particularly afraid of that for Phyllis."

"Never," said Mr. Johnson firmly. "We are far too careful. The boys and girls always have a rub-down after games, and the linen and clothing are most scrupulously aired."

Black shut up the book. He decided upon direct tactics.

"I like what I have seen of St. Bees," he said, "but I feel I must be frank with you. My wife was given a list of schools, with yours amongst it, and she at once struck it off the list because she remembered being very put off it by a friend many years ago. This friend had a friend—you know how it is—but the long and short of it was that the friend was obliged to remove his daughter from St. Bees and even talked of suing the school for criminal negligence."

Mr. Johnson's smile had gone. His eyes looked small behind the horn-rimmed glasses.

"I should be very much obliged if you would give me the name of the friend," he said coldly.

"Certainly," said Black. "The friend afterwards left this country and went to Canada. He was a clergyman. And his name was the Reverend Henry Warner."

The horn-rimmed glasses did not disguise the odd, wary flicker in Mr. Johnson's eyes. He ran his tongue over his lips.

"The Reverend Henry Warner," he said, "now let me see." He leant back in his chair and seemed to be pondering. Black, trained to evasion, knew that the principal of St. Bees was thinking hard and playing for time.

"Criminal negligence was the word used, Mr. Johnson," he said, "and oddly enough I ran across a relative of Warner's only the other day, who happened to bring the matter up. I was told that Mary Warner nearly died."

Mr. Johnson took off his horn glasses and slowly polished them. His expression had quite changed. The over-genial schoolmaster had turned into the hardheaded businessman.

"You obviously know the story from the relative's point of view only," he said. "Any criminal negligence was on the part of the father, Henry Warner, and not on ours."

Black shrugged his shoulders.

"How can a parent be sure?" he murmured.

His words were calculated to draw the principal further.

"How can you be sure?" shouted Mr. Johnson, all pretence at geniality gone, and slapping his hand on his desk. "Because I would have you know that Mary Warner's case was one isolated incident that had never happened before and has never happened since.

"We were careful then. And we are careful now. I told the father that what had occurred must have occurred during the holidays, and most definitely and finally not at school. He would not believe me, and insisted that our boys here were to blame, through lack of supervision. I had every boy over a certain age up here before me, in this very room, and questioned them privately. My boys spoke the truth. They were not to blame. It was useless to try to get any sense out of the girl herself; she did not know what we were talking about or what we were asking her. I need hardly tell you, Mr. Black, that the whole thing was the most frightful shock to myself and my wife, and to the whole staff, and the story is one which, thank God, we have lived down and which we had hoped was forgotten."

His face showed fatigue and strain. The story may have been lived down, but it had definitely not been forgotten by the principal.

"What happened?" asked Black. "Did Warner tell you he was going to remove his daughter?"

"Did he tell us?" said Mr. Johnson. "No, indeed, we told him. How could we possibly keep Mary Warner here when we found she was five months pregnant?"

The jigsaw puzzle was fitting together rather nicely, thought Black. It was remarkable how the pieces came to hand if you set your mind to the job. Finding out the truth through other people's lies was always stimulating. First Miss Marsh; he had to break through her iron curtain. The Reverend Henry Warner, too, had certainly gone out of his way to build a fictitious barricade. A train accident to one, rheumatic fever to another. Poor devil, what a shock it must have been to him. No wonder he packed his daughter off to Cornwall to hide her secret, and shut up the house and left the neighbourhood.

Callous, though, to wash his hands of her when the business was through. The loss of memory must have been genuine enough. But Black wondered what had caused this. Had the world of childhood suddenly become nightmare to a schoolgirl of fourteen or fifteen, and nature taken charge and mercifully blotted out what had happened?

It looked this way to Black. But he was a thorough man; he was being paid well for his time of research, and he was not going to his client with a tale half told. It must be the whole story. He remembered Carnleath was the place where Mary Warner had gone for her convalescence after the supposed rheumatic fever. Black decided to go there.

The firm for which he worked supplied him with a car, and Black set out. It occurred to him that another word or two with old Harris, the gardener, might prove fruitful, and as it was on his way to the West Country, he stopped off at Long Common, bringing as excuse a small rose tree which he had purchased off a market gardener en route. He

would tell the gardener this came from his own garden, as a small return for the advice given him the previous visit.

Black drew up outside the gardener's cottage at midday, at which
hour he judged the old fellow would be home for his dinner.

Unfortunately Harris was not at home. He had gone to a flower
show at Alton. The married daughter came to the door, a baby in her
arms, and said she had no idea when he would be back. She seemed a
pleasant, friendly sort of woman. Black lit a cigarette, handed over the
rose tree, and admired the baby.

"I have a youngster like that at home," he said with his usual facil-
ity for playing fictitious roles.

"Really, sir?" said the woman. "I have two others, but Roy is the
baby of the family."

They exchanged baby gossip while Black smoked his cigarette. "Tell
your father I was in Hythe a day or two ago," he said, "seeing my girl,
who is at school there. And curiously enough I met the headmaster of
St. Bees, the school where Miss Mary Warner was educated—your
father was telling me about it—and how angry the vicar was that his
daughter caught rheumatic fever—and the headmaster remembered
Miss Warner well. He insisted, after all these years, that it was not
rheumatic fever, but some virus the child had picked up at home."

"Oh, really," said the woman. "Well, I suppose he had to say something for the sake of the school. Yes, that was the name. St. Bees. I
remember Miss Mary talking about St. Bees often enough. We were
much of an age, and when she was home she used to let me ride her
bicycle. It seemed a great treat to me then."

"More friendly than the vicar then," said Black. "I gather your
father had no great liking for him."

The woman laughed.

"No," she said, "I'm afraid nobody had much opinion of him, though
I dare say he was a very good man. Miss Mary was a dear. Everyone
liked Miss Mary."

"You must have been sorry," said Black, "that she went down to
Cornwall and never came home to say good-bye."

"Oh, I was. I never could understand it. And I wrote to her down
there, but never had no answer. It hurt me quite a bit, and Mother
too. So unlike Miss Mary."

Black played with the tassle of the baby's shoe. The face was puckered to cry, and Black thought this might distract him. He did not want Harris' daughter to go back inside the cottage.

"It must have been lonely at the rectory all on her own," said Black. "I expect she was glad of your company during the holidays."

"I don't think Miss Mary was ever lonely," said the woman; "she was such a friendly soul, with a word for everyone, not stuck-up like the vicar. We used to have fine games together, pretending we were Indians and such. You know what kiddies are."

"No boy friends and cinemas then?"

"Oh no. Miss Mary wasn't that sort. The girls are terrible today, aren't they? Like young women. They chase the men."

"I bet you had admirers, both of you, for all that."

"No, really, sir, we didn't. Miss Mary was so used to boys at St. Bees, she never thought them out of the ordinary. Besides, the vicar would never have allowed anything like 'admirers.'"

"I suppose not. Was Miss Mary afraid of him?"

"I don't know about afraid. But she was careful not to displease him."

"Always had to be home before dark, I suppose."

"Oh yes. Miss Mary was never out after dark."

"I wish I could keep my daughter from coming back late," said Black. "In summer evenings it's sometimes nearly eleven o'clock before she is in. It's not right. Especially when you read the things that happen in the newspapers."

"Shocking, isn't it?" agreed the gardener's daughter.

"But this is a quiet neighbourhood. I don't suppose you get any bad characters around here, and didn't in those days either."

"No," said the woman, "though of course when the hoppers come it's a bit lively."

Black threw away his cigarette. It was burning his fingers.

"The hoppers?" he said.

"Yes, sir. It's a great district for growing hops. And in the summer the hoppers come down and camp in the neighbourhood, and they're quite a rough crowd, from some of the worst parts in London."

"How interesting. I had no idea they grew hops in Hampshire."

"Oh yes, sir. It's been an industry for a long time."

Black dangled a flower before the baby's eyes.

"I suppose you weren't allowed anywhere near them when you were young, or Miss Mary either," he said.

The woman smiled.

"We weren't supposed to, but we did," she said, "and we'd have got into a proper old row if we'd been found out. I remember one time—— What is it, Roy? Is it time for your nap? He's getting sleepy."

"You remember one time," said Black.

"Oh, the hoppers, yes. I remember one time we did go off to see them after supper—we'd got friendly with one of the families, you know—and they were having a celebration, what for I don't remember—someone's birthday, I suppose—and they gave me and Miss Mary beer to drink; we'd never tasted it before, and we got real tipsy.

"Miss Mary was worse than I was; she told me afterwards she didn't remember a thing that happened all evening—we were sitting round the tents, you know, where the people lived, and when we got home our heads were going round and round, we were quite scared. I've often thought since, whatever would the vicar have said if he'd known, and my old Dad too, for that matter. I would have got a thrashing, and Miss Mary a sermon."

"Deserved it too," said Black. "What age were you both then?"

"Oh, I was around thirteen, and Miss Mary had turned fourteen. It was the last summer holidays she ever had at the rectory. Poor Miss Mary. I often wonder what became of her. Married, no doubt, over in Canada. They say it's a lovely country."

"Yes, Canada's a fine place, by all accounts. Well, I mustn't stay here gossiping. Don't forget to give the rose tree to your father. And put that youngster to bed before he drops off in your arms."

"I will, sir, good day to you, and thank you."

"Thank you, on the contrary," thought Black. The visit had been worth while. Old Harris' daughter had been better value than old Harris. Hoppers and beer. Fair enough. Mr. Johnson of St. Bees would say conclusive. The time factor fitted too. The boys of St. Bees were absolved. What a damnable thing, though. Black let in the clutch and drove off through the village of Long Common towards the west. He felt it was important to discover at what point Mary Warner had lost her memory. That she remembered nothing of what must have happened at the hop-picking celebration was plain. A reeling head, a

black-out, and two scared kids making for home at top speed before
they were discovered.

Johnson of St. Bees, still warm in the defence of his school, had
told Black that there was no doubt Mary Warner had been completely
ignorant of her condition.

When the matron, aghast, had discovered the fact and taxed the
child, Mary Warner was bewildered. She thought the matron had gone
mad. "What do you mean?" she had said. "I'm not grown up, and I'm
not married. Do you mean I'm like Mary in the Bible?"

She had not the remotest idea of the facts of life.

The school doctor had advised against questioning the child further.
The father had been sent for. And Mary Warner was removed. That,
so far as Mr. Johnson and the staff of St. Bees were concerned, was the
end of the matter.

Black wondered what the vicar had said to his daughter. He suspected that the vicar had questioned the unfortunate child until he
had given her brain fever. The shock must be enough to turn any
child mental for life. Perhaps he would get the solution down at Carnleath. The only trouble was that Black did not know quite what he
was looking for. The Reverend Warner must surely have changed
their names.

Carnleath turned out to be a small fishing port on the south coast.
It had probably enlarged itself during the past nineteen years, because
there were three or four fair-sized hotels, a sprinkling of villas, and it
was evident that the populace now devoted themselves to the business
of catching tourists before catching fish.

Black's family, Phyllis and the boy, returned to the mythical land
whence they sprang. Black was now a newly married man, and his wife,
a girl of eighteen, was expecting her first baby. Black felt doubtful as he
enquired for nursing homes. But he was not disappointed. There was a
nursing home in Carnleath, and it did specialise in maternity cases only.
Sea View, it was called. Right out on the cliff's edge, above the harbour.

He backed his car against a wall, got out, and went to the front
door and rang the bell. He asked to see the matron. Yes, it was about
booking a room for a future case.

He was shown into the matron's private sitting-room. She was small
and plump and jolly, and he felt certain that he would be well advised

to leave his mythical wife—Pearl, he decided to call her in a sudden flight of the imagination—in the matron's capable care.

"And when do you expect the happy event?"

No Cornish woman this, but a hearty, ringing Cockney. Black felt at home with her at once.

"In May," said Black. "My wife is with my in-laws at the moment, and so I've come on this little trip alone. She is determined to be beside the sea for the great occasion, and as we spent our honeymoon here, she feels a sentimental liking for the spot, and so do I." Black gave what he intended to be a sheepish, prospective father's smile. The matron was undaunted.

"Very nice too, Mr. Black," she said, "back to the scene of the crime, eh?" She laughed heartily. "Not all my patients are so fond of the backward glance. You'd be surprised."

Black handed the matron a cigarette. She took it and puffed at it with relish.

"I hope you aren't going to shatter my illusions," he said.

"Illusions?" said the matron. "We have few illusions here. They all go west in the labour ward. What was sauce for the gander turns out to be a pain under the pinny for the goose."

Black began to be sorry for the fictitious Pearl.

"Oh well," said Black, "my wife's a plucky girl. She's not frightened. I may say, she's considerably younger than myself. Only just turned eighteen. That's the one thing that worries me about this business. Is that too young to be having a baby, Matron?"

"They can't be too young," said the matron, puffing a cloud of smoke into the air; "the younger the better. Their bones aren't so set, and they're not muscle-bound. It's the old ones that give me my headaches. Come to me at thirty-five and think they're in for a picnic. We soon show 'em. Your wife play a lot of tennis?"

"Doesn't play at all."

"Good for her. Had a girl here last week, she was local champion over in Newquay, and she was so muscle-bound she was in labour for thirty-six hours. Sister and I were worn to a frazzle at the end of it."

"What about the girl?"

"Oh, she was all right once we stitched her up."

"You have had patients as young as eighteen before?" he asked.

"Younger than that," she said; "we cater for all ages here, fourteen to forty-five. And they haven't all had pleasant honeymoons. Would you like to see some of my babies? I've a little fellow born an hour ago, and Sister is just making him pretty for Mother."

Black steeled himself for the ordeal. If Matron was as forthright as this over one cigarette, how would she be after two double gins? He knew he must ask her to dinner. He went round the nursing home, saw one or two prospective mothers, saw several more whose illusions had apparently been shattered, and when he had inspected the babies, the labour ward, and the laundry, he made a silent vow to remain childless.

He booked a room with a view over the sea for Pearl, he gave the date in May—he even paid a deposit—and then he asked Matron to dine.

"That's very nice of you," she said, "I'd enjoy it. The Smuggler's Rest is only a small place, nothing to look at from outside, but the bar's the best in Carnleath."

"Then the Smuggler's Rest it shall be," said Black, and they arranged to meet at seven.

By nine-thirty, after two double gins, lobster, and a bottle of Chablis, with brandy to follow, the difficulty was not to make Matron talk, but to get her to stop.

She launched into the finer sides of midwifery with a wealth of detail that nearly turned Black dizzy. He told her she should write her reminiscences. She said she would when she retired.

"No names, of course," he said, "and don't tell me all your patients have been married women, because I shan't believe you."

Matron tossed down her first brandy.

"I told you before we had all sorts at Sea View," she said, "but don't let that shock you. We're very discreet."

"I'm unshockable," said Black, "and so is Pearl."

Matron smiled.

"You know your onions," she said; "it's a pity all husbands don't. We'd have fewer tears at Sea View." She leant forward intimately. "You'd be staggered to know what some people pay," she said; "I don't mean the honest-to-God married people like yourself. But those who have slipped up. They come down here to get the business over, and they pretend to be aboveboard, and everything nice and pretty, but they can't deceive me. I've been in the game too long. We've had titled patients at Sea View, pretending to be Mrs., and their husbands think they are having a holiday in the South of France. Not a bit of it. They're having what they didn't reckon to have—at Sea View."

Black ordered another brandy.

"What happens to the unwanted baby?" he asked.

"Oh, I have contacts," said Matron; "there're plenty of foster mothers in this part of the world who won't say no to twenty-five shillings a week until a child reaches school age. No questions asked. Sometimes I've seen the face of the real mother in the papers afterwards. I show it to Sister and we have a quiet laugh. 'She didn't wear that pretty smile in the labour ward,' I say to Sister. Yes, I'll write my memoirs one of these days. I dare say they'd be worth something, and they'd sell like hot cakes."

Matron took another of Black's cigarettes.

"I'm still worried about my wife's age," he said. "What's the youngest you've ever had?"

Matron paused for reflection, breathing smoke into the air.

"Sixteen, fifteen," she said. "Yes, we had a fifteen-year-old once, barely fifteen, if I remember rightly. That was a sad case. Long time ago now, though."

"Tell me about it," said Black.

Matron sipped her brandy.

"She came of well-to-do people too," she said; "the father would have paid anything I asked, but I'm not a grasper. I told him a sum I thought fair, and he was so pleased to dump his daughter on me, he gave me a bit extra. I had her here for five months, which is a thing I don't do as a rule, but he said it was either that or a remand home, and I felt so sorry for the poor kid I took her."

"How did it happen?" asked Black.

"Co-ed school, the father said. But I never believed that yarn. The amazing thing was that the little girl couldn't tell any of us what had happened. I generally get at the truth from my patients, but I never got it from her. She told us at Sea View that her father said it was the greatest disgrace could ever come upon any girl, and she couldn't make it out, she said, because her father was a clergyman, and he was forever preaching what had happened to the Virgin Mary as being the most wonderful thing in the world."

The waiter came with the bill, but Black waved him away.

"You mean to say the girl thought the whole business was supernatural?" he asked.

"That's exactly what she did think," said the matron, "and nothing would shake her. We told her the facts of life, and she wouldn't believe us. She said to Sister that something horrid like that might happen to other people, but it certainly hadn't happened to her. She said she had sometimes dreamt about angels, and probably one had come in the night, when she was asleep, and that her father would be the first to say he was sorry when the baby was born, because of course it would be a new messiah.

"Do you know, it was really pathetic to hear her talk, she was so sure of herself. She told us she loved children and wasn't a bit afraid, and she only hoped she was really good enough to be its mother; she knew this time he really would save the world."

"What a frightful story," said Black. He ordered coffee.

Matron became more human, more understanding. She forgot to smack her lips.

"We became ever so fond of the child, Sister and I," she said, "you couldn't help it. She had such a sweet nature. And we almost came to believe in her theory ourselves. She reminded us that Mary had only been a year or so younger than she was when Jesus was born, and that Joseph had tried to hide her away because he was shocked at her having a baby too. 'You see,' she told us, 'there'll be a great star in the sky the night my baby is born,' and sure enough, there was. It was only Venus, of course, but both Sister and I were glad for the child's sake it was there. It made it easier for her, took her mind off what was happening."

Matron drank her coffee and glanced at her watch.

"I ought to be going," she said; "we're doing a Caesarean at eight tomorrow morning, and I must have a good night's sleep."

"Finish your story first," said Black. "What was the end of it all?"

"She had her baby, and it was a boy, and I've never seen anything so sweet as that child sitting up in bed with her baby in her arms; it might have been a doll given her for a birthday present; she was so pleased she couldn't say a word. She just said, 'Oh, Matron, oh, Matron,' over and over again, and Lord knows I'm no softie, but I nearly cried, and so did Sister.

"But I can tell you one thing, whoever was responsible for that bit of work was a redhead. I remember saying to the child, 'Well, he's a proper little Carrots and no mistake,' and Carrots he became to all of us, and to the poor little girl as well. I don't ever want to go through again what happened when we parted them."

"Parted them?" asked Black.

"We had to do that. The father was taking her away, to begin a new life, and of course she couldn't do that with a baby, not a child her age. We kept her and Carrots for four weeks, and even then it was too long; she'd grown too attached to him. But it was all arranged, you see; the father was to fetch her, and the baby was to go to a home, and Sister and I talked it over, and we decided the only way to do it was to tell the poor child that Carrots had died in the night. So we told her that. But it was worse even than we thought. She turned dead white, and then she screamed. . . . I think I shall hear the sound of that scream to my dying day.

"It was terrible. High-pitched, queer. Then she fainted dead away, and we thought she would never come round and that she would die. We called in the doctor, which we don't do as a rule—we attend to our patients ourselves—and he said the whole thing was monstrous and that the shock of losing her baby might turn her mental. She came to, eventually. But do you know what had happened? She had lost her memory. She didn't recognise us, nor her father when he came, nor anyone. She remembered nothing of what had happened. Her memory had gone quite dead. She was well physically and mentally, but for that. The doctor said then it was the most merciful thing that could have happened. But if it ever came back, he said, it would be like waking up to hell for that poor little girl."

Black summoned the waiter and paid his bill.

"I'm sorry we've ended the evening on such a note of tragedy," he said, "but thank you very much for the story all the same. And I think you should include it in your memoirs when you come to write them. By the way, what happened to the baby?"

Matron reached for her gloves and her bag.

"They took him in at the St. Edmund's Home at Newquay," she said. "I had a friend on the Board of Governors and got it arranged, but it was quite a business. We called him Tom Smith—it seemed a safe, sound name—but I shall always think of him as Carrots. Poor lad, he will never know that in his mother's eyes he was destined to be the saviour of the world."

Black took Matron back to Sea View and promised to write as soon as he returned home, confirming the booking of the room. Then he ticked her and Carnleath off the list in his notebook, and beneath them wrote the words "St. Edmund's Home, Newquay." It seemed a pity to come all this way to the southwest and not drive a few miles further on what would be only a matter of routine. The matter of routine proved harder than he thought.

Homes for the offspring of unmarried mothers are not usually willing to discuss the whereabouts of the children handed to their care, and the superintendent of St. Edmund's Home was no exception to this rule.

"It doesn't do," he explained to Black; "the children know nothing but the home that brought them up. It would unsettle them if the parents ever tried to get in touch with them in after life. It might lead to all sorts of complications."

"I quite understand," said Black, "but in this case there could be no complications. The father was unknown, and the mother is dead."

"I have only your word for that," said the superintendent. "I'm sorry, but it's strictly against the rules to break silence. I can tell you one thing. The last we heard of the boy, he was going steady, in a good job as travelling salesman. I regret I cannot tell you any more than that."

"You've told me quite enough," said Black.

He went back to his car and looked at his notes.

It was not only in his mind that the superintendent's words had rung a bell, but in his notes as well.

The last person to see Lady Farren alive, except the butler, had been a travelling salesman touting orders for garden furniture.

Black drove north, to London.

The firm who made the garden furniture had its headquarters in Norwood, Middlesex. Black obtained the address by putting a call through to Sir John. The catalogue had been kept amongst all the other papers and letters belonging to Lady Farren.

"What is it? Are you on to anything?" Sir John asked over the telephone.

Black was cautious.

"Just a final checkup," he said; "I believe in being thorough. I will get in touch with you again as soon as possible."

He went to see the manager of the firm, and this time Black did not disguise his identity. He gave the manager his card and explained that he was employed by Sir John Farren to enquire into the last hours of the late Lady Farren, who—doubtless the manager had seen in the newspapers—had been found shot a week before. On the morning of her death she had given an order for garden seats to a travelling salesman for this firm. Would it be possible, Black asked, to see the man?

The manager was extremely sorry, but three salesmen were all away, and when they were travelling it was not possible to contact them. The distances they covered were large. Could Mr. Black give him the name of the particular salesman he wished to question? Yes, Tom Smith. The manager consulted his book. Tom Smith was quite a young fellow. This was his first round. He would not be due back at Norwood for another five days. If Mr. Black cared to see Smith at the earliest possible date, the manager suggested he should go to see him at his lodgings, on the evening of the fourth day, when he might have returned. He gave Black the address.

"Can you tell me," said Black, "if by any chance this young man has red hair?"

The manager smiled.

"Sherlock Holmes?" he said. "Yes, Tom Smith has a shock of red hair. You could warm your hands at it."

Black thanked him and left the office.

He wondered whether he should motor down to see Sir John right away. Was there any purpose in waiting four or five days to question young Smith? The pieces of the jigsaw fitted. The story was conclusive. Lady Farren must have recognised her son, and that was that. Yet . . . had she? The butler had taken in Lady Farren's glass of milk to the drawing-room after the salesman had left, and had found her perfectly normal. The pieces fitted, but there was still one little odd-shaped bit that was missing. Black decided to wait.

On the fourth evening he went down to Norwood about half-past seven, on the chance of finding that Tom Smith had returned. His luck held. The landlady, who opened the door to him, told him that Mr. Smith was having his supper, would he please come inside. She showed Black into a small sitting-room, where a young fellow, hardly more than a boy, was seated at the table, eating a plateful of kippers.

"Gentleman to see you, Mr. Smith," she said, and left the room.

Smith put down his knife and fork and wiped his mouth. He had a thin, rather pinched face, like a ferret, and his eyes were pale blue and close together. His red hair stuck up from his head like a brush. He was quite small in size.

"What's up?" he said. He was plainly on the defensive before Black had opened his lips to speak.

"My name is Black," said the detective pleasantly. "I'm from a private-enquiry agency, and I want to ask you a few questions if you don't mind."

Tom Smith rose to his feet. His eyes looked smaller than ever.

"What are you getting at?" he said. "I've not been doing anything."

Black lit a cigarette and sat down.

"I'm not suggesting you have," he said, "and I'm not here to look at your order book, if that's what's scaring you. But I happen to know that you visited a Lady Farren on your rounds just recently, and she gave you an order for two garden seats."

"What about it?"

"That's all. Tell me what happened at the interview."

Tom Smith continued to watch Black suspiciously. "All right," he said, "let's say I did go to this Lady Farren, let's say she did give me a couple of orders; I'll make it all right with the firm when I see them, if they've got wind of it. I can say I asked the cheque to be made out to me, through a mistake, and it won't happen again."

Black was reminded of Miss Marsh. Reminded, too, of the Reverend Henry Warner. Even of Mr. Johnson and his touchy self-defence. Why did people invariably lie when questioned about something else?

"I think," said Black, "it would be much simpler for you, and for your relations with your firm, if you told me the truth straightaway. If you do, I won't report on you, either to the firm or to the superintendent at St. Edmund's."

The young man shifted uneasily from one foot to the other. "You've come from them?" he said. "I might have known it. Always down on me, right from the start. Never had a chance, not me." A note of self-pity crept into his voice. He almost whined. The baby destined to save the world, thought Black, had obviously not made a conspicuous success of the job up to date.

"I'm not interested in your childhood," he said, "only in your very immediate past, and the interview you had with Lady Farren. You may not know it, but the lady is dead."

The boy nodded.

"Saw it in the evening paper," he said; "that's really what decided me to do it. She couldn't split on me."

"Do what?" asked Black.

"Spend the money," said Tom Smith, "and cross the order off my book, and say nothing to no one about it. Easy done."

Black smoked his cigarette, and he had a sudden vision of crowded tents, and lorries, and mattresses, dumped in a field where the hops grew beside tall poles, and bursts of laughter, and the smell of beer, and a shifty-eyed, redheaded fellow like this boy, hiding behind a lorry.

"Yes," said Black, "easy done, as you say. Tell me more."

Tom Smith became easier in manner. The detective wasn't going to say anything. Not if he told the truth. All right.

"Lady Farren was on the list of the big nobs in that district," he said, "plenty of money, I was told, and she'd be sure to give me an order. So I called there, and the butler showed me in, and I gave the lady my catalogue, and she chose two seats, and I asked for a cheque. She wrote it out, and I took it. No more to it than that."

"Wait a minute," said Black. "Was Lady Farren pleasant to you? Did she take any particular notice of you?"

The boy looked surprised.

"Notice of me?" he said. "No, why should she? I wasn't anyone. Just a chap trying to sell her garden seats."

"What did she say to you?" persisted Black.

"She just looked through the catalogue, and I stood by waiting, and she marked two items with a pencil, and then I said would she make out the cheque to bearer—I tried it on, see; she had that dumb sort of face that's easy to fool—and she didn't bat an eye, but went to the desk and wrote out the cheque.

"Twenty quid it was. Ten pound a seat. And I said good morning, and she rang for the butler, and he showed me out. I went off and cashed the cheque right away. I put the money in my wallet, and even then I wasn't sure about spending it or not, but when I saw in the paper the lady was dead, I said to myself, 'Here I go.' Well, you can't blame me. It's the first chance I ever had to make a bit of money no one knew anything about."

Black extinguished his cigarette.

"First chance, and you use it dishonestly," he said, "your choice, and your future. Ashamed of yourself?"

"No one's ashamed till he's caught out," said Tom Smith. And suddenly he smiled. The smile illuminated the pale ferret face, deepened the light blue eyes. The furtiveness went, and in its place shone a strange, engaging innocence.

"I see now that dodge didn't work," he said. "I'll try something else next time."

"Try saving the world," said Black.

"Eh?" said Tom Smith.

Black said good-bye and wished him good luck, and as he walked away down the street he was conscious that the boy had come out on to the doorstep and was watching him.

That afternoon Black went down to report to Sir John Farren, but before being shown into the library, he asked the butler to have a word with him alone. They went to the drawing-room.

"You brought the traveller into this room, and you left him with Lady Farren, then after five minutes or so Lady Farren rang, and you showed the salesman out. After that, you came in again with Lady Farren's glass of milk. Is that correct?"

"Quite correct, sir," said the butler.

"When you came with the glass of milk, what was her ladyship doing?"

"She was just standing, sir, much where you are now, and she was glancing through the catalogue."

"She looked just as usual?"

"Yes, sir."

"What happened then? I've asked you this before, but I must just check again before reporting to Sir John."

The butler considered.

"I gave her ladyship the milk. I asked if there were orders for the chauffeur, and she said no, Sir John would be driving her in the afternoon. She told me she had ordered two garden seats, and she showed me them marked in the catalogue. I said they would be useful.

I saw her put the catalogue down on the desk, and she walked towards the window, to drink the glass of milk."

"She said nothing else? She didn't refer to the salesman at all who had brought the catalogue?"

"No, sir. Her ladyship didn't remark on him. But I remember I did, just as I was leaving the room, but I'm sure her ladyship didn't hear what I said, because she never answered me."

"What did you say?"

"I said, joking-like, her ladyship enjoyed a bit of humour, that if the traveller called again I'd know who he was because of his hair.

" 'Proper little Carrots he is, and no mistake,' I said. Then I closed the door and went to my pantry."

"Thank you," said Black, "that's all."

He stood looking out across the garden. Presently Sir John came into the room.

"I expected you in the library," he said. "Have you been here long?"

"Only a few minutes," said Black.

"Well. And what's the verdict?"

"The same as before, Sir John."

"You mean, we're back where we started from? You can't show me any reason why my wife should have killed herself?"

"None at all. I have come to the conclusion that the doctor's opinion was right. A sudden impulse, owing to her condition, made Lady Farren go to the gun room, take up your revolver, and shoot herself. She was happy, contented, and as you and everybody else knows, Sir John, she had led a blameless life.

"There was absolutely no motive for what she did."

"Thank God," said Sir John.

Black had never before considered himself a sentimentalist. Now he was no longer so sure.